The Last Poem

Also by Courtney Peppernell

Pillow Thoughts
Pillow Thoughts: Deluxe Edition
Pillow Thoughts II: Healing the Heart
Pillow Thoughts III: Mending the Mind
Pillow Thoughts IV: Stitching the Soul
Once Upon a Feeling: A Pillow Thoughts
Affirmation Deck for Reflection and Healing
The Road Between
I Hope You Stay
The Space Between Us
Watering the Soul
The Way Back Home
Time Will Tell
A Month of Sundays
Out of the Ashes

The Last Poem

COURTNEY PEPPERNELL

ATRIA BOOKS

New York   Amsterdam/Antwerp   London   Toronto   Sydney/Melbourne   New Delhi

THE LAST POEM
First published in Australia in 2026 by
Atria Books Australia, an imprint of Simon & Schuster (Australia) Pty Limited
Level 4, 32 York St, Sydney NSW 2000

10 9 8 7 6 5 4 3 2 1

New York Amsterdam/Antwerp London Toronto Sydney/Melbourne New Delhi
Visit our website at www.simonandschuster.com.au

For more than 100 years, Simon & Schuster has championed authors and the stories they create. By respecting the copyright of an author's intellectual property, you enable Simon & Schuster and the author to continue publishing exceptional books for years to come. We thank you for supporting the author's copyright by purchasing an authorised edition of this book.

No amount of this book may be reproduced or stored in any format, nor may it be uploaded to any website, database, language-learning model, or other repository, retrieval, or artificial intelligence system without express permission. All rights reserved. Inquiries may be directed to Simon & Schuster, 1230 Avenue of the Americas, New York, NY 10020 or permissions@simonandschuster.com.

© Courtney Peppernell 2026

All rights reserved. No part of this publication may be reproduced, stored in a retrieval system, or transmitted in any form or by any means, electronic, mechanical, photocopying, recording or otherwise, without prior permission of the publisher.

ATRIA B O O K S and colophon are trademarks of Simon & Schuster, LLC.

This book is a work of fiction. Any references to historical events, real people, or real places are used fictitiously. Other names, characters, places, and events are products of the author's imagination, and any resemblance to actual events or places or persons, living or dead, is entirely coincidental.

A catalogue record for this book is available from the National Library of Australia

ISBN: 978-1-76163-956-2

Cover design and illustration: Justin Estcourt
Interior design: Midland Typesetters, Australia
Printed and bound by CPI (UK) Ltd, Croydon CR0 4YY

The authorised representative in the EEA is Simon & Schuster Netherlands BV,
Herculesplein 96, 3584 AA Utrecht, Netherlands. info@simonandschuster.nl

For Claire, my second chance. I am so grateful to be loved by you, the kindest person I know. I love you. You are poetry to me.

And to my grandmother Jo, the "Winnie" in my life. Your zest for life, curiosity, and wide-open heart have been a guiding light. You taught me how to live with wonder and love with grace.

Prologue

Wren

We are all going to die—at some time, at some place, and in some way, because all life ends eventually. *How* is never guaranteed, *when* is a mystery, and *why* is one of life's most pondered questions. But what anyone will tell you is that the world will still carry on, even in our absence. The garbage trucks still collect the trash, the bills still arrive in the mail, the cars still fill the freeway, the sun still rises and sets.

Since the day my fiancée, Lucy, died, I knew that the world would carry on without her, but *my* world stopped. The trash piled up, the bills went unpaid, the car sat in the street for months on end, and the sky, like many other things in my life, lost all its joy and color. Since that day, I have been waiting for a morning when I open my eyes and her face is not the first thing I see. I have been waiting to listen to the rain and not hear her footsteps in between its soft patter. I have been waiting for a sun-drenched afternoon when I don't hear a knock at the door and think that it is Lucy coming home.

We lived in a townhouse in Manhattan. It was a beautiful brownstone, its timber finishes polished despite its age. Marigolds grew on the windowsills, and potted plants lived on the stoop. We had a balcony that overlooked a courtyard, wisteria twisting along the fences in lazy, fragrant spirals. In the summer I would sit and write from a small iron table on the balcony, shaded by the vines, and in the winter I worked from my office, nestled in front of the fireplace with Lucy often curled up nearby, reading or simply watching the flames. I wrote everything, novels, books of poetry, collections of essays, and at the center of it all was Lucy. I wrote about my love for her, about the life we built together, about the adventures we shared and the quiet, ordinary moments that made up our days. Those books became bestsellers. The poetry collections earned me literary awards, and my novels garnered critical acclaim. Lucy, always my biggest cheerleader, had begged me to try my hand at a young adult fantasy series, an idea that had lurked in my brain but which I'd nearly dismissed. In the end, *The Lost Archives*, a series about a secret academy, enchanted books, and a hidden history that was never supposed to be uncovered, somehow became a runaway success. It dominated bestseller charts, was translated into dozens of languages, and was eventually adapted into a movie trilogy. My essays were featured in *The New Yorker* and *The Atlantic*, and my name became synonymous with intimate, lyrical storytelling. The press loved me. I was B.W. Paisley, an author who, according to *The New York Times*, "could make even the simplest moments feel profound." I gave interviews, appeared at literary festivals, and attended galas, all with Lucy by my side. Together, we were the couple people admired, perfectly imperfect, unapologetically in love. We had a combined social media following of fifteen million.

Life had miraculously turned out the way I had always dreamt it would be: I was a successful author, I was engaged to the love of my life, and I was happy. On quiet Sunday afternoons, Lucy and I would stroll through Central Park, caramel lattes in hand, planning our wedding. We'd marvel at how we had managed to create such a life together, weaving our dreams into reality. We felt unshakable, as though nothing in the world could touch us. Until one evening, it all came crashing down.

We were driving home from a charity gala in New Jersey.

Lucy worked as an art dealer and, because of her job, we often attended those kinds of events: dressed up, smiling for donors, slipping shrimp cocktails onto tiny napkins. The city lights blurred past the windows, and I remember feeling tired but happy.

"I've been thinking about writing another poetry book," I said as casually as I could, though it would be my first in a decade. "With the wedding coming up, thinking about my vows has sort of put me back in the mood."

Lucy grinned. "I'm sure your editor will be excited to hear this."

"I may have already mentioned it to Peter," I admitted.

Lucy giggled. "I bet he squealed at the thought of his agent commission. So, how long have you been secretly writing poetry?"

I shrugged, a little sheepish. "Oh, not very long. I'd almost forgotten how to string a stanza together."

"You could never forget," she replied, softly. "You've always loved writing poetry."

I smiled. "I've always loved writing poetry about *you*."

Lucy laughed, her breath catching in her throat, her eyes glistening. "How many poems could you possibly write about me?"

But I was never given the chance to respond.

It was as though a bomb went off, and the world exploded. The sound of brakes screeching filled the air while glass shattered into sharp raindrops around us. Lucy's arm instinctively reached out across my chest, as though she could hold me in place as the vehicle skidded across the road. We slammed into something, and suddenly I was overwhelmed by the smell of motor oil, of burning rubber, of blood. Someone was screaming and I wondered in a daze who it was, until I realized the sound was coming from me.

Then complete silence enveloped us. It was as though time had stopped, like we were in a vacuum of empty space, and the only thought in my mind was of the woman I loved. I reached over to Lucy and—

"I love you, Brooklyn," she said, with her final breath.

I'd do anything to give her the answer to her question.

I could write about her forever.

I spent a week in the hospital. First responders had to cut us both from the vehicle. I had a fractured femur and a deep gash in my head that required twelve stitches, but that was it. My Lucy, though, was pronounced dead on arrival. My mind shut down and would only offer me bits and pieces of the accident in short bursts, my memories slowly and stubbornly returning as the weeks wore on. Once they decided I was strong enough to handle the truth, the investigators came to me. They told me a young pedestrian, all of five years old, had been struck and paralyzed, and that a John Doe had been injured in a separate vehicle, his condition critical. Their words were careful, their tone measured, as though there were pieces missing.

Of course, the media devoured the story. The accident wasn't just a tragedy; it became a spectacle. The press covered it relentlessly, twisting every detail, hungry for blame and scandal. They painted Lucy as reckless and irresponsible, her name dragged through headlines and talk shows. I became collateral damage, my grief laid bare for public consumption: "B.W. Paisley Injured and Her Fiancée Dead"; "Fatal Collision; A Night of Revelry Turns Sour"; "Tragedy on the Turnpike"; "B.W. Paisley Crash Being Investigated by NYPD." Paparazzi camped outside our brownstone, their flashbulbs lighting up the windows like strobe lights, chasing me down the streets of New York as if grief alone wasn't enough to destroy me. There were thousands of comments spiraling across social media; most were just people wanting to share their condolences, but others were accusations. The NYPD eventually claimed the accident had been Lucy's fault and that it was caused by her negligent driving. They even tried to insinuate that she may have been under the influence, despite the fact that she hadn't had a drop to drink at the event. I was no longer "B.W. Paisley, celebrated author." I was "B.W. Paisley, tragic survivor." The same press that had once built me up now dismantled my life, piece by piece.

I stayed numb in those weeks after the accident. I could barely remember Lucy's funeral. In the months that followed, my lawyers dealt with lawsuits that did not feel justified, but I didn't pay them much attention. I just couldn't; everything felt so dark without Lucy. There would be no more walks in Central Park, no more wedding planning, no more falling into her arms at the end of a long day and feeling as safe as I could ever hope to feel. Instead, I had effectively become a widow, at twenty-nine years old. And of course, I stopped writing.

One afternoon almost a year later, staring out at the withered wisteria in our courtyard, I got a call from our wedding caterer, confirming the recipe for my grandmother's pecan rum bars—my favorite treat growing up. Lucy had planned them as a surprise. It was such a Lucy thing to do, and the weight of her loss hit me harder than it had in all the preceding months. How was I supposed to exist in a world without her? I suddenly realized I couldn't be Brooklyn Paisley anymore. Not without Lucy.

I packed Lucy's clothes, everything but her favorite sweater, and left the boxes at Goodwill, fleeing before I could watch them be unceremoniously sorted into dollar bins and color-coded racks. Then I told Peter, my literary agent, that I was taking a couple of weeks off—to get some space, to return to writing the poetry manuscript. And he believed me. As though, somehow, a few days away was all I needed to grieve the fact that the love of my life had been gone a year. The truth was, though, I already knew I wasn't coming back anytime soon, I just couldn't bring myself to say it aloud. He spluttered something about how much faith my editor had in me, how she was ready to make me an offer for the poetry book, but I had already stopped listening.

I pushed away all other obligations into a corner of my mind and packed a single suitcase, taking Lucy's sweater, my favorite notebook, and a scrappy collection of cardboard drink coasters with me. Then I fled. What started as one week turned into two, then three, and then I stopped counting. I drove from city to city, then state to state, searching for Lucy. The highways were lined with tacky billboards, their clashing colors and chaotic layouts all blending together like a carnival gone wrong. Lucy, with her art dealer's eye, would have torn them apart. *Green on blue? What are we, in elementary school?* she would have quipped. Her job wasn't just about selling art, though; it was about connecting people. She was always traveling, networking with collectors, curators, and artists alike, raising funds to promote work she believed in. No matter where she went, she would always bring home a coaster from a local bar for me. It was her small way of letting me know she was thinking of me even when she was far away.

I visited upscale wine bars and sat on rickety stools at places with sawdust on the floor. I followed the coasters and drank at nearly all the bars she had been to, trying to find her in the bottom of a bottle of cabernet. I could almost see Lucy sitting beside me in the passenger seat or feel her hand resting on my knee as I drove. The farther southwest I drove, the stronger that presence became. The miles blurred together, and so did the days. I'd stop at roadside diners and gas stations and get coffee in paper cups that was so hot it scalded the roof of my mouth. I didn't know what I was searching for exactly. A sign? A miracle? Some proof that Lucy was still out there, somewhere? Every so often, I'd spot something out of the corner of my eye—a flicker of movement, a flash of dark hair—and my heart would skip, thinking Lucy really was there. Only it wasn't her. It was never her.

Until the day, six blurry weeks later, I arrived in Everston, Colorado, a small town tucked into the foothills of the Rocky Mountains, where the peaks rose sharp and jagged against the sky. The winding mountain road twisted through pine trees and rocky cliff edges, leading to a town of colorful and weathered buildings, nestled in the shadow of the hills. By chance or fate—I didn't know what I believed in anymore—I stayed. Because, as I drove down that final stretch into Everston, Lucy appeared beside me in the passenger seat—so real, it took my breath away. Her dark hair fell in soft waves around her face, her amber eyes sparkling with the sharpness I loved and missed. She wore my old flannel shirt, sleeves rolled up to her elbows; the gold necklace I'd given her last Christmas glinted in the sunlight. She looked at me with that familiar half smile, the one that always felt like it held a secret just for me.

"You found me," she said, her voice warm and teasing, as if she'd never left at all.

"Where have you been?" I asked, breathless.

"I've been here," she replied. "Waiting for you."

PART I

September

Chapter 1

Wren

The old gutters along the front of the house were falling apart and rusted in sections. It didn't matter how long I spent staring up at it, squinting through the bright sunlight was unfortunately not going to magically repair the gaping holes in the metal. There were little puddles of water pooling everywhere around the house, rotting the wood, creating muddy patches where the water had settled, having nowhere else to go.

"Miss?"

I turned to see Kyle, the plumber I had repeatedly called over the past month. His shirt was dirty, and flecks of mud and grime were splattered across his face, but he was grinning triumphantly from ear to ear.

"Fixed," he said proudly.

I stared up at the holes.

"Not the word I would use," I said dryly.

"I meant that the pipe in the laundry room shouldn't be leaking anymore."

I smiled, because *leaking* was a modest description, to say the least. A full-blown explosion was more like it.

"Well, I suppose one thing at a time," I said.

Kyle stared up at the gutters, shielding his eyes from the sun with a stained hand.

"This will need replacing too," he said matter-of-factly. "I can pick up supplies later today?"

"Please. Although I think a family of sparrows is taking up residence somewhere along the left side of the roof."

Kyle whistled. "There'll be a lot more than sparrows nesting around this house."

I shuddered at the thought of creepy crawlies, and quite possibly opossums or racoons, invading the house.

"I can hear things at night, moving around in the roof."

He considered for a moment.

"Could be haunted."

"That would be the least of my worries," I said. *I'm the only one here who is haunted.*

"What's that?"

"Nothing." I waved my hand at him. "Thank you for coming out so often. The owner really appreciates it."

"Real nice thing you're doing for Gill, you know, fixing this up. This house has been here for as long as I've been alive."

"I think it's probably been a bit longer than that," I said, laughing. "Gill has been really good to me, letting me stay, so it's the least I can do."

Kyle picked up his toolbox and threw a wrench into it before shutting it with a snap.

"I'll be back tomorrow with the supplies."

He began heading toward his truck but then paused a moment, looking at the front door with its chipped paint and the mesh screen full of holes. The hinges on it were so red with rust that the door was barely holding on.

"You know, my father always used to say that a fresh coat of paint could fix anything."

I stared hard at the front door. "He's probably right."

I watched as Kyle made his way down the cobbled path to the front gate, opening it and disappearing into the street.

Sighing, I looked back at the house, examining its steep gabled roof, arched eaves and Oregon pine trimmings weathered by time. It had to have been a beauty at some point in its life, with its big bay windows and large front porch, complete with a swing. I hoped that underneath the house's crumbling railings, somewhere in its weed-infested yard, past the shingles falling off the roof, there was still some charm left. If I restored the fir floors, wiped away the dust, shined the ornate brass, and repaired the stained-glass dormer windows, then maybe the house would come back to life. I had to believe this. I had to believe that things that were once broken could become whole again. Perhaps Kyle was right, maybe a fresh coat of paint would be the best place to start.

I was up to my arms in sawdust on the porch when I heard my name. It was Gill standing by the fence.

"Afternoon," he smiled. "I just saw Kyle. He said he's picking up some new gutters."

He looked up at the house, giving it a nod like they were two old friends.

"Word travels fast around here." I took off my safety goggles and put the circular sander down on the workbench I'd fashioned out of a couple of old sawhorses and some plywood I'd found forgotten in the shed.

Gill shrugged. "Oh, you know how small towns are."

I just smiled in acknowledgement and pushed open the gate to welcome him in, steering the moment away from myself. I had told Gill I was from the East Coast, but apart from this had only given him the barest of details about myself. He'd taken this in stride, never pressing me for more. I liked that about him.

"Everything okay?" I asked. "Is it the gutters? You don't want me to replace them?"

"Oh, everything's fine, just fine." He rocked back on his heels lightly, his hands in his pockets. "I was just out for an afternoon stroll and thought I would check in on you, see how the house is coming along."

I was about to respond when a loud screech erupted from what sounded like the vicinity of the attic. Gill raised his eyebrows.

"Or perhaps I should say what needs to be moved along."

"Opossums," I said. "Or raccoons, I'm not sure yet."

"Ah, I know it's the strangest thing, but Edith always liked opossums. Never could understand why. Ugly buggers."

A look passed over his face then, just for a moment, so fleeting that most would miss it. But I knew the look, the ache of remembering.

I had met Gill in Sam's, the local diner. After arriving in Everston without a plan, I had been staying at a local motel, barely able to keep track of the time or the days. One morning, I decided to venture out from the stuffy motel room, sat down in a booth at Sam's, and ordered pancakes. Lucy had a habit of asking for a stack of three pancakes with butter, maple syrup, and a dash of sea salt. *To even things out*, she said. It was her go-to order, and as the waiter set the stack in front of me it turned out this was how they were served at Sam's. Anything could remind me of Lucy and would send me spiraling—a fresh bouquet of orchids, the smell of cinnamon, her favorite song on the radio, moonlight shining through the window in the middle of the night, honeybees. Especially honeybees, because she always liked to call me Bee. Sometimes I could hold it together, but other times it felt as though I'd had the breath knocked right out of me. Staring down at those pancakes that day reminded me that she would never enjoy them again. She would never look at me from across the table with a glint in her eye and insist it was the only way to properly enjoy pancakes. It broke me all over again, and I sat there, sobbing over my stack. Gill had been sitting at the counter, and he turned around at the sound of my sniffling, setting aside the newspaper he'd been reading.

"You know, tears are like pancakes. They're best shared with someone else," he told me.

I gave him a weak smile and, with my wet napkin, gestured for him to join me.

"Dear, now why are you crying over a stack of pancakes?"

I thought for a moment about what I should tell him. I'd only just met this man, but I instinctively felt like I could trust him. Plus, it had been weeks since I'd had a real conversation with anyone. I had refused all calls from my publisher and agent. I texted my family periodically only to let them know I was still alive.

I told him the truth then, that they had reminded me of someone I loved who was no longer here. I didn't need to say anything else because Gill clearly understood.

From that day on, I met with Gill for breakfast each morning at Sam's. Sometimes we talked and other times we just sat together in comfortable silence. I learned Gill was a simple soul. He loved freshly baked apple pie with a dollop of whipped cream and a sprinkle of nutmeg on top. He liked football and religiously attended the local high school team's games every Friday during football season. He enjoyed fishing because, as he said, it brought him peace like nothing else could. Gill was a grandfatherly type, handing the local kids a few dollars for ice cream with a wink. He loved to play chess, and I had the feeling he was inclined to let his opponent win a game or two. He had been married to his high school sweetheart Edith for almost forty years. After she passed, he told me, everything became harder and the world looked duller, sounded muffled somehow. He still made their bed every morning with military-like precision, and he used Edith's favorite teacup for his coffee. But now that she was gone, he felt the pain in his knees more acutely, became aware of his slower pace, and that he'd somehow gotten a half inch shorter. It became more difficult to maintain the old house where he and Edith had spent their lives together. Cracks began to spiderweb across the foundation, overgrown ivy threatened to cover windows, and the gutters filled with leaves. Gill knew it was time to move on; he was due to join some of his friends in the local retirement home.

"It will be good for me," he told me. "I am too old to be standing on a ladder, fixing the damn roof and patching holes. I'll fall and break a hip and that'll be the end of me. Besides," he winked, "I'll have plenty of people to play chess with."

"You don't want to sell it?" I protested when he suggested I live in the house.

He shook his head slowly, eyes turning glassy. "I've had real estate agents come through. Photos, listings, endless back-and-forth. They all say the same thing: 'You'll get a good price if you just stage it right.' But every time someone walks through, poking around like it's already theirs, it just breaks me."

He looked at me, a faint, sad smile tugging at the corners of his mouth. "I'm not sure I can let it go just yet." My mind went to the tiny studio apartment in Queens that Lucy and I had rented before my career took off and royalty checks started coming in the mail. We loved that apartment and found it difficult to move. But our townhouse in Manhattan was something entirely different—it was a part of us. Even though I'd fled from it in a hurry, the thought of selling it and never being able to return, of losing that connection to Lucy, her presence carved into the walls, made me feel sick.

"But why me?" I asked. "You don't even know me."

Gill's expression was thoughtful. "No, I don't," he said. "But I know grief. And we certainly share that in common."

My head swam. *Am I out of my mind?*

"The truth is," Gill continued, "I don't need a tenant. I need someone who'll see the place for what it is. Someone who might even breathe some life back into it." He paused. "And I think maybe you need that too."

I took Gill's hand and squeezed it. He knew I understood.

It was then that I saw some light return to his eyes. He glanced at me, a small grin on his face.

"It needs a bit of work, but I may have some coupons for the hardware store you could use?"

The only tool set I'd ever owned was one I'd purchased from Amazon.

"I'll take all the help I can get."

I immersed myself in the house, pouring every ounce of my energy into its creaking floorboards and peeling walls. It became my refuge, the ultimate escape, a place where I could disappear from the world, and lock my heartache outside.

I learned a few things about my new home in that first month after Gill gave me the keys. One-third of Colorado is forest—more than twenty-two million acres of ponderosa pine, aspen, blue spruce, and cottonwood willow. The roads wound through canyons, and, without warning, a snowcapped range rose in the distance, stealing my breath. Everston was the kind of town that felt like a secret, tucked in between these swaths of forest and mountain peaks. It was the kind of place where Sam's Diner never closed, where there was always a fresh pot of coffee brewing and a slice of pie waiting, whether at noon or two in the morning. The local florist included little handwritten notes with every bouquet, and the only bookstore in town had a resident cat that slept on the windowsill. On warm nights, the town square hosted movie nights under the stars.

I also learned a few things about old houses. Like how century-old pipes don't care about your schedule. Wood rot spreads faster than you think. Sometimes I'd peel back a wall expecting a quick fix, only to find the whole structure held together by sheer will. The house needed more work than I had anticipated, but then again, so did I. As it happens, small town folk are curious about newcomers, which made staying invisible difficult. But I hadn't just picked a town no one would think to look for me in, I'd made sure I wasn't someone worth looking for. Grief had changed me. I'd lost weight in the way people do when they forget to eat, when exhaustion takes over hunger. I'd dyed my hair from dark to light brown. Swapped glasses for contacts. Traded my tailored jackets and polished pumps for thrifted sweaters and scuffed work boots. I started going by Wren, my middle name. It was easier that way, less explaining, fewer questions. Wren wasn't a name tied to fame or tragedy. It was a name that let me start over, to become someone unremarkable in a town where people knew each other by name and routine, not by headlines.

But calling myself Wren wasn't just about hiding. It was also about holding on to Lucy. Wrens were Lucy's favorite birds. She'd said so on our second date, and she loved that it was my middle name. She'd even gotten a delicate little tattoo on the inside of her wrist. She treasured all animals, but she had a quirky fascination with wrens; she thought their plump little bodies were adorable, and she loved the fierce protectiveness with which they watched over their nests.

She once told me that wrens were resourceful and would build their nests wherever they saw an opportunity—in a brush pile, inside a tree hole, or, if desperate, even in something like an old shoe. They could find a home anywhere. I wondered if I could do the same. I certainly didn't feel at home in Everston yet, but when a person is your home, where do you go when they're gone?

Gill cleared his throat and pulled me out of my reverie. "You're doing a great job on the old lady, you know. I can already see her coming back to life."

He walked over and placed a gnarled hand on the area that I'd been sanding and gave me a look of approval.

"She's tough, Gill, like me." We laughed. In working on the house, I'd already hammered my thumb—twice—and caught countless splinters, not to mention that I'd ripped my jeans on some old aluminium plates I tripped over in the shed.

But I didn't want it any other way. The hard labor allowed me to focus on something else apart from my own life; it gave me a sense of purpose while I was adrift. Gill letting me stay in his house in exchange for the work was just a bonus.

"You know . . . If you ever need other people to talk to, I know a few folks in town who—"

"Will play chess with me?"

He laughed. "Well, that too."

"You don't have to worry about me, Gill. I'm coping."

I could tell Gill that I'd found an elephant in his attic and it would be more believable than what I'd just said, but he nodded anyway.

"Well, if you ever change your mind, you know where to find me." He picked up the safety goggles I'd tossed aside and handed them to me.

"Best let you get back to it."

He smiled and waved, and I watched him as he slowly made his way down the driveway.

I sighed and returned to inspect my handiwork. I'd made good progress on the door: I'd scraped away the paint then sanded it down to the bare oak. The door had been stripped back down to its natural state—a clean slate, a blank canvas to start over—but I wondered if even a full restoration would really be enough to make anyone want to enter the house once more.

*

After taking another break, I gave the door a fresh coat of paint and replaced the wire screen window. I propped it back into place with new hinges and a shiny new brass knocker. Not bad. The evening rolled in then, bringing a familiar coolness to the air as the sun retired for the day. I decided I'd done enough work, so I went inside to wash off the grime that had caked itself to my skin.

As I had done for so many nights since I moved in, I sat on the porch swing, a blanket draped over my lap and a glass of wine sitting on the small wrought-iron table beside me. The swing was my favorite part of the house. It seemed to be the only thing that was untouched by age, as though it were deemed off limits to the elements. I stared out past the picket fence that encompassed the property, wildflowers snaking themselves through the palings.

"You should pick some."

I turned to see Lucy sitting beside me on the swing.

"I thought your favorites were marigolds?"

She shrugged. "These ones are pretty too."

I smiled, wondering how many I could pick if I started now. Lucy loved fresh flowers on the kitchen counter. I realized how much I missed always having fragrant blooms in the house.

"I should start putting fresh flowers on the kitchen counter again. The way you used to."

"It *would* brighten up the place a little," she said, tipping her head to assess the work I'd done today.

"I'll pick some in the morning. It'll tidy up the fence and brighten the kitchen."

Lucy shifted her gaze to me, her soft eyes narrowed in concern.

"Bee, why am I here?"

"Because I wanted to see you," I replied quickly, as if it were the simplest answer to the simplest question in the world. Because it was. "Besides, you said you would always be here. Don't you remember? You always said that to me. 'Bee, I'm not going anywhere.'"

She exhaled softly, her expression full of something I couldn't quite name. "Sometimes life doesn't let us keep the promises we make, Bee," she said softly. "You of all people should know that."

I swallowed hard. "Well, what do you want me to say?" My eyes burned, and I clenched my fists, willing the tears not to spill over.

"Goodbye."

"Well, I can't. I can't do that."

"You have to try."

"Why? Why do I have to say goodbye when I can sit out on this porch swing every night, looking at wildflowers, with you here beside me as more than just a memory? This is what makes Everston so special, because, of all the places in the world, I somehow found you here."

"That's not the reason you ended up here."

"Oh? And what is?"

I could see Lucy looking up at the sky, which was now dark and spattered with stars. "It's beautiful, isn't it?" she murmured. A car drove past us then, its headlights washing over me. When the light faded, Lucy was gone, and I was alone again.

Chapter 2

Henry

One afternoon, when I was nine years old and sitting cross-legged on the school library floor, cutting out small paper people, I asked our librarian a question.

"Mrs. Connolly, what does a librarian actually do?"

Sitting next to me, my brother Jacob scoffed.

"They obviously sort books, duh, Henry."

Mrs. Connolly looked at us thoughtfully.

"Well yes, we do sort lots of books, Jacob. But there are many other things a librarian does."

"Like what?" I pressed.

"Perhaps the most important thing we do is to help people find what they are looking for."

For a very long time after, I considered her answer. So long, in fact, that I carried it with me all the way through school, through college, and into my adult life, eventually becoming Everston's resident librarian. I made it my policy to help people find what they were searching for, no matter what it was. Over the years, I have found many things: a family's beloved missing border collie, sweaters in almost every color, answers to math equations, textbooks from one hundred years ago. I've taught more than half our local retirement home how to use computers and iPhones; I've helped with dozens of school projects; I've organized scavenger hunts, trivia nights, coding classes, free lunches for the homeless. I've printed life-size posters of various pop stars for fans, was once asked if I could supply fake IDs, and I've called 911 on more than a few occasions. I've heard, seen, and done it all—I have always tried to find the answers for people, because that's just what librarians do. We search, we find, and we deliver. In my own life, though, the answers haven't come so easily. I'm still searching, sifting through endless questions, hoping to find something—anything—that gives grief meaning. But the truth is, there are just some questions that don't have answers.

Everston had been home my whole life. It was small-town America, engulfed by steep peaks that touched the sky. The last operational mine closed in the early nineties, and since then, we stayed alive mostly through tourists filtering through the town on their way to Colorado backcountry. On Main Street, you could find all the things that made Everston, well, Everston. There was the Hobby Shop and Smithey's Furniture Store, and there was House of Glamor selling prom dresses, some of which had been on the rack since the eighties. There was one movie theater left in town, which mostly played black-and-white films, and there was a motel called the Green Leaf, run by Barbara Matthews, who won Colorado's state beauty pageant in the seventies. There was an old antique store filled with oddities and knickknacks, and paintings by our local artist Merrill, who is ninety-two years old and still judging our annual pickle-eating contest. We had Sam's Diner (owned by, if you couldn't guess, Sam), with checkered floors, red leather booths, and drip coffee. There were three bars, a café, and an auto repair shop that gave you a free donut every time you had your vehicle serviced.

If you headed farther into town, there was a church, painted white with a blue door, with bluebells growing in the gardens around it. There was a small fairground with a permanent Ferris wheel that lit up every night; the other rides came and went with the county's various fairs, with staff arriving from miles away to set up rides and games. We had a school that housed elementary and middle school students, with a tiny high school next door. Our fire station and sheriff's office were combined—if you called one, you were just as likely to get someone from the other department—and the sheriff and fire chief had both been there since before I was born. There was no hospital in town, just old Dr. Williams, who was hard of hearing. He could wrap a sprained ankle and reset broken bones, diagnose the flu, and hand out cough drops like they were candy, but that was about it. For anything worse, you'd have to head to the town over for a hospital.

There was no McDonald's to be found here, no Walmart or Home Depot, but there was Eddie's Hardware Store and Pat's Grocer, an alpine ski shop and gift shops. However, I believed that the greatest place in the whole town, even if I were a little biased, was the library. Everston Public Library was not a grand building that towered over the main square. It certainly didn't have marble flooring, spiral staircases, or stained-glass windows like some libraries in giant cities. In fact, the building used to be a bakery until it was bought by the town, renovated, and turned into what it was today. Although, from time to time, both myself and patrons alike would swear we could still smell fresh bread in the air. Ask anyone from Everston and they would tell you that our town was the heart of the high country, but if you asked me, I'd say Everston Library contained all the heart we needed.

The library sat on a corner of Main Street; an alleyway separated it from the Hobby Shop and the library's parking lot. I liked to arrive by seven thirty every morning. In those early hours, the library was still and silent, and I liked to imagine that it was asleep and softly dreaming. This morning was no exception, despite the cold chill in the air. There was a coffee shop across the road, and the grinders had been going since before dawn, singing out to the brick and stone buildings. The smell of coffee beans wafted into the street as I parked directly in front of the library and headed toward the front doors. Everston's businesses had taken to repainting the exteriors of their shops in the last few years and, as a result, Main Street had ended up looking rather colorful. When I saw this, I also petitioned to have the library painted. Unfortunately, the paint shop mixed up the colors, so we were left with bright terra-cotta bricks with teal green finishes. I felt like it only added to the charm.

Beside the front doors was a large metal box with a slot and a sign that read *Book Returns*. I had found all sorts of things in the library return box—trash, Ping-Pong balls, Barbie dolls, diapers, even half a cedar branch once. I had tried all sorts of preventatives, including nice signs that said *For Library Books Only!* and an old webcam that I fashioned into a mock security camera, but people still put all sorts of things into the slot. The worst, of course, was the occasional firecracker. This morning, however, I noticed a piece of paper stating *Read Me* duct-taped to the front of the box. Curious, I peeled the paper off and opened its folds.

Will be in today. Need to negotiate.

I had received notes like this before—*I can't find the book, sorry; I accidentally spilled my coffee on the book; My dog ate the textbook; If I bring my own headphones, do I still need to check out audiobooks?*—and also some rather colorful book reviews, but I had to wonder what someone possibly needed to negotiate with me.

Shrugging, I unlocked the front doors and reached over and hit the main power switch. The lights slowly flickered on, and the library awoke. The library had undergone many changes over the years, but one thing I always kept was a banner that hung above the entryway. It said: *All Are Welcome*.

After placing my things behind the reception desk, I made my way to the staff room, powering up the coffee machine and retrieving my mug from the cupboard. I was perhaps the only person on our staff who used the coffee machine for tea and not coffee. The machine whirred to life, rumbling and pouring the hot water into my mug, and I dunked a tea bag several times for good measure. I relished those first few morning sips.

"Morning, Henry."

I glanced up as Lana, the library's assistant director, popped her head through the door to greet me. Lana was in her late twenties, and she'd been my colleague and friend for the past five years, a steady presence in the library and an expert at keeping things running smoothly.

"Morning, Lana. You're here early."

"Pulled up just after you! I thought I'd better get a start on those final Imagination Week programs."

"That's probably a good idea," I said. Our Imagination Week programs were always very popular; it was an entire week dedicated to creativity and the books we loved. There was dressing up and events and it was all a lot of fun, but the prospect of how many schoolchildren would be funneling through the library over the next week sent a small shiver down my spine.

"Let me know when you've finished. I'll run the final programs by the board, and then we should be all set!"

I wandered over to investigate the contents of the fridge, searching for the other half of a bagel I had left the other day, and making a mental note to clean out any other bits of old food.

"Do you know what you're dressing up as?" Lana asked.

I glanced up, a bit sheepish.

"I'm thinking Paddington Bear because I have an old Halloween costume I could reuse."

"Oh, but that's cute," Lana said. "The kids will love it. I'm thinking Ms. Frizzle."

I grinned. "You know, I think Dev would go as the Magic School Bus if you baked some of those chocolate chip cookies for him."

She shook her head.

"He would do anything for those cookies."

Our tech assistant Dev was a ball of fun, and he really would do anything for Lana's chocolate chip cookies.

The library didn't open until nine, but arriving early meant I got to enjoy at least an hour of quiet time and read my emails without any interruptions. Once the doors opened, it was a free-for-all, and I spent most of the morning at the front desk. I didn't notice how much time had passed until my stomach grumbled around noon. Before I could sneak a snack under the desk, though, a man shuffled over to me. His silver hair sprawled across his brown suede coat, and he cradled something in his arms.

"Can I help you?" I adjusted my glasses.

"Hello. I left a note for you last night."

I tilted my head, then remembered the scrap of paper I had found this morning on the book return, something about a pending negotiation. This would be interesting.

"Oh, yes. What do we need to negotiate today?"

"Well, I have some library fines," he said, and handed me a printed receipt. I looked down then back up at the old man, trying to smother a laugh. His total came to $236; he'd had these fines for more than a decade.

"I see," I said slowly. "Well, sir, there are some options we could—"

"Here's what I was thinking," he interrupted. "I could pay it off with this."

He placed on the desk what looked like a mound of clay

accessorized with shiny pieces of plastic, all smushed together into something that loosely resembled a frog.

"One of a kind," he said. "I know how much libraries love original art."

I inspected the "art," trying to locate any evidence of value—a famous signature, rare materials, anything—and wondered if perhaps he thought we also functioned as a museum. I supposed I did have a habit of collecting knickknacks, so we did look a little bit like a museum, what with all the decorations I had accumulated over the years.

"Who is the artist?" I asked cautiously.

He smiled brightly. "Me! Made it myself."

I stared at him, trying to decide if this conversation was actually taking place or if I was dreaming, when suddenly I heard a loud popping noise, and the ceiling above the readers' corner exploded, water bursting through the panels, soaking everything in its direct path.

"What in the world?" I gasped, and raced around the counter toward the commotion. "Lana!" I called out urgently. "Go turn off the water supply!"

I saw Lana scramble out from the science fiction section she had been restacking, and she bolted toward the front doors in the direction of the valve.

I hurried to save whatever I could, moving armchairs out of the way, punting aside a small coffee table, and tripping over myself to rescue an antique reading lamp before the water could claim it. But the floor was already a lake and there was now a large, gaping hole in the ceiling. The water finally stopped shooting out like a geyser when Lana flicked the water main off, reducing itself to a trickle, then a drip. I stood with my hands on my hips, shaking my head at the damage. It was a disaster. The water had soaked the rugs and all our throw blankets and, most critically, some books.

"So," my silver-haired sculptor said, holding up his FrankenFrog statue. "Do we have a deal?"

It took me thirty-five minutes to get ahold of Kyle, our local plumber. Kyle was steady in a crisis, just like his dad had always been back when he was running their family business. I once had the misfortune of having pipes burst in my bathroom, shooting god only knows what over everything, but Kyle's dad, ever the efficient optimist, had me back up and running in no time.

I gazed up at Kyle on his ladder, praying that he could work that same magic in our library.

"Thanks for coming," I said. "Honestly it just sort of exploded."

Kyle muttered something inaudible as he continued to prod around up there.

"I mean, I know the building is old, but she's still holding up overall, don't you think?"

Kyle continued muttering, too low for me to catch all of it, but it sounded a lot like he was comparing the library to his great-great-great-aunt.

"How long do you suppose this will take to fix?"

Kyle shifted on his ladder so that I could finally hear him.

"Well, I need to replace all of the piping and the ceiling panels, so this section will be out of action for a little while."

I groaned.

"So, no chance of having us up and running tonight?"

I heard him laugh, echoing into the roof.

"I'm good," he called down. "But I'm not a wizard."

I sighed. "It's just that I host meetings here every other Tuesday, and I happen to have one tonight."

"Can you meet somewhere else in the library?"

"No. All the other areas are booked."

"Can you postpone the meeting?"

"Well, I could, but it wouldn't be ideal—might set some of our progress back."

Kyle shifted something in the roof, producing a loud thud, and suddenly, rusty orange water poured down onto the floor.

"Yuck," he said.

I looked down at the rugs; they would now absolutely need replacing. Yuck indeed.

"What about having them meet at Brandy's instead?" Kyle asked.

"Brandy's?" I repeated.

"Yeah, my girlfriend Sasha manages the bar—I'm sure she'd host your group."

I crossed my arms, realizing Kyle probably didn't know *why* our group actually met.

"Yeah, I'm quite fond of Brandy's, and Sasha, of course, but we're a grief counseling group, Kyle . . ."

"I see," he replied thoughtfully. "Well then, surely it's important for your group to meet, even if it's at a bar. It's not something you should cancel, Henry."

He fumbled for a moment before handing his phone to me.

"Just ring Sasha, Tuesdays aren't busy at Brandy's. Everyone is usually across the road at The Den for bingo night, so I'm sure she'll stay open for you."

I sighed again, pushing my hair back from my forehead. Brandy's it was.

I scribbled a note and left it at the front of the library to explain the venue change, before calling all the regular group members to let them know about the flooding and our temporary meeting location. Nearly everyone asked if I had called Kyle, and when he heard me confirming to everyone that I had, I saw his chest puff out just a bit, his smile growing a little wider.

"Don't let anyone into this area," Kyle said, making his way down the ladder. "I'll crunch some numbers and text you with a quote."

Even though Kyle always tried to be fair with his pricing, judging by the water damage, this wouldn't be cheap.

"I'll have to run this by the board as soon as you get back to me." I wasn't looking forward to it. Most of the board members were octogenarians and very cranky when it came to expenses.

He straightened his ball cap.

"I'm on it, Henry. We'll get it fixed. Don't worry so much, buddy."

I grimaced. Easier said than done.

Kyle grabbed his ladder and gave me what I supposed was a friendly arm punch and left.

I stayed there a moment, my shoes squishing into the soggy rug as I took in the damage. Water pooled around the legs of the chairs, and the bookshelves warped and darkened along their edges. But it wasn't the repairs I was most worried about—those could be managed, fixed with time and effort. I was more concerned with the thought of our grief group not having their safe, warm spots in the armchairs in their favorite corner of the library. It wasn't just the physical nature of the space, it was the solace it offered, the understanding nods, the shared stories, the unspoken comfort of being surrounded by others who understood. And now, as I stood in the mess, I wondered how to carry that refuge somewhere else.

By the time the day started to wind down, Lana and I had played tag team seamlessly, the product of having worked together for so many years. While she managed the rush of kids, ushering them to tables for an afternoon of origami, I had managed to mop up all the water and move the wet books into the staff room to dry. Eventually I was able to find a moment to myself and make a cup of tea.

"What happened to the readers' corner?"

I jumped as Dev, our tech assistant, walked into the staff room, dumping his bag in a corner.

"Sorry, Henry." He laughed. "Didn't mean to startle you."

I waved my hand over my mug.

"It's not you. Just . . . don't ask." I sighed.

"A busy day here at Everston Library, it seems," he said, grinning and handing me a brown paper bag.

"Mindy baked some apricot cookies last night."

"She's an angel," I said, fishing one out, savoring the sweet aroma over my tea.

I finished my cookie and watched as the sun started its descent, hitting the front doors, sending a fiery gleam of light spilling across the floor, warm and inviting. Whatever happened to be going on in the outside world, the library was the one place I always felt safe. It held my memories, the beautiful ones and the ugly ones, layered into every corner like the rings of an old tree, each one marking a moment of time.

Jacob made up so many of those rings. Even now, all my memories of him—both good and bad—haunted me. Two years had passed, and it still didn't feel real that he was gone.

It had started with fatigue. He grew tired more easily, which was unusual for him. Jacob was a runner. He would run everywhere, even in the middle of winter, when Everston was bitterly cold and the snow piled several feet high. When he stopped running for a few weeks, I became suspicious, but he brushed me off whenever I questioned him. Not that that was out of character for him. Jacob was born two minutes and twenty seconds before me, and therefore by birthright (according to him) he was always right.

He started making excuses. "I'm probably just working too hard. I'm sure it's nothing, and I'll be back to normal soon. I just need to get more sleep."

But normal never returned. One afternoon, while we were in my snug two-bedroom house, Jacob reading the paper as I busied myself making dinner, he suddenly fell off the kitchen stool and screamed. It was the kind of scream that makes every hair on your body stand up, the kind of scream that you feel right through your bones. I had never driven so fast in all my life, but the ride to the hospital felt as though it took decades, Jacob agonizing in the front seat, begging me to go faster, repeating that something was wrong.

After a battery of tests and days of stress, my emotions rocking me every which way, we discovered that my twin, the person I had entered the world with, and whom I had always counted on, had advanced stage IV pancreatic cancer. After our dad had suffered a minor heart attack a few years earlier, our parents had retired to Hawaii, determined to embrace a slower pace of life. Without them here, I slipped into caregiver mode without hesitation. It felt as though our small world had suddenly shrunk to just the two of us. Jacob moved in with me, leaving behind his apartment across town, so I could support him. I remember those final months as though it were a grim songbook—I can recall every dirge, every sour note. The doctor's appointments, the failed treatments, the arguments between Jacob and me.

He had wanted to savor every last minute and I wanted him to keep fighting. When Jacob died, I did what any librarian would do: I tried to find the answers. *Why did he have to go? What else could I have done? When will my heart stop feeling as though it's buried under twenty million tons of rubble?* The only problem was that, at the same time, I just wanted the world to end. I prayed for an asteroid, an explosion, every natural disaster I could think of, anything to turn the lights out. Jacob was my brother, my twin; in what world could I possibly exist without my other half?

Grief is a shadow and the world prefers the light. When you are grieving, people give comfort for a short amount of time and then expect you to return to normal, but they don't understand that things will *never* be normal again. Old habits need to be undone and new habits need to be formed—all while there is a hole in your heart completely consuming you, every hour of every day.

I buried myself in my work to forget the pain. I made finding answers for others the most important priority in my life, especially when I had none for myself. I told everyone who asked that I was fine, I was coping, I was moving on. People told me all the time, *You are so strong, Henry Briggs. Jacob would be proud. Look at you, such an example to this town.*

I suppose the only one that knew the truth was the library itself. It kept me company when I couldn't find the strength within me to go home. Instead, I'd sit in the middle of the history aisle, accompanied by a bottle of Glenfiddich—a gift from Mayor Ashcroft for helping to write her campaign speech—staring blankly at half a row of Van Gogh biographies.

On our thirty-sixth birthday, as I sat in that same spot, my vision blurring and my chest aching, I noticed a book on the shelf that was out of place. I reached for it and cracked its spine, flipping to a random page, settling my gaze onto a poem:

> *This is not the end, not at all.*
> *I have only ventured to the place*
> *between night and day—*
> *I still hear you when you call,*
> *I still listen to all you have to say.*
> *Cry for me if you need to, but laugh;*
> *hold my name in your heart,*
> *the way you have always done so.*

> *Think of me often, but do not allow*
> *these thoughts to consume you.*
> *Live as I have always wanted*
> *you to live.*
> *For I will see you again,*
> *somewhere, one day,*
> *and we will smile.*

My eyes welled up with hot tears that threatened to spill over. I forgot my whiskey, and for a moment I even forgot my grief. Or maybe it's not accurate to say that; rather, I realized that grief didn't have to rule over me. I could sit with it and we could talk to one another, grief and me, but it wasn't the only conversation partner I had to limit myself to.

That's not to say that I didn't still feel despondent—how could I not at times? My other half was gone. But I found that poetry could drag me out of the dark hole I was in; it could remind me to look at the sky, to go home and sleep in my bed instead of on the library floor. I wondered if others might feel like me.

I had no idea how my little idea might be received, so I started small. I put up a simple sign at the library desk: *Grief Support Group*.

First, one person inquired, then two more, and then another. I contacted Max Turner, a semiretired therapist who lived only a few blocks away, to see if he might be interested in joining us. Turned out he was.

Over the last four months, we'd settled into a steady routine. We met every other Tuesday evening, mostly to share how we were feeling. There were tears and jokes and snacks. And, as corny as it might sound, there was comfort. We were all looking for answers to our grief, and it seemed—even if our little group wasn't an answer itself—that we were on the path to finding them.

*

"I'm heading home, Henry," Lana said, putting on her cardigan. "Anna is supervising the study group and Dev is on desk. You need anything from me before I leave?"

"All good here. Do you have the spread list to give to the school?"

She nodded. "Emailed it to the principal this afternoon. There are no allergies to report, so I think your lemon poppy seed cupcakes are a go."

I laughed.

"I think they're more likely to go through the marshmallow squares than the cupcakes."

"Imagination Week is going to be great. Try not to lose sleep over it."

I raised my eyebrows. "We're librarians, Lana; we lose sleep over everything."

She just smiled and waved, heading out the door into the night, car keys in hand.

I went to the sink to wash my mug, leaving it on the dish rack to dry overnight. Sometimes I still felt the urge to sleep in the library, wishing I never had to leave. Things would be easier if I could stay hidden in the history aisle, rather than face the darkness that kept me up at night, but Kyle was right—I knew these meetings were important, not just for the members, but for me too.

I was still tallying how many lemon poppy seed cupcakes I would need to impress an entire class of middle schoolers when I got to Brandy's. I wanted to show the kids there was more to the world of confections than just sugar, that there was a particular kind of joy that came with picking poppy seeds out of your teeth.

"Henry," a voice called out. I looked up to see Gill standing outside the entrance.

"Hey, Gill, glad you're here. I brought you a little present." I handed over a Twix chocolate bar, the kind that Edith used to keep in the house to appease Gill's sweet tooth.

Gill smiled at me, the creases in his face deepening.

"You're a good boy, Henry. I'm sorry you're having to deal with such a mess. When will the library be back up and running? Kyle get back to you yet?"

I sighed. I didn't want to think about it right now.

"Yeah, hopefully next week or the week after. We'll just have to see."

"Brandy's is a nice replacement, though. Do you think Max will notice if I pop over for a whiskey?"

"He may." I grinned and held the door open for him. Let the old man have his nightcap.

Brandy's was the oldest bar in Everston. It was originally owned by a Brandy Johnson and then passed on through the family. The original Brandy was said to have been a firebrand, one of very few female business owners at the time. She could drink plenty of men under the table, and long after she retired, she coached her granddaughter through Prohibition. Now, it was run by Sasha, Brandy's great-great-great-granddaughter.

There were photos of bar patrons plastered on every inch of the walls, moose and deer heads keeping watch, old license plates tacked behind the bar. A neon Budweiser sign welcomed customers, flickering in the night, a constant beacon for those looking to drink. Floating shelves ran along the walls, with rickety bar stools placed underneath, coasters scattered everywhere, and rows and rows of bottles suspended on glass shelves behind the ancient oak-slab bar. It hadn't really changed in decades, but it was warm and inviting, and that's really all anyone asked for in this town.

As Gill crinkled open his chocolate, I gathered some barstools and set them up in a circle at the farthest end of the bar.

Sasha emerged from the back to oversee, folding her arms and smiling warmly. In the time after Jacob's death, I really appreciated that Sasha didn't try to avoid me, as some did, and also didn't go overboard with pity, holding my hand and whispering platitudes. She was just Sasha, the same as she was before Jacob passed.

"Everything okay, got what you need?"

"I think we are all set. I appreciate this, truly."

"It's not a problem, I'll be floating around, just trying to unclog the dishwasher in the back, so yell if you need anything." She wiped her hands on a towel and swung it over her shoulder, disappearing behind the bar.

The door opened and, one by one, our group members filtered in, waving and chatting, excited to be at our new meeting place.

"I'll have a gin and tonic, please," Rita said to the bartender on duty, hanging her coat on the rack just by the door.

"Oh, that does sound nice," Bobby said behind her, ordering one as well.

The thing about grief is that it doesn't care who it targets. It will visit anyone's doorstep, and, when you open the door, you never know who will walk in, and who might walk out.

That's why our group wasn't just for those who had lost someone due to death; it was for anyone carrying the weight of loss in all its forms. Sorrow has many faces, and each of us had been forced to confront one of them. In addition to Gill, our members included Bobby, whose parents were highly conservative and who hadn't accepted his sexuality. Winnie's husband, Cliff, just up and left one day—no note, no warning, just gone. Julian was from the next town over; his wife had had five miscarriages and didn't know he attended. Emerson, our youngest member, was in a horrific car accident a year ago. She was left with a broken body and a broken heart. Rita's sister had dementia and most days didn't recognize her. Olivia, our town reporter, joined from time to time but stayed mostly silent. Her mother, our nightly news anchor, died of a brain aneurysm three days shy of her sixtieth birthday. And then there was me, still trying to navigate a world that felt incomplete. We were a motley crew, and our first meetings had been awkward, with all of us unsure how to share our pain without stepping on someone else's. But over time, we relaxed, and the group became a rare place where we could be vulnerable without fear of judgment. No matter what heartache we brought to the table, we all understood its weight, and that each of us had a seat.

As I stole a glance at my watch, Max breezed through the door in his usual cashmere sweater and thin-framed glasses. He eyed the moose head on the wall suspiciously, then strode over and perched on a barstool with us.

When everyone was settled, and those who'd grabbed a drink had been served, Max looked up.

"Shall we begin?" he said, crossing his legs. "How is everyone?"

There was a low murmur in response before Julian's voice cut through.

"My daughter had her first ballet recital this week," he said. "I cried halfway through."

I smiled, shifting on my barstool. It wasn't as comfortable as a library armchair, but it would do.

Max looked at Julian, his eyes kind. "That sounds fun. Anything else interesting about your week?"

Julian was from Norvale, about thirty minutes north of Everston. It was a much bigger town, sprawling through the valley, with chain supermarkets, shopping plazas, and a steady stream of traffic weaving between the mountains that framed its edges. He had a daughter, Hazel, and a son, Miles, but he and his wife, Cara, had been trying to conceive another child for years, a journey marred with pain. In our last meeting, Julian mentioned that he told his wife he was working extra night shifts, because he didn't know how to tell her that instead he was driving to Everston for these meetings. He couldn't bring himself to tell her that he was suffering, too, in a different way.

Julian cleared his throat.

"I worked a lot this week. Sometimes it's easier to be at work than it is to be at home, but I feel guilty for that," he said.

"Why do you feel guilty?"

"Because it's difficult to grieve for a baby I've never met, and I can't tell my wife because she's in so much pain."

"That doesn't make your pain any less real, Julian," Bobby said quietly.

"It just doesn't feel real," Julian continued. "My wife, you know, she can barely eat, barely sleep, barely get out of bed, she cries all night long, she says the names we had picked out for the babies over and over again. But me?" he drew in a breath. "I just go about my day trying to get from one thing to the next. As though the baby never existed. How—how is that not the most horrible thing you ever heard?"

"Regardless of the loss we face, and even if that loss is shared with another, we all still mourn in different ways. Your own experience is valid," Max said, then gestured toward Gill. "Gill, what was the first thing you did after Edith passed?"

Gill thought for a moment. "I was angry. I remember going inside the shed in my backyard and screaming at the walls for hours."

"And you, Bobby? What do you do every time you think about your parents?"

"I cry," Bobby said. "And then I watch *Titanic*."

"I cut up photos of my ex or I blast some music," Emerson offered. Max nodded, slightly amused.

"Winnie?"

"I read a lot when Cliff left to distract myself. It worked sometimes," she said.

"I did a seven-mile hike and cursed at every tree on the way back," I said, shrugging lightly.

"You see, our experiences with grief are ever-changing. They can look wildly different from person to person, or sometimes they can look very similar. Just because your grief looks different from your wife's grief does not make you a monster, Julian," Max said.

Julian bowed his head and studied his hands in his lap. "I can't argue with that."

"Henry, how was your week?" Max asked, giving me a thoughtful look.

I adjusted my glasses, pushed them up the bridge of my nose.

"Well, nothing out of the ordinary, although Imagination Week isn't too far off, so I'm starting to look into ideas for it."

"Oh, Imagination Week!" Winnie interjected. "My neighbors' kids are so excited for it. Their mom's already started on their costumes."

"Ah, that's wonderful!" I replied. "Do you know if they enjoy lemon poppy seed cupcakes?"

Max diplomatically cleared his throat and I straightened on my stool.

"It sounds exciting," he interjected. "Did Jacob ever attend any library events with you?"

I nodded. "Yes, all the time. He had a special affinity for books, and he always wanted to work in publishing."

Max shifted and crossed his other leg. "Do you find these events difficult without him?"

I deflected. "Actually, I received a phone call this week, someone asking after Jacob. An old colleague of his who didn't know of his passing. I had to tell her he was no longer with us."

"And how did she respond?"

"Well, she said that Jacob will always be with us."

Emerson groaned loudly. "I hate it when people fucking say

that." Winnie clucked and Emerson turned red. "I mean, I don't like it when people say that."

I hid a small smile. I hadn't expected Winnie and Emerson to have grown so close in such a short amount of time, but I supposed that loss connects us to people we otherwise may have never known.

Max was unfazed. "Why does it bother us?"

When no one answered, I said, "Well, because that's half the problem, isn't it? My brother isn't with me. He's gone, and I need to accept that."

When I would first wake up in the morning, still groggy, I would sometimes forget that he had died, the knowledge having not yet kicked me in the gut. I could almost convince myself that he was just away on vacation, and any minute he would turn up on my doorstep, and grouse at me for not going to the gym more often. Jacob and I were like night and day. He was supremely confident, and I was utterly reserved. He liked beer; I enjoyed a nice brandy. He liked football, hockey, baseball, hiking, parasailing, and bungee jumping. I liked reading, old movies, sudoku, baking, and antique stores. We were not identical twins, but when Jacob kept his hair short and had forgotten to do laundry and needed to borrow my clothes, people would sometimes mistake him for me. No matter how different we were, we were still each other's other half. Jacob always knew what I was thinking before I'd even say it. We would finish each other's sentences, and, despite his need to always be right and to challenge me at every opportunity he got, he would always follow up with a smile, and say, "I never doubted you." I knew when Jacob was near, even if I hadn't yet caught sight of him—we had our own language. So how could I have not known that the other half of me was so sick? The thought lingered with me, a heavy guilt I had yet to be able to resolve, as our group session wound to a close. We ended with tea and a poetry reading, as usual, though Sasha didn't have an electric kettle, so she used the espresso machine. I swear it tasted faintly of coffee. *Not ideal.* This week it was Bobby's turn to choose, and he picked a poem by Maya Angelou. As he read about great trees falling, I thought of Jacob and what kind of tree he would be. Probably a redwood. He was always the strongest and tallest in the room.

"No Olivia tonight?" Rita asked, pouring hot water into a mug and dunking her teabag, staining the water.

I glanced at the door momentarily, thinking perhaps Olivia would arrive late in a flurry of golden hair, cheeks flushed from the report she had been chasing for the day.

I shrugged. "Not tonight, I guess. But there's always next session."

"I worry for that girl," Rita said. "All the pressure the station puts on her, trying to fill her mother's shoes. And you know"—she glanced around conspiratorially—"the last I heard she was seen kissing Sally Aslop!"

I peered at Rita through my glasses. "Rita, we don't meet here for gossip . . ."

"But did you know, Sally Aslop is married to the pastor in Norvale! My church ladies told me all about—"

I poured some sweetener into Rita's mug: two Splendas. I'd memorized everyone's order by now.

"It's none of our business," I said gently, handing her the mug. "Besides, didn't Max just remind us to give people space?"

Rita pursed her lips and looked down at her mug, stirring it absently. For a moment, I could see her as a little girl, caught sneaking an extra cookie before dinner, embarrassed to be chided by an adult.

"Everyone deals with things in their own way," I added with a small shrug. "Maybe instead of guessing, we just hope Olivia turns up next time. She'll feel more welcome that way."

"Of course," Rita said softly, her voice trailing off. "I just miss . . ."

For as long as I could remember, when I rode my bike home from school as a kid, I would see Rita and her sister Martha on their front porch, cups of tea between them, gleefully gossiping about the neighbors. These days, Martha stared out of the window from inside a nursing home, and never said a word.

Rita's eyes went misty. "It doesn't matter how many years I have lived, Henry, life is always hard when it takes a turn."

"I know. Believe me, I know."

"Goodnight," Max called out to the others who were slowly departing, bidding each other well until the next time. He stopped and placed a hand on my shoulder.

"I'll email you, Henry," he said lightly; I knew he was referring to the invoice for tonight's session.

"Great! See you in two weeks," I said.

He looked as though he wanted to say something more, but then he just smiled and followed the others out into the cool Everston evening.

My phone buzzed in my pocket, startling me.

> Henry, sorry to take so long. Had trouble sourcing piping. Can get shipment in a few weeks. Sorry, big job at the old house off Ducks Crossing Road taking up my time.
> Kyle

A shipment in a few weeks? How was I going to last that long? I was busy trying to find a polite way to ask Kyle if he could bump the library up the priority list when Bobby distracted me.

"Hey, Henry, are we meeting at Brandy's or at the library next time?"

"Here," I said, sighing softly. "But we'll be back at the library in no time . . . I hope."

The stragglers disappeared into the night and I returned the stools to their original places.

"I could have packed those away. Come have a drink," Sasha said from behind the bar.

I leaned on the oak. It was getting late, but I wouldn't turn down a drink. Sasha clinked down two tumblers in front of us and poured us each a glass of brandy.

"You look like hell, Briggs," she said.

"I feel like hell," I said, raising my tumbler to Sasha and taking a burning sip.

"You think it helps, all that talking?"

"Well, I think the alternative, at least for most of us, would be much worse."

"You know, a little birdie told me that the library pays for these sessions because it received some sort of mental health initiative from the state," Sasha said, arching an eyebrow. "How very generous of the government."

I sighed, swirling the last of my brandy in the glass. "Was the little birdie Gill?"

"Sure was. On a pension, having free grief counseling sessions goes a long way," she replied, her voice light but her expression sharp. "Although, really, does anything in this world come for free?"

I froze. *Busted.*

"Please don't say anything," I muttered, avoiding her gaze.

Sasha shook her head. "I would never. I think it's honorable what you're doing, Henry. Truly. But I am worried about you. Six people in the group already, and you're talking about adding more? That's a lot to take on. And let's be honest, librarians aren't exactly rolling in cash."

I managed a small smile and finished my brandy, setting the glass down with a quiet clink.

"Thanks for the drink, Sasha. And the space."

With that, I said no more, leaving Sasha staring after me, her concern etched into every line of her face. She didn't understand, and maybe she never would. This wasn't just about generosity or kindness—it was something I *had* to do. I couldn't save Jacob. I couldn't stop the cancer, no matter how many specialists I called, how many treatments we tried, or how much money I spent. But I *could* save this group. I could make sure no one felt alone, no one felt like they had to carry the grief in silence. Hiring Max and hosting small sessions in the library had worked for these people. If the sessions weren't "free," most of them wouldn't come, and how could they? Gill's pension barely covered his rent at the retirement home. Rita's savings went into her sister's care. Emerson and her mom were drowning in medical bills. If there were a price tag, they'd walk away. I felt like I was doing something, and I wanted to do more: welcome more people, create more groups with other counselors. But the truth was, even I had limits. My life savings wouldn't last forever. I needed a plan and, though it wasn't fully formed, I was working on it. I'd have to convince this group of people, who already found talking about their grief almost impossible, to share their stories with strangers. It wouldn't be easy, but if I could convince them, it could mean a future for these sessions. A future for them—and maybe, in some way, a future for me too.

Chapter 3

Emerson

I held on to the keys so tightly that they left a little zigzag across the palm of my hand. I breathed in deeply, then out again. *All you have to do is open the car door, get in, start the ignition, and just go. That's it; it's that simple.*

But nothing is ever that simple, is it? It had been months, and I had not yet managed to get behind that wheel again, even with all the people in my life telling me that I could. I just couldn't. For weeks, my mom had been driving me to and from group sessions, waiting patiently in the car, wondering if this session would be the one to make me want to drive us home. That night, however, she was doing some overtime hours at work, and couldn't wait outside. So instead, she dropped me off and handed me the keys on her way to the bus stop.

"You can do this," she insisted, squeezing my hand.

"It's not long. Just drive home, maybe put the radio on."

She was right; it wasn't a long drive home—twelve minutes, in fact. I loved my mom, of course, more than anything. She was the person who stroked my lips with ice chips and fed me through a straw when I couldn't feed myself. I felt guilty always begging her to drive me around, and I couldn't ask her not to go to work. But this overwhelming sense of positivity she had, that I could just slide back into the driver's seat if only I tried with all my might, was difficult to live with. My mom was the most understanding person I knew, but at the same time, she didn't get the fear or the mess in my head right now.

I would do anything just to drive myself down the road, but instead I was standing there, staring at my reflection in the window, completely frozen.

"I can drive you home, Emmy."

I turned and Winnie stood beside me, her floral tote bag slung over her shoulder, leopard-framed glasses askew, far down the bridge of her nose.

"With that prescription?" I countered.

She grinned, completely unfazed. "I'll have you know my eyes are still as sharp as they were at your age."

"Then why do you need me to read to you?" I asked.

She ignored my question and held out her hand.

"Go on," she said. "I'll drop you off and have some coffee and strawberry cheesecake with your mom."

"But what about your car?"

She shrugged lightly. "I can collect it later; I'll walk from your place. It's good for me, and it's only a couple miles." She tapped her legs. "If I don't move them, these old things will freeze up."

I sighed. "Strawberry cheesecake is Mom's Achilles' heel. You'll be talking for hours."

I offered her the keys, but then closed my fingers around them before she could pick them out of my hand.

"Winnie, do you think this is ever going to get better?"

She paused for a few seconds. "Yes," she said simply. "It will. It will never leave you, but you'll learn to live with it."

When? was what I really wanted to know, but of course she didn't have the answer. I silently slid into the passenger seat, and Winnie put the key in the ignition. This was my brother Sebastian's car, on loan while he was finishing his final year of college. I was supposed to go to college, too—UCLA, the same as him. I'd had it all planned out. I'd managed to secure a gymnastics scholarship at the end of my senior year, my boyfriend Brady securing one for football to the same college. We were going to drive my old Jeep Wrangler from Colorado to California together. A once-in-a-lifetime trip, he would whisper in my ear as he held my hand during those final months of senior year.

It's all gone now.

Five weeks after we had graduated, I was driving to Brady's house. It was a normal Friday afternoon. I'd finished a run, watched Brady play football, and was going to meet him at his house for dinner. I was eighteen. The weather was normal. It was not raining, it was not snowing, the wind wasn't even blowing. I was sober. My phone was in my backpack, which was zipped, on the back seat. And yet, somehow, I lost control of the vehicle. I plowed through the guardrail and into the forest. I hit several trees before slamming into a giant Douglas fir. I remember the glass shattering and the smell of pine, right before everything went black. I have no clear memory of anything else, although sometimes it comes back in pieces: the car skidding, the stars dotting the night sky as I looked up at them, and the feeling of heat. I woke up nineteen hours later in the intensive care unit, with third-degree burns across 6 percent of my body, mainly the left side of my face, my neck, and my shoulder. I'd fractured my pelvis, torn my ACL, and suffered a severe concussion. The hospital had shaved half of my head, and I was wrapped in bandages and covered in IVs and tubes. The detective investigating the crash had told me that upon impact my seatbelt had snapped; I had then been thrown through the windshield and onto the hood of the car, which had exploded into flames. He had told me that, because I had lost consciousness, I had slid off the hood of the car and landed behind the same tree the car had slammed into. It had been the only thing that had shielded me from even further injury and, as the officer put it, certain death. Ironic that a tree could both ruin and save my life.

When it comes to burns, I learned, there were many different kinds. There were first-degree burns, which damage the outer layer of skin, the epidermis. You might get a sunburn and have to rub aloe on yourself. Or maybe you scald your hand on a hot pan, drop some f-bombs, and run it under cold water. Easy peasy.

Then there were second-degree burns, which damage both the outer layer of skin and part of the underlying layer, the dermis. Those could sometimes be mild and treatable at home—think of when you're riding your bike really fast and you skid and fall onto the sidewalk, badly scraping your knees and getting gravel stuck in your skin. Not fun, but also not the end of the world.

Then we graduate to the big leagues with third-degree burns, which destroy both layers of skin *and* the nerve endings where you burned yourself. Ouch.

Oh, and you thought we were done? Nope. There were also fourth-degree burns, which destroy not just the skin but the muscle, tendon—even the bone. Those kinds of burns don't just scar your body, they change your entire life. That is, if you don't die.

I needed multiple surgeries on my face, neck, and shoulder, as well as my hands, and I also needed skin grafts. The bathroom cabinet at home was stocked with every kind of antibiotic out there. It was also stocked with antidepressants. My open wounds were replaced with lighter skin, which was starkly noticeable against my darker complexion. I had always wanted to stand out, and yet now all I wanted to do was hide. I was obsessed with trying to lessen my scarring, so I wore pressure garments and splints. Sometimes these hurt. I had invested so much of my life into gymnastics and now I wasn't even sure I could ever do it again. My injuries completely derailed my training, my scholarship, my ability to even think straight. It's like growing up near the ocean, living and breathing the ocean, and then being told you could never swim ever again. Also, people stared at me. All the fucking time.

But even after all of this, and with the medical bills stacking up and Mom's health insurance only covering some of it, the one thing that changed most drastically was, well, me. Before, I would walk into the gym at school completely unafraid. As a gymnast, I would spend hours of my life dedicated to tempting death: throwing myself into the air and trying to land on my feet on a thin wooden beam, raised four feet in the air. I would run and hurl myself into handsprings, then backflips, twisting gracefully in the air. Now I couldn't even bring myself to get back behind the wheel of a car.

It didn't help that Brady, who had visited me in the hospital only once, broke up with me two weeks later via text. He said it was too hard for him. Too hard for *him*. Getting my heart broken hurt like hell, but it was more than that: I felt ugly down into my bones. I felt like I really did die that night, and I had been reborn a monster.

I had always loved my skin. I had perfect skin. That might sound extra, but it was true—I *actually* had perfect, airbrushed skin and all my friends would constantly remind me about it. *You are radiant, Emerson. Have you ever had a pimple in your life? Your skin is perfect, you glow like the actual sun.*

I didn't feel like the sun anymore; I felt like an angry, dark cloud. The kind of cloud that brews a thunderstorm. Everybody runs from a thunderstorm.

When I walked in the door, I saw Mom asleep on the couch. The house was quiet, lit only by the soft glow of a lamp in the corner and the flicker of a pumpkin-scented candle still burning on the coffee table. She had draped a blanket over herself, her purple fluffy slippers poking out the end. A crisp breeze drifted in through a cracked window, carrying that damp-leaf woodsmoke smell I loved. It was the kind of cool that clung to your skin, reminding you that summer was over.

I shook her gently.

"Mom," I said softly.

Her eyes fluttered open, confused then triumphant.

"You did it! Oh, Emmy, you drove home. I'm so proud of you."

"Oh, well, I . . ." I trailed off, struggling to explain to my mother that, no, I didn't drive myself home; her daughter was still terrified of cars.

"She sure did!" Winnie said brightly, stepping out from the doorway. "And I was promised some of your strawberry cheesecake for dessert."

"Winnie, I didn't know you were stopping by!" Mom said, surprised. "Come on in."

"I won't be long, Meera, Emmy just wanted company on the drive home."

Mom beamed. "That's my girl! I'll go put the kettle on."

After Mom disappeared into the kitchen, I felt Winnie squeeze my shoulder.

"I'll pick you up. From now on, if you need a ride, you just let me know. I'll help you."

"Winnie—"

She stopped me. "Just until you're ready to do it yourself. It's nothing."

I felt shame prickle my skin. "What if I'm never ready?"

"You will be, Emmy, you will be." She stared into my eyes and gave me an encouraging smile. I nodded slowly.

"Cake is ready!" Mom sang out, and I hung back as Winnie went to join her in the kitchen. I wasn't in the mood for cake anymore.

My alarm trilled at seven thirty in the morning, and I automatically hit the snooze button. Rolling over, I was immediately confronted by fur in my face. Our cat, Mr. Socks, liked to rotate his bedtime visits between Mom and me. Lately, he'd been spending a lot of time in my bed. Mom thought it was because he knew I needed him, but I felt like he had a hidden agenda. He knew I left for work at the crack of dawn every morning, which meant he'd get my bed all to himself before his breakfast.

"Mr. Socks, will you go to work for me?"

He lifted one eye lazily and began to purr. I guess that was a no then.

I didn't mind. Even after everything I'd been through, Mr. Socks still slipped into my lap on the couch and rubbed against my legs when he spotted me in the kitchen. So many people had become stilted around me—there was always a pause when they saw me for the first time, as if they weren't quite sure what to say, or they needed extra time to process me. At least Mr. Socks treated me the same.

I wasn't the most popular girl in high school. I was hell-bent on gymnastics, so I didn't have too many friends outside of my team and Abbie Glenfield, who sat next to me in chemistry class and saved me every time there was a pop quiz—but I did date Brady, the school's quarterback. People knew who I was.

In those first few months after the accident, I didn't want to see anyone. I didn't want to be *seen*. I needed constant treatment, constant help, constant reassurance. I cried every day. I didn't want people to think I was weak. Especially not *them*, my new college team. The one I'd dreamed about joining for years. The elite girls I'd idolized in competitions, who had already proven themselves on national stages. My new coach reached out, checking in on my recovery and adding me to the team group chat early. Everyone had welcomed me before the season even began, sending messages filled with excitement, offering to FaceTime, asking if I needed anything before move-in. It should have made me feel included. After all, I'd wanted to show them that I belonged, that I wasn't just some high school standout who got lucky with a scholarship. But instead, it felt suffocating.

Gymnastics is not a sport in which you can exhibit weakness. It has an exhaustive checklist of requirements: balance, precision, strength, agility, flexibility, coordination, and endurance, and in an instant, all of that had been taken from me. I had been the best at it, and suddenly I was learning how to move my body without screaming in pain. How was I supposed to face a team of champions when my recovery wasn't even guaranteed?

So I didn't. I stopped answering their texts. I ignored their messages, their offers to call. I couldn't stomach seeing their perfect routines on TikTok, their medal posts, their glossy smiles on Instagram. I stopped posting altogether. I learned that when you shut people out, after a while, they stop trying to get back in. I didn't blame them: if you repeatedly visit a field to see sunflowers, but the sunflowers are never there, would you keep going back? I did the same with my high school friends. What was the point of staying connected to people who were moving on with their lives? They didn't understand what I was going through, and I didn't want them to. It was like cutting a cord: clean, final.

The only person I didn't shut out was Coach Tillman. She wouldn't let me. She texted almost daily, called every week without fail. She was always asking how I was, checking in with the latest from the doctors. She was always reminding me the scholarship was deferred, not lost. She was the one who wrote the glowing reference that helped me get the scholarship in the first place. The university was willing to defer my start, but I wasn't just worried about the training it would take to get back to where I was. I thought of the makeup, the sparkles, the perfectly coordinated leotards, the smooth muscles, all under close watch. It would be a joke, me performing. Most days, I couldn't even look at my own reflection much less subject myself to the scrutiny of judges looking over every inch of my body.

Brady, however, did go off to college. He left with his friends; they went on their own road trip and he posted it all over social media. Within a month, he had a new girlfriend. Meanwhile, I was still in active recovery. Between Brady, gymnastics, my friends, and the ache I felt every time I opened my eyes, it was too much.

And then I dropped an entire display of hiking poles on Henry during my first shift at Adventure Rudy's. Oops. With physical therapy, I had gained some of my strength back—not the kind required to complete a backward flip and twist, but enough to stock shelves, man the register, and pretend not to notice when customers stole granola bars from the impulse-buy section. Adventure Rudy's was an outdoor retail store catering to tourists and local hikers, selling everything from thermal socks to bear spray. People came through Everston every season, eager to take advantage of the nearby trails. Some came prepared. Others had clearly underestimated Colorado's terrain.

The store was chaos that afternoon. A busload of tourists had just come through, and I had been restocking a rack of trekking poles when I lost control, sending them clattering to the floor, right at the feet of a man flipping through a field guide. I knew who he was; everyone in town did. Henry. He was the local librarian and pretty much adored by everyone.

I bent down to pick up the fallen poles just as he knelt to do the same. "Sorry," I mumbled, "didn't mean to do that."

"No harm done," Henry replied, straightening as he placed the poles back on the rack. He was holding a trail guide to Stormy Peaks.

"Planning a hike?" I asked.

He glanced down at the book, as if he'd forgotten he was holding it. "Oh." He admitted, "My brother loved hiking. I'm trying to figure out where to scatter his ashes."

He said it so casually, I felt myself reel back.

Henry noticed and quickly added, "That makes me sound like a serial killer, doesn't it? I promise I'm not, he died of cancer."

"Well, what a relief," I replied dryly.

Henry grinned. "I don't hike all that much, to be honest."

"Well, grief makes us do weird things," I said. "I was in a car accident and now I can't even touch the door handle of a car, let alone drive one."

He studied me for a beat before speaking again. "I'm starting a grief support group at the library," he said. "It's not only for people who are grieving death, and it's a no-pressure space. It's free; you should stop by sometime."

Coach Tillman had suggested therapy for my mental health after the crash, and so had my doctors, my nurses, and even my new boss. Mom already had two jobs, and insurance was barely covering the medical bills, so I couldn't add anything else. What Henry was suggesting was a different kind of therapy, with no bills attached. I didn't think I had anything to lose.

I hadn't lost anything since. I just hadn't found it yet, either.

That morning, I spent most of my shift in the hiking gear section, answering customer questions about trekking poles (ones that were still standing upright this time), shoes, and other equipment. *Yes, this style comes in a nine wide. No, you don't need special socks to wear them. My favorite trail? Eagle's Head.* That sort of thing. A tourist came in midmorning asking what our best hiking boot was— *Speedgoats? Merrells? Danner Trails? Nikes?* He bought the pair I didn't recommend, didn't even try them on, and never once looked me in the eye.

What a fulfilling exchange.

I moved on to a lady and her kids looking at the raincoats.

"What's on your face?" the little boy asked, squinting up at me.

"Andrew!" the mother exclaimed, grabbing the boy's arm and yanking him away from me.

"I am so incredibly sorry. Kids are . . . you know . . ."

I wasn't bothered by kids asking direct questions about my burns; they were just naturally curious and honest. I was much more bothered by people who obviously pitied me. Far beyond those who wouldn't meet my eye, like Hiking Boot Man, they were the ones who made me feel fragile, like a broken bird fallen from its nest.

"It's fine. I had an accident. But I'm getting better."

"Does it hurt?" he asked.

"Not anymore," I lied.

"Wow, you are really brave," his sister piped up, before handing her mom a sweater. "Can I have this?"

"Sure, honey," the woman answered quickly.

"Just these please," she said to me, handing over the raincoats and sweater. I had a feeling she would probably buy the entire store if it meant she could leave faster.

I rang up her items, and the woman paid. As they left the store, I heard her turn on her son.

"Andy, do you really think that was appropriate—" And they disappeared from view.

By the time my shift was nearly over, I had almost finished taking stock.

"You all good, Emerson?"

I glanced up to see Jarrod, the store manager, hovering by the door.

"Yep, everything's fine!" I chirped. Jarrod was nice, but he asked me if I was okay at least four times per shift. If you couldn't actually kill someone with kindness, I was pretty sure you could make them nauseous with it.

"Okay, well, you can finish up early if you'd like. Darren got in early."

He probably asked Darren to come in earlier just in case I couldn't handle the full shift. Normally, that would have irritated me, but it was Thursday, which meant I'd be heading to

Winnie's house soon, where we'd drink tea and talk about the book we'd picked out for the week.

I handed Jarrod the stock list. "Thanks. I've done most of it already."

He nodded. "You still okay for Saturday's shift? It'll be busy."

"More than capable," I said, a little too dryly.

Jarrod blushed. "Of course. Yeah, I know that. I'll see you Saturday!"

A year ago, Winnie's husband, Cliff, left her. After forty-something years together, he just disappeared while Winnie was at the supermarket. Wild. I thought Brady was the worst person on Earth, but my vote now went to Cliff (though Brady was still a close second).

When I joined the grief group, I didn't expect anything to happen. I was only going to make Mom happy. But then Winnie sat down next to me, and she handed me a bright-red lipstick.

"What's this for?"

"You've been fussing with your neck for ten minutes. Wear red. Everybody will be looking at the red, not your burns."

This was the first time someone had acknowledged the elephant in the room. I immediately found myself drawn to Winnie and, despite our nearly sixty-year age gap, she became my new best friend. Imagine that: nineteen years old and my favorite person in the world was seventy-eight. After work, I'd bike to her house. We'd hang out all the time, under the guise of our so-called book club (which, let's be honest, was just the two of us). We'd swap novels and poetry books, bird-watch from her back porch, and experiment with whatever new recipe she'd find in some decades-old magazine. Somewhere along the way, I got her hooked on reality TV—*Real Housewives*, anyone? *Beverly Hills* was her favorite. Given that Henry invited us to share poetry in our sessions, we also had plenty on our list: Mary Oliver,

Audre Lorde, Sylvia Plath. Our favorite poet at the moment was B.W. Paisley. Her work just felt so accessible. Reading her words, you could tell she deeply felt the emotions that she'd written onto the page. She was a real person, not some old dead white guy like John Keats or Percy Bysshe Shelley.

"How was work?" Winnie asked, as I plopped myself down on her couch and reached for the cookies she had already placed on the table.

"Fine, same old same old."

I bit into the cookie, relishing its gooey chocolate center. Being with Winnie was so comforting. She wasn't your quintessential grandma. She was small, with soft lavender-gray hair that was wavy and full of life, and wore half-moon glasses that always seemed slightly askew. She baked like she owned her own patisserie, knitted like it was an Olympic sport, and cruised around town in a beat-up mustard-yellow Volkswagen Beetle. She also had the cutest tees, colorful scarves, and to-die-for boots. She attended the Sonic Bloom Festival in Denver every year without fail, played video games like a pro, and had the energy of someone born thirty years later than she actually was.

"What's on the agenda for today?" she asked.

"Whatever you like! We can either watch a movie, or we can read some poetry?"

What I liked most about reading poetry with Winnie was that she'd always relate the poem to a story about her life, and I loved listening to her wild tales about former lovers and the time she met The Rolling Stones *and* Madonna in one night. And yes, all of her adventures with Cliff too. I knew that she was devastated about him, but I think it helped her to share, so I always listened.

She was halfway through telling me about the first time she and Cliff went to New York City when my phone rang. Mom.

"Hey, I'm just at Winnie's—we're doing our Thursday book club thing."

"Oh, that's okay, honey, but I need you to come pick me up."

I looked over at Winnie, slightly panicked.

What is it? she mouthed.

"Um, I can't, we're just in the middle of a really important chapter," I stammered.

"What?" Mom and Winnie said simultaneously.

"Emerson. My car broke down, I'm just past Highland Street. I need you to get in your brother's car and pick me up." Her sentences were getting choppy, which meant she was already irritated.

"I can't," I said.

"What do you mean you *can't?*"

"Because—"

"Emerson Marie Coleman." She drew my name out in a dangerously quiet voice. Yikes. "You will come pick your mother up, right now!"

I knew when I was defeated.

"I'm sorry, Mom. I really can't, I don't have Sebastian's car."

"What do you mean you don't have the car?"

I sighed. "I lied. I rode my bike here. And I didn't drive the car home the other night after group, either; Winnie did."

She was silent. Silence is the worst because it holds both the blessing and catastrophe of the unknown, and you have no idea what you'll get stuck with. I would rather she started yelling.

"You need to get in the car and come get me. I'm stranded on the side of the road, Emerson," she said finally.

"I *can't.*"

"Emerson, this has gone on for too long, you hear me? Enough of this. You need to get over this fear."

"You don't understand!" I said, anger bursting out of my chest. "You'll never understand what this feels like!" I hung up the phone, jumped up from the sofa, where only moments before

I'd been happily nestled, and rushed out, furious tears escaping despite my best efforts.

"Emmy, wait!" Winnie called after me. I knew she'd heard the entire conversation, but I didn't turn back. She couldn't help me. I jumped on my bike and pedaled away.

When I did a salto on the balance beam, it felt like I was flying. Now it felt as if my life was split between the two sides of the beam. On one side was the life I had before, with perfect skin and a triple-twisting double layout that would drive a crowd wild. On the other was the life I had now. I was barely holding on to either.

I rode for at least twenty minutes, but instead of going back home, I found myself at the library. The library was open late. I first discovered this when I'd had a panic attack some months ago and needed a temporary refuge. It was quiet, it was safe, it was somewhere I could just be—thoughts of gymnastics, my accident, even my skin, put aside while I immersed myself in a book.

I parked my bike near the entryway, fitting it neatly into the bike rack, and went inside, making my way to the poetry section. I'd always hated poetry in school. I couldn't understand why we needed to write an essay about a door being blue and how that meant the poet was suffering from depression. Sometimes a door is just blue, you know?

But Henry introduced me to a new kind of poetry. Maybe in exchange for all the crap life had given me, the universe gifted me with these books, because when I read them they made me feel seen. And, despite all the moments I spent curled up in a ball avoiding the mirror, they never made me feel ugly.

I trailed my fingers across the poetry shelf, not stopping until I found what I was looking for. I pulled out a book and found a secluded spot to sit down but hadn't even made it ten pages in when I read something that hit every nerve in my entire body.

*On all the days
you can't bring yourself
to look into a mirror.
On all the nights the tears
stream like a river—
I hope someone reminds you
that the life you have is worth living.
I hope they listen to your fears
and reservations in the way
they listen to your dreams
and aspirations: with purpose,
with a knowing that they are
equally as important.
I hope you cut the strings tying
you to the person you used to be;
they are not there anymore,
long gone, but you are more beautiful
than you were before.
Because you have carried on;
despite the world telling you not to,
you have risen for a new dawn.*

"Emerson?"

I hurriedly wiped away my tears.

"Oh, hi, Henry. Um, sorry, are you closing up now?"

He checked his watch.

"Still have another hour or so. Doesn't look very comfortable down there."

"The readers' corner is out of action," I said, and he grinned, rolling his eyes.

"Yeah, yeah, I know." He studied my face, his grin fading. "Are you okay?"

I shrugged. "Had a fight with my mom."

"Ah. That can happen with moms."

"She just doesn't understand what it's like. You know? She doesn't get it."

Henry knelt down beside me, resting his elbows on his knees. "I felt like my mom didn't understand either. I was pretty callous about it—I really thought I was the only one in the world dealing with Jacob's death. Like my grief somehow held more weight, more anguish. I barely spoke to her. I shut her out because I thought she couldn't possibly understand what I was feeling. And in doing that, I think I made her feel like she'd lost me too. She was already mourning one son, and I made her feel like she was mourning another."

"My mom hasn't lost me, though. She just doesn't see me anymore."

"Well, maybe that's how my mother felt about me. Maybe she felt like she had failed because she couldn't take on my grief in addition to her own," he replied gently.

"Maybe," I conceded reluctantly. "It's just—it's always been my mom, my brother Sebastian, and me. My dad left when I was little, and ever since then, it's been the three of us against the world. And now it's like, ever since the accident, she doesn't even look at me the same way. I don't know if she's disappointed or just tired of me."

Henry's expression softened. "I'm sorry. It's hard when you feel like the person who's always been there suddenly doesn't get you."

I hugged my knees. "I just hate fighting with her."

He gestured to the book in my lap. "What are you reading?"

I turned the cover over. "It's another book by B.W. Paisley. This one is called *Hope for Tomorrow*."

"Poetry?"

I nodded.

"She writes about loss in the way that I feel it. She understands."

"The beauty of poetry is that it can evoke feelings like that sometimes. Perhaps you could read this out next week?"

"At the meeting?"

He nodded. "If this poet is important to you, I'm sure the group would love to hear her words as well."

"I don't know. What if the others hate it, and it makes them feel worse?"

Henry rose to his feet. "You know, I started the group specifically because of poetry. I read a poem and it was the only thing at the time that got me back up off this exact floor. I think if you've found a book that does the same for you, then you should share it with others who may need it too."

I nodded distantly, watching him as he moved back toward the counter to serve someone.

Henry's words lingered, but so did my doubts. Sharing wasn't just about reading lines on a page—it meant opening up, even just a little; something that I was trying so hard to do more of, but still found so difficult. I stared down at the book in my lap, brushing my thumb over the embossed title. *Hope for Tomorrow*. The irony wasn't lost on me. I'd spent so much time lately thinking about what my life had been like before the accident. The certainty I felt each day. My body had been a finely tuned machine then, every movement deliberate, and I knew what I wanted from my future. But could there really be hope for tomorrow when that future had changed so drastically?

My coach said moving forward would be just like riding a bike. That I would be able to drive again, perform again, feel comfortable enough to get back into the life that I'd once had. But I wasn't getting back onto the same bike. This bike had different gears, different speeds—I was wobbling. I missed how it felt to fly, but I knew that I would be safer on the ground.

Chapter 4

Wren

I was told the firsts were always the hardest—like the first letter that arrived in the mail addressed to her; or the first evening I found myself in our favorite restaurant without her; or the first joke that made me laugh before I realized I couldn't share it with her. Of course, there were also the obvious firsts, like the first string of holidays without her, the first birthday, and the first anniversary of her death. The firsts went by in a haze, as though they weren't even real, and perhaps they weren't, because I spent so much of that time ignoring my pain. What no one tells you, or at least what I was not prepared for, was that the *seconds* are, in fact, the hardest. Fourteen months had somehow passed since Lucy died. To me, the firsts seemed easier to gloss over. People expected you to be struggling. They were patient. But by the time it all rolled around again, the same people would expect that you'd recovered, as if somehow grief was simply linear and not infinite.

Lucy would have been twenty-nine today. *Would have.* She passed two months before her birthday. She would never be twenty-nine. She would never get older. This date would always be there on the calendar, a constant reminder that I would grow older and she would not, she would forever be frozen in time.

Lucy loved birthdays. She loved her birthday, my birthday, anyone's birthday. She would always cheer, *It's your birthday! Today is about celebrating you!* She could make anyone smile and enjoy their birthday, whether it was our neighbor dreading the big 4-0 or her mom, who would obsessively tally her grays.

After the accident, I stopped paying attention to birthdays. My friends, my editor, my cousin Marnie, they all celebrated their birthdays and I ignored them all. I ignored my own birthday too. I felt tiny under the weight of my grief; even a single person appeared like a giant by comparison, and large groups? Almost unthinkable. Time continued to march forward, and on so many days I was either completely untethered from it or desperately trying to hold on to everything that had not been catastrophically upended.

Everston was so far away from the life I knew. It felt simple, quieter, like I could do nothing here, except restore the old house during the day, and drink wine on the swing as the evening rolled in.

Today, the evening was fresh, a cool breeze coming down from the mountain ranges. Stars dotted the sky, growing brighter as the night became darker. It was a curious thing, the idea of mourning: stuck between wanting to remember and wanting to forget.

I loved celebrating Lucy's birthday. Every year, we went to Momo & More, a dumpling bar tucked down an alleyway, marked only by a flickering neon dumpling sign. I don't even remember how we found it, but to us, it had the best dumplings in New York. One year, the chef surprised Lucy with a cake shaped like a dumpling. I took a Polaroid of her pretending to take a bite, laughing as everyone worried her hair would catch fire from the candles. That photo lived on our fridge until the day I took everything down and packed it all away in a box. I could still picture it perfectly. Her wide smile, the glow of the candles, the way her eyes sparkled in the dim light. Part of me clung to that memory, desperate to keep her alive in my mind. But another part would give anything to forget—because tonight, I wasn't at

Momo & More. Lucy was gone, and I was there on the swing, drinking alone. On cue, Lucy appeared beside me on the wooden seat. She was blurry at first, as though my eyes couldn't quite adjust, or perhaps that was just the wine.

I raised my glass to her. "It's your birthday," I said, and it came out more slurred than I had intended.

"You shouldn't drink so much," she replied.

I scoffed. "Since when do you oppose a glass or two of red? We'd always drink this much at Momo & More."

"But not because we were sad."

"I'm not sad," I objected, "I'm celebrating your birthday."

Someone must have been barbecuing somewhere. The smell of tangy glaze and burnt wood drifted into the front yard.

"Did you notice the fence?" I asked, pointing to it. I'd spent nearly the whole week gutting the weeds and clearing all the refuse in the front yard. The fence was visible now; I'd also given it a fresh coat of white paint, and it gleamed in the moonlight.

"It's beautiful," Lucy replied.

"And I've sanded the decking along the porch," I said. "Tomorrow, I'm going to stain it, it'll look just as it did before. And I'll patch the railings, have the missing ones replaced."

Wouldn't that be simple, if you could replace the hole left by a loved one in the same way you could replace a broken railing.

Lucy didn't respond for a moment, and I looked to her, afraid she was gone again.

"I don't want you to feel this way anymore," she said. "I want you to live again, to be out in the world."

"I am," I responded. "Did I not just tell you I've repainted the front fence?"

"I don't mean the progress on this house."

"Well, what then?" I said. "Because here I am in this town, very far from Manhattan, and I sure think I'm 'living,'" I used air quotes because they always drove Lucy crazy.

"I want you to find love again," she said.

"I could date if I wanted to," I replied, though even I could hear the doubt in my own voice. "I just choose not to." I had my reasons—dating felt like too much risk, too much vulnerability. And really, what would I even talk about? *Hi, I'm still grieving my dead fiancée, what do you do in your spare time?*

"You don't know how to open your heart again."

I waved my hand at her. "I don't need to. I still have you."

I reached for the bottle of wine and realized that it was now empty. Sighing, I stood and moved into the house, beginning to search the kitchen cupboards. I was sure I had another bottle in there somewhere. I reached for the top cupboard, pulling it open, but the door snapped from its hinges. Startled, I let go and the cupboard door came crashing down onto the countertop, knocking three mugs onto the floor, and sending shards of ceramic pieces everywhere.

I stared down at the mess on the floor. "This house is me." I laughed, the effects of the wine sending jittery sensations through my body. "I am as broken as this house."

Lucy stared at me.

"What's the point?" I said. "It doesn't matter how many parts of this house I fix, something else breaks. Perhaps it's better off staying broken, just like me." I stormed to the foyer and reached for my coat. The cool evening air would do me good. Main Street wasn't far, a twenty-minute walk at most, but the night air might sober me up, clear my head. Maybe that's what I needed.

"Where are you going?" Lucy asked, standing in the kitchen, arms folded. It's an image I had of her, only we weren't in this house, we were home.

"Town," I said, twisting as I shrugged myself into the sleeves. "Want to come with me? I'm sure we could find Everston's own Momo & More. We can start again, here, somewhere new." I turned to face her, but the kitchen was empty.

*

Everston didn't have many bars. In fact, it had a grand total of three. The sports bar was too loud, and the dive bar, also known as The Den—sticky floors, flickering neon sign—didn't appeal to me all that much, so I chose Brandy's. It was well lit and warm, and there was only a trickle of people inside, most of whom were huddled on the far side on stools. I shook off my coat and settled at the bar, ordering a glass of wine from Sasha, the owner. We'd only spoken once, weeks ago, when I was there on a rather difficult day, and I'd asked about an old photograph on the wall. She'd told me her family had owned Brandy's for decades and the name had stuck.

A young man approached the bar and asked Sasha for more water for the group of people. I wondered what kind of group they were. Maybe it was an after-work drinks thing, or some kind of club. It was odd to see them gathered in such a small space, with stools in a sort of half circle, and I couldn't help but try to guess their purpose. While I was observing them, Sasha and the man exchanged easy banter about books. She called him Henry. He was wearing a turtleneck and glasses, was clean shaven, and had a nice smile. He was just the type of person you could create a character about, but I shut that thought down immediately. I hadn't written in well over a year, and perhaps I would never write again. What was the point, when every time I even thought about a pen, or a laptop, or a journal, it set my insides on fire? I suddenly spotted Gill among the group. Instinctively, I shifted slightly, turning away so he wouldn't notice me. The last thing I needed was for him to see me drinking alone in a bar and to start asking questions.

I shifted my focus back to the conversation at the bar. Henry was gesturing to a paperback he'd set on the bar counter. "Do you want to borrow it after I'm finished?"

"That book is good," I said, before I could stop myself. "But the author is not."

Henry looked over at me. "How do you know?" he asked.

"I've met him," I replied. "He's very rude to his fans."

Henry appeared interested. "Oh, wow. That's a shame, but good to know," he said, and he extended his hand. "I'm Henry, I work over at the library."

I shook his outstretched hand. "Wren," I replied, wondering if I would ever get used to it, introducing myself as this new person.

"Any particular reason you're drinking alone at Brandy's?" he asked.

It was a very pointed question, almost rude for any other sort of situation. But in this moment, I realized it wasn't meant to be prying. Something in me could tell: *he knows*. I could see it in the careful way his eyes lingered on me, as if he recognized the weight that I carried. Grief was all over me, like a permanent badge that only those who wore one, too, could see. He seemed to understand, like I understood, in a way that those who were not in mourning could not. And I could see it on him, too, in the way he spoke—carefully, cautiously—as though trying not to disturb something fragile.

"I'm celebrating a birthday," I replied.

"Yours?"

"No, my fiancée's."

Henry looked at the door, as if expecting someone to walk in at any moment.

"She's not coming," I said quietly. "Not unless you can conjure the dead."

He nodded, his expression shifting. "My brother passed away a couple years back. I have celebrated two of his birthdays, alone, in this very bar."

"One of them he spent two hours singing through a Bon Jovi set list," Sasha remarked.

Henry shrugged. "Jacob would have liked it."

"We used to go and get dumplings," I said, staring into the wineglass. "She loved birthdays."

"There's no shame in continuing to celebrate them," he replied.

I hastily changed the subject. "Are you some sort of wine connoisseur group?" I asked.

"Oh, no." He laughed. "We're a grief group." He looked over at them momentarily. "It's connected us in a way that we wouldn't have been otherwise. They're my friends." His green eyes shone when he said this.

"A grief group . . ." I echoed.

"Loss, heartache, bereaved partners, identity struggles." He smiled. "There's lots of reasons people grieve."

"Yes, I suppose that is true," I replied, and I noticed Gill sitting next to a young man with bright-pink hair. These must be the folks he wanted to introduce me to.

"Would you like to meet the group?" Henry asked. "We meet every other week, on a Tuesday, usually at the library."

I suddenly felt more sober. A grief group? An extra reminder that Lucy wasn't coming back? Oh, that was all I needed.

"I'm sorry," I said, reaching for my coat. "Maybe another time."

"There's no fee," Henry offered. "And often there are baked goods."

I slipped into my coat quickly, offering a small smile. "I really should be going," I said, and I turned from him, toward the door. I momentarily stopped in the doorway, glancing back at Henry returning to the group of people. There was a young woman reading from a book; the words had a rhythm I almost recognized, as if from something blurred by time. I knew I'd heard them before, I'd just long forgotten them. I stepped out into the cool night and disappeared into the shadows.

Chapter 5

Henry

We were told that metastatic pancreatic cancer was the hardest to detect. Jacob's was so advanced, they gave him less than a year. It didn't matter how many times doctors, nurses, or friends told me I couldn't have known—I still felt like I should have. He was my twin. I could always sense when he was sad or angry or excited. Why hadn't I sensed this? But tragedy often arrives in the middle of an ordinary day. One moment, life is just as you've always known it. The next, it leaves you gasping for air.

I straightened the picture frames along the windowsill, pruning the daisies a nurse had delivered earlier. "What about skydiving?" I asked. "You always said you'd love it. When we get you out of here, we should go together."

Jacob smiled weakly. "You know I'm not leaving here, Henry."

"You don't know that," I said, forcing lightness into my voice. "What about Australia? We could go somewhere far away, anywhere you want."

Jacob huffed a small laugh. "Henry, you hate leaving Everston. You won't even go visit Mom and Dad in Hawaii."

"But I could," I insisted. "We could go to Iceland, or Egypt, or—"

"Think you could get me a coffee?" he interrupted.

Jacob loved coffee. He tried for years to convert me. He would offer me lattes, cappuccinos, espressos, macchiatos, iced coffee, drip coffee, even Irish coffee. He tried ordering different flavored beans, pairing the coffee with pastries, adding sweetener and syrups, you name it. But I refused them all. I was a tea drinker. There was nothing about that bitter, acrid, nauseating stuff that I would ever enjoy.

"You're not supposed to have . . ." But I trailed off when I saw the look on his face.

I smiled. "Of course. I think there's a travel magazine in the waiting room; we can pick a destination while you sip."

Jacob coughed, his whole body shaking with the effort. "Henry," he said finally, taking a deep breath. "I'm not leaving this room. I'm dying. The sooner you accept that, the easier this will be."

"For who?" My voice cracked. "It's never going to be easy."

"It doesn't mean I won't be with you."

"You can't say that like it makes any of this okay," I said, my eyes burning.

He gave a tiny shrug.

"It's not over yet. You have to keep fighting."

Jacob sighed, wincing as he shifted. "I'm tired, Henry. That doesn't mean I've given up. It just means I'm ready."

"Well, I'm not," I whispered, tears spilling over. "I still need you."

He held my gaze, something in his eyes softer than I'd ever seen—acceptance, maybe. Or goodbye.

I slipped out of the room and found the vending machine at the end of the hall. It was out of coffee. I pressed my forehead against the glass, listening to the hum of machines down the palliative care ward. I had failed Jacob again. I couldn't even bring him the one thing he'd asked for.

And there was nothing I could do to fix what was happening to him, no matter how desperately I wanted to.

*

If I couldn't change what had happened to Jacob, I could at least try to create something good in the space he left behind. The library became an anchor. Something to pour myself into. The steady routine of the library became the foundation that kept me from crumbling completely.

Sunday became my second-favorite day. It used to be the first, but Tuesday claimed that honor after I started the grief group. I liked Sundays because the library was usually quiet and it gave me more time to restock shelves, catalog new materials and books, refill the stationery supplies, and prepare new displays for popular genres and books. Once I papier-mâchéd a large Saphira for our Eragon display and strung it up above the YA fantasy section. But the main reason I loved Sundays so much was because I had time to sneak out for an almond croissant from Brew Haven, the café across the road.

Kyle was tinkering with the ceiling again, and I'd been hovering next to him for the last twenty minutes.

"Henry," he said, without looking down. "It's hard to fix things with someone watching."

"Sorry," I replied sheepishly. "I'm just really anxious to have our reading corner back."

"I should be done this week, and you'll be back to normal next week."

I clapped my hands triumphantly, a little too loudly, causing a nearby patron to jump and scowl at me.

"Oh, that's great news! I can't thank you enough."

"Well," Kyle said. "Don't thank me until you see the final bill."

"Can I get you a coffee or a tea, Kyle?"

"Double shot espresso with chocolate syrup and three sugars would be amazing, Henry," he replied. I felt myself grimace and couldn't help but think of the way Jacob would have laughed at this.

I popped my head into the staff room. "Lana," I said, catching her with half a sandwich raised to her lips. "Coffee?"

She smiled. "I'd love one."

"Maybe a cookie too?" I offered.

She sighed. "Oh, go on then. Ask them if they have any of those macadamia and pine nut ones."

I laughed. "Yes, ma'am, I'll be back in ten minutes."

The day was crisp, with the sun casting a gentle warmth across Main Street as I stepped out into the light. A smattering of people were strolling about, enjoying the mild early autumn weather. Brew Haven was buzzing with customers, many of whom were savoring the sunshine at tables and chairs in the adjoining courtyard. As I ordered the coffees, I glanced momentarily to the back of the café and saw Max sitting in the far corner.

I'd met Max when the group was still just an idea. I'd found him online—searched "grief therapist" and clicked on the first result that popped up for a clinic in Norvale. When I emailed him about starting the group meetings, he'd requested to meet me individually first. I'd walked into his office with my hair sticking out in every direction and mismatched socks. It had been a *day*.

Max had looked at me thoughtfully, before opening his notebook.

"You mentioned in your email that you're starting a group," he said. "For people who are grieving?"

"Well, that's the basic idea, yes," I replied. "I put a sign up at the library I run, and I have had some interest."

He nodded and scribbled something down.

"What do you think you might talk about?"

How I'd do anything to have my brother back.

"Oh, all sorts of things," I said. "Feelings, I suppose."

"That's a good start," he responded. "How many people do you think will be in the group?"

"Well, I've had four people inquire. So, it would be five, including myself," I replied. "I guess I'm not sure where to begin."

"I would imagine so." Max looked up from his notebook.

"But I think it's important," I continued, "to share grief with others who have experienced it."

"It's natural that we form bonds with people who can understand us," Max said. "It's innately human."

"Great," I'd replied. "So you'll help?"

Max had nodded. "Just on one condition, Henry," he replied.

"Anything!"

"You understand that every grief process is different. We can't always help everyone."

I thought about the first few times people had begun to inquire about the sign. *I could use someone to talk to*, one person said, their grief heavy, almost tangible, like a weight they didn't know how to carry. I remembered the way some voices had wavered when they asked about the meetings, and I could see that their pain felt all-encompassing, nearly swallowing them whole. And then when I said *yes, a place for you*, I watched as something shifted. Small at first, barely noticeable. A little more ease in their shoulders, a spark in their eyes; hope. Of course, there was a long road ahead, but it was the start of something.

I pushed the memory aside as I approached Max, deeply engrossed in the book he was reading. "The reading corner should be fixed by next session," I said brightly. "So it's back to books instead of whiskey."

"Henry." Max smiled, looking up, and he closed his book. "Day off?"

"Never," I replied. "Just enjoying a moment of peace and quiet, and grabbing some coffees and pastries."

He pointed to the remains of a donut. "Have you tried the jelly donuts?"

"Of course," I said. "They've supported me through many after-school days."

Max chuckled. "I'm considering having another."

"I'm glad I saw you, I wanted to run something by you," I said. "An idea I've had." Max gestured to the empty seat, and I sat down. "I was going through our outreach programs for the next six months, and I thought that perhaps the library could host a poetry evening."

Max looked at me blankly. "A what?"

"A poetry evening," I repeated, enthusiastically. "Of course, I'd need to run this by the board, but I could make flyers, talk to patrons and local businesses about selling tickets. And the best part? The poetry readings could be done by members of the group."

Max's expression didn't change, so I pressed on. "You know how hard it is for people to talk about their pain," I said. "But poetry? Poetry gives people a way to say things they don't know how to say otherwise. It's not just words—it's a way to process everything, a way for people to share something without feeling like they have to lay it all out. It wouldn't just be an event. It would be a chance for them to express their grief in a way other than just . . . talking about it. It could be healing." I hesitated, catching myself. "I even think I could convince Olivia to write an article on it." I paused, reconsidering. Olivia was elusive at the best of times, but it was worth a shot. "I mean, if she's not too busy, of course," I added.

Max was listening, but his brow had furrowed slightly, and I could tell he was weighing his words carefully.

"You hate the idea," I said, flatly.

He shook his head. "I don't hate the idea, Henry. I think it's admirable you want to support the group. I just wonder if you're taking too much on."

"I'm not sure I understand. I've got time to do it, so why shouldn't I?"

"Well, I just wonder if you're compensating for the pain of losing Jacob? Maybe you don't realize it, but you might be trying to fix something you couldn't fix with him . . ."

I opened my mouth to argue, but his steady knowing look stopped me. It was the kind of look that had pulled me out of countless spirals before, a mix of understanding and brutal honestly. Max could read me like a book.

"It's okay to care," Max continued, gently, "but it isn't your job to fix everything."

"I know that," I replied. "But look at all the progress everyone's made since we started meeting. These group sessions, they've been a lifeline for all of us. If we don't keep finding ways to connect, I'm worried we'll lose that momentum."

Max set his coffee down carefully, tilting his head. "I think the sessions have been going well just as they are. Do you think we really need a poetry evening as well?"

I thought about the cost to run the sessions.

I nodded. "Yes, I do. Grief is isolating. But the evening would be a way to remind everyone it doesn't have to be. It can bring us closer, help us see the positive in sharing those experiences."

He leaned back, considering. "I think you're right that connection is key. Vulnerability takes courage, though, and not everyone will feel ready to share on such a public stage. You need to be mindful about that."

"Absolutely," I agreed, smiling brightly. "Will you help me introduce the idea to them?"

Max raised an eyebrow, the corner of his mouth twitching in amusement. "And when exactly are you planning to spring this on them?"

"This Tuesday," I said quickly, almost sheepishly.

He cleared his throat, his eyebrows climbing higher. "So, in two days?"

I shrugged. "No time like the present."

He opened his mouth to reply but closed it again as my order was called from the front of the café. I stood to retrieve it.

"We'll try, Henry," Max said. "Don't take it personally if not everyone's ready."

I nodded. Not everyone might be ready, but I wasn't just doing this for the group's progress. It was about keeping the group *alive*. The poetry evening wasn't just a chance to share; it would be a way to raise the funds we needed to continue the sessions, and maybe to expand. I wasn't ready to let go of what we'd built together.

Sometimes grief makes you feel helpless, but this—this was something I could do.

That afternoon, I busied myself with refilling staplers, restocking the books that had been returned to the book bin, no surprise that I also found a sweater in there with a sticky note that read *"accidentally took home,"* and I made a mental note to visit the thrift store, since we'd be needing a new rug for the reading corner. As I was in the middle of choosing between budget planning or writing a very enthusiastic email to the board about the poetry evening idea, the bell rang and I saw the woman from Brandy's—Wren?—walk in through the front doors. She stopped momentarily at the secondhand book display, looking at the titles, before she wandered across the floor to the aisles.

She carried herself the same way so many of us in the grief group did; her step was a little slower, her eyes a little glassy, her smile hidden in the corner of her mouth.

Wren reemerged eventually at the front counter, just as I was wrestling the last of the staples into the magazine.

"Hi there," she said.

"Hi," I replied. "Welcome to Everston Library."

"Henry, isn't it?"

"Yes." I smiled. "Wren?"

She nodded. "Sorry for just taking off the other night at Brandy's. It was getting late, and truthfully, I'd had a few glasses of wine. I didn't want to lose my way back home."

I straightened my glasses. "Oh, don't even worry about that."

"I was hoping to borrow a book."

"Well, you'll need a library card first," I replied, and I bent down, finding the application form and sliding it across the counter. "Just fill out your details for me."

She nodded, and picked up a pen from the holder near my computer.

As she started writing, I said, "So, what brought you to Everston?"

"Well, I thought I might end up back home," she replied. "I'm originally from Montana, but my family moved to New York when I was seventeen, and I suppose I needed a quieter pace. I stumbled upon Everston, if I'm honest."

"Everston has a way of finding people who aren't looking for it," I said.

She paused in her writing. "Have you always lived here?"

"Oh yes," I smiled. "I've lived in Everston my whole life, can't imagine going anywhere else."

"It is a quaint place," she said, handing me back the form.

"I just need your ID too," I said, and she paused.

"I'm sorry, Henry, I must have forgotten my wallet."

I shrugged with indifference. "Not to worry, we can let it slide this once."

"I'm always forgetting things lately," she murmured. "It's like I can't seem to remember the most basic of things."

"Grief can do that sometimes."

Her smile faded and I wondered if I had been a little too direct.

"I'm sorry," I said apologetically, hoping I hadn't overstepped.

"You mentioned your fiancée the other night, and—" I gestured at the book she was holding, titled *Grief and How We Survive It*, "—that's also a little bit of a giveaway."

Wren laughed wryly. "I thought I'd be better at this by now," she said. "She died sixteen months ago, in a car accident. But it still feels like yesterday."

"Time never seems to line up with loss," I replied.

"I still see her sometimes," she said. "As though she is right in front of me." She blushed, and took a deep breath, as though surprised by her own candidness. "I haven't admitted that to anyone."

I began to copy her information into the computer so I could print a new card. "My twin brother, Jacob," I said gently, "he died two years ago. Pancreatic cancer. I was still talking to him up until late last year, about three months before I started the grief group. I would have entire conversations with him in the middle of the grocery store."

Wren's eyes brightened. "I drink wine with Lucy and talk about the state of the house I'm living in."

"We're open to newcomers," I said. "The grief group I mean. Why don't you stop by?"

The printer whirred and popped out Wren's new library card, so I scanned the book she passed me into the system before handing it back to her.

"You meet at Brandy's?"

"Normally we meet in the reading corner here in the library," I said. "But we've had a slight plumbing issue, so until next week we're meeting at Brandy's again. On Tuesday night."

"I see."

"Kyle, our local plumber, has been quite busy of late."

She blushed momentarily. "That might be my fault," she said. "I'm renovating the old house off Ducks Crossing Road. The plumbing there has been a nightmare."

"Gill's place!" I exclaimed. "So *you're* the New Yorker up to your arms in sawdust and weeds."

"Word travels fast," she replied, with a smile.

There was a small commotion near the science fiction aisle as two teenagers knocked over a stack of books sitting on the library cart.

"Maybe I will see you Tuesday, Henry," Wren said, and she walked away, the book tucked under her arm.

I can work with this, I thought as I made my way over to the spilled books. *A maybe is always the first step.*

Chapter 6

Olivia

I was five when I almost died. My brother and I had been playing on the balcony at home, and I tripped, hitting my head on the guardrail. The memory is broken, just fragments that sometimes came back to me in dreams.

My brother's voice was small, childlike: "Olivia? Olivia, wake up!" I remembered his finger prodding into the side of my arm, and the warm feeling underneath my head, where the blood had pooled.

Then my mother screaming.

After this, all I remembered was white walls, bright lights, and face masks. A woman telling me that *everything is going to be just fine* and a man shining a flashlight into my eye.

Next, I remembered stirring in the hospital. I was still in the emergency department, because another child had been wheeled in with two broken ankles and was screaming curse words, most of which I had never even heard before. The doctor was at my bedside, and so was my mother. She was dressed the way she was usually dressed: immaculately. She was the kind of woman who could walk into any room, and people's heads would turn. When she was talking to someone, they would often stutter. That was the reaction my mother evoked from people, and it didn't matter who they were, where they were from, or what they did: they would always respond in the same dizzy way, as though she had put some sort of spell on them. My mother had checked her watch. "The babysitter should be here soon," she told the doctor.

"Ms. Piroso, your daughter has a concussion and required seven stitches."

My mother had looked at the doctor, momentarily confused, before replying, "And I'm on the air in an hour."

Bonnie Piroso, the first female TV anchor from Everston.

I loved my mother, and I will always love my mother.

But I never liked her.

"Liv." I looked up from my desk. Josh was standing there with a paper bag. "You eaten?"

"If that's a tuna sandwich, I don't want it."

He grinned. "Meatball."

I grimaced. "I don't really want that either."

He pulled another paper bag from his satchel. "Well, lucky for you, I got you turkey."

"Extra mayo?"

"Always."

I sighed and took the sandwich from him. "Take me with you."

He offered a rueful smile. "You know there's no one else I'd rather be driving all over the state with."

"Drinks this week?" I asked.

He looked back at me, sheepish.

"You have an assignment, don't you?"

"Denver," he replied. "Interview with Serena Williams."

My jaw dropped slightly. "And Cassie got that?"

Josh sighed. "You'll be back soon; just keep trying to get back into Colin's good graces."

I groaned as he gave me a solemn look and left me to my sandwich. I was not supposed to be sitting at my desk, doing baseless tasks; I was supposed to be out in the field, with Josh, our cameraman, finding and reporting on stories. I'd been a reporter for High Country Broadcasting, or HCB, for the last ten years, and I'd had more than my share of interesting stories and assignments—scores of hiking injuries, wildlife running rampant, plane crashes, three murders (not connected), car wrecks, politics and sporting events, even a fisherman once who caught a triple-headed trout. I'd interviewed everyone from the governor and Peyton Manning to The Lumineers and the entire cast of *The Hateful Eight*. I'd mingled with everyone from A-list celebrities to social media influencers (including spending the entire day with Doug the Pug), to local business owners, schoolteachers, and the entire Everston Fire Department, and yet I still lived in the shadow of my mother. HCB was based in Norvale, thirty minutes outside of Everston. We were a regional TV station, and Norvale was the biggest town in the region. This didn't mean that HCB hadn't had its fair share of prize-winning stories; we even topped larger networks at the NAB awards for our on-the-ground reporting during the largest wildfire Colorado had ever seen. My boss, Colin, who was our station manager, was thrilled by this. But perhaps the greatest legacy to HCB was having one of the first regional female anchors. My mother, Bonnie Piroso, a woman who became a household name across the region. Her portrait still hung in the hall, her dressing room still smelled of her—a soft, powdery scent of jasmine—and everybody who worked at this station aspired to be like her. Even me, although I never quite understood whether it was out of adoration or spite. And yet, my mother would never have been assigned desk duty, because Bonnie Piroso would never have been suspended from active reporting, or, as Colin had eloquently put it, "Suspended until you get a grip."

Eight weeks ago, news had been painfully slow. It was off-peak season, which meant there were fewer injuries related to skiing or traffic accidents, or just tourist chaos in general. I had not had any out-of-state stories planned, nor any "wow factor" stories on the horizon, just your run-of-the-mill local news. Lots of simple puff pieces, which so many reporters complained about but, truthfully, I enjoyed. You never knew who you were going to connect with when doing a story on the winner of the state's "best ice cream flavor." The story that I was covering at the time was a neighbor dispute in Norvale. One neighbor kept placing dog poop on the doorstep of Mr. Pritchard, who, after a previous run-in, had wound up in a neck brace and was unable to bend down to remove the feces, which were now stinking up his front porch. I did ask Josh whether the neck brace was real, because I'd seen Mr. Pritchard bend down to grab a beer half an hour before we interviewed him, but Josh insisted this only added to the story. Before I was due to interview him, Wendy from hair and makeup had found an old coat of my mother's in wardrobe and was positively delighted at the prospect of me wearing it for the segment. As I'd slipped it on, checking that it fit me, I'd dug into the pockets and found a note. It was a note my mother had written decades prior.

Livy,

I am writing this on your prom night, filled with joy at seeing how beautiful you have become. I'm so proud knowing my remarkable daughter came from me. As you step into the limelight (prom queen, I'm sure), remember all that I have taught you. You will turn heads and capture hearts, just as I did. You're captain of the cheer squad and dating Jasper Delaware, just as I always wanted. All the sacrifices I have made have been worth it to ensure you have the best of everything. You deserve nothing less. Always know that greatness is your birthright.

All my love,
Mom

Perhaps if my relationship with my mother had been normal, this note would have filled me with fond memories and joy. But my relationship with her was anything but. In truth, I didn't receive this letter on my prom night. I called her at eleven that night because Jasper Delaware had dumped me. I called sixteen times and got her voicemail each time. She'd flown to New York the same night to interview Duran Duran. For my mother, the job always came first. I read this note an hour before I was due to go on air for the segment. I'd then found a bottle of champagne in the news truck and decided to drink the entire bottle. No one noticed at first. I wasn't stumbling, wasn't slurring, just coasting on the kind of numbness that made everything feel slightly removed, like watching myself from a distance. It turned out that Mr. Pritchard, my subject for the interview, had attempted to poison the neighbor's dog—hence their retaliation of dog feces on his doorstep. I didn't have a dog. But I loved dogs. So, in the spirit of loving dogs, and in the spirit of champagne, I launched a battle against Mr. Pritchard, which included throwing the dog poop *at* him. By the time the camera crew realized I had gone completely off course, it was too late, the segment was live, and chaos had already ensued. The video went viral, naturally, because who doesn't want to see a drunk reporter, especially one who was the daughter of a decorated regional TV anchor, flinging dog poop in righteous fury? Colin had been apoplectic. He ranted and raved for close to forty minutes (it could have been longer, but I wasn't sober enough to be sure). My punishment was swift: suspension from active reporting and a one-way ticket to desk duty "until further notice" or, as Colin so delicately put it, until I could "handle my affairs." The problem with handling such affairs is that no one really explains *how* you're supposed to handle your mother abruptly dying of a brain aneurysm, particularly when you harbor both love and resentment toward her. Complicated feelings with a capital C. Add to that the fact that everyone I'd ever known absolutely adored her.

Now, eight weeks after the incident, I sat at my desk, relegated to menial tasks and missing active reporting. Colin emerged from the broadcasting studio and approached my chair. He handed me a stack of papers.

"You know, I'm feeling super good," I said. "And I bet New York would make me feel even better, and—"

"You're still suspended," Colin replied, without looking up from his phone.

"Colin, with all due respect—"

"I knew your mother for twenty-five years," he interjected. "I miss her terribly, but I'm not out here flinging dog feces at strangers and ruining the reputation of HCB!"

"He tried to poison the dog!"

"That doesn't give you the right to throw shit at him!"

"But I—"

"I'm late for a meeting." Colin stalked off, and I buried my face in my hands with a groan. I was really going to have to sit here for the entire afternoon. Again.

I always thought I'd end up in a big city, chasing the thrill of crowded streets instead of pickup trucks lining Main Street. But with my mom constantly coming and going throughout my childhood, I craved stability. Every now and then I found myself dreaming of faraway places, but then I'd catch that first glimpse of the sun rising over the mountains and I was reminded of why I stayed.

Apparently, the pipes in the library burst the other week, and Henry had temporarily set up our meetings at Brandy's. I couldn't pretend I didn't often find myself at Brandy's, but Henry, or Max for that matter, didn't need to know this. I handled this group the same way I handled just about everything in my life, by keeping it at arm's length. It was better this way. The only reason I ever attended was because of Colin, who, after the viral incident, insisted that I needed to talk about my mother's death with someone. It turns out that, although I could research just about anything, when it came to myself I was not so eager to delve in deeper. But tonight, I'd decided to attend. I was halfway out of my car when my phone buzzed in my pocket. Aunt Nell. I swiped to answer, wedging my phone between my shoulder and my ear, so I could pull my handbag from the front seat.

"Hey," I said.

"Oh, sweetheart, I was just thinking about you," she said, her voice warm. She had a mother's voice, despite never having had children. "You know me, I don't like to pry"—which was a lie—"but I wanted to check in. How's work? How's, uh, everything else?"

"I'm fine," I said, which was a carefully curated response I gave to just about everyone. "I'm actually about to walk into my grief support group."

There was a pause, and then, delighted, she said, "Olivia! Look at you, taking care of your well-being."

I bit my lip. Was group therapy really improving your well-being if you never talked about yourself?

"Well, don't let me keep you," she continued. "But call me later, okay? Riot and I want to come visit soon."

Aunt Nell's new boyfriend, Riot, was a heavily tattooed mechanic with a soft spot for stray animals and my aunt's chaotic energy. She adored him. I still wasn't sure how I felt about him yet, but Nell was happy, and that was enough for me.

"Will do," I said, then hung up and shoved my phone back into my pocket.

I sighed, steeling myself, then pushed open the door to Brandy's. The meeting was already underway when I slipped in. Henry gave me a small smile; I think he was just happy I showed up. Rita, on the other hand, scowled at me as I scraped one of the barstools noisily across the floor and sat down next to her. I dug into my handbag, retrieving the latest copy of *Us Weekly*, and handed it to her. She softened almost immediately. I did not want to join this grief group. I'd always believed I was resilient and strong, able to remain poised even with a lifetime of my mother's remarks—*Livvy, why don't you wear your hair this way? Livvy, why are you not head cheerleader yet? Livvy, at your age I was the best in the field!*—and yet I simultaneously sighed relief and sobbed hysterically when she died. But, despite all my efforts, I couldn't help but want to know the stories of each member of this little group, and not because that's what I loved to do but because they'd grown on me. Emerson was nineteen, she had the entire world at her feet, and it was ripped away from her in an event that took thirty seconds. Winnie spent just about her entire life with someone she believed was her soulmate, only to wake up in the morning and find he'd left—no note, no explanation, just gone. Julian was unable to tell his wife he wasn't sure he wanted to keep trying for more children, because the loss of each one was more painful than the last. Bobby was stuck between the relief of finding himself and the pain that he wasn't accepted by those he loved. Gill lost his wife, Edith, and wasn't sure what to do with the rest of his life, considering she was the center of it for nearly fifty years. Henry was trying to fix everybody else around him, because he couldn't fix the cancer that took his brother Jacob from the world. And Rita drove me up the wall with her constant need to gossip, but her sister had dementia, and most of the time didn't even recognize her. Imagine someone you loved your entire life not even remembering your name. So yeah, I couldn't help but collect a copy of her favorite magazine every time I saw it. Strange, this thing called grief. Most days I just wanted to be alone, and yet the moment I was surrounded by these people, I suddenly couldn't think of being anywhere else.

There was someone new today. She stood apart from the

others, shy, seemingly unsure if she really wanted to be there. I knew that feeling all too well.

While she seemed to be listening, the woman remained quiet. She had soft caramel-brown hair, threaded with golden highlights, honey eyes, and the same quiet exhaustion etched beneath them as everyone else in the room. But she was also beautiful. Max suddenly asked how I was, and because I was too busy staring at our new member, I didn't answer. Max probed again, pulling me out of my reverie, and prompting Rita to nudge me with her elbow. I blushed.

"Hi," I said clumsily, and Henry gave a little wave. "Hi," I repeated. "Yes, I'm Olivia." The words were out of my mouth before I realized I'd said them, and everyone looked at me quizzically.

"Thanks for reminding us, Liv," Max said. "How have you been?"

"Fine," I replied.

"Just fine?"

"I heard a joke at work the other day," I spluttered. My brain had gone into total malfunction.

Henry sat taller. "I love jokes," he said.

I had no choice but to entertain what I had ungracefully started.

"Why did the scarecrow win an award?"

There was a ripple of murmurs, and I heard Winnie say, "Because he was scary good!" to Emerson.

"Why?" Max asked, with zero emotion across his face.

"Because he was outstanding in his field."

Henry, to all his credit as the world's kindest human being, laughed enthusiastically.

The new member gave the smallest of smiles, but it was probably out of sheer pity.

I sunk into my barstool, as Bobby, noting my utter lack of

ability to function, offered to read from the latest poetry book he'd found. *Thank god for poetry*, was all I could think.

I was half hoping Henry might surprise us with the announcement of an open bar after the meeting. But of course, this was Henry, which meant the familiar clink of teacups was already making its way around the room. I avoided the tea tray, knowing Gill would corner me if I lingered too long. He would want to know if I was back to active reporting, and I didn't have the strength to tell him I wasn't. He was utterly delighted about the dog poop throwing incident and thought the suspension was unfair. But that was Gill. Instead, I made my way to the back of the bar. In the corner, Emerson and Winnie were sitting close, their heads bent together in low conversation. Winnie was gesturing animatedly, and Emerson was listening with wide-eyed fascination. They were probably in deep discussion about birds. Between Winnie's encyclopedic knowledge of every species in Colorado, and Emerson's ability to spot nests and feathers like she was born with binoculars glued to her face, they could spend hours swapping facts and bird-watching stories. I sat down next to Emerson and leaned in to her ear. "Who's the new woman?"

"Wren," Emerson whispered. "Her fiancée died."

"About a year back, or close enough." Winnie sighed, and it never ceased to amaze me how sharp her hearing was for a woman going on eighty.

"So, she just ended up in Everston?"

"Henry says she's staying at Gill's in exchange for fixing up the place," Emerson replied.

"Interesting," I said.

"I swear I've seen her before." Emerson narrowed her eyes. "I just can't figure out where."

I looked back over her shoulder, searching for Wren. There was something about her—something magnetic—that pulled at me, a quiet curiosity I hadn't felt in a long time.

Chapter 7

Wren

The raccoons or opossums, whatever they were, had seemingly moved on. Or at least, that's what I told myself after a full night's sleep, free of screeching from the ceiling.

They say New York never sleeps. Its heartbeat thrums through taxi engines, street vendors, and the occasional wail of sirens, but Everston woke up differently. Here the light broke over the mountains and stretched through town quietly. There were swallows in the trees, the distant rumble of a hay truck, and—for now, at least—no sign of the opossums.

When I first moved into this place, Gill hadn't set foot in the master bedroom for months. He said it was too hard to sleep without Edith. I understood. Waking up without Lucy made mornings feel pointless. I had since changed the curtains, replaced the bedspread, stripped the wallpaper, and repainted in soft linen tones that brightened the space. But I left the four-poster bed; its dark wood and intricate carvings felt like something worth keeping. A new rug, a few plants, and the room felt lived in again.

As I made my way down the stairs, I caught myself in the mirror, but I hardly recognized the woman who stared back. My hair was shorter, now threaded with highlights, and it was thin and messy: I had lost so much of it in all the stress. I wore contact lenses, hiding whatever once sparkled within my eyes. I favored clothes that swallowed me, because it felt easier to move through the day hidden.

I'd had no intention of going to Henry's grief group last night. But yesterday, while tending to the wildflowers as the evening grew dim, I'd waited for Lucy and she hadn't arrived, so I'd found my feet carrying me back to Brandy's.

Max was very clearly semiretired, and he didn't wear socks with his loafers, but he had simply smiled at me when I sat in the corner, and perhaps that was enough in the moment, no pressure to unveil my deepest pain to a room full of strangers. He started by asking how everyone was, and then most of the group introduced themselves to me. Henry gave a little speech about how books and poetry had become a focal point of the sessions, at which point a man named Julian interrupted.

"I'll admit," Julian said, leaning forward on the stool slightly, "I never thought I'd say this, but I've been enjoying reading poetry. Lesley caught me with my nose in a book the other day and couldn't stop laughing. She said, 'Who are you and what have you done with my husband?' I think she might be expecting some lines in our anniversary cards from now on."

The group laughed, and Julian brushed his hands through his sandy hair. "I think . . . I think it helps," he continued. "You know, when words can say what you can't. Especially with everything Lesley and I have been through and continue to go through." His voice wavered, but he pressed on. "The miscarriages—it's been a long road. But hearing her laugh, even over something as ridiculous as me reading love poems . . . I haven't heard her laugh like that in so long. Maybe it's worth it."

I closed my eyes momentarily, blinking back the echo of Lucy's laughter. It is often the smallest things that haunt you after they're gone.

Bobby cleared his throat, his voice pulling me back. He had the silkiest, loveliest voice. He could be a narrator. "It's funny," he said. "I freaked out when Henry told me the pipes had burst at the library. I thought that meant this was all canceled. This—this group—it's the first time in years I've felt like I belong anywhere, and the idea of losing that . . ." He trailed off, then shook his head. "Well, honestly, I nearly had a meltdown."

Henry flushed a little, the tips of his ears turning pink. "I, too, nearly had a meltdown," he admitted, which earned a small chuckle from the group.

Bobby grinned. "Not to get sappy, but I realized it doesn't matter if we're at the library, here, in a park, or sitting on cardboard boxes. My real family never quite figured out how to be around me, but you all—you get me. And that's enough for me."

I thought of my own family. I sent a few text messages to my parents every now and then to let them know I was still alive, but not much more, much to their dismay. They asked me often when I'd be coming home, but I still didn't have an answer. I'd left New York abruptly, telling them things had not become easier, that I needed more space, that I needed time to figure things out on my own. And while that was true, the simpler, harder truth was that it was easier than admitting that after all this time, I didn't know how to let them back in. Marnie, who'd always been more of a sister than a cousin, had called me just last week. Her voicemail was bright and cheerful, a gentle plea for me to call her back. "I just miss you," she'd said. "Even if it's just a two-minute call to say hi, I'll take it." We'd grown up together in Montana before my dad's job took us to New York. Despite the distance, we'd stayed close. We used to send each other letters, scrawled in messy handwriting, then emails, filled with inside jokes, dreams, and teenage frustrations. As adults, it became texts—quick snapshots of our lives. But since Lucy's passing even those had stopped.

And it wasn't just Marnie or my parents. There was an entire world I'd left behind in New York: a glittering, high-paced world that now felt like it belonged to someone else entirely. Book launches at the Strand, cocktail parties in sleek SoHo lofts, rooftop events overlooking the skyline. My publicist, Dana, used to drag me to gala dinners, literary award ceremonies, and high-profile events where I'd sip champagne and mingle with all sorts of other authors, publishers, journalists, and magazine editors. But I used to walk into those rooms with Lucy by my side. People would smile, offer congratulations on my latest book, or ask about my process, and then Lucy would speak and I would watch nearly every person fall under her spell. Listening to her command an entire room would always make me fall in love with her all over again. And we'd leave those events late at night, sliding into the back of a cab while laughing over some ridiculous conversation we'd had.

Grief has a way of building walls, and I'd let mine grow sky high.

"We're glad you're here, Bobby," Henry said, interrupting my thoughts. Somewhere behind the bar, Motown funk was playing faintly, its upbeat rhythm a strange contrast to the weight of the conversations being had. "But I do promise we'll have the library fixed soon," he added. "And we'll start fresh."

There was a small murmur of relief among the group, as Henry's words seemed to reassure them.

Winnie raised her hand theatrically, her bracelets jangling. "Well, speaking of starting fresh," she said, "I've decided seventy-eight is the perfect age to reinvent yourself. Tell me, Bobby, would Tinder be your app of choice?"

The room laughed, and Winnie feigned an incredulous look. "I'm being serious!" She winked. "If I'm still figuring myself out at this ripe old age, that means all of you have years of reinvention ahead. That's life, isn't it? Things happen, and we have to keep finding new ways to be ourselves."

"You don't have time for Tinder," Emerson quipped. "We're much too busy."

Winnie patted her shoulder in response.

"Shitty things happen," Emerson added. "I've had to rethink my whole life. It's made me pretty angry, to say the least." Her words hung in the air as she absentmindedly brushed her fingers across the burn scars down her neck and across her forearm. They looked like delicate rivers etched into her skin, branching out in uneven trails. Yet Emerson's eyes were full of armor. She glanced at Henry and then at the rest of the group and shrugged. "But being here is low-key great. Talking helps."

"A much better alternative to silence," Max agreed.

Rita, who had been quiet, spoke up, her voice cracking slightly. "I just want one day," she said. "One day when my sister looks at me and remembers who I am. When we can gossip about all the things we used to gossip about. That's all I want."

The room grew still, heavy with her words. Then Gill, with his silver hair and bright-blue eyes, broke the silence. "Well, if anyone is wondering, it's perfectly reasonable to cry into a stack of pancakes every now and then. Therapeutic even."

"Is that your professional opinion, Gill?" Max asked, his lips pulling into a smile.

"Absolutely," Gill replied, and he glanced at me knowingly.

Henry clapped, which startled me, but he looked at the group with a soft, satisfied smile. "You know, I've said it before, but showing up—even when our normal spot is otherwise out of order—showing up for each other is half the battle. The rest we can figure out, together." It was clear that Henry, for all intents and purposes, was the glue of the group. There was something steady about him. A kind of calm in an otherwise chaotic world. He didn't force anyone to share, but somehow, he made you want to. I almost raised my hand to speak, and then the door opened.

I felt the atmosphere shift the moment Olivia entered. Her presence filled every corner, drawing all eyes to her. She was late, but she didn't offer an explanation. She just slipped onto an empty stool, handed Rita a copy of *Us Weekly*—to which Rita guffawed in delight—and offered the room a soft, easy smile that somehow found its way directly to me. My breath caught in my throat when I saw her, and it was both elating and terrifying. She was endearing. Beautiful, actually. The kind of beauty that sneaks up on you, unassuming at first, but then makes you pause for a split second longer than you should.

And then the guilt hit me. There is so much guilt in grief. You feel guilty if you laugh, if you wake up wanting to seize the day, if you haven't cried in over an hour, or if you find someone gorgeous and they are not your partner. I spent the rest of the evening listening and nodding and then, when everyone had finished with their cups of tea, I slipped out the door without a word, and into the night.

This morning, I decided I was going to deal with my feelings about the grief group, and my apparent attraction to Olivia, with a steaming cup of coffee and extra whipped cream.

I drove to Main Street, waiting patiently at the end of the road for ducks to cross as they disappeared into the overgrown tumbleweeds. The buildings were bright and vibrant against the backdrop of the mountain ranges. I parked in front of the library, crossed the road, and stepped into Brew Haven. The café greeted me with its weathered wooden floors and mismatched furniture. It was bustling this morning, with a hum of chatter and the occasional clinking of ceramic mugs. In one corner, a couple sat nestled in worn-out armchairs, smiling at each other in a way that suggested decades of shared mornings. I had to look away. It was the biggest question after you lost someone you loved so deeply: could you ever really find forever with someone else?

I ordered my coffee and waited near the big bay windows, happy with myself for including the extra whipped cream with maple drizzle. Suddenly, though, I heard my name.

"Wren?"

I turned to see Olivia standing behind me.

"Oh, hello," I said.

"Hi," she replied. "I didn't get a chance to properly introduce myself last night." She stretched out her hand. "I'm Olivia," she said, and I shook it, a little flustered that she was suddenly standing in front of me.

She motioned to the empty table. "Do you want to sit with me?"

My legs moved faster than my thoughts, and I was seated before I could change my mind.

"Have you been in the group long?" I asked.

She shrugged her jacket off and folded her arms in front of her. "A couple of months," she replied. "Although if I'm honest, sometimes I just can't bring myself to go."

"I wasn't so certain I was going to go last night, and then I just suddenly found myself sitting on a stool among everyone."

"Henry can be rather convincing," Olivia smiled, and then paused. "My mother, she died of a brain aneurysm six months ago."

"My fiancée Lucy died in a car accident," I responded. "A little more than a year ago now."

"Still feels like yesterday, doesn't it?"

"In a lot of ways, it does," I replied. "There are days I wake up and it's as though Lucy has just died and I am right back in those first moments; then there are other days that I can see how much space is between the time she was alive and now. And then of course there are days when I can't quite believe it's happened."

"I know," Olivia said. "It's like I went to bed one night with a mother, and I woke up without one. How do you even grapple with something like that?"

I shifted in the booth. The time I had spent recovering in the hospital I was mostly sedated. I didn't remember too much of it; all I had left was a faint scar along my hand and the occasional ache in my thigh if the weather was too cold. When they told me that Lucy had not survived, it ripped through me, and then I would sleep, and I would wake up, and it would rip through me all over again.

"I'm sorry," Olivia said. "I just started dumping all of this on you."

"No," I replied. "It's nice to talk to someone who understands the abruptness of it all. Were you close with your mother?"

She looked out the window for a moment. "To be honest, we had a complicated relationship. It's part of the reason I have found it hard going to the meetings. Everybody there is grieving for someone they loved very deeply. I did love my mother, but she could be cruel to me."

I was reminded of a bookstore in Toronto. Three years ago, during a book tour, a young woman approached me and asked me to sign a specific page in one of my books. When I turned to the page, it had only been a simple poem; in fact, I couldn't quite remember what had stirred me to write it. But to the woman, it described her relationship with her mother and for that reason the poem meant everything to her. I felt the need to tell Olivia this for some reason.

"I read a poem once," I said. "One of the lines was—*For in her eyes, a mirror I see, a reflection of her, a shadow of me, a dance of love, but riddled with ache, how do I make sense of the steps we take?*"

Olivia looked at me curiously. "So, you do like poetry."

I realized then that perhaps I had lost myself in talking with her, straying far too close to accidentally revealing who I was. I felt slightly panicked, until we were interrupted by the barista bringing over our coffees.

"We ran out of whipped cream, Liv," he said, seemingly sympathetic under his mustache. "We used the last on your friend here."

I blushed. "Oh no, I feel terrible."

"New in town and already costing us all our whipped cream." Olivia smiled.

I plucked a spoon from the caddy sitting on the table. "I'm willing to share," I said, handing it to her. Our fingertips brushed, for only a second, just skin on skin, but it was enough to send a pulse racing up my arm. Heat pooled low in my stomach, and my breath caught until I forced myself to steady. "I hope you like maple drizzle."

I couldn't quite believe the blush creeping into my cheeks, but I pushed it down, because Olivia smiled and said, "It's my favorite!" She took a scoop of the cream as though it were the most natural thing in the world.

"How did you come to be in Everston?" she asked.

"I'm not so sure," I said. "After Lucy died, everything was a blur. I left New York with no plan and drifted through hotels and bars, if I'm honest. Lucy collected coasters from her travels, so I started trying to find her in those places. The last one she had was from Everston."

"She'd been here before?"

"Yes. I suppose I was trying to find her again."

"Have you?"

I took a sip of coffee. "I actually think I'm finding myself more. I seem to know a lot more about how plumbing works in old houses these days."

She laughed and the sound warmed me.

Olivia's phone started to vibrate between us. She silenced it and took another scoop of whipped cream. The phone rang again.

"Do you need to get that?"

Olivia waved her hand. "It's just my boss. He's not very happy with me at the moment."

"Where do you work?"

"I'm a reporter," she said. "My mother was the morning show anchor for the same station: HCB. We're based out of Norvale."

"That sounds like a big legacy," I replied.

Olivia's eyes told a different story. "It is. They're really big shoes to fill," she said. "There are so many people who knew my mother for the powerhouse she was, but they have no idea who she was behind closed doors."

"So you're stuck between wanting to live up to all the things she did but not wanting to actually be her."

Her shoulders relaxed slightly. "Yes, actually, that's exactly how I feel. What about you?" she added. "Where is your family?"

I had to still myself. I suddenly wanted to tell her everything about myself, but how could I without revealing who I really was? And the small amount of peace I'd found here in Everston . . . I wasn't willing to give it up. If people found out who I was, it wouldn't take long for the press to find me. And I couldn't go back to that frenzy. Not yet.

"My parents still live in New York," I replied. "I have a cousin—who's more like a sister, really—who lives in Montana. I think it's hard for them to understand why I needed the space, but they respect it."

She didn't press the matter. "My brother left home when he was eighteen. He works on cargo ships out in the Pacific somewhere."

"What about your father?" I asked.

"I never knew him," she said. "But I made peace with that a long time ago."

"Do you think it helps? The grief group?"

Olivia didn't answer at first, but then she looked up at me. "If I've learned anything from Henry's group, it's that there is no expiration date on grief. People seem to think you can wrap it up neatly and store it away, but it doesn't really work like that. At least with this group, I know that there are others that feel just like this."

"Sounds like you've been plenty of times then, if you've learned that much."

She grinned. "Either that, or the people in this group just have a way with words. Do you think you'll go to another meeting?" Olivia asked.

"Will you?"

"Well," she replied, "I do owe Rita another copy of *Us Weekly*, wouldn't be right to deprive of her it."

I smiled. "Maybe I could also add a copy of *People* magazine."

"See." Olivia smiled. "You'll fit right in."

Strangely, it seemed, after spending nearly the entire morning nestled in a booth by the window of Brew Haven, that I might also fit with Olivia.

October

Chapter 8

Henry

The day that Jacob died, I didn't wear a watch. I knew that I would be checking it constantly, which is an outlandish concept—how many times do you check your watch while you're waiting for someone to die? Instead, I sat beside him, a constant vigil. I had spent weeks reading to him in this very spot, but today there was no reading. Grief had stolen my voice. I held Jacob's hand, and it felt heavy as he lay motionless in the hospital bed. Every so often I would fall asleep and then awake with a start, thinking perhaps he'd gone and I hadn't had the chance to tell him I loved him one more time. I wanted those to be the last words he ever heard; a reminder of how much he was loved.

The room was warm. I'd opened the curtains to let in the sunlight. I noticed the flowers along the windowsill had begun to wither. I felt guilty for not replacing them, but I couldn't leave his side. He looked small beneath the thin white sheets, almost as if he'd faded overnight. His hair was gone. Jacob and I had both inherited our father's thick curls. Dad would run his fingers through his hair when he was stressed, and we'd both picked up the habit. At this point, Jacob had lost even that privilege. He hadn't wanted our parents to see him like this, to remember him this way. But I'd called them anyway, telling them it probably wouldn't be long. They were trying to get a flight, to make it in time. It's strange, time, isn't it? I ached at the thought that

Jacob was slipping away, moving toward somewhere none of us could follow.

Every so often the nurses would come into the room. They would offer me things like water, tea, magazines, a crossword puzzle, perhaps to go and sit in the room down the hall and watch some TV. But it all seemed trivial. Was I really going to sit there asking "part of a transformer" for five letters while my brother was taking his last breaths? I thought not.

Jacob had barely eaten anything but Jell-O all week. I'd fed it to him as he lay exhausted against the pillows. I'd run ice chips across his lips and moisturized his dry hands. His palliative care consisted of a constant rotation of medications and painkillers. They would be interchanged, increased and decreased and swapped out. He had cried in discomfort or pain sometimes and then the nurses would fiddle with his IV bag and suddenly he would go quiet, and the cries would stop. This had felt at first like a never-ending cycle, but now I knew the cycle would end. This is what I had come to accept. There would be no miracles now. We were not fighting or hoping, we were just waiting. One of the nurses had come into the room and checked on his vitals, stroking Jacob's arm gently.

"We're doing all we can to keep him comfortable," she reassured me.

But not alive, I thought, because we were beyond that point now. But Jacob didn't seem to be in any pain that day. His breathing had become shallower, and his skin had changed. It had been yellow for so many months as a result of the treatment, but he had turned a pale gray, and I knew that it wasn't going to be much longer. I'd thought about what Jacob would have wanted to know in his last moments. Would he want his favorite song—"Viva la Vida" by Coldplay—playing? Would he want to smell pine needles, because all he ever did was hike? Would he want me to remind him of that time when we were kids and we'd found a twenty dollar bill while playing in the park? We'd debated over whether to turn it in or spend it on candy, but eventually we did turn it in to the sheriff, who accompanied us to the candy store and let us buy whatever we wanted, a reward for being honest. I'd settled on my original plan, to talk to him softly, to tell him that I loved him as he slipped away. As it happens, *I love you* wasn't the last thing I had said to him; instead I'd said: *I'm just going to get you a coffee.* He wasn't really conscious by then—I knew that—but I'd said it anyway. It felt stupid and symbolic all at once, but I wanted to give him something normal, something he loved, even if it was just the idea of it. When I had returned, the nurse was in the room. She'd looked at me knowingly and touched my shoulder, as I slumped into the chair again next to Jacob's body.

"Do you want a minute?" she'd asked.

"I'll just have a coffee with my brother," I'd replied.

And I had—I drank that coffee next to Jacob. It almost made me puke. He would have thought that was brilliant.

By the time the formalities were done, and the undertaker called, it was just after three in the afternoon. I'd left the hospital, and walked into the sunlight, and the world had felt different. The sun was warm, but it didn't feel warm to me; I felt cold. The streets around the hospital were busy, but people's faces were blurry, as if I was hoping that somehow one of them would be Jacob and all of this had just been some long, drawn-out nightmare. I'd left with some of Jacob's things, and his hospital bag, and it had felt as though it was filled with boulders. I drove home from Norvale, where the hospital was, to Everston in silence. When I returned to an empty house, I couldn't bring myself to sleep. How was it fair that Jacob would now sleep forever—lost to the world—while I still had the privilege to close my eyes, drift into dreams, and wake up to another day he'd never see?

Three days after Jacob's funeral, a delivery came for me. It was a brand-new coffee machine, and a note from Jacob: "Isn't it lovely."

I laughed out loud. It was such a Jacob thing to do. For the first time since his passing, I thought of him and smiled. The absurdity of it all, that even in death, he had found a way for one final prank. I'd give anything to tell him one last time, I'm still never drinking coffee.

In the weeks that followed, the condolences poured in. Bright flowers, homemade casseroles, lasagnes left quietly on my doorstep. I had texts from people I hadn't heard from in years. Regular library patrons would stop by the front desk, offering soft words, unsure if I wanted them. I appreciated all of it. Truly. But none of it filled the hole Jacob had left behind. There were so many who could empathize with the loss of my brother, as my sibling—but not the grief of losing a twin. We were innately "us" before we had even entered the world. Our lives had always been parallel, intertwined. Jacob knew what I was thinking before I said it. The loss of him created a vacuum, and it rewrote the very shape of my existence. It was the kind of grief that carved jagged edges where once there was certainty. I wasn't just grieving him, I was grieving the part of me that only existed because he did.

The hardest part came in sifting through his belongings. I found all sorts of things, some I expected, and others I really didn't. Like the chemo bag he wore, or the hoodie he took to both the clinic and then the hospital, which he called his cancer uniform. I'd bought him a thermos for his cold water—the only thing he could bear to drink during chemo—with the word "coffee" printed on it as a little joke. He thought it was hilarious, and the day I found it in his wardrobe, I sobbed for hours. It felt like I couldn't or shouldn't keep those things, but I couldn't possibly throw them away either.

It was the dilemma I was facing now, staring down at the very last box of Jacob's things that I had been holding on to. Should I keep them, or discard them? What if throwing them away meant I would forget the way he looked in that hoodie, or the silly war we had over his love for coffee and my disdain for it? I thought about asking Max and the group that evening. Maybe they would know what to do when holding on starts to feel just as painful as letting go.

When it came to our meetings, the library was the only true home for them, and I was thrilled the readers' corner was back up and running after three weeks. Winnie had even made a lemon meringue pie to celebrate our return, and I couldn't wait for a slice of its tangy richness. At six p.m. on the dot, Rita bustled in with Bobby and Gill, her hands waving about, telling a story that sounded grandiose but in reality was probably about her neighbor's pumpkins growing along her side of the fence. Winnie and Emerson arrived together, deep in conversation; I'd wager a guess it was probably about birds or poetry. Julian arrived carrying a cardboard box and a backpack, and he motioned to me as he sat it down on the table.

"Henry," he said, his voice a little higher pitched than usual. "I need your help."

"What's wrong?" I asked.

"My kid," he said. "Her science fair is tomorrow, and we stayed up all last night working on her project together, but the dog wrecked it this morning and she is just devastated. You got anything I can replace it with?"

I paused momentarily to make sure I had heard him correctly. "You need some sort of science project that she can take to school?"

Julian nodded. "Please Henry, Lesley's not doing so great, and she didn't have time today to redo it, and work was just chaotic and I—"

I held up my hands. "You know, I think we actually have some leftover projects from the World Science Day we just hosted. I'll see what I can do."

He sighed in relief. "You're a legend, Henry," he said, and he went to find a chair in our corner.

Olivia arrived on time for once, and, to my curiosity, Wren followed directly behind her.

"Henry," Olivia smiled, and she handed me one of my cashmere sweaters. I stared at it in confusion.

"I borrowed it last month."

"I've been looking for this," I said.

"I was cold." She patted my arm before walking over to the rest of the group.

Wren approached me quietly as I was still staring at my missing sweater that had been in Olivia's possession this whole time.

"Still taking on new members?" she asked.

I smiled at her. I was quietly thrilled she'd returned. "We absolutely are. Go take a seat, Max will—"

Max breezed through the door in the same way he always did, perplexed that everyone wasn't already sitting down and ready to begin.

"We'll be starting shortly," I said, softly.

She smiled and wandered over to where Olivia had sat down, sitting next to her.

"Ready, Henry?" Max asked.

"Of course," I replied, and I took a seat.

"I think we will start with a poem," Max said. "Emerson, care to pick something at random?"

Emerson shifted in her seat. "You bet," she replied. "I've just recently found this new poet and I'm really enjoying her book."

Max joined his hands in his lap. "Take it away, Emerson," he said.

Emerson cleared her throat and read the first line. *"And then one day you were gone—"*

"Emerson," Rita interrupted. "Is this really poetry or one of those millennial self-guided books? What about e.e. cummings or Sylvia Plath? Back in my day—"

"Well, it's not your day anymore, Rita," Emerson snapped. "If you don't like it, then go sit somewhere else in the library."

I caught the shock on Wren's face, as Olivia turned around in her chair to stifle a laugh.

"What Emerson probably meant, Rita," Max interjected, "is that poetry comes in all different kinds of forms, these days."

"No, I literally meant she could go sit somewhere else. This is, like, my favorite book right now."

Winnie placed a hand on Emerson's shoulder and squeezed.

Rita looked at me with her nose scrunched and annoyance written all over her face. "Henry, as the librarian, surely you would appreciate what is and isn't poetry."

"Yes, I am a librarian," I replied softly, patiently, "but I happen to think Emerson's book is definitely a book of poetry."

Emerson grinned triumphantly.

"I also happen to think that we should be a little patient introducing new forms of art to people who perhaps may not be familiar with them." And I looked at Emerson pointedly.

She sighed sheepishly. "I'm sorry, Rita," she said, "I promise that this book is really good."

Rita shrugged. "Well, I do enjoy listening to you read, Emerson," she replied. "I'm happy to listen to this one too."

I couldn't tell if Max was thrilled at this interaction or annoyed, but he indicated for Emerson to continue the poem. She began to read again:

And then one day you were gone—and I was filled with all the reminders of you.

I found your scarf, and letters, books and photographs, your toothbrush and favorite sweater, and I put them all in a box.

You were everywhere and yet gone. I desperately wondered what to do—for if there was no trace of you, then surely the grief would leave—so I got rid of the box.

But I was wrong; the grief never left.
It stayed, and I wish I'd kept your sweater.

There was a clunking sound and I noticed Wren had dropped her water bottle. She appeared flustered, almost as though she was about to be sick. She quickly stood and disappeared behind the fiction aisle toward the bathrooms. Max continued and asked the group how the poem had made them feel, and I wondered if I should check on Wren.

"What did you think, Henry?" Max asked, and I was brought back to the circle.

I cleared my throat. "I have a box of Jacob's old things, the last box in fact that I have held on to, and today I stood staring at it for well over half an hour, wondering if I should keep it or throw it away. But I think my question has been answered."

"What are you going to do?" Bobby asked.

"I'm going to put Jacob's picture back on my mantelpiece," I replied.

Bobby smiled at me. "I think that's a great idea."

Wren eventually returned to her seat, and Olivia whispered something in her ear. She nodded in response, and I could only assume everything was okay. Before I could announce that Winnie had made lemon meringue pie, Max gave me a pointed look, as if to say that it was my turn to announce my grand plans. I stood up and clapped my hands together. This was often something I did: I'd clap to get people's attention, despite the fact it always made at least half of our little group (mainly the older folks) jump out of their skin.

"I have something I want to suggest to you all," I said. "I've put some thought into this, and I'm hoping you'll all consider it with enthusiasm."

"You're going to start providing dinner?" Bobby asked, hopeful.

"Pizza would be nice from time to time," Gill agreed.

"Well, no," I stammered, "that's not exactly—"

"It could be one pizza," Winnie suggested. "We'd all get a slice. Emmy and I could share a slice for even numbers."

"As long as it's cheese," Emerson replied. "I don't like too many toppings, it just ruins the entire experience."

"It really does," Julian interjected. "It should be a rule of three toppings or less."

"Well, what about those of us who enjoy lots of toppings? Perhaps we could get two pizzas, one with minimal toppings and one with lots," Rita debated.

We were way off track as usual.

"How about we let Henry tell us what he's thinking?" Max said, with a smile.

Thank you, Max. Ever the diplomat.

"A poetry evening," I said, and everyone gave me a quizzical look. "Held here at the library, of course," I continued. "We can each write our own poem, or even a couple of poems, about what we have felt since joining this group, maybe even what we have discovered or are continuing to discover, and we'll read them out here in front of an audience." I paused, gauging their reactions. "I just think it could be a really meaningful way for us to celebrate how far we've come, and to connect with other people in town. Poetry gives us a chance to process things differently, to say the things we sometimes can't in conversation. And sharing it with others might be scary, but it could also be powerful. A reminder to ourselves and anyone listening that we're not alone in this."

The room fell silent for a beat. I could see some skeptical faces, but also a few glimmers of interest—curiosity, maybe even possibility.

"You mean get up in front of people?" Emerson asked. She sounded horrified.

"Well, yes," I replied. "But it wouldn't just be for us. This could be a way to connect with others in the community who are grieving, too, or even just those who want to support us. Maybe it's a chance for the library to start something bigger—other grief initiatives, more support groups, who knows? Maybe the library could be not only a place for book borrowing but a place of healing too."

Emerson still looked uncertain.

"We'd sell tickets, have some catering, and tea of course," I added.

Julian cleared his throat. "But we aren't poets," he said.

"We don't have to be poets," I replied reassuringly. "It doesn't have to be perfect. You could write together or pick a favorite poem from a book and talk about it, or even write a letter. It's about expression, not perfection."

Julian seemed to relax, his shoulders loosening. "Oh. Well, that seems okay, then. I'm not much of a writer."

"What would we wear?" Rita wondered, and then her face brightened. "We could get all dressed up! Like they do at the awards shows."

Bobby shifted uncomfortably in his seat, his voice hesitant. "Are we going to have security?" he asked. "What if . . . what if someone shows up who isn't there to support us? Someone who just wants to cause trouble?"

I hadn't thought about this. I knew Bobby's story: family members who didn't accept his queerness, the fear of being ridiculed or hurt in a space that should feel safe. I'd need to make sure that wouldn't happen.

"Will there be enough seats?" Gill wondered. "I'm sure half the retirement home would like an evening out."

"Just as long they understand that it's not all poetry from the fifteenth century," Emerson remarked.

I held up my hands in surrender. "Lots of questions," I agreed. "And a lot of planning, but my main point tonight was just to bring the idea up."

They were all looking at me as if they still needed convincing.

Max suggested everybody go home and think about it, and we could reconvene to discuss at the next meeting. He added that he believed the idea was a positive step in everyone's healing. Although, frankly, I think he just added that in to make me feel more hopeful.

When everyone broke away to talk amongst themselves, I found Wren.

"Are you okay?" I asked, remembering her dash to the bathroom. "Sometimes these meetings can be a little overwhelming in the beginning."

"Oh, I'm fine," she replied. "I just . . . was moved . . . by the poem . . ."

I smiled. "Oh yeah, it's a lovely little book. It's called *Hope for Tomorrow*. Emerson brought it in one day, and I noticed how worn the cover was, the pages warped from being read so much. You can tell it's well loved. I've met a lot of librarians who say there is nothing like a new book, which is true, but I have always got a soft spot for the ones that have been read over and over. There's just something about them . . . like they've lived, you know?"

She softened. "I've always loved well-worn books too."

"You know I've been struggling with getting rid of the last of Jacob's things. It's serendipitous, I think, that Emerson picked that particular poem."

"I've always found it rather amazing, actually, that what we need can come to us just by a simple piece of writing."

"Well, that's exactly why I've ordered more of B.W. Paisley's books. She has quite a few that I haven't read but I'm sure Emerson will enjoy."

Wren went pale again.

"Are you sure you're okay?"

"Yes," she responded. "I've just remembered I left the lids off the paint cans this afternoon, and I need to get back, or else it'll all dry up."

"I really hope you'll come back, Wren," I said. "And the poetry evening, I think it would bring a lot of joy to Everston."

She nodded slowly. "I can't promise anything, Henry," she said.

Olivia suddenly appeared beside me. "A poetry evening," she said. "I don't suppose you've contacted any local reporters?"

I folded my arms. "Well, why would I do that, when we've got the best right here?"

She looked at me with her eyebrows raised. "This has nothing to do with the fact that most other networks would be thrilled to see me in a mandatory grief counseling group because of the incident."

I feign insult. "You think so low of me."

Olivia sighed. "I'm still on desk duty," she admitted.

"I know," I replied. "You forget that Colin comes in here once a week with his grandkids."

"What incident?" Wren asked, and my face broke into a grin.

"One day I'll tell you," Olivia replied.

"Oh, come on Liv," I pleaded. "It's an amazing story . . ."

She held up her hand. "I'll speak with some colleagues and see what Colin would think of this. But you know what he's like, he's only after ratings."

"You're just going to have to sell it to him," I quipped.

Wren looked from Olivia to me and then back again. "You're really not going to tell me the story?"

Olivia only returned a smile.

"Henry," Winnie called, "where do you keep your cake slicer?"

I excused myself from Olivia and Wren. I could only imagine what Winnie was trying to use to slice up the lemon meringue pie.

Chapter 9

Olivia

Death didn't frighten me. At least, not in the existential way; I was not afraid of whatever comes next. What did frighten me was grief. Because, in my experience, grief compels you to pick apart every single detail of yourself, and it forces you to confront things you never knew existed.

Hundreds of people attended my mother's funeral. It was held in Everston, at the local church. Its arched windows and time-weathered stones were gray against the blue of the sky. The wooden pews were filled with mourners: townsfolk, colleagues, friends, and people she had met during her travels. The church was decorated with hundreds of roses, her casket draped with a huge arrangement of lilies, soft sunlight filtering through the stained-glass windows. The Everston choir sang songs, and people were invited to place handwritten notes in a box beside her casket. A slideshow of memorable on-air moments played in the background as guests lit candles for her. It was an elaborate affair. The flowers had bothered my seasonal allergies, and my eyes watered the entire time. I used a pack and a half of tissues. At least I looked the part. My brother, Matty, didn't come home for it. That was his choice. Probably one last chance to say, *You were never there for me, so I'm not showing up for you*. Good for him. I, however, was tasked with reading the eulogy. The week before, I had sat down multiple times to write it. How would I summarize her life? Where would

I even begin? I imagined writing my own eulogy, and the things I would say—would it be possible to squeeze everything I had seen, heard, and felt into such a small space of time? I mean, can you ever really sum up a life in just three minutes?

As I sat in my living room, the blue light from my computer straining my eyes, I had started and deleted, started and deleted. When I was fourteen years old, I had been cast as Juliet in our school's production of *Romeo and Juliet*. On the night, the auditorium had been filled with all of my classmates' parents, beaming up at them. My mother was two years into her role as anchor at HCB, having been promoted for her coverage of the Indian Ocean tsunami. By this point, all my friends knew who she was; their parents too. I had babbled all week about the play, about how I was so excited for her to be there. She had said she wouldn't miss it.

Well, she did miss it. She wasn't even there to collect me from the auditorium. Romeo's parents dropped me home.

On my sixteenth birthday, I blew out the candles in front of all my family and friends, but not my mother. She sent a huge arrangement of flowers and a pretty dress three days later, wishing me a happy birthday. She hadn't even remembered the date.

When I got the keys to my first apartment, I moved everything in with Josh's help. My mother had called me from somewhere in California, promising that we were going to go out to celebrate when she returned: a nice dinner and champagne. She returned, but she never made dinner plans.

Of course, I didn't tell those stories in my eulogy. I went along with the picture-perfect existence that she had created. I was the daughter who was successful, but not as successful as her. I was the daughter who was beautiful, but not as beautiful as her. Those in attendance believed everything I'd said in the eulogy; including that I was afraid to live in a world that didn't include Bonnie

Piroso. This wasn't entirely untrue—I *was* afraid to live in the world without her, because she had told me who I was supposed to be my entire life. If she was no longer telling me, then who was I? Following the service, the whole community spilled into Main Street and lined the road for a procession. The pallbearers were dressed in crisp black suits, with dark sunglasses and sprigs of evergreen in their pockets. One of them was Colin. The procession moved slowly through Main Street. All the shops closed their doors as a mark of respect.

At the wake, people approached me with stories of my mother. The way she ran coverage for the O. J. Simpson trial, how she saved a boy's life in Oklahoma during a tornado, how her investigation led to the safe return of another American journalist taken hostage in Libya, the time she was stranded in Alaska during a snowstorm and saved the day. Or personal stories of her—how she could make an entire room laugh, how inspiring she was, how warm and gracious and full of elegance she was. There were one hundred different versions of her, and I didn't know any of them. The only version of my mother that I knew was the one that was always absent, and so the only version of myself that I knew was the one that was always alone. This was the most difficult thing about picking myself apart—if I wasn't honest with those around me, how could I be honest with myself? And if I wasn't honest with myself, how could I even begin to heal?

When Henry suggested the idea of a poetry evening, it was immediately clear who was comfortable with the idea of public speaking and who was not. Winnie seemed rather enthused; so did Gill and Rita. Bobby seemed uncertain, almost afraid. Emerson looked as though she had been asked to walk a tightrope, and Julian seemed a little confused by the whole picture. Yet out of everyone, Wren looked the most aghast at the idea. There was something about Wren that I couldn't quite put my finger on. She was articulate, but not in a lawyerly or doctorly sort of way.

She had to have been something impressive in New York, and I didn't know why, but I was so determined to find out what that was.

Winnie sent Henry off to find a cake slicer for the lemon meringue pie, and before I could ask Wren what she did in Manhattan, Winnie had already cornered us both.

"So," Winnie said. "Bet you're wondering if talking in circles with strangers makes the dead any less dead."

Wren looked like she had been smacked.

"Do you like chicken pot pie?" Winnie added brightly, and Wren recovered.

"Yes."

Winnie smiled. "Emmy always joins me on Friday nights for some chicken pot pie; would you like to join too?"

Wren glanced at me as though she didn't know what to say.

"Wren is busy fixing up Gill's place," I offered.

"You're welcome, too, Liv," Winnie said. "Unless you're working late on all that desk duty you've got going on."

I scowled slightly. "I'll bring some red, shall I?"

Winnie seemed to approve of this, which meant I didn't have any other choice.

On Thursday, I realized I'd completely run out of everything. Milk, eggs, coffee, salad; even those fun little packets with crackers, cheese slices, pastrami pieces, and olives. And I suddenly had a real craving for pesto pasta. I normally did my shopping at the Safeway in Norvale after work, but the thought of having to drive thirty minutes there and back didn't sound appealing. Pat's Grocer on Main Street would still be open and would have to do. I fetched my car keys and a sweater and slid into some Ugg boots.

There was a hand-painted sign that sat on the curb outside the store promoting a sale on mozzarella. *Tempting*. The building itself was unassuming, with faded paint and window boxes filled with seasonal blooms. If it weren't for a row of shopping carts near the entryway, you'd suspect this was someone's residence. Although, this was probably the way the owner, Pat, liked it. Everybody knew Pat. When Pat laughed, it could be heard for miles, one of those hearty laughs that made people turn their heads and often laugh along with her. The creaky door swung open and a bell announced my entry. I collected a handbasket from the corner and strolled past the bulletin board crammed with community notices, with no doubt in my mind that Henry had already put up some printout regarding the poetry evening. The overhead lights warmed the neatly stacked aisles, and I squinted at the various handwritten signs marking every produce section. I found my way over to the deli counter, considering the half-priced brie for a moment, before deciding that my original thought of pesto pasta was a winner. I turned around to find the pasta aisle and promptly smacked into something, hard. A basket flew in the opposite direction, sending apples all over aisle three.

I'd just walked directly into Wren.

"Wren!" I exclaimed. "I'm so sorry!"

"It's no problem," she replied, although her voice was muffled as she scrambled to prevent the apples from rolling away.

"I'm so clumsy," I said, picking up two stray fruits and handing them to her. "You can't let me loose anywhere."

"I knocked over a stand of Tupperware in Macy's once," she grinned. "This hardly tops that."

"I slipped on a doormat while interviewing someone once, literally fell on top of him in front of his wife."

Wren's eyes crinkled at the corners as she grinned. "Well, perhaps you do have me beat," she replied.

"Can't find what you need?" she asked, nodding to my empty basket.

"More like I can't decide," I replied. "Although I did leave my apartment with a craving for pasta and basil pesto, but I'm not entirely sure Pat's will stock the sauce I need."

Wren hummed to herself. "We can always ask." She walked up to the checkout area, a small nook with only one wooden counter, slightly worn with age, and a bowl of free peppermints sitting on the edge.

"Do you have any basil pesto?" she asked.

The cashier was Pat's grandson, Mickey. But of course, Wren didn't know that. Which meant she also didn't know that Mickey wouldn't have the faintest idea what basil pesto *was*, much less any brand names.

"What's that?"

Exactly.

To Wren's credit, she was very patient. "Well," she said, "it's a sauce. It's made from basil, garlic, pine nuts. Looks green in color, almost like a paste."

"That sounds pretty good," Mickey replied, and I almost thought I hadn't heard him properly.

"Oh, it's great!" Wren said. "Very popular in New York."

"You're from New York!?" Mickey sounded very impressed by this, and I was still surprised he was engaging this much with a customer; I'd never heard him say more than three sentences prior to tonight.

"Yes." She blushed.

"Is it true that New Yorkers will push people off the sidewalks because they're in such a hurry?"

"Well, we only push tourists off the sidewalks," she replied with a wry grin.

She walked away for a moment, gathering ingredients. "I used to make my own," she smiled, handing me the produce. "Give that a go."

I wasn't sure how to respond. But the way she was smiling warmed me from somewhere deep inside.

"You'll have to show me," Wren added brightly, and I was momentarily confused. "You know," she said, "take a picture when you make it?"

"Oh, yeah," I replied. "I'll send it to you." I pulled my phone out of my pocket and held it out to her. "Put your number in."

There was a flash of something in her eyes—curiosity, or maybe even hesitation—but whatever it was, it passed quickly, and she took my phone, typing her number in.

"Perfect," I said, feeling heat rush to my cheeks. I must have been grinning like an idiot, but I couldn't help it.

Wren's eyes lingered on me for a moment, a flicker of something playful in her expression. "Don't let me down. I want to see that masterpiece."

"I'll try my best," I said, which made her laugh.

She gave me a small wave and started down the next aisle, leaving me standing there with a basket full of ingredients and a faint, unexpected sense of warmth.

Let's just say, I was glad I ended up going to the grocery store.

After dinner, I poured a glass of wine, curled up on the couch, and flicked on the TV. The soft glow bathed the room as I scrolled mindlessly through Netflix, skipping past rom-coms about small-town love, runaway brides, and broken-hearted widowers. As my mind wandered, it went to Wren. I smiled, remembering her at the grocery store in denim overalls speckled with paint, one strap undone, a Smashing Pumpkins T-shirt underneath. The way she'd been so concerned about whether I had pesto for my dinner had been almost painfully adorable. I wrestled with the urge to text her. She was probably busy. Or maybe she wasn't. Maybe she'd been thinking about texting me. Or maybe she wasn't thinking about me at all. I sighed dramatically, resisting the urge to scream into my large sofa pillows at my own ridiculousness. I was a grown woman. I could text Wren. Right? I took a deep breath, unlocked my phone, and brought up Wren's contact.

Doing anything interesting tonight? I typed and then immediately erased it. *Cringe*.

It was so lovely to see you! I tried again . . . and erased it again. *Absolute cringe*.

I tried once more: Hey there, just watching some TV, any recommendations? I erased this, too, and groaned to myself. That was the worst of them all.

My thumb hovered over the keys, wondering why I had suddenly lost all my ability to formulate words. I took another sip of wine, and then typed:

> You know I forgot to ask you an important question . . .

I hit send and put the phone down a little too forcefully. I shouldn't have texted. I barely knew her. Wren barely knew me. She was going to think I was some sort of weird reporter creep with mommy issues. Half true, none of it entirely my fault. (Throwing dog poop while intoxicated on live television, completely my fault.) And yet my phone lit up with a reply almost immediately.

> Oh?

> What were all the apples for!?

> The horse next door . . .

I grinned.

> Really?

> Yes, really!
> His name is Mr. Patches

And he enjoys apples?

> He loves them

I swiped to find the photo of the pesto I'd made for dinner and sent it to Wren.

You weren't wrong. Homemade pesto is infinitely better.

Wren reacted to the photo with a love heart. I don't know why, but seeing the little heart appear on my screen made me smile into my wineglass.

> Wow. I'm impressed.
> Do you take orders?

There I went, smiling into my wineglass again.

So do you actually enjoy chicken pot pie or were you being polite?

> I really do love chicken pot pie

Tbh I've never had Winnie's pie
I guess I need to thank you for my invite

> Don't thank me until we know
> it's actually good :)

> Fair point :)
> I can at least thank you for the pesto ingredients!
> Do you like to cook?

> I love cooking, my mom taught me
> It was something we always did together

I paused for a moment, trying to imagine what that would have looked like, or felt like. For my own mother to have taught me to cook, or to have at least been around to sit at the dinner table on a normal evening.

My phone buzzed again.

> I'm sorry. I didn't mean to bring up my relationship with my own mom

> You don't need to apologize. Just because I didn't have a good mom doesn't mean you can't talk about yours

> Do you miss her?

How to even answer that.

> I miss what she could have been
> Do you miss Lucy?

> Every day

I couldn't help but feel like I was intruding. How could I even be entertaining the idea of flirting with Wren, when it was clear she was still in love with her fiancée?

> I should let you get back to the apples and Mr. Patches

> He's asleep, why aren't you?

> I struggle to sleep sometimes

> Me too

The thing was: I didn't want to stop talking to her.

> I lied before

> About what?

> My mom. I don't miss her in the way most people would miss their mom if she died. It's hard for me. She was never really part of my life to begin with

> I understand. How can you miss someone who never took the time to know you?

> Exactly. It's hard for me to admit, because the whole town loved her

> Just because their memory of her is different, doesn't mean yours isn't true

She started typing something and the dots flashed across the screen. They disappeared and then reappeared, and disappeared again. Finally, Wren texted:

> Do you think people deserve second chances?

For forgiveness?

> For love

I think everybody deserves to find love again

That was the end of our conversation, and I can't tell you how many times I replayed it over and over in my head.

Chapter 10

Emerson

So, I'd been thinking a lot about hash browns. Specifically, Sam's Diner hash browns—crispy, golden, with just the right amount of cheese and a side of hot sauce. If there's one thing in Everston that had never let me down, it was them. And trust me, I'd had my fair share of hash browns: I was qualified at this point. *Nothing* compared to Sam's.

This, I told myself, was the reason I agreed to meet Coach Tillman at the diner this afternoon. Not because I was ready to face her. Definitely not because I wanted to talk about my future. Just because I wanted hash browns.

The bell rang as I entered Sam's, and the smell of coffee and dough hit me in all the right places.

"Emmy!" Mrs. Wilks said as she noticed me. "The usual, hon?"

"Yes, please," I replied. "Any free booths, Mrs. W?"

She laughed, and looked around at the mostly empty diner. "We're pretty full today, but I'll make special room for you."

I grinned, sliding into my favorite booth, the one with coffee rings etched into the surface of the table.

Mrs. Wilks brought a pot of coffee over. "You doing okay, sweetheart? Haven't seen you in a while."

"I've just been busy," I replied, which was sort of true considering I'd picked up loads of extra shifts at Adventure Rudy's.

Between work, meetings, and hanging out with Winnie, I really hadn't even had time to drop by Sam's.

Mrs. Wilks's eyes lingered on me a moment, and I could almost read her mind. I knew she wanted to ask me about treatment, about doctors' follow-ups, about whether they thought my scars would heal over. But she didn't ask me whatever she wanted to know; she just said, "How about I give you some extra hot sauce?"

"You're the best," I replied.

I watched as Mrs. Wilks disappeared around the counter and into the kitchen, calling to her husband for a serving of hash browns. I basically lived at Sam's my entire senior year. Brady and I would hang out there after nearly every football game. There was a crash from inside the kitchen as Sam cursed. I felt my body lock up at the sound of glass shattering. Mrs. Wilks rushed from the kitchen and fetched a long-handled broom.

"Always dropping things," she mumbled and disappeared to clean up the mess.

My mind flashed back to those early days at Adventure Rudy's.

I was restocking carabiners when something heavy hit the floor behind me. A metal shelving unit had tipped, sending a row of water bottles clattering to the ground. I froze. The impact jolted through my body, the crash triggering something deep and instinctual. My heart pounded. The noise dragged me back to the accident; the sickening crunch of metal, the sound of my own breath catching as my world turned upside down.

"Emerson?"

Jarrod, the manager, stood near the back, watching me with concern.

"You good?" he asked.

I swallowed, forcing myself to move. "Yeah," I replied. "Just spaced out for a second."

"Did you hurt yourself?"

"No more than I already have," I said dryly, holding up my arm to show where I was still wearing pressure garments.

He blushed slightly, and I sort of felt bad for being a brat.

"How about you just mind the store?" he said brightly. "If you need any help, just call out to me."

"Sure thing," I responded.

By the time I rang up the twentieth customer of the day, my arm and neck were hurting. I was sweating, and those beads of sweat over my burns? Well, not a feeling I recommend. The bell above the front door rang again, and I braced myself. This customer was elderly, and I really did not think she should be considering skiing or hiking or anything outdoorsy . . . like, at all.

"Hello," she said.

"Hi, how can I help you?" I replied.

She placed a tote bag on the front counter; it had a hummingbird embroidered on the side. She removed a shoe box and opened its contents.

"I'd like to return these," she said. "I purchased them for my husband."

The woman had panache. She was dressed in a striped maxi skirt, with a well-worn vintage leather jacket. Around her neck she wore layers of mismatched beaded necklaces in various bright colors, and she peered at me through oversized round glasses perched on the bridge of her nose. She fumbled in her pockets and handed me a receipt.

Her weathered hands were adorned in an assortment of rings that I would absolutely wear myself, and on her wrist she had a tiny tattoo of a hummingbird, which matched her tote bag.

"They didn't fit?" I asked, looking over the receipt.

"Oh, they fit," she replied.

I was confused.

"So why are you returning them?"

"Because my husband left me, and he has no intention of coming back, so I don't think he will be needing his boots, and I could use the refunded money to get myself one of those yummy-looking cinnamon rolls from Lou's Bakery next door."

I didn't even know what to say, but the words, "What an asshole," came out of my mouth before I could control myself.

The woman chuckled.

"He *was* an asshole," she said. "He never appreciated me, always made everything about him. Nearly fifty years I wasted with that man, yet I'm the one having to deal with the mess of it all."

"Those cinnamon rolls from Lou's can probably help you with all that grief," I said, and I rung up the refund on the computer.

Her eyes twinkled. "They're that good, are they?"

"They're very good," I said. "I pretty much lived on them in my recovery."

Why had I just blurted that out to a random customer? I didn't know why I felt immediately at ease with this lady. But her eyes didn't move to my scars, they didn't linger on my pressure garment, or fill with pity in the same way everyone else's did.

"Well then, I'll be getting a few to take home as well."

"I won't be long," I said. "I'm new and I just have to figure out how to put the refund through."

"Could have fooled me, pet," she said. "Don't rush yourself."

As I was entering the item number into the system, the bell signaled another customer. He walked in wearing a football jersey from my old high school. He could have been Brady, with the same tousled chestnut hair, broad shoulders, and almond eyes. I overheard him asking Jarrod if we stocked cleats. My stomach sank. There was nothing in this world that could prepare you for how to live with life-altering change. Nothing. My mom had told me that everything was going to be okay, that I would regain use of my fingers again, that I would grow into my new skin and learn to feel beautiful in it, and learn to filter out the staring and the comments. But she didn't know that I often heard her crying at night, and hearing Mom cry brought me a new type of pain. So much of me didn't want to live with this new skin. It was as though I now shared a body with sadness, and I infected anyone and everything that came into contact with me.

"Never liked football," the woman quipped, and I'd almost forgotten she was standing there.

I laughed. "It's totally overrated," I said. "I prefer gymnastics . . . or at least, I did. Just waiting to see if my doctors will ever let me do it again."

She scoffed. "What do they know?" and her eyes shone. "You can do anything, so long as you put in the work, and reward yourself with something sweet."

I smiled. "I'll take that advice," I replied.

This woman had fixed my whole day, and I probably was never going to see her again. I handed her another receipt and her refund in cash, moving the shoebox underneath the counter.

"All set," I said.

"Thanks for all your help." She smiled. "You take care now."

Turned out, I did see that woman again, because it was Winnie.

Mrs. Wilks placed my hash browns in front of me: a double serving, with extra hot sauce. The sound of the plate clinking in front of me brought me out of my daydream. I smiled at her, suddenly realizing how hungry I was.

Do you ever wonder if you've met someone in another life? Or whether life is all predestined: the stars align and you are set on the path that was already written for you . . . those kinds of things? The series of events that led me to working at Adventure Rudy's, meeting Winnie, and then somehow seeing her again at one of Henry's meetings, seemed so unlikely, and yet, all in all, it saved my life. Was it fate? Destiny? Chance or luck? Or maybe a combination of all those things? What was it going to take to get me to drive again, or to get me to love gymnastics again?

My coach suddenly sat down in front of me, talking at a million miles an hour—apologizing for being late, explaining that her four- and six-year-olds had gotten into the pantry and smeared peanut butter all over the countertops, and that her teenager was allergic to peanuts.

"Nightmare," she concluded.

"It's all good, Andi," I replied. "Mrs. Wilks served me my hash browns as soon as I walked in the door."

Andi smiled. "Yes, I do remember you, Brady, and the gang coming in here quite often."

I tried not to let my face fall at the mention of him.

Andi waved at the waitress and quickly ordered a coffee and a muffin.

"How are you?" she asked.

It's like, the most common question to ask someone, and yet half the time people either don't give an honest answer, or the questioner doesn't want to hear an honest answer.

"I'm better, sort of," I replied.

"Sort of?" she asked.

"Well, I mean, I'm functioning," I replied. "But I still can't drive, and I haven't thought much more about UCLA."

Andi smiled as the waitress placed her coffee and muffin in front of her. She added sugar and stirred for a moment.

"It's been tough on you Emmy, I know, but one way or another we are going to have to let UCLA know about that scholarship."

"I know," I said, sinking into the chair.

"What does your mom say?"

I shrugged. "She says I'm an adult and it's my decision."

This wasn't entirely true. Mom did say I was an adult and

that it was my decision, but she also said that it was a once-in-a-lifetime opportunity that I shouldn't give up.

"Gosh, I just remember your Yurchenko vault during that Arizona competition," she said. "I'd never seen judges so stunned."

"Won by a landslide," I grinned. She was referring to a Yurchenko double twist (also known as an "Amânar"), which basically went like this: you run toward the vaulting table (must have, like, perfect speed and momentum), place both hands on the springboard shoulder-width apart, push off the vaulting table, elongate your body with your arms upward, tuck your knees and twist, then extend your body again, and tuck your knees to complete the second twist, before sticking your landing, which means both feet have to simultaneously land with minimal steps. You needed perfect form, height, and landing.

"You really do deserve that scholarship, Emerson," she said.

I wasn't just *handed* that scholarship; someone like me never got handed anything. I had everything they were looking for: technical skills (I was near perfect on vault, bars, and beam, and I could execute complicated routines with precision), strength and conditioning (my core strength and flexibility were next-level), resilience in the face of challenges, leadership, and adaptability.

And finally, I was consistent. I was always consistent before my accident. I consistently got good grades, I consistently maintained high scores at competition, I consistently worked well under pressure, my friends were consistent, Brady was consistent. And now look at me: I couldn't even consistently wake up on time.

"Andi, I'm just not even sure I want that path anymore," I said, and it was the first time I had said it out loud.

"What path do you want?" she asked softly.

"That's just it, I'm not sure."

She smiled at me, reached out her hand and gave mine a little tap. "I'll be here whenever you decide, Emmy."

She gathered her things. "I have to run though; left the younger two with the teenager while I was here, and god knows how she's retaliated after the peanut butter incident." She gave my shoulder a light squeeze. "I'm here, Emmy."

I watched her leave into the fading daylight. Mrs. Wilks placed another stack of hash browns in front of me, and I looked up at her.

"On the house," she smiled. "Exactly as you like them."

At least I could count on my hash brown order always being the same . . . but maybe that was the problem? The picture I had in my head of the way my life was supposed to go didn't match up with reality at all any more. And I was so busy trying to remember what that old picture looked like, I'd forgotten to take a new one.

The afternoon dipped into dusk, and I knew Winnie would be expecting me. I hopped back on my bike and rode to her house. If my fear of driving had done anything good, it was that it really shaped my quads again. I mean, I was fit, because I was an athlete, but honestly, biking everywhere—who even needs leg day at the gym?

Winnie didn't live very far from Main Street. I opened the weathered wooden gate and pushed my bike up the river-stone pathway leading to the front porch. She had different-colored potted plants scattered everywhere and two cane chairs underneath the front window. There was a birdbath in the middle of the front yard, and trellises supporting climbing roses on the side of her house. The window shutters were painted bright blue and her front door was wide open.

I called out to her as I entered, but she didn't answer; probably busy rolling the pastry for the chicken pie. The living room was cluttered with an assortment of old furniture and, right in the center, an overstuffed couch covered in floral patterns. Her fireplace mantel was covered in random trinkets and sculptures and tiny teacups. I tossed my jacket over one of her armchairs and called out to her again.

"Winnie!" I said, louder this time.

Still no response. I walked into the kitchen looking for her, and the smell of pie filled the small space. It was definitely in the oven already, but where was Winnie?

She'd been making cookies for dessert and was clearly peeling potatoes for mash, as they both sat on the counter waiting to be finished.

"Hello?" I called again, and I couldn't help but start to panic.

I looked around in concern and noticed a bunch of letters from Norvale General Hospital sitting half opened on the counter, so I reached for one of them.

"You're here!"

I jumped. Like, basically through her roof. I could have catapulted myself back into the gymnasium on the vault in that moment, I swear I got airtime.

"Jesus fucking Christ," I said.

"Emerson," Winnie scolded. "Back in my day my father would have washed my mouth out with soap."

"Where *were* you?" I demanded.

She looked at me blankly. "I was hanging laundry."

"What are all these letters from the hospital?" I asked.

Winnie peered over at me through her glasses. "Oh, it's just some old mail."

"But they're from the hospital."

"I was cleaning out some cupboards the other day and happened across them. Probably from the time Cliff hurt his knee."

I squinted at the labels, trying to find the date they were issued.

"Come help me set the table, Emmy," she said, and she plucked the envelopes out of my hand, storing them away in a drawer.

"Are you sure you're okay?" I asked.

Winnie waved the question away. "I'm just fine, Emmy,"

she replied. She checked her watch. "Our dinner guests will be arriving soon!"

"Come on in, girls!" Winnie greeted Olivia and Wren at the front door.

Winnie was practically my best friend these days, and I liked to think of her as mine. So, as her best friend, I wanted to tell her that trying to set up a woman mourning the death of her fiancée with a washed-up reporter angry at her mother for, like, so many reasons, didn't exactly seem like a match made in heaven. But I also knew that Winnie loved rom-coms, and ever since that dirtbag Cliff left her after nearly fifty years, she'd been trying to believe in love again. This was also probably the highlight of her week—other than hanging out with me, of course. I took Wren and Olivia's coats and hung them in the small closet by Winnie's front door, as she led them into the living room.

"You have a lovely home," Wren commented, and she sat down on the sofa.

Olivia handed a bottle of red to Winnie, who looked most appeased. I would never understand people's obsession with wine.

"Do you need help?" Olivia asked Winnie.

She shook her head. "Make yourselves comfy, I'll be in the kitchen."

I watched, kind of amused, as Olivia considered sitting next to Wren, and then awkwardly decided to sit in the armchair next to her instead.

"Emmy, come open this bottle and pour a glass for us old gals, will you."

"What about me?"

She looked at me flatly. "Please," she said, "I wasn't born yesterday."

I grunted and followed her into the kitchen.

Once I'd settled next to Wren, and handed both her and Olivia a glass of wine, Olivia brought up the poetry evening.

"I wouldn't have the first clue how to write a poem," she said. "Maybe I could manage a limerick, but how long does Henry think this evening is going to last? All night? There's only nine of us."

"I mean, Rita could probably talk for several hours," I said, and she smirked.

"I think he just wants to put on something that'll draw a crowd," Wren replied. "Raise some awareness for mental health initiatives in Everston."

"But why?" Olivia pressed. "Who's this even for? Is it for us, or is it for him?"

"Maybe it's both," Wren said thoughtfully. "Max could've suggested it. Poetry can be therapeutic, right? It could be his way of getting us to dig a little deeper into what we're feeling."

"Or Henry's just trying to invite other people in the community and let them know there's help?" I added. "He was there when I needed someone. He was there when you needed someone."

Olivia feigned insult. "I don't *need* anyone," she replied, and then grinned at me. "Besides, if he wants to fundraise, why can't it be a bake sale? We could sell cookies. I'm much better at baking cookies."

"We could also have brownies," I said. "There would *have* to be brownies."

"I don't think Henry's expecting anyone to win a Pulitzer," Wren said. "It's not about being good at it. It's about putting something out there—your feelings, your story. Even if it's messy, it's still yours."

"I like that," Olivia said softly. "You can still be something, even if you're messy."

Wren smiled, "I think you can be anything."

Olivia held her gaze a moment too long. "Me?"

Wren blushed and said little too quickly, "Well, any of us, really."

I cleared my throat, because someone had to, and if they kept looking at each other like that, I was going to throw a cushion at them.

"I'm more worried about the whole public speaking thing," I said. "I can be catapulted into the air in front of a huge crowd, but if I have to talk, I might puke."

Wren smiled kindly. "You'll be okay, Emerson."

"What would I even write about?" Olivia questioned. "Surely he doesn't think I'm going to write about my mother?"

"Maybe I could write the gruesome details of my car accident," I offered, and Wren seemed to pale.

"Emerson, I don't think—"

"What would you write about?" Olivia asked her curiously. "If you had to write a poem, what would you write about?"

Wren downed the rest of her glass.

"Ladies!" Winnie called, interrupting. "Dinner's ready!"

Winnie did make the best chicken pot pie—golden crust, creamy filling, the works—and tonight she'd served it with roasted carrots and green beans on the side. I could tell Wren and Olivia were both enjoying it from the way they talked quickly in between mouthfuls so they each could have another scoop.

"This is wonderful, Winnie," Wren said. "Truly, I don't think I've ever had chicken pot pie this good."

"Well, they say food is the way to the heart, don't they?" Winnie replied.

"Are you trying to worm your way into Wren's heart, Winnie?" Olivia smirked.

"Not any more than you are," she quipped.

Olivia coughed into her food.

It was so obvious to me that Olivia was into Wren. The way she lit up around her. Please. She practically melted the other day when Wren complimented her hair. And Wren wasn't subtle either—I mean, she was still grieving, sure—but she laughed at Olivia's worst jokes, and stared at her whenever she wasn't looking. It was kind of impressive, really, how two people could be so obviously into each other and still pretend they weren't. Why didn't anyone just say what they felt anymore? Why all the circling and hint-dropping? Just say it. You *like* her. Boom. Done. Revolutionary.

"Have you done any hikes?" Winnie asked, changing the subject.

"Not yet," Wren replied. "I've been quite busy with Gill's house."

"Ah, yes, I did hear about this," she said. "Although if you don't have time for a hike, there is a lovely lookout up on Everston Overlook, it's a very scenic drive."

Wren smiled. "Well, Emerson, maybe the lookout can provide some inspiration for your poem?"

I sunk slightly in my chair.

"I can't drive," I said quietly.

"Oh, I'm sorry," Wren stuttered. "I didn't know."

"I mean, I *can* drive," I corrected. "But I just haven't wanted to since my accident."

"I see," Wren said.

"We're getting there, Emmy," Winnie said. "If you'd only remember to put some gas in your car!"

I pouted at her in response.

"You could drive my car," Wren offered.

"What kind of car do you have?" Olivia asked, glancing at me with a grin. "If Emmy's going to practice, it might need to be a little beat-up."

"Rude," I muttered, heaping more green beans onto my plate.

Wren hesitated a moment, then said, "Oh, it's an old 1960s Cabriolet. A silly decision really, considering Lucy already had a car, and we lived in a brownstone, so there was really no need. But she loved that thing, and I haven't been able to part with it."

Olivia blinked. "Wait, a Mercedes-Benz Cabriolet? That's not just 'old,' that's collector-level."

Wren moved some of the carrots around on her plate. "I suppose."

Olivia looked at me and I shrugged. I wouldn't have the first clue about cars. And then Olivia looked at Winnie, who seemed interested, but she wasn't really much of a car person either. Come to think of it, I didn't realize Olivia *was*.

"Well, you must have been doing well, if you owned a Cabriolet as a second car."

Wren seemed uncomfortable, as though she knew what the next question would be.

"What did you do in New York anyway?"

Olivia was being such a reporter and completely missed Wren's discomfort. I reached for my water, shooting Winnie a sidelong glance, attempting to send her a telepathic *Do something!* message.

"Oh, just the odd things here and there," Wren replied, avoiding eye contact.

Olivia frowned. "A 1960s Mercedes-Benz Cabriolet is worth a small fortune, easily two hundred grand."

I choked mid-sip, water shooting down the wrong pipe and spluttering back into my glass. *Holy shit*.

"If you lived in Manhattan, and owned a brownstone, plus a vintage Mercedes, that doesn't exactly scream 'odd jobs' to me."

"Olivia," Winnie interjected gently. "Perhaps Wren isn't quite ready to talk about her past."

Olivia looked as though she wanted to say something more, but she closed her mouth. I don't think I'd ever seen Olivia back down from any line of questioning. When I told her once that my doctors had called and wanted to switch my medication, she took the phone from me and grilled them for forty-five minutes on what exactly the medication was and what it would do and whether it was the right thing for me.

Although one thing I did know: Winnie's schemes were absolutely off the table.

November

Chapter 11

Wren

When I was younger, all my classmates had grand dreams of becoming doctors, astronauts, or firefighters. But I never knew what I wanted to do. I wish I could say that I had always wanted to be a writer, that I had dreamed of becoming a writer since I was a small child. But the truth was, I wanted to be many things before I wanted to be a writer. I wanted to be a chef, a veterinarian, a pilot, or Piper Halliwell from *Charmed*. In fact, I vividly remember telling my mother I was going to be a pirate when I was five years old. That dream ended when I threw up on a cruise we took to Hawaii. I wasn't a grade-A student, either, but my English teacher had high hopes for me.

When we're young, we're told to find what it is that we are passionate about. They say if you love what you do, then you never work a day in your life. This seemed to be the case for me when I found writing. But what if the thing you love doing is the reason you lose the person you love the most?

Everston Library was fast becoming a regular feature in my day. Its large arched windows were currently decorated with posters and artwork relating to popular kids' books like *Percy Jackson and the Olympians*, *Charlotte's Web*, and *The Cat in the Hat*, in honor of Book Week this month (something Henry apparently looked forward to every year). There were armchairs and sofas decorated in vintage cushions, inviting reading nooks; the subtle fragrance of aged paper hung in the air.

"What are in these?" I asked, as I lifted a box onto the counter.

"Books, of course," Henry replied. "I've ordered in a rather large shipment this quarter." He looked at me quizzically. "I've been struggling with those boxes all morning and you just lifted that one up like it was filled with marshmallows."

I laughed. "Yes, well, fixing up Gill's place has made me a little tougher I suppose."

"What would I do without you?" Henry replied.

I smiled, pretending to ponder his question. "Probably hire a forklift, I suppose."

"When can you start?" he replied. "I am down three staff members, and I have at least another five boxes of new shipments to catalog." He leaned over the counter toward the printer and collected some documents, filing them into a drawer.

"I'm happy to lend my help, but only if I am paid in those cinnamon rolls Winnie keeps insisting I try."

Henry laughed. "From Lou's?"

"Yes, those ones."

"They *are* a treat," he confirmed. His expression grew more thoughtful. "Jacob loved cinnamon rolls too," he said. "He'd insist on a weekend hike, followed by a cinnamon roll."

"It's always the little things," I replied, "that I miss the most. Lucy's love of knitted sweaters, or how she always needed to have a peppermint cookie with her tea."

"Jacob always had odd socks on," Henry said. "I'd always find mismatched socks strewn throughout the house, it used to drive me crazy."

"Isn't it funny how we'd give anything for those little quirks now?"

Henry nodded. "It's a strange thing, missing someone—I could cry over mismatched socks, and in the same breath smile remembering weekend hikes and cinnamon rolls."

There was something about Henry's gentle nature and his curious smile that made it so easy to open up to him. I felt as though we'd been friends for years, even though we'd only really known each other a few weeks.

"It's the guilt I struggle with most," I said. "I blame myself for what happened to Lucy."

Henry looked at me thoughtfully. "But you weren't driving, Wren."

"No," I agreed. "But I was reading something to her in the car, and then we crashed. She was distracted. It was my fault."

He was quiet for a moment, as he leaned against the counter. "It's easier to blame ourselves," he said. "I blamed myself for Jacob's death too. If only I had noticed earlier. We were twins. I should have known that he was sick."

"How could you have possibly known?" I asked.

"Yes, exactly," Henry replied, opening a box. "How could *you* have possibly known Lucy would lose control of the car?"

I wished I could tell Henry that after the accident I had a sudden zest for life. And maybe, at first, I could convince myself I was shaken but grateful to have survived. But that gratitude was quickly overpowered by survivor's guilt, and the debilitating pain of losing Lucy. The car was totaled, a squashed piece of metal. The wreckage alone was enough to make passersby gasp and wonder how anyone had survived it. Maybe one day I'd see the wonder in that myself. But for now, I was haunted by the question I couldn't stop asking: Why did I survive, and Lucy didn't?

Henry eventually broke the silence. "So," he asked, "do you think the poetry evening is good idea?"

I curled my finger around a strand of hair, nervous suddenly.

"The others seemed to think so," I replied tentatively.

"I know you've only recently joined, Wren," he said, "so I would understand if you didn't want to contribute a poem. But I also think poetry could be healing for you."

I stared down at the boxes filled with books, the spines neatly aligned, their bold, bright fonts calling out to me like forgotten memories. Once upon a time, there were few things that brought me greater joy than writing—a dance between words, a way to untangle the chaos, a place to make sense of things, a home. But now, even the thought of poetry gave me a sinking feeling. How could I find healing in something that now only reminded me of pain?

"Perhaps I'll just observe," I said softly.

Who was I if I could never write again?

After a thoughtful pause, Henry said, "I am just glad you're part of our little group, Wren, whether you write a poem or don't."

He looked at his watch. "I daresay we've earned a cinnamon roll. Should we wander over to Lou's?"

"I think we should," I replied.

"You know," he said, fetching the sweater he'd draped over a chair earlier, "we may even be able to request some peppermint cookies."

My eyes brightened at the thought. "I'd love that, Henry."

Rita was trying to force-feed Gill her home-baked zucchini bread when I walked into the library later that evening. I noticed Winnie sitting near Henry, bundled in one of her thick knitted shawls. She looked a little paler than usual, her eyes slightly sunken. Emerson was sitting on one side of her, and as I sat down on her other side I caught the way she pressed a tissue against her nose. Emerson was wearing a bright-red sweater with Bert and Ernie stitched into the front. She handed me half a granola bar as I crossed my legs.

"You look tired," she observed.

"I was helping Henry this morning, and then I was on a ladder all afternoon," I replied.

Emerson smirked. "You know, you could paint that whole house yellow, and Gill would think it's great." She considered for a moment. "You know, Wren, maybe you *should* paint the whole house yellow, just to see what he would do."

Before I could respond, Olivia walked in. The soft lighting of the library caught the golden-blond waves of her hair as they waterfalled down her shoulders. I felt myself inhale sharply as she moved toward me. We hadn't spoken since dinner at Winnie's.

"Hi," she said, sitting down in the spare seat next to me, draping her sweater over the back of the chair. Her hand brushed the edge of my arm as she leaned past, and the contact was so slight it shouldn't have registered. But it did. I felt it everywhere. "I'm sorry about the other night," she said. "I pushed too hard about the car, and it's just a car. I'm sorry if I made you uncomfortable."

How could I answer that? *Yes, you did make me uncomfortable, but only because you don't know who I really am.* I felt suddenly half inclined to tell her everything, to let her see every part of me, every truth I'd worked so hard to keep hidden. But what then? What if she looked at me differently? What if she didn't understand? I'd wanted to disappear, and yet I wanted Olivia to *see* me. Her eyes held mine, steady and unblinking, and for a breath I couldn't decide what unsettled me more, the pull of her gaze or the way my own lips parted under it.

"I just find you interesting," she added, at an almost whisper. "I'm sorry if I pressed too hard."

"I *did* do more than odd jobs in New York," I replied softly, "but I came to Everston to start again. Maybe we can just start again too?"

She smiled. "I'd like that."

Max walked in and half of us gasped. He'd shaved his beard. He looked ten years younger.

He waved us all off, as we peppered him with compliments.

The Last Poem

"Right," he announced, sitting down. "Poetry evening!" he exclaimed. "Anyone started their poems?"

"I have," Julian said. "Got a little something, at least."

Emerson sat up in her chair. "Really?" she asked.

"Yeah, do you want to hear it?"

"Obviously," she replied.

Henry clapped (predictably). "Read it for us, Julian!" He was grinning from ear to ear, so excited by all of this.

"*What is a poem?*" Julian recited, "*but for a bit of my heart. What is a poem but for where my journey starts?*"

He sat back down, looking at us all with anticipation.

"Like that?" he asked, hopeful.

"Yes, but you can probably do better," Emerson replied.

"Emmy!" Olivia scolded. "It's great, Julian," she added. "Just, maybe you could add something more?"

"Well, it's not finished," he said. "How would *you* write it, Emerson?"

He asked this as more of an accusation than a question, but Emerson sat up a little straighter.

"Write a letter to your wife," she replied, and Julian seemed shell-shocked for a moment.

"A letter?" he said slowly.

"Yes," Emerson replied. "Write a letter to her, and to the children you lost. But also write a letter to the children you've got here. Tell them what is really in your heart. I think that's a better way for your '*journey to start*,'" she said, adding air quotes to the last words.

Everyone was silent. For a moment, I thought Julian was going to get defensive. But he didn't. He leaned back in his chair.

"You always surprise me, kid," he said, and truthfully, Emerson surprised me too.

The hour melted away, filled with excited chatter about the poetry evening, what food could be served, how to create a stage—Bobby suggested fairy lights—and who in town could moderate the event. Henry said he would do it, but Rita suggested the mayor, which seemed a little grandiose.

Winnie suddenly stood, swaying slightly before gripping the back of her chair. She pressed a hand to her temple.

"I think I'm going to call it a night," she said.

Emerson frowned. "You okay?"

"Oh, I'm fine. Just a bit of a headache." She waved a hand. "Weather's getting colder, probably just the flu." She slipped into her coat. "I'll see you soon," she said, patting Emerson's shoulder, before heading out.

Emerson watched her go, chewing her lip.

"What's wrong?" Olivia asked.

"My mom's working late again, and Winnie usually takes me home." Emerson glanced at me. "I came with her, and so I don't have my bike; she must have forgotten because she's not feeling well."

"I can drop you off at home," I offered.

Olivia looked at me. "Well, maybe we can both drop her home and then you can drop me back at my car?"

I was confused.

"Well, you know, with you being new and everything."

Still confused.

"She's either implying that you're some lunatic that's going to kidnap me and chop me up into little pieces, or that she wants some time alone with you after you drop me off." Emerson smirked. "Or that you need directions and wouldn't possibly have Google Maps."

Olivia and I simultaneously turned bright red.

"Thank you, Emerson," Olivia replied. "I'll remember not to do anything nice for you ever again."

"It's okay," I said. "I mean, I can assure you I am not going to chop Emerson up into little pieces, and I actually don't need to rely on Google Maps in a town so small, but we can all go. It's no problem."

I couldn't hide my smile, and I noticed the corners of Olivia's mouth turned up at the same time.

The days were growing cooler, turning the nights even colder, with leaves crunching underfoot and a hint of moss and damp soil drifting through the evening breeze. I unlocked the car door and pulled the front seat forward.

"You'll have to climb in," I said to Olivia.

She stepped closer, brushing past me to slide into the back. Her hand skimmed my hip, the scent of bergamot trailing behind her. She smelled like a Sunday morning—bright, soft, and lingering. I swallowed and climbed into the front seat, my heart ticking a little faster.

"This car is actually so fire," Emerson said, settling into the passenger side.

"Thank you," I replied lightly. They didn't need to know that just two days ago the back seat had been overflowing with take-out cartons, crumpled receipts, and the faint smell of soy sauce that seemed to haunt me. Some burst of energy earlier today had forced me to clean it, lemon-scented detailer, a vacuum, the works. Maybe it was my idea of moving forward. Or maybe it was the thought that if I wanted to offer someone else space, I had to start by making some for myself.

Emerson glanced out the window, her fingers fidgeting with the hem of her jacket. "I don't think I'll ever get over this fear of driving again," she said. "It makes me feel so stupid."

"It took me a while to drive after mine too," I replied, and it felt strange to say that out loud. I had always thought of the accident as *Lucy's accident*, because she had died and I had not . . . but I had been in the car too.

"It's so weird," she murmured. "One minute I was on the road, and the next I was flying. I don't even know how I lived."

"But you did," Olivia said from the back seat. "You're still here."

Emerson glanced over at me. "I'm sorry about your fiancée," she said quietly.

I nodded, my chest tightening. "I'm sorry about your accident," I replied. "And that you now fear driving. I'm sorry about your mom too," I added, meeting Olivia's eyes in the rearview mirror.

Emerson looked down at her hands. "You know, my ex, Brady, he didn't really get it. None of my friends did either. They tried, but . . . they've never really lost anyone or anything. Not like this. It's like grief is this . . . weird, unofficial, shitty club."

"It really is," Olivia agreed. "And nobody truly understands until they've been through it themselves. That's the worst part. And maybe the best part too, when you find people who actually get it."

"It does have its perks," I said with a faint smile. "Like, maybe you can practice driving again in this car?"

Emerson's eye widened. "Are you serious?"

I shrugged. "Why not?"

"We could both help you," I added, and I glanced back at Olivia again. "You know, so Olivia can make sure I don't chop you up into tiny pieces."

Olivia's gaze met mine once more, her olive green eyes warm and steady, catching the moonlight in a way that made it impossible to look away. A small smile curled on her lips, and my heart tipped off balance, desire threading through me in places I hadn't let myself feel in a long time.

"It's probably best I chaperone," she agreed.

*

The Last Poem

The sunrise was beautiful the next day, light spilling between the houses like golden paint. Everston was barely awake as I pulled my car onto the empty streets. Emerson only lived four miles away. I pulled into her driveway and waited patiently for her to emerge. Her front door opened, and a ginger cat came hurtling out into the driveway, disappearing into the neighbor's bushes. Emerson yelled something inaudible after the feline before opening the car door.

"Are we thinking bagels?" she asked.

I checked the time on the car's dash. "It's six a.m.," I replied.

"And? Do you not like bagels at six a.m.?"

"No, no," I said. "Bagels would be nice."

There was a knock on the window—it was Olivia.

"Of course, she's, like, late for everything else, but not when it involves you," Emerson grinned dryly.

I shushed her, leaned across, and unlocked the car so Olivia could slide into the back seat. Emerson didn't even get out—just shoved the passenger seat forward and smushed herself against the dashboard.

Olivia grumbled as she climbed in. "You couldn't just get out?"

"What?" Emerson said, completely unbothered. "It's cold out there."

Olivia sighed as she got herself situated in the back seat. "I thought you were driving," she said to Emerson.

"That is still up for debate," I replied.

"There's no way I can drive this car right away," Emerson said.

"Well, we don't have to today," I said. "The plan was to drive and see where the highway took us."

"The plan was to drive at the crack of dawn because there would be no traffic and Emerson would feel better," Olivia objected.

I glared at her in the rearview mirror.

"I can't drive this car period. If I crash it, there's, like, no way I could pay you back."

"I have insurance. But how about we just start with bagels?" I said.

"And coffee," Olivia added.

The morning slipped away from us as we drove the scenic route. The evergreen trees carpeted the valley as we navigated the bends around the mountains, Olivia sharing stories of her time in college. Emerson was calm, unfazed by the roads. Along the roadside, the wildflowers were an array of colors—asters, sunflowers, and goldenrod—and a hawk flew somewhere above us. We stopped for an early lunch in Norvale, and dipped in and out of shops. Emerson insisted on stopping by the bookstore, and we became lost among the shelves for at least half an hour.

"I got something for you guys," Emerson said, as we piled back into the car. "As a thank you for helping me, but also, I figure you probably need some inspiration for poetry night." She leaned down to grab something out of her tote bag. "Like, because we can't all be good at writing poetry like me."

I knew what was in the bag before she had even pulled them all the way out. I had spent days deliberating on the color of the cover, the font of the title, the feel of the pages. It was one of the first poetry collections I'd ever written, years ago, back when the world still felt whole. For so long, all anyone ever wanted to talk about was *The Lost Archives*. It was strange—but also oddly comforting—that something I'd written in the beginning of my career could still reach someone like Emerson. Before the six-figure book deals and the intense deadlines, there had been poetry, and so much of it had been about Lucy. I'd always hoped to return to poetry, but when she died, I'd shelved the thought, literally and figuratively. And yet, somehow, it had found me again in Everston. Emerson handed each of us a copy of *Hope for Tomorrow*.

"You didn't have to do that! But it's beautiful," Olivia said.

"Thank you, Emmy," I barely managed. I didn't need to look at the book; I knew every page, every sentence, every word.

I turned on the ignition and pulled out into the street to return to Everston.

"Have you read this one?" Olivia asked.

"Obviously," Emerson said. "It's, like, one of my favorites. I just ordered three of her other books too."

"B.W. Paisley," Olivia read aloud. The way it sounded on her lips was enough for me to have to wind down the window. The air whipped into the car and through my hair.

"Great name for a writer," she said absentmindedly.

Emerson cleared her throat and read. *"You are so far away now; as though we are in different lifetimes—split between the stars. I close my eyes and find forever with you."*

The car continued its journey through the winding mountain roads. My eyes remained fixed ahead, as the wildflowers continued to dot the roadside. The view was breathtaking, and yet my mind was racing as fast as my pounding heart.

"Do you think she, like, always wanted to be a writer?" Emerson said. Her question lingered between us.

Olivia flicked through the pages in the back seat.

"She probably wanted to be one hundred things before she became a writer."

"Yes, probably," I said. My chest felt heavy with the weight of my secret.

"But, like, imagine she never became a writer, or a poet," Emerson said. "And there was never this book, or any others she had written."

Olivia grinned, distracted by a happy memory. "I used to love to bake." She smiled. "All kinds of things, in my Easy-Bake Oven."

I laughed. "Sounds scrumptious."

"What's an Easy-Bake Oven?" Emerson asked.

"Never mind," Olivia and I said in unison.

"So, anyway, I've been thinking that if the gymnastics scholarship doesn't work out, maybe I could, you know, study poetry?" Emerson said, tentatively.

"That's a great idea!" Olivia replied. "I mean, who loves poetry more than you, Em?"

Emerson's eyes sparkled. "You really think so?"

"Absolutely," she said. "I could totally see you running a poetry workshop at the library one day. Henry would be thrilled."

Henry really would. Hosting a poetry workshop would probably make Henry's entire year.

"Everyone has to start somewhere," I added.

"Even B.W. Paisley," Emerson said. "Maybe she wanted to be a gymnast!"

"Or perhaps," I said, as the mountains stood tall in front of us, "she wanted to be a pirate."

It was only then, as I was laughing along, and watching the road blur past, that I realized it was the first time in almost a year that I'd been on the road and not thought about Lucy.

Chapter 12

Olivia

Whenever I told people that I was a reporter, the first thing they'd ask me about was the craziest person I'd ever met. I don't like the word *crazy* to describe someone. *People* aren't crazy, *life* is—and sometimes life is too *crazy* to go through alone. Every person has baggage in one way or another. Whether they appear to be put together or falling apart, underneath it's all the same. We all have breaking points and sometimes they happen at multiple points in our lives. When I think of my own breaking points, I think of the time I was fifteen and, in one short week, my best friend decided I wasn't cool enough to sit with him anymore, Mom didn't show up to parent-teacher night for the fourth year running, and my brother, Matty, joined the Navy and left me all alone. It felt like the end of the world. There was another time, right after I graduated college, and Mom hosted a big party to celebrate. The first thing she said during her speech was how proud she was that I had graduated with a degree in journalism; she followed that very sentence up by listing all her *own* accolades. I'd cried in the bathroom for an hour. Then, there was a year ago, when my ex-girlfriend had come home one day and said she was no longer attracted to me—probably one of the cruelest things you can say to someone. I was completely blindsided. Or, more recently, Mom dying. Opening the door to our sheriff, who looked as though he himself might cry, and hearing those words.

The first thing I thought was . . . *finally*. Yet what I have learned is that it's often less about the breaking point, and more about what comes next.

The afternoon's sky swirled with dark, angry clouds, crawling closer to town as the day dragged on. The storm cast a dull gray light throughout the station, although you could spot our weather reporters from a mile off—storms gave them a bounce in their step. I stared absently out the window at the brewing chaos while my computer screen glared back at me, my eyes burning from hours of fact-checking for various potential stories across the state. Josh appeared at my desk and handed me a candy bar, fudge brownie flavor. He knew me so well.

"I hope the sugar in this replaces my brain cells," I said.

He grinned, running a hand through his curly chestnut hair. "Well, I did try to suggest you for mentoring some of the interns today."

I sat upright in my chair. "I totally would have done that—whose idea was it not to pick me?"

Josh blushed slightly and I sighed. He didn't even have to say it. "Colin."

He nodded. "Sorry, Liv. I'm just the cameraman, he isn't going to listen to anything I have to say."

"I need to get back out there," I said. "I am going to lose it behind this computer."

"What about socials? That might be nice and cruisey?"

I scrunched up my nose. "Colin wouldn't let me within an inch of the station's social media accounts, let alone control them."

Josh toyed with the stapler on my desk. "Have you checked that source for Cassie yet?"

I grimaced and said, "No," before letting out a dramatic sigh. "Do you have any idea how hard it is, to watch her prance around here, acting like she's already got the promotion?"

"Well, she has to actually deliver the scoop of the year to

secure that job. I don't think stories about potential measles outbreaks will do that."

"Obviously!" I replied. "But she's just so infuriating!"

Josh gave me an exasperated look. "Why'd you have to throw shit, Liv?"

"You don't think I ask myself that every day?"

He stood to leave. "Just hang in there, Liv. Sometimes a great story is just around the corner."

"We'll see," I said. I unwrapped the candy bar and shoved half of it in my mouth.

The hour crawled by, and I absentmindedly emptied staples one by one onto the desk; they lay scattered like broken stitches.

My phone buzzed with a text from Wren.

> Still on for dinner?

I suddenly felt warm, and I texted back.

> Of course! Sorry about this brewing storm :(

> I love the rain! See you soon :)

I smiled to myself, pushing Wren's text to the back of my mind—something and someone to look forward to—as I turned to Cassie's story. The source, Claudia, claimed her child had contracted measles at St. Christopher's, a private school where she insisted an outbreak was being covered up by the principal, who vehemently denied it. But we hadn't verified her story or tracked down any other cases, and Claudia's recent dismissal from the PTA only made the whole thing more suspicious. I had a name and a phone number, so I dialed. The line rang for a few moments before a woman answered.

"Hello?"

"Is this Claudia?" I asked.

"Yes, who's calling?"

"Claudia, this is Olivia Piroso from High Country Broadcasting. I'm calling regarding the measles outbreak at St. Christopher's. Do you have a moment to answer a few questions?"

"Oh, I sure do!" she said, her tone suddenly perking up. "The principal has kept the doors open, putting every single student at risk!"

"I see," I said, keeping my voice neutral. "The thing is, Claudia, none of the other parents have confirmed there's been a measles outbreak. So, we're trying to corroborate your story."

"It's *definitely* the measles! My son had spots!" she replied indignantly.

"Any other symptoms?" I asked, scribbling on my notepad.

"He was irritable."

"Okay. And when did this all begin?"

"It started after we went to the lake," she said quickly, her voice sharpening. "Will this be on the news? Because that principal is absolutely incompetent, and I want everyone to know!"

"What was the name of the lake?"

"Silver Mist, up north," she replied.

I frowned. Silver Mist Lake. I knew it well; I used to camp there with an ex and her family. The place was infamous for its high concentration of mosquitoes.

"Claudia, is there a chance it isn't the measles?" I asked, leaning forward in my chair. "They might actually be mosquito bites."

There was a long pause, followed by a sharp click as she ended the call. I groaned, dropping the phone back onto the desk and crossing out my notes. With a sigh, I scribbled "*dead end*" next to the story. It was obvious, wasn't it? There was no measles. Just a parent with a bruised ego after being dismissed from the PTA, desperate to drag the principal's reputation through the mud.

Cassie would not be pleased. In the same moment, I spotted Colin emerging from his office. I decided to take the opportunity to corner him again.

"Boss, got a second?"

He looked like he was about to say *no* but instead he just raised his eyebrows at me.

"I see Cassie got the Serena Williams interview, so I was wondering . . ."

"No big interviews until you bring me a good story."

"Yes, I've heard you on that loud and clear."

"Then hear me again," he said. "Bring me a good story. Find one and we can talk about it."

"I have one!" I spluttered. "It's about the grief group I'm in."

Colin turned toward me, seemingly interested.

"Oh? Has the therapist crossed a line with one of the members?"

I thought about Max, and how professional and kind he was, and pushed down a flash of anger.

"No," I replied flatly. "He would never do that."

Colin looked disappointed.

"We're organizing a poetry evening. As a group we have found that reading poetry has helped with managing our grief."

Colin didn't seem impressed in the slightest. I continued.

"So, we're hosting an evening, and inviting the whole of Everston to hopefully encourage others to talk about their grief as well."

He folded his arms. "I don't know, Olivia. I mean, it might be a feel-good puff piece but not exactly the story I was looking for from you."

"But isn't the point of the news to share good stories as well?"

"Yes, like a golden retriever rescuing a three-year-old from a burning house," he replied. "With a picture of a happy, smiling retriever, and the words 'Dog Saves Three-Year-Old' as the headline."

"It would mean a lot to Henry," I said. "It's great press for the library . . ."

He sighed. "Henry is a good man. I'll think about it, but in the meantime bring me something with juice."

As I watched him walk away, I thought of my mother. If she had been faced with the same dilemma, she would have thrown her friends under the bus and then reversed back over them just to save her job. Every day, I tried to be the opposite of her, and yet I had this sinking feeling that I was still my mother's daughter.

Cassie happened to be in the break room as I made my way over to the coffee machine.

"Would you like a coffee, Cassie?" I asked.

She sighed. "Oh, we've run out of oat milk," she replied. "No good."

I filled the pot with water. "That's too bad," I said, and didn't do a very good job of hiding the sarcasm in my tone.

"Did you contact Claudia?" she asked.

"Yes," I replied. "A bust. Son had mosquito bites, not the measles."

Cassie rolled her eyes. "I doubt I'll be bothering with these mediocre stories for long," she said, flipping her hair. "Not after my Aiden Callaway interview last week."

I hated that attitude. It reminded me too much of my mother. Her career took off, and she stopped caring about the smaller stories. But those are just as important as the bigger ones.

"Aiden Callaway was incredible," Cassie continued, gushing. "I mean, he's gotta be the biggest name in country music right now. I swear he was totally into me. He kept smiling at me with that gorgeous face of his."

I resisted telling Cassie that Aiden Callaway was just genuinely nice and she was nobody special.

"And," she added, "we stayed at the Four Seasons! Must be doing something right!"

I almost dropped the mug. I didn't realize the station was spending that much on assignment these days.

"It sounds like you had a great assignment," I replied.

"Well, only the best for the future anchor, I suppose. I mean, I guess they're trying to bribe me. Didn't you stay at Motel 6 on your last assignment with Josh? Shared a room, too, right?"

Urgh. Motel 6 wasn't even THAT bad.

"Oh," I replied slowly. "So you *are* going for the promotion?"

"Of course. I just figured after your mom died, you'd step away from the fast lane. You know, to work on yourself. And, I mean, the station is going to need someone with serious experience."

My eyes were steady out of pure skill, but they had figuratively rolled right to the very back of my head. "I'm still very happy in the fast lane. Thanks, though."

"Colin is just such a great boss, isn't he?" she replied, ignoring me. "Honestly, he has been super sweet to me, and I just can't wait to keep working alongside him. We work so well together." Cassie paused, and tried to express what I could only assume was a look of warped empathy. "I'm sure we can find something for you, Olivia. When you're ready that is."

There was nothing in the world I wouldn't have given to throw dog feces at her and wipe that smug look off her face.

Like most things in Everston, the restaurant I picked to meet Wren had been there a long time. It was frozen in that same timeless charm of the early 1900s, with its rich mahogany, ornately framed golden mirrors, and leather upholstery. Wrought-iron chandeliers were suspended from the ceiling above, casting a glow over white linen–draped tables. The room was dim as I wove through the tables toward her. They made their own pasta by hand, which I already knew was Wren's favorite.

"I'm sorry I'm late," I said as I sat down. "The highway from Norvale can get a little congested in this kind of weather."

"If we're being honest, I was early. I hope you don't mind that I ordered us some wine."

I looked at the bottle sitting on the table, a pinot noir from the North Fork Valley. She'd picked one of my favorite wines, completely by chance—or maybe fate just had great taste.

"I don't mind at all," I said.

Wren smiled, showing her dimples. Her nose was sprinkled with freckles, and the gentle curve of her lips made me want to memorize the way she looked at me just then. Her hair fell loosely above her shoulders, framing her face like sunlight catching the edges of a picture. She was wearing a light-blue cotton dress, with a gold necklace. She was effortlessly beautiful.

"How was work?" she asked, and I was brought back to Earth.

"Honestly, horrible," I replied. "My boss is still refusing to let me go back to active duty, and today I found out that my archnemesis is also gunning for the anchor role."

Wren poured me a glass of wine. "Is that the role that your mother had?"

"Yes," I said, "and I don't even know if I want it, I just know that Cassie Johnson would be a terrible anchor for HCB."

"Can you finally tell me what you did to get saddled with desk duty? Please?" Wren said.

I sighed, dreading recounting this story. "There was an incident on air. I was reporting on a neighbor dispute. A man was complaining that his neighbors were leaving their dog's poop on his doorstep. Turns out, they were only doing this because he had tried to poison their dog. So I just started throwing it at him."

"You threw dog poop *at* him?" she asked, her eyes wide and her mouth brimming with humor. "On live television?"

"It's on YouTube somewhere."

Wren laughed. "That *is* a story," she agreed. "A brilliant one."

"I wasn't myself," I said. "I'd found a letter my mother had written to me the night of my prom, and she'd never given it to me. I suppose I'm glad that she never did, because the letter was nothing short of praising herself, not me, but I guess it just brought up things for me. I found a bottle of champagne and . . . well, next thing I knew I was in a dog poop-flinging fight."

Wren's eyes held a depth of understanding. "You are allowed to both grieve your mom and be relieved that she is no longer in your life, Olivia."

"I know," I said, softly. "It's just hard to reconcile both the grief and the relief, you know? Sometimes I feel like I mourn the mom I never had more than the one I lost."

Wren nodded thoughtfully, reaching her hand across the table, her thumb grazing the tops of my fingers.

"Grief is messy. It doesn't follow a script, it just demands that you feel all of it."

She brushed the hair from her face, and I noticed a small scar along the edge of her hairline.

"Do you think about it a lot? The accident, I mean," I asked, cautiously.

Wren swirled the wine in her glass, her gaze momentarily distant. "I do," she replied. "It's hard not to. One moment, everything was fine, and the next, we were skidding along the road. It's difficult to piece it all together sometimes."

"That's normal," I said gently. "It was traumatic. Of course you wouldn't want to remember it."

She nodded slowly, then hesitated before speaking again. "The thing is . . . the police said that Lucy caused the accident. But I don't remember it that way. I don't ever remember her losing control of the car."

I leaned forward slightly. "What do you mean?"

"My memory may be fractured," she said, her voice quieter now, "but I remember the explosion. I remember something crashing into us. Our car was knocked off the road and we flew into an electrical pole. But I don't remember everything the way it was reported. The police said Lucy lost control—plowed into an oncoming vehicle, then onto the sidewalk, hitting a young boy and finally the pole. But . . . I don't even remember the boy."

"Was anyone else injured?"

"Two people," she replied, swirling her wine again, as if she was trying to untangle her memories. "The young boy and . . . well, the police just said a 'John Doe.' I never found out who he was."

I sat upright, my curiosity sparking. "And what did the crash report say exactly?"

"That Lucy lost control of the vehicle, hit the other car, mounted the curb, and hit the young boy, and then the pole. The boy was paralyzed, and the other man was injured," she said, her brow furrowing as she tried to remember.

"Did they say how the John Doe was injured?"

"No," Wren responded, shaking her head. "But—" she added, a shadow of guilt passing over her face, "I think, maybe, I distracted her. I was reading to her that night, in the car, maybe she looked at me instead of the road."

"But you said your car was hit first?"

"I think so," she replied. "We ended up wrapped around the pole. But the boy was on the opposite side of the road, with the other vehicle."

I frowned, trying to piece it together in my mind. "But if he was on the other side of the road, how could you have hit him?" I paused. "And what about your car? The damage to it . . . wouldn't that show whether you were hit, or if you hit someone else? Did the police say anything about that?"

"They didn't go into details, at least not with me," Wren said. "All I was told was that it was Lucy's fault."

I leaned back slightly. "It doesn't make sense," I said, meeting her eyes. "I mean, if your car ended up wrapped around a pole, and the boy was on the opposite side of the road, it sounds like you were hit, pushed into the pole, and the other vehicle struck the boy. Not the other way around."

"Do you think so? I haven't thought about it that much. I try to avoid thinking about it at all, if I'm honest," Wren said.

There was so much more I wanted to ask. My instincts were burning, hungry for the truth. Something about her story didn't add up, and the missing elements pulled at my mind. But I could see she was feeling overwhelmed by all this talk of the accident. And I also wanted to know what her favorite color was, what she liked to do when she wasn't renovating Gill's old house, what her favorite season was. There were so many things about Wren that I wanted to uncover.

The candle on the table between us had burned right down, so that the wick was making tiny popping noises. I had lost track of the time, as we had been talking, eating and pouring more wine. There was an ease to being with Wren; I felt like I wanted to be near her all the time. The waiter delivered the check to the table, and I realized our evening was about to be over. I didn't want it to be.

"Do you mind if we stop by the bookstore on the way out?" I asked, anything to just spend a little longer with her. "It's just next door."

"Of course," Wren replied, and she gathered her keys and bag.

The Book Nook was open late on Fridays. The exterior, painted in a regal shade of purple, stood out, further accentuated by a vibrant hanging sign just above the entrance. Colorful bunting adorned the doorframe and fairy lights had been strung in the window frames. The moment we walked inside, there was the unmistakable scent of freshly baked cookies and pastries. Positioned on the front counter, in between a vase of flowers and some business cards, was a tray with a tempting stack of oatmeal cookies. I wasn't going to deny myself a sweet treat, so I plucked one without hesitation and extended another one to Wren. The Book Nook unfolded with rows upon rows of books, and generous leather armchairs had been placed in various corners with coffee tables. The store assistant was sitting at the front desk, playing solitaire. She glanced momentarily toward us before returning to the game. Wren's demeanour shifted subtly as she scanned the rows of books, a sense of unease creeping into the corners of the bookstore. I had hoped that by asking her about the accident, I hadn't crossed a delicate line. Her hand reached out toward a row of B.W. Paisley books, but she pulled away almost instantly, as though they'd burned her.

"What are we looking for?" she asked, her voice carrying tension.

"It's my aunt's birthday soon," I said, wanting to lighten the mood. "She loves plants, and wants a Venus flytrap, so I thought why not get her a book all about them."

Wren's eyes brightened. "Interesting choice."

"Do you like Venus flytraps?"

"Oh, they're fascinating," Wren said, and suddenly the tension evaporated, and she'd returned. "They can count, you know."

I laughed, her unexpected trivia catching me off guard. "You sure seem to know a lot of things, Wren."

She turned from me, her fingers delicately trailing along the rows of books. It was a movement that looked like it had been done a thousand times. I found myself wondering about her past—perhaps she had been a botanist, a scientist, a bookstore owner, even a florist. There was an intrigue about her that was magnetic, a pull that I couldn't seem to turn away from. And yet some people's histories are closed books that they prefer to leave undisturbed.

Distracting myself, I focused on the search for plant books, only realizing Wren had disappeared when I found a title I wanted to share with her.

"Wren?" I called, but there was only silence.

"Wren?" I tried again.

Suddenly, she popped her head around the aisle with a mischievous "boo" and I involuntarily jumped.

"Biscuits!" I yelped.

Wren laughed. "Biscuits," she repeated, a playful note in her voice. "I'll need to remember that one."

I thrust the Venus flytrap book into her hands, and she inspected it, a thoughtful expression on her face.

"Oh, yes," she said. "Donna Plumberry is a wonderful botanist."

Curiosity welled up inside me as I was once again impressed by how much she knew about authors and books, but before I could ask, our phones chimed, disrupting the moment. It was a text from Henry saying that he had received permission from the library board to host the poetry evening at the library.

I cleared my throat, reading out the text dramatically, mimicking the way we recited breaking news.

Wren smiled. "You don't need to follow in your mother's footsteps, Olivia. You're already good enough."

There was something in the way she said my name, as though her lips held it there—safe, warm, secure. Wren leaned on the aisle shelves, and the overhead light washed over her, in a way that made it difficult for me to look away.

She smiled lightly. "What are you staring at?" she asked.

"Nothing," I replied. *You.*

She paused, opened her mouth, closed it again. I looked at her quizzically.

"I have to tell you something," Wren said quietly, leaning toward me.

There are certain people whose stories you could read for a lifetime. You open your eyes one day, and you're changed because their story has intertwined with yours, like two chapters that fold together to create a novel you can't seem to put down.

Wren was shorter than I was, so I had to lean down toward her. My heart thudded in my chest, loud enough that it felt like the books around us were reverberating. I leaned in, slowly, giving her time to pull away if she wanted to. But she didn't. Instead, her thumb brushed against my skin, like a promise, until our lips met and everything else fell away. I had kissed people before, but this—this was different. It was full, deliberate, and electrifying, like a current moving through me, grounding me and making me soar at the same time. Her hand found its way to the back of my neck, her fingers gentle but firm, anchoring me in the moment. My hand slid around her waist, pulling her closer, and suddenly nothing else existed—the room, the world, even time itself seemed to dissolve. Her lips moved with mine in a rhythm that felt effortless, as though we'd done this a hundred times before. It was tender and intimate, but there was something hungry in it, too, like we were trying to pour everything we couldn't say into that one perfect moment.

It might have been hours before we pulled apart, or minutes or seconds. It didn't matter. All that mattered was whether I could kiss her again, ideally every minute of every hour of every day.

"What were you going to tell me?" I asked, my voice barely above a whisper.

Wren's lips curled into a faint, almost dazed smile as she pulled me closer.

"I forgot. It can't be that important."

Chapter 13

Wren

Last night's storm had littered the ground with branches and filled the gutters with trickling water and leaves. I ran along the hiking trail closest to the house, kicking up mud with my heels. It wound through dense forest, marked by a weathered sign at the entrance. The path narrowed as it ascended higher, the spiced scent of pine and the faint sweetness of aspen leaves filling the air. I veered farther, passing an old heritage-listed house, to make the shortcut over the bridge near a stream. The kids in Everston told stories of the house being haunted, but the only haunting thing about it was that it used to be somebody's home and now it wasn't. The ground was still damp and soft beneath my feet as the sunlight played tag with me through the trees, darting in and out between the branches.

There were two things that made me feel free: writing and running. When I was writing, I felt so lost in the words, I almost forgot to breathe. When I was running, I bounded steps ahead of my own thoughts, praying that they wouldn't catch me. When I came up for air, it was like starting my life over anew; like being reborn again, every single time.

Back in New York, running was something I did nearly every day. Lucy used to tease me about how I'd lace up my shoes no matter the weather—the bitter cold of January or the sweltering heat of July, neither deterred me. *Are you going to run down the aisle?*

she would joke, her eyes glistening. But she knew running was where I found myself, where I felt alive. When Lucy died, I stopped running. I stopped writing. I stopped being the person I used to be and doing the things I loved to do. It was as if every part of me that wasn't directly tied to surviving just . . . disappeared. I told myself it didn't matter, that nothing mattered without her. But now, as my feet hit the ground beneath me, and the wind brushed against my skin, I felt something stirring, something I hadn't felt in a long time.

Lucy's death still hurt, but not in the way it did a year ago, or five months ago, or even three weeks ago; I was making room for it, and in the newfound space I had created, the only person I could think about was Olivia.

I liked her. That much was undeniable. Her laugh, the way she looked at me like I was someone worth seeing, someone worth knowing—it had been forever since I felt seen like that. And that kiss. It had left me breathless, weightless, like for the first time in so long my world wasn't just consumed with grief. That there could be a spark of something. But that's exactly what scared me. My breath hitched as I pushed harder, running faster than I probably should. The memory of the kiss flashed through my mind, as though the thrill of it was running alongside me; but so, too, was an intense guilt. I wasn't supposed to feel this way. Not yet. Maybe not ever. Right?

The trail curved ahead, the tree line beginning to thin, as the sunlight broke through the gaps. I slowed down, my lungs burning, but it wasn't just the run taking the breath from my lungs—it was Lucy. I stopped, hands on my knees, as I tried to catch my breath. My heart was pounding. How could I kiss someone else and feel good? How could I let myself be in that moment with Olivia, knowing how much I still missed Lucy? It felt like I had betrayed both of them. The ache in my chest tightened, and I straightened, staring out at the trees. The colors of fall surrounded me, bright and alive. The fiery reds of maple leaves, the golden yellows of birch, and the deep, burnt oranges of oak—each tree a promise of renewal, a stark contrast to the heaviness in my chest. Why did moving forward, with all its vibrancy and promise, feel so impossibly complicated? I started walking, my steps slower, more deliberate. The truth was, kissing Olivia had made me feel alive again, the way trees breathe again after winter. I didn't want to forget Lucy, or the love we shared. But I also didn't want to not know what it would be like to kiss Olivia again. I leaned against a tree, my breath steadying, the rough bark pressing into my palms as I absorbed its quiet, grounding pulse. Maybe it didn't have to be one or the other.

When I arrived home, my clothes were splattered in mud. They seemed to be covered in all sorts of materials these days: sawdust, paint, mud, opossum poop (not ideal). I had a feeling there would be more sawdust coming my way today, as repairing the wooden porch railings was top of my to-do list.

Railings were designed to keep people safe. To support almost-falls and trips and when climbing or descending stairs. But I wondered if they were also supposed to act as arms to this house, wrapping all around to keep the soul of it intact. I had dismantled the porch railing and installed a new one. Fresh pine from town. Half the morning was gone, and I was in the middle of painting when I realized I'd missed one of the panels for the railing, and there was a gap between the end paling and the banister. I grumbled to myself, kicking the door slightly as I stomped into the kitchen to find the measuring tape. I would have to cut a new piece of wood and attach it before finishing the painting.

Lucy was suddenly standing in the doorway and it startled me, the measuring tape almost dropping from my fingers.

"The new railing looks great," she said.

"It's not finished," I replied, and my voice was harsh, almost accusatory.

"Angry about it?"

"Yes," I responded curtly. "It's very frustrating."

"You were always the calm one," she said. "Nothing seemed to faze you. If there was a problem, it could be handled."

"I don't understand your point."

"Why are you angry at the railing?"

"I'm not angry *at* the railing," I said. "I'm angry that I'm still imagining talking to my dead fiancée."

"And?"

"And nothing," I snapped. "I have work to do."

"Why can't you just admit who you're really angry at?" Lucy asked.

I stared at her, my eyes brimming with hot, angry tears.

"You!" I exclaimed. "I am so angry with you!" I slammed the measuring tape down on the counter, the cabinets rattling. "You left me," I said, the ache in my chest pounding so hard I felt it might burst through my skin. "You left me, Lucy."

"I know," she said softly.

"And I know you didn't mean to. Of course you didn't want to die. But in some fucked-up way, you got off easy. You weren't left behind. I was. I was left behind, to try and live in this world without you."

"But you are," she murmured. "You *are* living."

"But I feel so guilty about it!"

Lucy looked at the kitchen. "Yet you've managed to start making something of this place, Bee," she said.

"There's still so much to do: painting, repairing cracks, replacing the carpet upstairs, updating the countertops, and swapping out windows. It's ongoing."

"Grieving too."

I looked away from her, at the light filtering in through the kitchen. It glossed over all the new cabinets I had installed.

"I like her," Lucy said. "Olivia, I really like her."

I huffed in response. "Well, she asks lots of questions."

A very clumsy attempt at deflection.

"*You* ask a lot of questions," Lucy replied. "You love asking questions, you love answering questions, you love pondering and writing and storytelling, and Olivia likes all those things too. Ever think that perhaps she could help you write again?"

I sucked in all the air around me.

"I am not writing about anyone ever again. Look at where that got me."

"I didn't stop you from writing, you stopped yourself."

I opened my mouth to argue, but I suddenly heard the front gate creak, and saw Henry walking up the driveway. I'd laid new pebbles, and the crunch of his shoes echoed throughout the garden and into the house.

I rushed to the door, in an attempt to appear as though I had been busily working on the railings.

"I thought you'd show up eventually," I called to him, feigning nonchalance.

"Well, Gill is rather impressed with the work you're doing." Henry smiled, reaching the front porch. "I thought I'd come see for myself."

I looked up at the house. "I no sooner fix one thing than something else pops up."

He laughed.

"Do you want some lemonade?" I asked.

"I'd love some," he replied. "Who were you talking to?"

My breath hitched—I felt caught out. "When?"

"Just before, I thought I heard you talking to someone?"

I knew that I could admit to Henry that I had been talking

to Lucy. He had admitted that it had taken some time for him to stop imagining his brother walking in through the door. But today was one of those days when I didn't feel like admitting to myself that, after a year, I was still having visions of my dead fiancée.

"Oh, just the birds," I replied. "It helps me to concentrate on the housework."

He looked at me as though he didn't quite believe me, but he didn't press any further.

I walked into the kitchen, fetched two glasses of lemonade, and brought them back outside, handing one to Henry.

"So." He grinned broadly. "What did you think?"

"I would replace the entire porch," I replied, "but it might be too costly."

Henry squinted at me through the sun rays. "I don't mean the porch, Wren, I mean the meeting last Tuesday; everyone seems really excited by the poetry evening."

"Oh," I replied. "Yes, well, they do. Julian has already started, which is encouraging."

"And I bet Emerson will write a great piece." He nodded.

"You know, I was thinking . . ." I began. "Everyone's poems will be so personal, so raw. It feels like we're creating something bigger than just one evening's entertainment. What if we made it into a book?"

He rubbed his hands together, obviously intrigued. "A book?"

"Something like that," I replied. "The common thread that ties everyone to the group is the feeling of being understood—of sharing the loss, instead of being alone in it. People need books like that."

It was one of the reasons I'd started writing poetry in the first place. Losing Lucy had closed me off from poetry for a long time. But now, I felt something beginning to stir in me again.

Henry looked at me curiously. "Do you mean to say that you would write it?" he asked. "I didn't know you were a writer?"

I nearly dropped my glass. "Ah—" I stammered, laughing awkwardly. "Well, I'm not. Not really. I enjoyed writing in school, and in journals and things, nothing serious"—*a total lie*—"but I have been writing some poetry lately. I'm sure I could pull it all together and shape it into something meaningful. Perhaps you could write a poem or two yourself? We could add everyone's poems."

Henry's eyes lit up. "Yes! What a wonderful idea. Well, we'd need to get everyone's poems in before the event. We could give them a copy ahead of time, as a bit of motivation before reading on the evening. And you'd be able to print the book yourself?"

I nodded. "I believe it's possible."

Of course, it was possible. I knew exactly what went into making a book—formatting, layout, print specs, distribution, marketing. I'd done it all before, several times over. But I couldn't tell Henry that. Not yet.

I stared into the garden, looking at the statues I had stumbled upon at a yard sale. They were an odd collection of mythical creatures: a fairy, a unicorn, and a griffin, each softened by time and weather. They were an odd collection, much like our group, and yet they somehow felt right. Out of place, yet perfectly fitting.

"I think it's brilliant, Wren," Henry said, grinning at me. "This could even be something shared with other grief groups. If I can get them going, that is. But it'd be such a great resource, a reminder that there is always a way forward."

"Yes, I think so too," I murmured.

"And I'll help you, of course. However I can. That's what librarians do, you know, we find answers."

That made my chest tighten. I felt a flicker of guilt, like a thread pulled just a little too tightly.

Henry paused, his smile softening. "You know, you came into the group at just the right time. It's like you were meant to be part of this poetry evening. You've got such great ideas—are you sure you didn't work as an editor back in New York? Maybe *The Guardian*, *New York Times*?" He chuckled, but his words hit me like a warning bell. I knew I had to change the subject, and fast. This conversation was veering too close to a place I wasn't ready to go.

"Oh, no, nothing like that," I said quickly, waving my hand. "Just happy to contribute where I can." I glanced away toward the garden, feeling my cheeks starting to flush. I felt like an impostor. "Anyway," I said, "I need this group"—I let out a small sigh, steeling myself—"because I was talking to Lucy."

Henry looked perplexed.

"Before," I added. "When you asked who I was talking to . . . it wasn't the birds."

He looked out into the garden as well.

"I suspected as much," he replied. "Were you triggered by something?"

Was I ever. I was still thinking about Olivia and our kiss last night. Not because I was trying to lose myself in someone else, but because I'd wanted to kiss her from the moment we met. And since that kiss, something inside me had shifted. Words had been flooding my mind, swirling like flashes of light, stringing themselves together in ways I couldn't quite explain. I finally wanted to write again. To capture the way her lips had felt on mine, how good she smelled, the way my heartbeat seemed to sync with hers as the rest of the world fell away. It wasn't just the kiss; it was everything she ignited within me. For the first time since my life had fallen apart, I was running, thinking about writing, and wanting to be part of the world again.

But I was still mourning Lucy.

"Can you fall in love and heal from heartbreak at the same time?" I asked Henry.

He considered this a moment. "Well, it begs another question: can you love the light and learn from the darkness at the same time?"

"I suppose you can," I replied.

"Why?" he asked curiously.

"Oh," I stuttered, suddenly self-conscious. "Just a thought."

Again, Henry looked at me as though he didn't believe me.

"I think you can open yourself up to someone new, even if you are still healing from the absence of someone else, but only if you ask yourself the right questions—am I using this person to fill a void, or do I genuinely enjoy spending time with this person?"

"I love spending time with Olivia," I admitted absently, staring at the slice of lemon in my glass.

Henry gasped. "You didn't!"

I suddenly realized what I had just admitted.

"Oh my," I replied. "Well, we just . . ."

He grinned from ear to ear. "You what!?"

"Kissed." I sighed. "Last night, and I've felt like a schoolgirl ever since."

Henry clapped, and it rang out through the front yard. He was always clapping.

"You know, I just knew it."

I smiled into my lemonade.

"I'll do it, Henry," I said, to answer his earlier question. "I'll help with the poetry evening."

PART II

Chapter 14

Henry

At first, I tried to see my brother in everything. I wanted to carry him with me; I looked for him in everything that I read or heard or saw. I would always bring Jacob up in conversation, trying to remind everyone about him. I found him in the lyrics of his favorite song, or a paragraph from his favorite book, or even the light breaking over the mountains. I couldn't let his memory disappear. I've learned many things about memory since then, mostly that I didn't always remember specific days but rather small moments and the way I felt.

I don't remember the specific date of our first grief meeting, but I remember that it was raining. The front door of the library had blown open and leaves had scattered through the entryway. I'd set up chairs in the reading corner, at first in a circle, then pulled apart, then scattered around the tables, unsure of how this was supposed to go. Gill arrived first, looking sharp in a collared shirt, dress shoes, and a hat, but he embodied uncertainty with a sheepish smile.

"Wasn't sure what to wear," he confessed, sitting down. He reached over to the candy bowl I had left strategically in the middle of all the chairs and plucked a chocolate bar.

I wanted to tell Gill that I wasn't sure of anything either. That when I'd placed the *Grief Support Group* sign at the library desk, I hadn't expected anyone to respond. I had never attended a grief support group, much less organized one. I knew that grief looked different on everyone, and that it was slow, so slow that sometimes you wondered if it was happening at all, like the way your hair or nails grew. But I also knew that when pain had nowhere else to go, it led you to things you didn't know you needed.

Emerson arrived next. She was wearing a thick scarf around her neck, despite the library being a cozy temperature. She sat down as far away from us as possible. Part of me wanted to encourage her to sit closer; however, a larger part was just surprised she came at all. Bobby arrived after that. He was equally as reserved and unsure, but he sat closest to the front. Winnie arrived last. She sat down next to Emerson despite the fact there were at least five other chairs available. I wondered what to do. Should I introduce myself? Should I tell them that the reason I was here was because my twin brother was dead and part of me was dead too? How do you even begin to share the darkest parts of yourself when you have spent so much time trying to hide them from the world? Thankfully Max arrived, and he interrupted the silence. He sat down in the front, adjusted his glasses, and peered at everyone.

"Grief is messy, isn't it?" he remarked. "It's like spilling barbecue sauce on your favorite jacket. At first, you think you can clean it up—scrub it out, make it disappear. But no matter how hard you try, there's always a stain. Fainter, maybe, but it's still there. And you're left figuring out how to live with it."

He looked around the room. "That's what heartache is like. It lingers. It changes how you see things, how you feel about the things you loved. It is still the same jacket. But it looks different."

"So, what do you do with the jacket?" Bobby inquired.

Max fixed his gaze on him, and responded, "You wear it anyway. You learn that the stain is going to stay, but it doesn't stop you from wearing the jacket."

That inaugural meeting was inherently simple. It softened

the edges of our vulnerabilities. There was an unspoken understanding between us, a thread from one struggle to the other. As I listened to Winnie and Emerson discover their mutual love of birds, and Gill complimenting Bobby on his pink hair, I sensed the potential of what these meetings could achieve.

Toward the end of the evening, Gill posed a question to Max. "How long am I going to grieve?" he asked.

"Forever," Max replied. "But it won't always feel like the biggest thing in the room."

I looked at Gill and Bobby, Winnie and Emerson—all of them from completely different walks of life, but each carrying their own burdens of death, rejection, abandonment, and disfigurement, and I realized that profound sadness was not just confined to death. So much of the world treated loss as though it belonged only to death, as if the two were inseparable, a club just for two. But really, loss was an overflowing club, and I suddenly felt determined to maintain this little group as a refuge for anyone who found their way through those library doors, no matter their story.

It had been one of those days. The universe seemingly plucked the day from hell and handed it to me. I'd arrived at the library to discover someone had left three trash bags full of garbage in the library return box. If I wasn't so perplexed about how they'd even managed to fit them in there, I would have cursed all the way to the dumpster to remove them. Then, not even an hour after opening the doors, I had a gentleman arrive and argue with me for forty-five minutes about why the library needed to refund him for the books he lost. He said he wanted to be compensated for the time he had spent looking for them. I'd sent him away with four books from the ones on sale at the front, just to get rid of him. By ten thirty, a class of third graders had arrived, but they were accompanied by a substitute teacher, so their commitment to causing trouble was airtight. Two boys actually drew on the wall, another placed some sort of sticky pastry on the chair of his classmate before she sat down, and as a collective they were so loud I had another patron ask for earplugs. By the time three o'clock rolled around, all I could think about was collapsing onto my couch with a large glass of wine. Which is why I was both surprised and embarrassed when Lillian from Sweet Moments, the local catering company I wanted to hire for the poetry evening, suddenly appeared at the library desk. I'd completely forgotten about our scheduled meeting.

There she stood, holding a sizeable tray laden with delectable finger foods.

"Henry?" she inquired with a smile.

"Yes," I replied, rising so abruptly that the chair behind me careened into the filing cabinets with a distinct crunch. "Lillian, it's nice to finally meet you."

"I apologize for being a few minutes behind schedule," she offered. "I was preparing the items we'd discussed and decided to add an extra one, thinking it would be a hit, but I underestimated the time it would take to get here."

"No need to apologize," I assured her. "Thank you for driving all the way in."

"You know, I haven't been to Everston in years," she gushed. "My family used to take vacations here during ski season. I've forgotten how quaint it is."

I thought of all the children who had chosen to terrorize the walls and throw books across the room that day and forced a smile. "Yes, I suppose we do have a quaint little town. Let's set up over here," I suggested, guiding her to set down her tray on a nearby table. She was a little out of breath, but there was an easy grace to the way she moved, someone comfortable in her own skin.

"Now," she began. "I know we agreed that chicken wings,

stuffed mushrooms, and sliders were an absolute must—and don't worry, I've included those—but I also thought we could add mini quiches because, honestly, they're always a hit."

She unveiled the contents of the tray, and I was met with all sorts of delicious smells. My stomach growled, traitorous and loud enough that I was glad she didn't seem to notice.

"You've outdone yourself," I replied, enthusiastically, leaning over the tray to get a better look.

She waved a hand, dismissing the praise, though the slight pink of her cheeks said otherwise. "I love to cook," she replied. She leaned closer to the tray, too, as though inspecting her handiwork.

Up close, she looked to be in her late thirties, if I had to guess. Her dark hair—almost black but softened by a natural shine—was swept into a casual braid, with a few loose strands escaping and flowing around her face and hazel eyes. Her skin was fair, a faint dusting of freckles across her nose, and as she reached to adjust the tray, I noticed a small tattoo on the inside of her wrist: a delicate outline of a whisk. Just above it, partially hidden by the sleeve of her cardigan, was a birthmark, deep purple and shaped almost like a crescent moon. She wore a soft yellow cardigan over a black dress, the fabric hugging her soft curves. There was flour dusted faintly on the sleeve, a signature of someone who'd been baking all morning.

"So do I," I said. "Although I am no professional like yourself."

Lillian tilted her head and laughed softly. "Well, I do a lot of catering for events, but my real passion is baking."

"Really?" I asked, curious. "What do you bake?"

"Cakes, mostly," she said, and her eyes shone, like the word itself brought her joy. "Cakes for birthdays, weddings, anniversaries, you name it."

My face brightened at that. "Oh, I love cake. I'd sell my soul for a triple-layered chocolate cake."

Her laugh was louder this time. "You know, I think I would too," she replied playfully. "Here, try this."

She handed me one of the mini quiches, and as I bit into it, my mouth was filled with creamy spinach and salty feta, all wrapped in a buttery crust that melted on my tongue. Suddenly I'd forgotten all about every hellish thing that had happened that day.

"You know, I think I've changed my mind. Forget the chocolate cake, I'd sell my soul for these."

She grinned. "They're good, aren't they?" she replied, reaching out and giving my shoulder a friendly squeeze, her touch lingering just long enough to make my thoughts scatter like a stack of papers caught in the wind. I'd found her catering company, Sweet Moments, online, when I'd been scrolling through pages of businesses, desperate for something that felt, well . . . right (but also affordable). Her pastries had caught my eye—soft frosting swirls, buttery croissants, flaky cheddar-and-chive scones. There was nothing particularly flashy about what Lillian did, but her food seemed honest, made with care. I was as enamored with her as I was with her quiches.

"You know, Henry," she said, with a twinkle in her eye, "I could probably make you that triple-layered chocolate cake. Might cost you your soul, though."

She winked, and I grinned, feeling a pull again, one I hadn't felt in a really long time. Before I could even consider what might be happening between us, I suddenly felt a hand tug at the hem of my shirt and a small voice say, "Where would I find the adventure books?"

It caught me off guard, and I let out a startled yelp. I looked down to see a sandy-haired, pint-sized little girl standing in front of me, her head tilted up expectantly. She looked all of eight—possibly seven—wearing a yellow sundress, floral socks, and brown loafers and clutching a well-loved book under her arm.

"What kind of adventure book are you looking for?" I asked, straightening up.

She stared at me blankly. "The kind that has adventure," she said, like I was dense.

Lillian and I exchanged amused glances. "Well, we have plenty of adventure books," I said. "What about *Where the Wild Things Are*?"

The girl looked at me as though I'd spoken in a different language.

"I read that book when I was, like, five."

"Oh," I said, feeling my cheeks grow warm. "I suppose you're looking for something a little more advanced then?"

"Yes," she replied, matter-of-factly. "That's why I'm asking you."

Today was not my day.

"Well, I'm Henry. I'm the librarian, so I can definitely help you." I craned my neck, hoping Lana might appear to bail me out.

"I know," the girl replied.

I frowned, surprised. "You know my name?"

"Your picture's on the wall," she said, as if it were the most obvious thing in the world.

Of course, the staff photos on the library noticeboard. I kept forgetting about those.

"I need a book that will take someone to a different place," she said earnestly. "You know, when someone doesn't want to be here anymore, so they go somewhere else."

I stilled slightly. The conversation had taken an unexpected turn, and out of the corner of my eye, I saw Lillian's expression shift, a flicker of concern crossing her face.

"What's your name?" I asked gently.

"Bailey," she replied.

"Well, Bailey," I said, crouching slightly to meet her eye, "why do you want a book like that?"

"It's not for me," she replied. "It's for my mom. Her friend is sick, and she is sad about it, so I want to get her a book. Then she doesn't have to think about her friend for a while and can take a break."

I let out a small breath I didn't realize I'd been holding and smiled at her. "I see," I replied, gently. "That's a very thoughtful thing to do."

"Well, when I read books, they make me forget about everything else. So, I want to do that for my mom."

I glanced at Lillian, whose expression had softened as she watched Bailey.

"You know, I might have something for your mom," I said, standing and leading Bailey to the poetry section. I plucked three titles from the shelf and handed them to her.

"Are these adventure books?" she asked, inspecting the covers.

"They're poetry books," I explained, "but you'll go on a journey when you read them."

Bailey cradled the books in her arms, seemingly pleased. She glanced down at my shoes briefly. "Henry," she said, with a hint of mischief, "did no one ever teach you to tie your shoelaces?"

I watched in mild amusement as she trotted off toward the library desk, where Lana was checking out another patron.

I found my way back to Lillian. "Sorry about that," I said.

"Don't be," she replied, smiling. "I bet you get all kinds of questions all day long."

"You wouldn't believe half of them," I said.

She studied me for a moment. "I think this poetry evening is going to be important to your town, Henry." She smiled. "You're doing a great job."

Jacob used to say that. It didn't matter if I was mowing the lawn, orchestrating some sort of community event, or overhauling the library shelves, he'd always tell me I was doing a good job with the same enthusiasm and encouragement. I could almost picture him now, jumping into the planning with both feet, pushing me to go big or go home. I hired Lillian on the spot, and after she left, I took the rest of the finger food into the staff room for Lana and me to indulge. I was halfway through my third mini quiche, thinking about how good a glass of wine would taste right now—and debating whether it would be inappropriate to follow Lillian on Instagram—when the front desk phone rang. I almost let it ring out. It was probably the same man attempting to settle his overdue fines with "art"—he was now offering owls made of papier-mâché. But something told me to answer, so with a sigh, I picked up the phone.

"Everston Library, this is Henry."

"Would it shock you right now if I told you I was calling from the top of Mount Everest?" Winnie's voice, warm but raspy, crackled through the line.

I felt my legs buckle slightly, because for Winnie this wouldn't be entirely beyond the realm of possibility.

"Winnie, you've been on my mind!" I replied, my grip tightening around the phone. "Are you feeling better?"

"Oh, well, silly old me has been without my phone," she replied breezily. "Would you believe the only number I know off the top of my head these days is the library's?" She cleared her throat. "I do wonder if you could help me with something, Henry?" she continued. "But best not to tell Emerson just yet."

"A surprise party?" I guessed, racking my brain as to when Emerson's birthday was.

She paused. "Not quite," she said softly.

I stopped searching for the late fees, glancing toward the staff room. The mini quiches and stuffed mushrooms I'd consumed earlier suddenly felt like lead in my stomach. "Everything okay?" I asked.

There was another pause. Then, softer: "I'm in Norvale."

I straightened. "Norvale?" My mind was already cycling through reasons—an errand, a day trip, a bookstore visit?

"I'm in the hospital, Henry," she clarified, and this time, she wheezed, one of those deep, raw coughs that rattled her chest. The way Jacob sounded in those final weeks. My heart dropped.

"I came this morning," she continued. "And the doctors keep blabbering on about a whole lot of nonsense. I'm quite high on something—" she paused and giggled, "—morphine, I think, but I figured you'd be able to help me make sense of it all."

I swallowed. "Winnie . . ."

"I just need you to come up here," she said lightly, as if she were asking me to pick up a carton of milk. "No need to alert the cavalry just yet. Emerson will fuss, and I don't have the energy for fussing right now. It's Norvale Hospital," she added, and I felt chills run down my spine, all the way to the tips of my toes. I hadn't set foot in that hospital since Jacob had died.

But this was Winnie.

"I'm on my way," I whispered, my pulse roaring in my ears, drowning out everything else.

Thirty minutes later I pulled into the parking lot and switched the engine off, yet kept the radio playing. I had been so unprepared for all the tasks that came with Jacob's death. It was a strange thing, to tie up the pieces of someone's life. It was unbearably painful. And every task was a constant reminder that he was no longer with me. While Jacob had still been alive, he wanted to map as much out together as possible. We planned his funeral: minimal flowers; double-crusted pizza had to be served; Tim McGraw's greatest hits album was the only thing allowed to be played, specifically the song "Live Like You Were Dying" (Jacob was not a subtle person); and the pastor had to tell at least six jokes throughout the service. But there were things Jacob and I couldn't do together. Between the will, and the life insurance, and all his belongings, it was the little tasks that set me off. Like the night I logged into his Netflix account to cancel it, and I saw the last thing he'd watched was *End Game*, a documentary on terminally ill patients and their families. I drank an entire bottle of red wine that night and cried myself to sleep. I can admit that. I had tried to block out the things I felt in that hospital—the fear, the agony, the deep ache—and yet there I was again.

A song played on the radio, and I recognized it: the same rich, gravelly vocals that had played on repeat as I said goodbye to my brother, on a warm July day, among all the people who loved him. The lyrics filled the car, Tim singing about living as though you were dying.

I ran my hands down my face. *Good one, Jacob*, I thought. I'd always been very practical; I could usually find an answer for just about anything . . . but sometimes there's no answer to be found. This was one of those moments. I wondered if perhaps my brother was trying to tell me something from wherever he was.

Winnie needed me, and that was a good enough reason to go inside the place I swore I'd never step foot in again.

Chapter 15

Emerson

I thought birds were honestly the coolest things in the world. I didn't consider myself a bird *expert*, but definitely a bird *fanatic*. For example, I learned that there are, like, five hundred species of bird in Colorado alone. The arctic tern holds the record for the longest migratory journey, covering 27,000 miles per year. Little blue jays collect paint chips, ravens can mimic human speech and even recognize individual faces, and some birds can even fly while they're sleeping. Wild, right? Winnie taught me all about birds. We spent so many afternoons discussing them, among all the other things we chatted about, of course.

It had been two whole days since I'd heard from her. I'd called multiple times. Her phone rang out. I'd texted too—no reply. I mean, she was an old lady; she could do whatever she wanted. Sometimes she'd get on these baking kicks, really take it seriously. Or sometimes she went on long bird-watching expeditions. And she still went camping sometimes. The woman was seventy-eight going on twenty.

But something felt strange, because Winnie always asked me to bake with her, and we always bird-watched together. Maybe I'd done something wrong. Upset her in some way. Which is why I found myself at Gill's old place, the one Wren was fixing up. She seemed surprised to see me when I walked up the cobblestone driveway.

The Last Poem

I leaned my bike against the porch railing, careful not to knock over the small bundle of pine saplings Wren had stacked near the steps. Their roots were wrapped in burlap, waiting for the ground to soften in spring.

"Are you going to start a Christmas tree farm?" I asked, grinning.

She scowled. "They're just trees."

"Sure," I teased. "That's exactly what someone starting a Christmas tree farm would say."

Wren rolled her eyes. "I can bet this place gets buried in snow during the winter. I'm just getting prepared to liven the yard up when it melts away."

I looked up at the cloudy sky, the wind carrying that familiar sharp bite. "Usually yes," I replied. "The most snow days we ever got in school was, like, seven. But the last couple of years have been low-key. There'll be no burying this year."

Not that I was a weather expert. But it was late November already, and we'd barely gotten a dusting of powder.

Wren seemed to breathe relief. "Are we supposed to be having a driving lesson?" she asked.

"I'd need to actually drive for it to be a lesson," I replied.

"Yeah, it's been a few weeks since we hatched that plan," she replied, moving a box of tools off the swing on the porch. "I just thought maybe you weren't ready."

I sighed dramatically, watching my breath curl in the air.

"No, hey, listen," Wren said, shifting toward me. "You've come a long way just by sitting in the front passenger seat," Wren said. "Olivia thinks so too." A nice sentiment. I knew Olivia did genuinely want to help me, too, but I had a suspicion her enthusiasm about these so-called driving lessons had more to do with how hard she was crushing on Wren than anything else.

"Olivia would think that," I said, with a smirk, "because she just wants an excuse to see you."

Wren scrunched up her nose. She did this a lot when she was thinking about something intently. I could see why Olivia liked her; she was cute, for, like, a thirtysomething.

"How's your mom?" Wren asked, throwing the conversation in the complete opposite direction. Deflection.

"She's fine," I replied. "She's working."

Wren sat on the swing and indicated for me to sit with her.

"I love this swing," she murmured. "It's my favorite part of the whole house."

"Not the opossums?"

She grimaced. "Gill seems to love telling everyone about my war with the opossums."

"I think he just loves talking about anything that reminds him of Edith," I said.

There was a nest of swallows in the tree beside us, and I watched them for a while.

"Winnie loves birds," I said. "We talk about them all the time. There's something about them. The way they just . . . go. Like the whole sky is theirs. Winnie says they represent freedom. For me, maybe it's the possibility. Trying to figure out what's next, where to go, how to get there—it's like watching them makes me believe a second chance is out there somewhere."

Wren watched the birds for a moment too. "What's your favorite bird?" she asked me.

"Ravens," I replied. "And not because they are all dark and emo, but because ravens are actually super smart. Did you know that ravens can remember specific individuals and events? They can problem solve, too, and have even been known to use tools."

Wren nodded. "Actually, I did know this; I quite like birds myself."

I sat a little straighter on the bench. "You do? What are your favorites? Wait, let me guess, wrens?"

She smiled. "Actually, no, but those were Lucy's favorite birds. If I had to pick, I would say bluebirds. You know they can spot a caterpillar from at least fifty yards away?"

"That's impressive," I said.

"Some people think that bluebirds connect the living to those who have passed away; they are supposed to be a symbol of joy and hope."

I contemplated her words. "Ravens symbolize death," I countered.

Wren smiled. "Yes, but also change and rebirth."

"They also have one hundred different vocalizations, and can live up to, like, thirty years old, or more."

"I hear they also collect shiny things."

"Well," I shrugged, "they have to impress the other ravens."

Wren laughed, before shifting slightly on the swing. It moved gently, rocking backward and forward; I lifted my legs so they were off the ground. It reminded me of the afternoons Brady and I would spend at the park: he would see how high he could make me fly on the swing.

"Can I ask you something?" I said.

"Anything," Wren replied.

"You loved Lucy, right, more than anything?"

"I did."

"So how do you know if you could ever love anyone else? Like, is there more than more?"

She was quiet for a moment. "I don't think there's more than more," she said. "There's just different. I loved Lucy for all the things she was, but that doesn't mean that I can't love somebody else, for all the things they are."

"I thought I was going to marry Brady and be with him forever," I said. "But then the accident happened, and I'm not the same Emerson I was back then. I'm burned, inside and out. I am not sure anyone would love the new Emerson."

"Perhaps you're asking the wrong question," Wren said. "You should start by asking yourself, why did you love him?"

I shrugged. "Well, he would always smile when I turned up to his practice, and he would always tell me how great I was for bringing extra snacks for him at lunch, or helping him do his homework. He was just really grateful for me."

Wren looked at me curiously. "What did he do for you?" she asked.

"What do you mean?"

"I mean, you have just listed all the nice things you did for Brady, but what did he do for you?"

I tried to think, but nothing came to mind. Instead, all I could think about were all the times I'd begged him to watch a movie with me at my house and he would choose to go out with friends instead. Or he would call me drunk and ask me to pick him up. Or he would say football was the most important thing in his life, *You understand, babe?* and then he wouldn't even say he was joking.

"Nothing," I said truthfully.

Wren folded her arms. The smell of honeysuckle wafted from somewhere in the garden. "Well, I think that's a good place to start," she said. "Someone needs to think of you, Emmy."

"Winnie thinks of me," I said. "Although she hasn't been answering my messages."

Wren stiffened, eyes narrowing as a spider scurried along the wall behind us, and scrunched her nose. "She was a little under the weather, wasn't she?" she said. "Maybe she's all bundled up on bed rest watching *Real Housewives*."

I grinned. "Did she tell you about that?"

"Oh, it's all she can talk about. I think she wants to be one of them." Wren smirked. "Why don't you bike over to her house? Go check on her yourself."

"You're right," I replied. "And if she's mad at me, better to talk about it, right? Life's too short, as Henry always says."

Wren nodded. "Yes," she replied, her eyes glazing over, as though thinking of someone. "Life really is too short."

*

I rang the doorbell, no answer. I rang again, still no answer. I went fishing for the spare key in the pot of lavender Winnie had growing around the side of the house, but it wasn't there. I walked back to the front door and realized it was open, so I let myself inside. The house was quiet. There was no scent of freshly baked cookies or pecan pie. Instead, there was a damp, musky smell, as though the windows hadn't been opened in a while. I made my way through the living room, and even checked her back courtyard, looking for her. The floorboards creaked beneath my feet. The silence was unsettling, an eerie contrast to the afternoons we had spent baking, reading, and laughing. I ventured into the kitchen, half expecting to find Winnie bent over the sink, scrubbing baking dishes with her headphones on. But instead, I discover her untouched grocery list, its pages weirdly blank. She wrote everything down. *Everything*. My eyes scanned the counter, and that's when I found them. At least three pill bottles. They had never been there before. I immediately looked at the labels: *doxorubicin, prednisone, cyclophosphamide*. I googled the names and my heart stopped. Cancer medications? Lymphomas? But Winnie didn't have cancer. What the fuck was going on?

I fumbled for my phone, my hands trembling as I called Winnie's number for the hundredth time. This time, instead of ringing into an empty void, I heard it inside the house. A muffled chime came from down the hall. I whipped around just as someone stepped out of Winnie's bedroom; a scream strangled itself in my throat. But it was Henry, a duffel bag slung over his shoulder. He froze at the sight of me, Winnie's phone in his hand.

"What are you doing here?!" I demanded.

Henry looked flustered, caught off guard, his grip tightening around the strap of the bag. "Emmy, I—"

Without thinking, I grabbed one of the pill bottles and shoved it at him. "Do you know what this is?"

His face fell, as though he wanted to sink into the floor beneath us.

"You do," I accused angrily. "Henry—*tell me*."

He exhaled slowly, staring down at the label. "She made me promise not to say anything."

A sharp, hot anger seared through my chest. My scars felt on fire. "Where is she?"

Henry hesitated.

"Henry, where the *hell* is she?"

His shoulders slumped. "Norvale Hospital. She's been there since Wednesday morning."

"Wednesday morning?" I repeated. "Two whole fucking days?" My voice cracked, tears choking my throat. "And no one thought to tell me? You let me worry, let me think she just—forgot about me?"

"She didn't want you to worry," Henry said, exasperated. "She instructed me not to. I'm sorry, Emmy, I know I should have . . ."

"Well, I fucking know now, don't I," I replied, turning away from him and storming outside.

I called Wren.

"Emerson?" There was a loud crash and Wren cursed, then apologized. "I really thought I had dealt with these opossums, but it appears I haven't."

"Do you think the opossums could wait and you could help me?"

"Oh, I am sure they'd love it if I left them alone, what's wrong?"

"I need you to drive me to the hospital."

Wren suddenly sounded alarmed. "Emmy, are you hurt?"

"No," I replied, and a lump swelled in the back of my throat. "It's Winnie."

Everston didn't have a hospital. After the accident, I was airlifted to Norvale Hospital, and I spent most of my time recovering in the burn unit. I remember that, for the first few weeks, I would close my eyes and the only thing I could see was the outline of a Douglas fir. I would feel heat in the areas of my body that had been burned. It was strange: no pain, just heat. Eventually the pain set in. I'd since gone through several debridement surgeries, and I continued needing laser surgery to repair the skin (not that it would ever fully be repaired). I was no stranger to Norvale Hospital; my stint here earned me some double-chocolate brownies from the nurses nearly once a week *and* multiple high fives from Dr. Bradman. They loved me there, and I guess you could say I grew to love them, too, for sticking with me, even in the moments I wanted to unleash the hell inside me. But I knew why I was there then. Walking in through these doors now, I just wanted to scream into the long corridors: *Why the fuck are we here again?*

The nurse directed us to the oncology ward, Room 17: the same number of books Winnie and I had read together. The walk there felt like several lifetimes. I pushed open the door gently, and I could see Winnie in the bed. She looked so small, the blankets and pillows practically swallowed her.

She sat up a little when she saw us, her expression shifting to one of guilt.

"My dear Emmy," she said softly. "I suspected I wouldn't be able to keep this from you for very long." She smiled softly. "And Wren! You've come along too."

I couldn't even speak.

Wren cleared her throat. "How about I go get us a coffee?" she said.

"That would be lovely, thank you, Wren," Winnie replied.

Wren excused herself and disappeared out into the hallway. I heard her footsteps become lighter the farther away she walked.

"I was so worried about you," I finally said.

"I know," Winnie replied. "I'm sorry. I just wanted to be sure I knew the facts before I saw you. You've got so much on your plate, kid."

"What is it?"

"I'm sick, Emmy," she said softly. "Have been for quite some time, only it's spread a bit too far to hold it off now."

I shook my head. "You can't be sick."

"Well," she said, and she winked at me, "how about we just pretend I'm not?"

"Why didn't you tell me?"

She sighed. "And ruin all that fun we were having?"

A nurse moved into the room, checking vitals and adjusting cords. She smiled brightly at Winnie. "This must be the famous granddaughter," she said. "Nice of her to visit today, isn't it, Ms. Langford?"

Winnie looked at me, her eyes light, twinkling. "Oh yes," she said. "I always love seeing my granddaughter."

I just wanted to crumble in that very moment. How many other things had I never asked her? How many more moments was I going to get with her?

Wren returned with the coffees and set them on the table beside us. I noticed the nurse was looking at her with an odd expression.

"Do I know you?" she asked, and Wren looked up at her.

"I'm not sure," she replied casually.

"You look so familiar, do you act?"

Wren pushed her hair behind her ear. "Never in my life!" she said, but the nurse continued.

"You just look so familiar; I've seen you somewhere before."

"I've forgotten sugar," Wren suddenly said. "I'm just going to go grab some, Emmy, I'll be back."

She disappeared again, and I wanted to ask the nurse where she thought she'd seen Wren before, but then Winnie reached out her hand, with a small smile, and I felt my heart sink in my chest.

"What are we going to do?" I said, barely above a whisper. I could feel myself shrinking into the chair beside her.

She tapped the book next to her, a slim collection of poetry about birds.

"We're going to read, of course."

Chapter 16

Wren

It is a universal truth that news never sleeps. In every corner of the world, there is always a story of some kind, something newsworthy, like an accident or a tragedy, or a profound and unexpected twist of fate. You might be in your kitchen, your living room, walking, running, driving, or simply going about your day . . . news finds a way to seep into your awareness. You might feel momentary sorrow or shock, but mostly you'll return to whatever you were doing—some ordinary thing—because such events belong to others, not to you. Such tragedy, or bereavement, or disaster only ever happens to other people. Until one day, it doesn't. And you realize tragedy doesn't discriminate; it can happen to anyone. Even you. And suddenly, you're the headline no one ever wants to be, left searching for answers that may never come.

A week ago, I had been out searching for replacement banisters for the staircase, something sturdy with a bit of character. It was one of those tasks I kept putting off, but that day, I'd finally decided to tackle it. On my way back, I stumbled across a garage sale tucked into a corner of a quiet street. I wasn't intending to stop—I hadn't planned to buy anything except the banisters, but something about it caught my eye. Among the usual clutter of mismatched chairs, chipped dishes, and boxes of books, there it was: an old writing desk. It was scratched and weathered, the kind of thing that most people wouldn't give a second glance. But I couldn't stop looking at it. It reminded me of the desk I used to write on back in New York, the one Lucy had convinced me to buy because she said it *looked like a place where stories could begin*. I bought it without much thought, just as I bought this one, as though some part of me knew I needed it. I brought it back to the house, sanded it down, repainted it, and placed it in front of the big bay windows in the living room. It overlooked the front garden, with the wildflowers and the pine trees, and the busy honeybees. I had danced with this writing desk all week. Approaching it every morning, and then turning away. I was busy with painting, and was still trying to fix the patio and repair the broken railings, but every now and then I'd wander inside and stare at the damn desk. Do I sit down? Don't I? Do I? And so on and so forth. Today was no different, only I'd managed to actually sit in the chair. I stared down at the notebook in front of me. I'd written the date at the top of the page. I'd always hated my handwriting, but Lucy loved it. She would insist that I write on paper first, so that she could keep the journals and notebooks I wrote in. She did keep them all, in a trunk at the foot of our bed. Her keepsakes, she called them. I closed my eyes, picturing the trunk. It was made from beautiful cedarwood, its brass bindings dulled by time. It was etched with scratches and wear, and we'd carved our initials at the very bottom.

The trunk snapped shut, and I turned from where I had been sorting through our laundry.

"What are you doing?" I asked.

Lucy smiled, a glint of mischief dancing in her eyes. "Just organizing things," she replied. Her tone was casual, and yet I knew she was hiding something.

I arched an eyebrow. "Organizing what exactly?" I replied, and I stepped around the bed to the trunk.

"What are you hiding in there?"

She tried to stop me from opening it, laughing as I wrapped my arm around her waist and pulled her gently aside, before opening the lid. There were journals and notebooks stacked neatly inside, all the ones she had insisted I use to write poems and annotations and whatever else came to mind.

"These are all my notebooks," I said curiously.

"Yes," she replied. "They're memories, all here, tucked away in this trunk. I want to make sure you can always return to them."

I laughed, pulling on her sweater. "Why would I need them, when I have you?"

"Because what you write is important," she said. "And one day you will realize you don't need me to write."

"Impossible," I replied. "You're the muse."

She shook her head, cupped my face in her hands. "You're the writer," she said softly. "If not me, then something else. It's in your heart, Bee. Just always write what is in your heart."

I blinked away the memory. Since Lucy had been gone, I'd wondered what to do with the guilt. It started with days, then weeks, then months, and then a whole year went by, and more. How long was long enough? Or will it be forever? But forever wasn't long enough while she was still alive, so whatever made me think it would be long enough when she was gone?

But there was Olivia.

And then there was my heart.

And somehow, the two had collided.

*

There were two ravens picking at something on the fence line, their glossy black feathers glistening in the pale light of the cloudy day. They cawed, jumped, alighted onto the fence once more, before taking off into the sky. I watched them from the window, still looking from the notebook to my computer, to the garden outside. I sat down, exhaled slowly, and opened the notebook.

The news of Winnie crushed Emerson. Henry was devastated, and I knew the rest of the group would be crushed too. Olivia was shocked when I told her. I knew that there was no way to shield any of us from the grief, but there was still something small I could do: I could write about it. I could give them words, banded together; comfort, something to hold on to. I could write them a book; I knew how to do that. The manuscript I had been reading to Lucy on the evening of the accident was a poetry collection. My first in over a decade. The publishers were thrilled; my team couldn't wait. There was an electricity to it all—something special. I had already known what I wanted to call it: *Thinking of You*. Back then, it was about Lucy, every word a reflection, a love letter. But time had passed, and I was not the same. I still thought of her, but I also thought of them, this group of people who showed up carrying grief in their arms but who still found ways to laugh. It occurred to me that *thinking of you* is something we say when we're in love, and also when we're grieving. We say it for anniversaries and funerals, for hospital beds and wedding days, for beginnings and endings. It means *I care, I miss you, you're in my heart*.

There was a flutter, a commotion outside the window. I saw a flash of blue before noticing a small bluebird perched on a branch just outside. Its vibrant plumage lit up the garden. One of the ravens had returned, and also settled on the same branch, and the contrast stirred a thought: could grief and joy exist together, like this raven and bluebird? I wrote *Thinking of You* at the top of the page. I tried to breathe steadily, the softness of the late morning sunlight filling my lungs. It was time to finish what I had started, even though it was different now, reshaped by what I had lost, but also everything I had gained. Once I began to write, I couldn't seem to stop, not even when the sun began to sink, and the birds had long parted ways. But even so, the more I wrote across the pages, the more it began to feel like I was finally coming home.

When I arrived at the library for our meeting, Henry was rummaging in the return box. He was making loud clanking noises, and I realized that he was trying to pry something out of it.

"Do you want some help?" I asked.

He turned, slightly startled. "Wren," he said, with a relieved smile. "Hi, yes, actually, could you just hold this for me?"

He indicated to the hinged flap, and I awkwardly pushed it inward as he reached farther into the bin. After a moment, we heard a gurgled squeak, before Henry pulled out a neon-colored rubber chicken.

"Why?" I asked simply.

He smirked. "You know, I have thought about putting a camera on this return box, just to see who in this town deems it appropriate to shove a rubber chicken in."

"If she wasn't dealing with everything right now, I'd say a prank like that wouldn't be so far out of the realm of Emerson," I replied.

Henry laughed, but it was a sad laugh. "I'm going to tell the group this evening," he said.

"Yes," I replied. "I suspected you would. Has she spoken to you?"

"Oh, eventually," he replied sadly. "When I dropped off Winnie's things, she was still there."

I nodded. "You were just doing what Winnie asked."

"I know," he replied. "But Emerson is sensitive. I should have said something."

I could see him wrestling with himself as I checked my watch. "Let's get inside before everyone arrives to find you digging more garbage out of the return box."

He nodded quickly and followed me inside. Max was already sitting in the reading corner; Max was never early. He had one leg crossed over the other, writing in a notebook. I'd never asked what he wrote down in that book, but I thought that perhaps one day I would. I found a seat and sat down. Gill and Rita arrived next, bickering over the rules of basketball. Bobby and Julian followed just after them. My heart fluttered when Olivia rushed through the doors; we locked eyes, and she came to sit down beside me.

"Are you okay?" I whispered.

"Yes," she said softly. "Are you?"

I had called Olivia the night I returned from the hospital. We'd stayed on the phone for hours: talking, listening, trying to devise some sort of plan for Emerson, anything at all we could think of. It was the first time in such a long time that I had relied on someone else for an answer. Lucy was always practical; she always knew what to do in the moments I was afraid. Since she had been gone, I'd relied on only myself. But perhaps, slowly, I could allow myself to rely on Olivia.

She reached over and squeezed my hand. Her thumb lingered, tracing lightly against my skin, and somehow that small touch settled me. "I'm okay," I said softly.

Henry suddenly cleared his throat. Now that he was under the lights in the library, I could see the circles under his eyes, the blotchiness of his face, and his ruffled hair. He had clearly not slept very well.

"I have some news that might be a little hard to swallow," Henry said. "But Max is here, and we are all here to support each other, so I am just going to come out and say it."

The Last Poem

I felt Olivia move closer to me, so that our shoulders were touching.

"Winnie is sick," Henry said.

"Oh." Rita sighed. "She probably got the flu from me I'm afraid. I dropped some recipes over the other week, but I'd had this nasty cough."

Henry smiled faintly. "She doesn't have the flu," he replied softly.

"Do you think we should drop some soup over?" Gill offered. "Edith always said chicken soup could cure anything."

Henry's shoulders slumped. "She isn't going to be cured from this," he said.

Silence enveloped our little corner of the library. A corner I had grown to love, to look forward to, to feel safe in.

"I see." Gill was the first to speak. "And Emmy?" he asked.

"Is with her," Henry said. "At the hospital."

"Oh dear." Rita sighed again. "She's grown quite attached to Winnie."

"She will be here for the poetry evening, right?" Julian asked. "I mean, she has to be, she just has to."

This seemed to spark the group into chatter, deliberating on how to get Winnie here, dedicating poems to her, even some sort of PowerPoint presentation.

Max cleared his throat. "It will be quite impossible for Winnie to make it."

Everyone fell silent again.

"This doesn't mean she hasn't given strict instructions to pass along," he added, with a gentle smile. "Instructions being that the show must go on."

"Exactly," Henry nodded. "We will carry on," he said. "So keep working on your poems, and we will keep organizing the event."

There was a murmur from everyone, as they slowly dispersed.

Rita and Bobby headed over to Max to discuss something and Gill and Julian bowed their heads to talk in low voices.

I felt Olivia gently stroke the back of my neck as Henry walked toward us.

"Tea?" he asked.

"None for me," Olivia replied. "My stomach is churning."

"Mine too," he responded. "I suppose it won't quite be the same without Winnie's baked goods," he said dismally.

"Have you been in touch with Emerson?" Olivia asked.

Henry shook his head. "Not since I saw her at the hospital."

"We can't seem to reach her either," she sighed.

Olivia's phone rang, and she stepped aside to answer it, in between the aisles.

"Are you okay?" Henry asked me directly.

"Me?" I replied.

"Yes," he said. "You are as much a part of this group as anyone."

Something about the way he said it, with such sincerity, made me feel like I really did belong. I hadn't expected to meet someone like Henry when I moved to Everston, but that was the thing about friendship: it blossomed when you least expected it.

"I'm worried about Emerson," I said, my voice low so the others couldn't hear. "About everyone, really. Haven't we all endured enough grief?"

"We certainly have," Henry said thoughtfully. "You know, I've been thinking even more about the poetry book. It's going to be really special, and I think it will resonate with a lot of people."

"I hope so," I agreed. "Poetry has a way of making sense of things." It felt like an old friend, the kind you stop calling when you're distracted and life gets too heavy. I'd turned my back on poetry a long time ago, convincing myself I couldn't face the words, when maybe the words were what I was missing all along.

Henry was looking at me curiously. I felt my cheeks redden.

I suddenly couldn't stand the idea of maintaining a facade with someone who had become such a good friend.

I cleared my throat. "Let's see how it turns out, anyway."

He shrugged lightly, grinning. "We can stumble through it together."

Henry informed me that Everston was hosting its annual Last Leaf Festival on Saturday as something of a farewell to fall. The air had turned, and everyone knew it was only a matter of time before heavy snowfalls became routine. The festival marked that in-between period, after the leaves had mostly fallen but before the first winter storm. A carnival rolled into town, with a caravan of trailers loaded with rides, games, and stalls selling everything from mulled cider to cinnamon popcorn. Henry handed us printed flyers for the poetry evening and assigned Olivia and me the task of not only distributing them around town but also handing them out at the festival.

"You know, he could have just made a post on social media," Olivia remarked as she stapled a flyer to an electrical pole.

"I think he's doing that too," I replied with a small smile. "And anyway, aren't you supposed to be covering the story for HCB?"

She grimaced in response. "I'm working on that," she said.

"Maybe you could bribe them with one of those giant teddy bears," I teased.

Olivia looked back at me. "Are you suggesting that I wouldn't be able to win one of those things?"

I handed a flyer to a couple walking by us. "I'm not suggesting anything," I replied, trying to hide my smile.

The fairgrounds were small, but they were bustling with activity, pockets of crowds surrounding food stalls, rides, and market stands. Folks pushed strollers, held hands, munched on corn on the cob and cotton candy, while teenagers paraded around with oversized stuffed animals slung over their shoulders. Laughter weaved its way through the crisp air, rising above the music and chatter. Suddenly, a small child dashed past us, squealing with delight as she clutched a warm paper bag full of cinnamon donuts, sugar dusting her fingers and cheeks. As we watched the scene unfold, Olivia's eyes lit up as she spotted a ring toss stall amid the bustling fair. The stall was decorated in colorful banners and twinkling lights. Giant brown teddy bears hung from the roof, and a carnival worker beckoned people to try their hand at winning one.

"Okay, Wren," Olivia declared, handing me her stack of flyers, "I'm going to get you that bear."

She stepped up to the booth, and the worker smiled. "Five dollars a turn or twenty for five."

"Twenty bucks?" Olivia asked incredulously, and the worker just shrugged, adjusting his hat.

She pulled out a twenty dollar bill and handed it to him. "How many rings do I need to get that bear?" she asked.

He looked up at the bears on the ceiling. "Three in a row," he replied.

She eagerly picked up the rings and sized up the rows of bottles arranged against the back wall.

"You know, for twenty bucks we could have just gotten another bottle of wine," I protested.

She shushed me and sent the first ring sailing through the air. It missed completely and the carnival worker grinned. "Come on," he encouraged her. "Flick your wrist."

"What if I had carpal tunnel?" she responded.

She sized up the bottles again and sent the second ring into the air. It landed squarely around one of the bottles, to the surprise of both Olivia and the worker, and I squealed in response.

Olivia looked at me. "Did you just squeal?"

"Go again!" I insisted.

She lined herself up, threw the next ring, and again it looped straight around the neck of the bottle.

By now some kids had also joined the booth, watching Olivia.

"Maybe make it four rings," the worker said sheepishly, but Olivia shook her head.

"Nope! A deal is a deal, bud; if I get this, I get a bear."

She threw another ring, and somehow, it landed around the bottle. We both cheered as the carnival worker presented her with a giant brown teddy bear.

Olivia grinned at me as we moved on, handing the bear to me.

"Thoughts?" she asked.

"I'm impressed," I responded. "I'm also calling him Freddy."

Later, as the sun set, we ordered cider from this little van near the cluster of pop-up bars. I took a sip and scrunched up my nose at the tart flavor.

"No good?" Olivia asked, and she sipped hers. I watched in amusement as she grimaced at the taste too.

"Definitely no good," she agreed.

A young group of teenagers passed us, accidentally knocking into Olivia, and the cider cup sloshed, spilling liquid all over the teddy bear.

"Oh, come on." Olivia sighed. "Really guys, I'm standing right here."

I laughed. "Somehow Freddy copped most of the cider."

She tossed our cups into a nearby trash can. "I've always been more of wine girl," she said. "Three years ago, we did a segment on one of the wineries in the area. They'd won some awards that year, but our coverage helped boost their profile, so they sent me some of their best bottles. Do you want to have a glass at mine, while I wash poor Freddy?" She paused a moment, unsure. "Unless . . . you need to go?"

"No, I want to stay," I replied.

"At the fair?"

"With you," I said, and Olivia's eyes lit up.

Olivia's condo was open and airy with large windows. The space was filled with tasteful decor and sleek countertops, with a living room that opened to a large balcony overlooking Everston. Outside, sleet started to fall, light and scattered. It tapped softly against the glass, a quiet reminder that winter was here. We'd made it inside just in time, it seemed. I scanned her bookshelf, dark and overflowing with various trinkets from travels, along with encyclopedias and autobiographical books. My eyes fell on my own books. She had three of them. The spines faced outward with the name I had left behind in New York, and my stomach churned with the shame of my deception. For every day I kept my real self hidden from the group, I felt more and more uncomfortable with my lie. I had never anticipated that I'd feel the way I did about them; I'd originally just wanted to sink into the shadows of this town and hide forever.

I sat down on the couch as she poured the glasses in the kitchen, the warmth of her apartment a welcome change from the cold outside. She had a Venus flytrap sitting near her TV, and when she saw me looking at it, she laughed.

"My aunt," she said. "She's trying to get me invested in them as well."

"How's that going?"

Olivia handed me a glass of wine. "There's just a part of me that wishes it were bigger, so I could casually leave it in my boss's office."

I grinned into the glass, inhaling the rich plum scent before taking a sip.

"Much better," I said.

Olivia sank down into the couch next to me, our knees touching.

"There's something about you," she murmured softly, her thumb stroking my arm, "that feels familiar."

Time seemed to stall as we were swallowed by the moment. I was lost in her gaze, heavy and wanting. I was pinned there, by the promise in her eyes, the curve of her lips, the faint freckles across her nose. Olivia leaned closer, her lips inches from mine, and I could feel the air pull in around us. Then, in an instant that felt like eternity, our lips met. Kissing Olivia was like diving headfirst into a sunlit ocean. Time slowed, and the world fell away, until there was only her. It was like discovering a secret garden, or like coming home to the lights being left on, so you knew someone was waiting for you. It was like rediscovering springtime after months of ice and snow. Our bodies could not get close enough. Olivia pressed me back, her weight delicious and grounding as she crawled on top of me, lips trailing from my mouth to my neck, her hands buried in my hair. She murmured something I couldn't catch, the syllables dissolving against my skin, as her hips rolled harder into mine, like she wanted to feel every inch of me. Heat surged through me until my fingers fumbled at the buttons of her shirt. I could see where this was going, mapped out before me, and it filled me with anticipation, need, desire . . . and fear.

"Wait," I whispered.

Olivia paused, her forehead resting against mine. "Do you want to keep going?" she asked softly, her eyes searching mine for reassurance.

"No," I said, then quickly corrected myself. "I mean yes, of course, yes." I hesitated, the words catching in my throat. "There is just . . . something that I need to tell you." Of course, I needed to tell her. The truth had been weighing on me from the moment we first met. Every kiss, every laugh, it all felt tainted, because she didn't know anything about my past. I had told myself I was protecting her, but really, it was me I was protecting. Now, with her so close, I couldn't carry the secret anymore. She deserved honesty, and if I wanted this—us—to mean anything, I had to tell her.

She looked at me quizzically, her brow furrowing. "Please don't tell me you actually work for Fox News . . ."

I smiled faintly. "No. But you might think it's worse."

Olivia eased back, shifting off me, but her hand lingered, warm against my arm. I ached to close the space again, to feel her pressing into me, moving against me the way she had just moments before. "Tell me," she said.

I inhaled sharply. "My name isn't Wren. Or at least, not exactly. Wren is my middle name. My real name is Brooklyn," I admitted, my gaze falling to where our skin met. "My fiancée Lucy *did* die in a car accident, but I didn't leave New York just because I was grieving."

Her eyes poured into mine, confusion blending with quiet curiosity.

I glanced over at the coffee table, where Emerson's gifted copy of my book now sat prominently. The sight of it sent a shiver through me. "I left New York because my work is known by a lot of people," I continued, my voice tightening. "Especially the press. After the accident, they were relentless. They tore Lucy's reputation apart, blamed her entirely, even though I remember it differently. I couldn't fight back, not with how vulnerable I was. So, I ran."

Her brows knit together. "Who are you?" Olivia murmured.

"B.W. Paisley," I said, the name landing heavily between us.

Her eyes widened slightly but did not leave mine, and I rushed to fill the silence.

"I have wanted to tell you," I stuttered, "but . . . there's been this part of me trying to start over, to figure out who I am without all the noise. My world has been colorless since Lucy died, but then I found myself here, and for the first time, there were bursts of color again. And when I met you . . ." My voice cracked, my heart pounding. "It felt like everything came back at once. I just . . . I didn't know how to tell you." Tears started to bead at the corners of my eyes.

Olivia didn't say anything at first. I'd grown so used to her facial expressions that I could see the moment her brain kicked into overdrive, processing everything I'd just laid out. I might have even seen a flicker of hurt, and confusion. My heart could barely handle it. She shifted slightly, her eyes filled with the same look she got when she was about to read a poem in front of the grief group, like the words were delicate, and she was determined to handle them with care.

"I understand if you're angry . . ." I began, but my voice faltered.

She reached up, brushing a strand of hair away from my face, her touch light and deliberate. "I'm not angry," she said gently. "I knew there was something about you. I just didn't know it was this. And I understand why you'd protect yourself, we all do that. I've got you, okay?"

I blinked at her, unsure if I had heard her correctly.

"You know that, right?" she asked, her fingers tracing the sides of my face. She had the softest hands; they sent electricity skimming through my veins.

"No one's said that to me in a long time," I murmured. A strange mix of relief and apprehension settled in my chest. Now that Olivia knew—really knew—who I was, would she see me differently?

"Well," Olivia said, her lips curving into a small smile, "it must have been exhausting, carrying this secret for so long. Not being able to fully be yourself. Your work is a pretty big deal, and you've written so many books, some we've shared at the meetings. That had to strike a nerve."

"The first time I heard Emerson read from one of my books, it felt like it belonged to someone else," I admitted. "Like it was from another lifetime. Those poetry books are more than ten years old. I started with poetry very early in my career, before all the success from *The Lost Archives*. But, a couple of years ago, I decided to move back into poetry. My publishers thought it would be something exciting for longtime fans. A book of love poems. And then Lucy died."

Olivia reached toward me again, her fingers brushing lightly against that same spot on my arm. A quiet reassurance, an unspoken *I see you*. She smiled playfully. "Speaking of Emerson, you know she's going to absolutely lose her mind. I can't believe she hasn't realized it's you."

"Please don't say anything," I said, my stomach twisting at the thought. "Not yet anyway. I've changed so much—cut and dyed my hair, lost weight, dropped the glasses—it's no wonder I look like a completely different person. I want to stay that way. Just until I tell her, and the others, but . . . I need time."

She nodded. "I understand," she replied. Her gaze grew more serious. "But, you know, if you remember that night, the accident, differently, it might be because it *was* different. Maybe the press got it wrong. Maybe it wasn't Lucy's fault."

"Maybe," I said softly, my hand trailing along her cheek, marveling at the way her hair framed her face so perfectly.

"Does it change how you see me?" I asked.

Olivia's eyes glinted as she climbed back on top of me. "You mean how you just let me in? I think that's sexy, if you ask me." Her lips grazed mine, the heat of her breath coiling low in my stomach. "And besides," she added, "I do like Wren. It suits you."

I blushed, my hands slipping beneath her shirt, wanting to explore more of her.

"And just while we're being honest . . ." Her lips hovered so close I could taste her. "I think there are other ways you can let me in."

December

Chapter 17

Emerson

Every winter in Everston, the snow buries everything. Although this winter was shaping up to be unusually dry, more of a powder than the heavy blankets that normally coated the town. The hospital halls were slightly chilly and smelled like antiseptic and stale coffee, but someone made an effort with Christmas decorations. Tinsel strung haphazardly along the nurses' station, a little tree in the waiting room with an assortment of mismatched baubles and handmade ornaments, its branches bent at all angles. Someone even taped a paper snowflake to Winnie's door, upon which was scrawled in a child's handwriting: *Merry Christmas, Winnie!*

Inside, her room was dimly lit, the weak afternoon light spilling in from the window. Despite the festive touches, there was no disguising how tired she looked. The sharpness of her collarbones, the hollowness beneath her eyes. It was strange how quickly a body could change. A month ago she was in her kitchen, covered in flour, arguing with me about whether a lemon tart needed more zest. And now she looked so small, like a tiny little bird.

A collection of gifts from the group was gathered on the table beside her. Julian and his wife sent a bouquet of fresh white lilies, their fragrance softening the clinical scent of the hospital room. A box of chocolates from Gill sat unopened, but, knowing Winnie, she'd already rationed them in her mind—one piece per visitor, no exceptions. Wren and Olivia brought a stack of books, some well-loved, others brand-new. Rita had sent a pile of glossy magazines, and Bobby had delivered an assortment of baked goods, because, as he put it, *If you can't bake, the least you can do is eat.* Henry left a crossword puzzle book with a note on the inside cover: Don't cheat! Normally I would have asked him to stay and help me figure out the answers with Winnie, but I was still so mad at him.

"See," Winnie said. "Plenty to be merry about this season."

I hadn't had the heart—or the stamina—to argue with her, even though every part of me wanted to scream. How could this be happening? How could the world keep turning, the town keep decorating, people keep stringing up lights and hanging garlands, as if nothing had changed? As if time wasn't slipping through my fingers in every conversation, laugh, or moment that we shared? Christmas songs played faintly from a speaker down the hall, cheerful and out of place against the hum of the hospital machines. Someone walked past carrying a plate of sugar cookies, and I hated how normal it all seemed. Because nothing about this was normal. Nothing about this should be happening.

"You need to go home," Winnie rasped, her voice weaker than it had been even yesterday. "It's been four days."

I stopped staring out the window and made a point of sniffing my T-shirt dramatically. "Eh," I shrugged. "Who am I trying to impress anyway?"

"A lady should always pride herself on her hygiene," she replied primly.

I scoffed. "Lady? Who are you and what have you done with my best friend?"

She smiled, but it was tired. "Oh fine," she said. "You've won over the nurses, I suppose."

I grinned. "Oh, I did that with these baddies," I said, pulling up my sleeve to flash my scars. "They love me here. I can get away with anything. Maybe we could look up your ex-husband's medical records and prank call him?"

Winnie chuckled, but it turned into a painful-sounding cough. I sat up straighter, worried, but she waved me off.

"Don't fuss," she scolded lightly. "I'm not made of glass."

I swallowed hard. She wasn't glass. But she was breaking all the same.

I cleared my throat. "You know, the poetry evening is—"

"Months away yet," she said softly.

"Yes, but we could—"

Winnie gave me a look, one that said we both knew better.

"Emmy, we both know I won't be going," she said.

My chest tightened. I guess we were done with pretenses.

"I don't know how to do any of this without you," I said, staring at the blanket. "I don't know how—" I gestured vaguely, trying to find the words.

"Nonsense," she said. "You have your whole life ahead of you."

"Yes, but—"

"You don't have to know, Emmy," she said. "You just have to keep going."

"I feel like a failure."

Winnie squeezed my hand, surprisingly firm. "You can pick a new dream," she said.

"Oh, yeah?" I murmured. "Like what? Gymnastics was my whole life."

She tilted her head, looking me over. "Have you still not learned?" she asked. "Gymnastics was *not* your whole life, Emerson. You love poetry and birds, you love reading and baking and debating. There are so many more things to you than bouncing around on one of those beams."

I bit my lip, the lump in my throat impossible to swallow. The ache of everything—of this moment, of what was slipping away, thudded in my chest. I had no idea what I was doing.

I mean, I used to. I used to have a plan. A good one. A full-ride scholarship, a shot at UCLA, a future that looked so damn bright I could barely see past it. And now? Now I was sitting in a hospital room, watching the one person who always seemed to know the answers slip away from me, and I had no idea what came next. It wasn't just gymnastics. It wasn't just school. It was everything. Who was I without it? Without the competitions, the training, the structure? Without the dream I'd had since I was a kid? People don't really tell you what to do when your whole life gets yanked out from under you. They just say things like *You'll figure it out* or *You're young, you have time*. But time feels like a joke when you're watching someone you love run out of it.

And my mom—god, my mom was trying. She was working late again tonight, texting me updates between shifts, pretending like she wasn't worried sick about me, about Winnie, about everything. Pretending like she wasn't holding down two jobs and holding me together at the same time. And I was just . . . stuck. Stuck in this weird limbo where I wasn't a gymnast anymore, wasn't a college student, wasn't anything really. Just a girl sitting in a too-bright hospital room, counting down the days she had left with her best friend. I wanted to tell Winnie all of this. I wanted her to tell me what to do, to shake me out of this funk, to remind me who I was, like she always did. But she was the one in the hospital bed, barely able to keep her eyes open, and I couldn't ask her to fix me when I couldn't do a damn thing to fix her. I blinked hard and sucked in a breath. Maybe she was right. Maybe I'd figure it out eventually. Maybe I had to.

But first, I had to figure out how to say goodbye. I choked out a small cry. Winnie, of course, wasn't having it.

"None of that now," she murmured, her fingers lightly tapping the blanket. "Hand me my water, will you?"

I reached for the cup on the table and passed it to her, watching as she took a slow sip. She still had that same dry humor, that same sharpness in her eyes, even as her body betrayed her. I tried to hold on to that, to pretend, even for just a second, that this was a normal afternoon between us.

I pulled a crumpled ten dollar bill from my pocket and handed it to her.

Her brow furrowed. "What's this?"

I forced a grin onto my face. "You won the bet."

"The bet?"

"You said Olivia and Wren were perfect for each other." I shrugged. "Classic you, always knowing."

Winnie let out a small laugh, shaking her head. "Well, someone had to be the voice of reason."

"Someone did," I agreed, my smile wavering just slightly.

She took the bill in her hand for a long moment, then reached into her handbag and pulled out a small, folded piece of paper. Her fingers smoothed over it as she studied me, her expression unreadable.

"I have something for you too," she said, pressing it into my palm.

I turned it over, curious.

"Make sure Henry gets this," she continued. "It's my poem for the poetry evening."

I clutched the paper, willing my hands to stay steady. "You can give it to him yourself."

She gave me a look, one of those unimpressed, knowing glares that could cut through any illusion I tried to build around us. "Emmy," she said, her voice softer now. "Be kind to Henry. He's racked with guilt over my choices. You shouldn't blame him."

"How can I not?" I argued. "You were in here for two days and I had no idea, thanks to him."

"He was doing what I asked," she replied. "If you want to be mad at someone you can be mad at me."

I slumped in the chair.

"And in any case," she continued, "Henry is helping me get my affairs in order." She said it so casually, like we were discussing next week's baking list. A silence stretched between us, thick and heavy, until she shifted slightly, reaching toward her handbag again. She plucked out a set of car keys and pressed them into my palm.

"What's this?" I asked.

"It's yours."

My heart stumbled. "Winnie, I can't—"

"One day, you'll get behind the wheel again, Emmy. And if it's in my car, then I'll be right there with you."

I blinked the tears away rapidly, staring down at the keys in my hand.

I moved to climb onto the bed, lying down beside her.

"Are you sure you want to stay?" Winnie said. "Aren't there a million other things you could be doing?

I snuggled into the pillow and clicked on the TV, turning on *The Real Housewives of Beverly Hills*. I reached out my hand and closed it over Winnie's frail, tiny one.

"None that matter," I replied.

Chapter 18

Olivia

The best memory I have of my mother is on a home movie. It was taken the day we moved into our new house. I was two years old, and my parents had saved enough to move from their apartment into a four-bedroom house with a wraparound porch. The tape was so old, the picture was grainy, and the colors were so washed out. In the footage, my mother is laughing behind the camera as I stumble around the living room, climbing over moving boxes. She then appears in the frame, wrapping her arms around me. I can hear my father calling to us; he's the one holding the camera. She places me on the ground again and walks toward the camera, telling my father the last boxes are too heavy for her to carry. They exchange the camera between them, the room momentarily turning upside down. I am still babbling, words that don't make sense but still make my mother laugh. The camera pans to my face, bright red and puffy.

"March 16th, 1990," my mother says. "The day our dream begins."

I am still babbling away, digging my fingers into the carpet beneath me.

"Where are your dreams, Livvy?" she asks. "Tell Mama your dreams."

My face breaks into a wide smile and I laugh over something she is doing behind the camera.

"My dream was always you," she says, and the camera shuts off.

The whole video only lasts six minutes, but I have always wondered why, five years later, my father left, and my mother changed her dream.

There was one silver lining to being my mother's daughter: she had a sister, my Aunt Nell. For as selfish and absent as my mother was, Nell was the direct opposite. Everston was once a mining town, but since the early 1990s the mines had all permanently closed. There was still the old railroad that traveled between Everston and Norvale, usually transporting passengers through the remote wilderness of the San Juan National Forest. Nell used to work on the railroad and now did volunteer shifts at the rail depot museum, which she lived next to. When I arrived at my aunt's house, she was bent over her succulents humming a song.

"Darling," she said, as she noticed me in the doorway. "What a surprise."

"Free afternoon," I said, crossing the lounge room and stepping into her arms.

"It's good to see you," she replied.

"New plants?"

"The nursery was having a sale."

"Well, this might just inspire your next purchase," I said, handing her the gift-wrapped book. "This one won't need watering."

"Oh," she replied happily. "You know me well, thanks, Livvy."

She turned her attention back to the plants, placing the book on the table next to them, and continuing to repot a succulent into a bright-blue jeweled pot.

For being the complete opposite of my mother, my aunt resembled her in ways that were sometimes a little unnerving. When my parents divorced, my mother was fragile, like she had aged ten years too soon. She slipped so far into herself I didn't think she would return. She did, eventually, but she was never the same. Instead, she became the woman the rest of Everston knew:

intimidating. I like to think I became a reporter to help others share their stories, but it's only partly true. I wanted to understand how grief could trigger someone into chaos. That someone being my own mother.

"How's work?" Nell asked, dusting her hands of soil and gliding into the kitchen.

I followed, watching as she began to brew us a pot of coffee.

"Difficult," I replied truthfully. "I'm a little lost."

She looked up curiously. "How so?"

"I'm still on desk duty."

She scowled. "Oh, Colin is a spindly jerk, isn't he?"

I laughed. "He's just protecting the reputation of the station," I replied.

"And that grief group," she said. "How's that going?"

I thought of Wren.

"It's going well, actually."

Her face lit up. "Oh, that's wonderful," she replied. "Meditation saved my life."

I smiled, as she extended the mug to me. "It's not exactly meditation." I paused, thinking about the poem Wren had read the night before, how the words just seemed to flow from her. "But it is something."

"Why don't you do a story about that?" she suggested. "About your grief group?"

"Well, Colin doesn't think there's any story there," I said.

She scoffed. "What would Colin know."

"I mean, how could he?" I replied. "He hasn't seen how far these people have come, or the way they've leaned on each other."

"You mean the way you've also leaned on them?"

I smiled. "Maybe. Even so, trying to convince Colin there is a story amid a bunch of random strangers all dealing with their own grief journeys is like trying to convince Riot to go back to using a car."

The Last Poem

My aunt met Riot at a speed dating event downtown, two years ago. He was divorced, had three grown sons I'd never met, owned a Harley he was obsessed with, and made my aunt the happiest I'd seen her in years.

"Maybe you should just ask Riot to take you for a spin." She grinned. "The freedom on the back of that bike."

I scrunched up my nose, imagining my seventy-year-old aunt flying down the streets of Everston with her big, bulky, bearded boyfriend.

"There's also a woman I've met," I said. "Her name is Wren." Even though I knew her real name now, I couldn't imagine calling her anything else.

Nell turned to me. "Oh?" she asked, her eyes bright.

"Her fiancée, Lucy, died in a car accident, and she wound up in Everston, joining our grief group." I left out the part about Wren being famous author B.W. Paisley. That wasn't my story to tell.

"But there's something about the accident," I continued, the thought burning at the edges of my mind. "The police and press blamed Lucy. They said she caused it. But the details don't add up. There was a child involved but also another victim, a John Doe. Who is he? He was never identified in the media. How does an accident get so much press, and yet one of the victims stays nameless?"

Nell shrugged, her hands busy arranging pots as she listened. "Maybe his family didn't want him identified," she suggested lightly.

"Maybe," I admitted, pacing slightly, "but it still feels . . . off. If it were that simple, why not just say so? Instead, it's like someone buried it. There's something not right."

Nell gave me a sharp look, one that said she'd heard this tone before. She picked up her spray bottle and began misting her plants. "Perhaps that's the story you need to tell," she said evenly.

"Better yet," Nell added, glancing at me over her shoulder, "maybe it's the kind of story Colin would be interested in?"

Her words hit like a challenge, and I felt my pulse quicken. In a perfect world, reporters could keep their emotions at arm's length, but this world wasn't perfect. We're human. And sometimes, someone else's pain seeps into your skin, becomes part of you, and refuses to let go. I thought of Wren, everything she'd lost, everything she'd endured. There was something inside me, fierce and unrelenting, that wanted to fight for her. Not just because she deserved it, but because it felt as though I *needed* to. The feeling settled heavily in my chest, and alongside it was something else—a fire. This wasn't just about Wren anymore. This was about finding the truth.

On my mother's fiftieth birthday, she became so intoxicated that by seven p.m. she was already vomiting. I found myself in her suite, holding back her hair as she leaned over the toilet. In a moment of drunken honesty, she confessed to me that she had slept with the host of *Good Morning America* last year while on assignment, and she had been the mistress of the front man of a famous band, and the reason the band dissolved. In so many of our interactions, I felt more like her friend than her daughter. Yet, during the same evening, she told me how proud she was of me, that she couldn't imagine having anyone else for a daughter. I'm not sure how one person can feel like two. One moment, she was trying to control every aspect of my life, molding me into something that I wasn't. But then, in moments of vulnerability, she showed me a softness that weakened my guard. We repeated the same cycle over and over again. Even now, after her death, I still found myself simultaneously trying to please her and piss her off at the same time. There was an old saying: "like mother, like daughter." I hoped I was nothing like my mother in many ways. However, there was one trait I did possess that I was proud of, and that was the ability to ask the right questions. In life, if you ask questions, you might get answers. But if you ask the *right* questions, you will always uncover the truth.

I decided to make Sam's Diner my headquarters for the day. While I was actively avoiding Colin, I was also craving pancakes—three fluffy discs stacked high, generously smeared with butter and drenched in maple syrup, the only proper way to eat them. As I settled into my booth, laptop open, I typed "B.W. Paisley" into the search bar, and a whole world unfolded before me. Articles, interviews, a dormant website, long-inactive social media accounts, all of it showcasing a life far removed from the unassuming woman renovating an old house in Everston. There were countless reviews of her literary works, each one heaping praise on her novels, poetry collections, and essays. And then there was the plethora of photos, image after image that stopped me cold. I must have stared at them for so long that tiny specks of light began to dance in my vision by the time my pancakes arrived. It was Wren, but at the same time, it wasn't. The Brooklyn Paisley in the photos was striking, almost luminous. Her dark hair was glossy, styled in loose waves that framed her face perfectly. Her makeup was polished, her features enhanced just enough to seem effortlessly elegant. She wore tailored outfits—sleek dresses, sharp blazers, pantsuits—that gave her an air of sophistication befitting an author who regularly graced bestseller lists and literary events. She looked like someone who belonged in New York, walking into a gala or onto a stage. She also, in many images, wore brown-rimmed glasses.

And then there was Wren—lovely, beautiful Wren. The woman I knew.

Wren's hair was shorter, unevenly cut, as though she had done it herself. The glossy waves were gone; sometimes there were flecks of paint in her strands. She rarely wore makeup, and when she did, it was minimal, just enough to hint at some effort. Her wardrobe was simple: usually jeans, flannels, and well-worn boots, better suited for hauling paint cans or repairing broken railings. She wasn't polished or glamorous; she was raw, grounded, and real.

It was like she'd peeled away every layer of her former self, trading Brooklyn Paisley's poised confidence for Wren's quiet anonymity. She'd become someone who could fade into the background of a small town, someone completely unrecognizable from the woman the press had relentlessly photographed and dissected. But even so, it was her. The eyes were the same—intelligent, soft, carrying depth.

I stabbed a fork into one of my pancakes, the sweetness of syrup barely registering as I chewed. Determination burned in my chest as I scrolled through the sea of online content, hunting for anything that might untangle the truth of Wren's story. Among the flood of headlines, one jumped out: "Tragic Car Accident Claims Life of Author's Fiancée, Involving Multiple Victims and Young Pedestrian." The article was by Lachlan Davis of the *New York Times*. I remembered meeting Lachlan when I was covering Hurricane Sandy. I spent weeks in New York reporting on the impact of the storm and subsequent recovery efforts. We'd shared tips and coffee in the chaos of post-storm coverage. Figuring it was worth a shot to ask about Wren's accident, I emailed him. To my surprise, his reply landed in my inbox within minutes.

Hi Olivia,
Nice to hear from you! Yes, I covered that story. It seemed like an open-and-shut case, according to the police. Here's what I gathered: Lucy Halloran was reportedly driving a green Jeep while intoxicated. She collided with the vehicle of John Doe and then veered onto the curb, striking a five-year-old boy. The boy, Alec Lewis, was left paralyzed, while John Doe sustained minor injuries. Halloran was pronounced dead on

arrival, and Brooklyn Paisley was rushed to Mount Sinai for intensive care. The family of the boy seemed at odds with the official version of events, though nothing ever came of it. The mother, Kirby Lewis, owns an art gallery on Fifth Avenue and still resides on the Upper East Side. It was a horrific crash, that's for certain.

On a lighter note, I have to say, the "crap-flinging incident" of yours was legendary. We couldn't stop watching the video up here. Absolutely hilarious!

Let me know if you're ever back in New York—we should catch up.
Lachlan

I groaned at the mention of that incident, sinking lower into the booth. Lachlan had included a phone number for Mrs. Lewis at the bottom of his email.

"Another coffee, honey?"

I looked up to see Mrs. Wilks standing over me, coffee pot in hand.

"Please," I replied, sliding my mug toward her.

"Anything else to eat?" she asked with a knowing smile.

I stared at my empty plate. "I don't suppose I could order more pancakes?"

She laughed. "You can order whatever you like, Liv. I'll have some more out soon."

As she walked away, I tapped the number into my phone. After a few rings, a crisp, polite voice answered.

"Mrs. Lewis?"

"Yes, speaking?"

"Hi, Mrs. Lewis. My name is Olivia Piroso. I'm a reporter with High Country Broadcasting in Colorado. I'm calling about your son Alec and the accident he was involved in."

There was a pause, her tone cooling. "What about it?"

"I've been investigating the accident and just had a couple of questions, if you have the time?"

"We've spoken to plenty of reporters," she said curtly. "It didn't change anything."

I took a breath. "Did any of those reporters know B.W. Paisley personally?"

She hesitated. "No, they didn't."

"Well, if it means anything, Mrs. Lewis, her favorite color is yellow," I said softly. "She loves rainstorms, old books, and coffee cups that fit perfectly in her hands. She hasn't been able to write the same way since the accident. She remembers it differently too. I'm trying to find the truth—not just for her, but for Alec as well."

And Lucy, I thought.

"I knew her fiancée, Lucy Halloran," Mrs. Lewis said. "Professionally, that is. She was a well-known art dealer in the state. I own an art gallery and I often bought pieces from her. She was always professional, but she was also sweet. Obviously, I knew of B.W. Paisley. I have several of her books. I never met her, though. But Lucy would often talk of her in our interactions. They were planning a wedding, for crying out loud. And then this happened. It's been a nightmare—the police report insisting Lucy was at fault, that she's the reason Alec will never walk again. No amount of so-called 'investigative journalism,'" she added, her tone sharp, the air quotes practically audible, "will change that."

"I can't imagine it," I said. "The difficulty in having to relive this, but I am just trying to understand what happened."

There was a long silence. When she spoke again, her voice was laced with emotion. "Alec doesn't remember much about the accident. He was running ahead of us, along the sidewalk. We'd just bought him a new bike. My husband and I were just a few steps behind, but we were arguing over the fact that the chain had already broken. We didn't see it until we heard it. This explosion. Screams. The police said Lucy was drunk and caused the crash, but Alec keeps saying it wasn't her fault." Her voice wavered. "He still has nightmares. Sometimes they're so bad, I can't calm him down for hours."

"I'm so sorry," I replied. "I can't imagine what he's been through, what you've all been through."

"His nightmares are always about the car," she continued. "He calls it a monster. A big silver monster. Which is just the thing—Lucy's car wasn't silver, it was green. It doesn't add up to us."

"Has anyone ever looked into this further?" I asked, leaning forward.

"The police told us not to talk to the press," she replied. "They were very forthright about it. Said that it would only do more harm to Alec than good. I got scared. We wanted to focus on Alec's immediate recovery."

"I see."

"That, and I didn't think anyone would believe us," she admitted. "But there was an EMT, he was on the scene. He was kind and he believed Alec. He might remember something."

"Do you have his contact information?"

"Yes," she said, "but we haven't spoken to him in over a year."

She gave me the number, and I quickly jotted it down.

"Thank you, Mrs. Lewis. I'm sorry again for everything your family has gone through."

"We're lucky we still have Alec," she said, her voice softening. "I can't imagine what Ms. Paisley went through. Losing your fiancée like that, and then having her memory slandered in the media. That kind of grief is unimaginable."

I swallowed the lump in my throat. *It's earth-shattering grief*, I thought, *the kind that brings you halfway across the country, running from it.*

"Thank you for your time," I said, and I ended the phone call.

Immediately, I dialed the EMT's number. It rang several times before going to voicemail. I left a message, my voice steady despite feeling queasy.

Mrs. Wilks set another plate of pancakes in front of me, their golden warmth rising in soft, curling steam. But as I stared down at them, all I could see was Wren in that accident—how she must have lived through it. The terror as everything spiraled out of control, the agony of waking up to a shattered world, and the crushing weight of grief when she realized what had been taken from her. It was overwhelming to contemplate. I felt like I was at a crossroads. Should I pursue the story and uncover the truth buried beneath the wreckage of that night? Or should I stick to the safer piece, the one about Henry and our grief group, the one that wouldn't threaten to unravel lives? Two stories. Two paths. But only one I could present to Colin. I knew which one he'd prefer. But what would it cost? Whose pain would it amplify, and whose secrets would it expose? The more I dug, the more it felt like someone worked hard to bury the truth, and the harder it became to walk away from it.

I searched online for any detectives tied to the accident. One name kept appearing: Detective Bill Andrews. After digging through old articles, I learned he'd retired from the NYPD a year or so ago. I tried to call the department, hoping they'd have some contact information, but it was a dead end. Frustrated, I turned to social media. There wasn't much to go on—Detective Andrews didn't seem like the Facebook type—but to my surprise, I found an old profile under his name. It hadn't been updated in years, but there it was: a blurry photo of him holding a fish. Classic. A small detail made my stomach drop. His high school? Everston High. *Small damn world.*

As I stared at the screen, trying to figure out my next move, a familiar voice interrupted my thoughts.

"Wren eats her pancakes like that, you know," Rita said, sliding into the seat across from me, her gold bracelets jingling as she gestured toward my plate. "Isn't that funny?"

"Rita," I said, startled. "Can I help you?"

"Oh, I just wondered how your poem was coming along," she said, though I knew better. She had that glint in her eye she always did when fishing for gossip.

"I'm working on it," I replied vaguely, knowing she wouldn't leave without more.

"Well, I've been working on mine," she said, producing a piece of paper from her pocket and unfolding it on the table. The handwriting was unmistakably hers, a mix of endearing loops and squiggles.

"Do you want to hear it?"

I looked at her. "Sure," I said. "Let's have it."

She cleared her throat dramatically and began to read:

> *From grief something new can be born,*
> *A silver lining amid the ache and mourn.*
> *From the shattered pieces of broken dreams,*
> *Joy takes root, at first timid, unlikely it seems,*
> *Until blooming freely, unafraid to flow,*
> *Love finds its place and begins to grow.*

She stopped, looking at me expectantly.

"It's great," I said quickly.

"Does it stir any feelings within you?" she asked, leaning forward like a talk show host waiting for some sort of reveal.

I wasn't entirely sure what she meant by the question. I hesitated, picking at my pancakes. "I suppose I find it hopeful?"

Rita groaned, exasperated. "It's about you and Wren!" she said. "Finding new love even through grief."

I nearly choked on the pancakes. "What?"

"Oh yes," she grinned, clearly delighted by my reaction. "You two are my muses."

"Rita," I began, "I appreciate the sentiment, but Wren and I are . . ."

"Smitten," she interrupted. "We can all see it. And how lovely for Wren after everything she's been through. None of us really know her backstory, though, do we? Do you?"

I was trying to find out.

I kept my tone casual. "I prefer to know who she is now."

Rita waved a hand dismissively. "You could write a poem about her," she said thoughtfully. "That would make a nice follow-up to mine. I could even help you, if you want? I mean, we don't know how good a poet Wren is, do we?"

I bit back a laugh and decided to steer the conversation somewhere more useful. "You know, Rita, there is something you could do for me?"

She perked up instantly, learning forward enthusiastically.

"I'm looking for someone," I said. "A retired detective named Bill Andrews. He's originally from Everston and used to work for the NYPD. I think he might have gone to school here."

Her eyes lit up. "Ooh, I love a good mystery," she said, practically buzzing with excitement. "I know just the person to ask."

I grinned. "I thought you might."

Wren was hosing down the side of the house when I arrived. The tall, slender windows at the front of the house caught the fading golden light as it dipped below the mountain ranges. The lawn, once overgrown, was now neatly trimmed, the flower beds replanted, fences freshly painted, and the front porch restored. I was in awe of how she'd managed to restore the old house.

She noticed me as I walked closer and switched off the pressure washer, her face lighting up with a smile.

"I have a pie baking," she said, pulling a few stray hairs out of her face. "I fixed the oven, installed a new range vent, and the hot water is finally working. Can you believe the kitchen is actually functional now?"

"I can't believe the whole house is actually functional," I replied, stepping closer to kiss her softly.

Her smile widened as she held me for a moment. I leaned back slightly, digging into my pocket and placing a bracelet on her hand. "You left this on my nightstand," I smiled. "I'm surprised I noticed it actually, what with how worn out I was."

Wren bit her lip, the corners of her mouth tugging up despite herself. "Do you want some pie?" she asked quickly.

"I'd love some," I replied. Then, hesitating, I added, "Have you heard from Emerson?"

"No," she said, leading me up the porch steps to the front door. "She's not answering my calls or texts, but I called her mom, and she said Emerson's been at the hospital nearly every day and night."

Wren guided me into the kitchen. It was almost unrecognizable—new cupboards, freshly painted ceilings, modern appliances—but she'd kept the original wood, its weathered patina marked with age. She placed two plates on the counter, and carefully served slices of pie onto each.

"I googled you," I said, taking a bite.

Wren nearly dropped her fork. "Oh."

"I like your hair better now," I teased, grinning. "And the cozy sweaters and overalls."

She glanced down at her paint-smeared denim overalls, laughing. "Really? You didn't like the Armani or Chanel?"

I pulled her toward me, pressing a kiss to her neck. It didn't matter if she had been working on this house all day, all week, hours on end, she always smelled like lavender and rain, something so distinctly her.

"You're an extraordinary writer, Wren," I whispered. "I hope you never forget that."

She leaned in to me, brushing a strand of hair behind my ear. "I'm just not so sure that's where I belong anymore," she said softly, and the ache in her voice made my chest tighten.

"Well, maybe I can help with that," I said, my own excitement bubbling to the surface. "There's something I want to talk to you about."

She pulled back slightly, curious. "What is it?"

"I've been doing some research," I began. "About the accident. A journalist I know covered the story, and he gave me the details of the family of the young boy. I called them today."

Wrens face paled. "You did what?"

"They don't believe Lucy caused the accident," I said quickly. "The boy, Alec, remembers a silver car, not Lucy's green Jeep."

Her voice wavered as she set her plate down. "We should just leave things be," she said quietly. "That family has been through enough."

"So have you," I replied gently. "You said yourself that things didn't add up, that you didn't think Lucy was at fault."

She turned away, her shoulders tense. "I said I didn't think Lucy was drunk driving," she said. "I was reading my manuscript to her when it happened. It was my fault she crashed."

"Wren," I pleaded. "I don't think it was your fault. I really don't."

She picked up the pie plate and moved it toward me. "Have another piece, if you like," she said, shutting the conversation down. "I have laundry to hang."

Without another word, she left me standing in the kitchen, confused by her reaction. I glanced at the pile of bar coasters she had neatly stacked on the kitchen table, a frame sitting nearby. Wren had arranged them carefully, a collection of memories from Lucy's travels—Phoenix, Trenton, Boulder, Maine. Each one brought back for Wren upon Lucy's return. I knew they held so much meaning for her. Just because someone dies, it doesn't mean the love you have for them disappears. If I wanted Wren, I would always have to share a part of her with Lucy, and I was prepared to do that. Which is why I needed to clear Lucy's name. She couldn't speak for herself. She didn't have a voice anymore. But I did.

I had to find out the truth.

Chapter 19

Henry

Jacob had asked to be cremated. His final wish was to have his ashes spread over Stormy Peaks, one of Everston's most popular hiking trails, known for its challenging ascent and breathtaking views. I think he requested this just to see if I would actually do the hike. Well, I did. I drove out to the trailhead, the crunch of gravel beneath the tires echoing in the quiet stillness of the forest. I was terrified I would blow a tire before even reaching the parking lot. Jacob loved the smell of pine mingled with the crisp mountain air, said he could breathe better out here. He wasn't wrong. Stretched out before me were 7.3 miles, a winding trail ascending 4,000 feet into the sky. Seven hours passed in a blur of sweat and tears as I carried my brother's ashes up the mountain. When I finally reached the solitary peak that loomed over Everston with outstretched arms, I released his ashes into the wind and screamed, "I told you I could!"

The memory still lingers, but what haunted me more than the echo of my voice being swallowed by the mountains was the silence that followed. Jacob hadn't been there with his trademark grin to say, *I never doubted you.* Jacob always believed in me. Even when I doubted myself, he never wavered. And if he could trust me to climb that mountain, then surely, I could trust myself to pull off this poetry evening.

The event was definitely attracting attention. I'd like to think it was a testament to the solidarity in our town—and even the neighboring towns, for the urgent need for grief counseling groups. But if I was being honest, I'd also witnessed Rita standing at the library entrance accosting patrons with flyers, and Gill swore he convinced the entire retirement village to secure tickets with the promise of free chocolate bars. I had yet to check with Lillian if they would make the menu. Even so, Mayor Ashcroft was coming, and I'd managed to secure Max's clinic as a sponsor for the event, which felt fitting, considering it was really a community outreach program. And, as if guided by some unseen hand, an anonymous donation had miraculously appeared in the library return box, the one and only welcome item I'd found in there to date. If Jacob could see me now, he'd be grinning that same grin, clapping me on the shoulder, and saying, *See? I never doubted you.* But despite all the excitement and anticipation that swirled around our poetry evening, we were now faced with a shadow. Winnie was slipping away from us, and there wasn't anything anyone could do about it.

I'd known Winnie prior to her joining the grief group. She was a regular library patron. Each month, like clockwork, she would arrive in search of the latest books on birds; she was particularly fond of warblers and hummingbirds. Her visits were always accompanied by an abundance of bird facts, which she eagerly shared each time she wandered up to the front desk to greet me, along with all manner of stories from her travels around the world when she was younger. When her husband left, Winnie disappeared. I didn't see her for quite some time, and I missed looking up from the front desk to see her eccentric self walking in through the doors, a great big smile on her face. Eventually she returned by way of the grief group. Usually Emerson was with her, and together they would borrow books on birds, but also books of poetry. Knowing that Winnie wasn't going to walk through those library doors again was a painful reminder of life's comings and goings. Winnie had asked Wren and I to pack up some of her belongings at the house. She didn't have any family left, and had told me that there were things she wanted passed along to specific people. Of course, when I had to pack up Jacob's things, I'd wondered where they would go, what would become of them, and who would own them next.

"I donated most of Lucy's belongings," Wren said beside me. "But I kept her favorite sweater."

I turned to her. "Isn't it strange to think that someone else might have those things now . . . and to them it might just be a T-shirt or a vase or a book, but to us it was so much more."

"My father used to say that it was just a sweater," she replied, "but it still smelled like Lucy for so long afterward. It was more than a sweater; it was a way to remember her."

"Do you wish you'd never gotten rid of her things?" I asked.

"No," she replied after a moment. "Because they did just become things in the end."

"I still thought that holding on to all his stuff would keep him here, tie him to me somehow," I said, "but the more time has gone past, the more I have thought that perhaps that isn't how it works at all."

Wren sat down on the edge of Winnie's bed, picking at the brightly colored wool of the crochet blanket. "I tried to tie myself to Lucy too," she said. "I tried to keep her memory alive. I thought about her all the time; I would see her wherever I went, I felt her, dreamt of her, willed her back into existence so much that it blurred everything."

I stopped gathering items from the closet, and I moved to sit down on the edge of the bed next to Wren.

"But now I wake up every morning and instead I see Olivia," Wren continued. "And I feel so happy. But then I think of Lucy, and I can't picture her face as clearly, and it crushes me. I don't know how I can be so happy and still so sad at the same time. I don't know what to do with that."

"They say if you name things, they last longer, as if by holding that name upon your lips and speaking it into the world, they're still here, still alive. I said Jacob's name every night before I closed my eyes, but Jacob isn't here anymore. Neither is Lucy. But Olivia is."

She smiled softly. "I know she is," she replied.

I paused for a moment before adding, "You know, there are things I've told you about Jacob that I haven't even shared with Max. I don't know why, exactly. I just . . . trust you."

Wren was quiet for a moment.

"It's not easy for me to let people in," I continued. "I'm always the fixer, not the one who needs fixing. But honestly, Wren, you seem pretty good with power tools."

She laughed loudly—like a honk—and immediately covered her mouth, eyes crinkling. "Sometimes we meet people and things just click," she said, still smiling. "Maybe we've met in another life, if you believe in that sort of thing."

I wondered if all of us in the grief group had met in previous lives. As if on instinct, I picked up a necklace from the bedside table. "Winnie wore this all the time," I said, running my thumb over the bright orange and green beads. "She would strut into the library on a mission, and it always caught the fluorescent lights."

"You should keep it," Wren replied. "If it means something to you."

I sighed. "I am not so sure I can let that kind of hurt in again."

"Well, perhaps you aren't letting it in again," Wren said, standing and opening another cardboard box. "I think that grief stays with us. Lucy's death was not just one day," she continued, "it wasn't the day of the accident, or the day in the hospital when I woke up and found out she'd died. It was and has been every day since."

She folded a pair of jeans and placed them in a bag. "It wasn't just Lucy I mourned either. I mourned the life we were supposed to have, the dreams we were supposed to achieve. And her family." She added, "For so many years they were my family, too, but when she died, the devastation divided us, sent us all in different directions."

I stood again and opened the bedside table drawer; it was filled with postcards. Some dated sixty years ago. They were all scrawled in Winnie's handwriting, pictures from towns and cities far from Everston. I handed some to Wren.

"Perhaps there are some things we could keep?" I said.

She looked down at them. "Do you know what Winnie said to me, during those early days I came to the group?"

I shook my head.

"She hadn't said a word to me, and then suddenly she asked if I thought talking in circles with strangers made the dead any less dead."

I snorted, and nearly dropped the postcards I was holding. "That cheeky little—yes, well, that does sound like our Winnie."

"And then she invited me and Olivia over for chicken pot pie with Emerson."

"Trying to set you up?"

"I suppose," she replied. "Although I've never asked how she knew."

"She is rather perceptive," I responded.

"She stopped by the house not long ago," Wren said, a small smile tugging at her lips. "She was giving me advice on what color I should paint the window frames. She suggested this wild shade of turquoise, and then to add polka dots along the side wall."

I laughed. "Turquoise? Polka dots? That *really* sounds like Winnie. She's always loved bright things."

Wren chuckled softly, her gaze distant, as if picturing the house with the vivid color. She continued to pile things into the cardboard boxes. "I have a little update for you," she said, almost bashfully, not looking at my face.

She moved across the room to her tote bag, pulled out a notebook, and handed it to me.

I looked at the pages: there were at least fifty arranged poems. There was a loose sketch of two birds on the front cover. I was briefly lost for words.

"I mean—" I stammered, "I'm floored you've managed to write all of this already!" I looked at her. "You just came out with all this?!"

She shrugged. "Just some thoughts," she replied.

I had a feeling Wren was downplaying her so-called hobby, but I didn't press her.

"Just so you know, I've been holding up my end of the project too," I said. "I've been looking into the self-publishing thing, and I think I know how we can print a small number of copies on our own!"

"Amazing!" she said.

"I was thinking we could give a copy to everyone who comes to the poetry evening," she added.

I felt my face light up. "Oh, see, that's a good idea. The promise of a free book!"

"We're actually doing this, Henry! I'm excited," Wren said.

She smiled and resumed digging into Winnie's closet, pulling out a leather jacket.

"She really does have amazing taste," she said, running her hands over the sleeves.

I found a cashmere scarf and wrapped it around her neck, then forced her to try on some oversized sunglasses from the eighties, as well as a fedora.

Wren was laughing as we danced around the bedroom in Winnie's clothes. We filmed the fun to send to Winnie, knowing she would find it all rather humorous. Suddenly, my phone vibrated with a text from Emerson. It only said two words.

She's gone.

Chapter 20

Emerson

I wish I could say that once you've hit rock bottom, it's smooth sailing from there. Like, hey, you survived the worst, now kick back with a margarita and enjoy the rest of your life. But no, life isn't that easy. Winnie taught me that. And honestly if she hadn't, I'd be cursing the universe big time for handing me such a crappy set of cards. I was angry, you know? Imagine this: car wreck, major burns, a year of recovery, dumped, no college scholarship, and to top it off, losing a friend who helped me through said crap. Yeah, I was steaming mad. But here's the deal—life just keeps throwing stuff at you. It doesn't matter where you are from, who you are, or what you do; good things, bad things, they keep coming. Winnie's lesson? You grab all the good stuff, hold it close, and keep moving forward anyway. That's how you ride off into the sunset.

I stood in front of my mirror, scrutinizing the dress I'd put on. Dust and smudges marred the glass, distorting my reflection. The dress itself was a riot of different colors, the neckline daring enough for me to don a bright beaded necklace. It was all Winnie's idea. She insisted we match for the poetry evening, but now I realized she had another event in mind for me to wear this outfit to. "I know you don't feel like the brightest person in the room, Emmy," she had said. "But the brightest person *never* feels that way, and yet they stride on in anyway. That's what you do with these scars. You walk into the room, and you show them off."

I'd obviously argued, complaining she didn't understand, that she didn't have visible ugly scars like mine. She'd just shrugged and said she would be gone soon, and she wanted me to wear the damn dress anyway. We'd laughed about it then and cried about it too. That's the thing you think about when you lose someone: How many times *didn't* I answer their call? How many times *didn't* I go to lunch with them because I was busy doing something else? If you had a magic mirror that would tell you exactly when all the people you loved would leave you, would you live your life differently?

There was a soft knock at the door, and it opened with a nudge. Wren stood on the other side.

"Your mom let me in," she said softly, walking into the room.

"It's a bit of a mess," I said, gesturing to the piles of clothes.

Wren wasn't paying attention to the mounds of my wardrobe littering the floor, but rather she was looking at all my gymnastics medals and trophies.

"Bit of a waste," I said, nodding to them.

"Or," she replied, "your story could make a good book."

Wren finally took a good look at my dress. "Wow," she said. "I didn't realize there was a color theme for today."

"Winnie didn't want her funeral to be filled with doom and gloom, so she wanted me to wear this bright dress. Even though it shows these hideous scars; the pastor will probably douse me in holy water thinking some demonic monster has risen through his church floors."

Wren looked at me blankly, as though I'd spoken in a different language.

"But you know, working on the old self-esteem," I added, half laughing, half wanting to cry over how exposed this dress made me feel.

"You don't have to wear this, Emerson," she said.

"But I do," I said. "This was the dress I was going to wear to the poetry evening. Winnie picked it out."

"But if you're not comfortable, you can wear something else. Something that feels more like you."

"That's the thing, this is something I *would* wear. I just haven't since the accident. Everyone kept telling me to just be myself, to just show off my scars, that they made me beautiful! But Winnie was the first person who told me I was right, that I was allowed to be angry, that I *did* look different, that they *were* ugly, but that didn't mean *I* was."

I sucked in all the air around me and my lungs felt heavy. This was some otherworldly kind of sadness I was feeling—what the fuck was I going to do without Winnie? What was I going to do without my friend?

"She just left me," I said, as tears began stinging my eyes. "She left me, and I don't feel fucking beautiful, and I don't know who the fuck I am anymore."

Wren wrapped an arm around me, pulling me into a tight hug as I began to sob in earnest. "I don't really know who the fuck I am either," she replied softly.

Up until then, I'd never heard Wren cuss. She'd always been this quiet, mysterious person who blew into our group without saying much about herself. But she was just . . . here for me. The sound of footsteps drew my attention, and Olivia appeared in the doorway. Wren let go of me, and the two of them stood there, looking at each other for a moment. There was this weird tension in the air, like they wanted to say something to each other, but didn't know how.

I obviously cracked a joke. "Did one of you forget to pick up the urn?"

Nailed it.

Olivia blushed, and Wren's lips curved into the faintest smile.

"How are you?" Olivia asked, and Wren answered by kissing her a soft hello.

"As Winnie would say: the boat still finds its way."

"I never knew what that meant," I replied. "She always had these random sayings."

Wren turned to me and said, "The whole saying is: 'Though the river may be rough,'" she looked pointedly at Olivia, "'The boat still finds its way.' It means that even if life is difficult, we can still navigate through it."

"You're, like, really deep," I said.

She started picking up clothes from the floor and hanging them over my occasional chair. "It was my job to think very deeply about things once upon a time. Now I mostly just think about new paint and window trimmings."

I wanted to ask her what she meant by "once upon a time"—if it had to do with whatever she did in New York—but my mom called up the stairs, interrupting the moment.

"We best get going, Emmy!" she yelled.

I sighed, the familiar tightness in my chest returning. "Do we have to?"

"And be late for Winnie's party?" Olivia replied, raising an eyebrow. "Not worth the risk."

Both Wren and Olivia extended their hands at the same time. I took them, one in each of mine, letting them guide me down the stairs.

It was kind of like poetry, you know? Having words to hold on to was just as important as having people to hold on to. That's what the grief group had shown me, and what I'd discovered through having these people in my life. When it felt like I was drowning, someone extending a hand—giving me hope—was the thing that saved me.

As far as funerals go, I've only been to, like, two my whole life. The first was for Mom's great-uncle Ravi, and all I can recall is how insanely good the pie was. The second was for my neighbor

Katie, who was pretty young, and I just remember feeling super sad, because she'd always been really nice to me. But Winnie's funeral? Man, that was something else entirely. Even though we were saying goodbye, it felt like we were saying hello. The chapel was hushed, the scent of pine hanging in the air, birdsong drifting in through the open door. Winnie's picture at the altar was vibrant, decorated in dried flowers and winter greenery that Wren had carefully arranged from what remained in her garden. We had the wake at Wren's house, with the fire going, and we served chicken pot pie. It was cozy, and honestly . . . kind of nice. She would have been very impressed. When you're missing someone, time just gets all messed up. Whether it's been five minutes or a whole week, it feels like they've been gone forever. Everywhere I looked, it was like Winnie was there—our favorite books stacked on the shelf, photos of us plastered all over my mirror, even the birds outside reminded me of her. It was like she was everywhere and nowhere all at once, and nowhere more so than at our next group gathering.

Henry clapped to get everyone's attention, and I felt Wren jump beside me.

"I'm going to have to talk to him about his clapping," she muttered under her breath.

I smirked. "He's just very excited about the poetry evening," I replied.

"Catering and decorations are organized," Henry announced. "Olivia, you are still okay to do door tickets?"

Olivia nodded.

"And press?" he added, hopeful.

"Still working on that," she replied, although Henry seemed to approve of this.

"And I'm going to emcee the event," he said.

"What order is it going to go in?" Bobby asked. "Like, who is reading their poems and when?"

"Yes, I'd like to know this too," Julian replied. "Who's going first?"

"Should we draw it out of a hat?" Gill suggested.

Henry held up his hands. "One thing at a time," he said, before gesturing to Wren.

Wren cleared her throat. "Okay, so, the order for the poetry evening," she said, pulling a small notebook from her tote bag. "We've got Rita and Bobby starting with their joint poem. Then Julian, you'll do your letter. And Gill, you will follow him. Then Henry is going to read, Emerson . . ."

I let out a groan in response, but Wren pointedly ignored me. "Then Olivia and then me. And then finally we will do a group reading of Winnie's poem."

I felt my chest become heavier.

Wren looked up at everyone briefly, squinting and blinking.

"Do you need glasses, Wren?" Julian joked.

"No, no," she laughed nervously, "never needed glasses in my life."

Strange, I thought.

She put the paper away, and Henry took over the conversation with Max, wanting to check in on everyone after last week.

"I'm not sure what to write," I said quietly to Wren. "I can't think very far beyond a couple of minutes at the moment, let alone to the night I actually have to read it out."

"I'll help you," Wren reassured me.

"But what if I don't know what to write?"

She patted my arm. "You will."

I nodded, feeling a lump form in my throat at the mere thought of writing something about Winnie.

"We've got this, Emmy," Wren said. "It's going to be a wonderful evening."

The library entrance bell rang, and we all glanced in its

direction, surprised to see someone entering this late. A man suddenly emerged from the aisles, clutching a briefcase.

"Sorry to interrupt so late," he said, his voice apologetic. "I'm Anders. I'm from Wilks & Reynolds Attorneys. I am handling Ms. Langford's estate."

Henry rose from his seat, extending a handshake. "Henry Briggs," he introduced himself. "I'm the library director."

"Oh yes, quite right, Mr. Briggs," Anders replied. "Sorry for barging in like this, but I'm headed back to Denver tomorrow, and wanted to catch you all. This is one of the more unusual will readings I've had, but Ms. Langford's notes specifically mentioned reading the will at one of your Tuesday meetings."

I looked around and everyone wore puzzled looks on their faces.

"I have Ms. Langford's will," Anders explained. "I need to read it to you, as she has left some things for you all."

Everyone gathered around closer, exchanging curious glances. Anders opened the briefcase and withdrew a stack of papers. Clearing his throat, he began to read aloud the contents of the will. I mean, most of it in the beginning was legal mumbo jumbo, but then he unfolded a letter penned by Winnie herself and addressed us each individually. Our readers' corner was completely silent; all I could hear was my heartbeat thumping in my chest.

Winnie had instructed her house be left to the Everston community, specifically to be managed by Henry, as a poet's retreat. She had asked Wren to manage the garden. She'd left various items for everyone, each referencing something specific they had shared with Winnie.

"And," Anders said, fumbling in his bag before pulling out a small stack of papers, "just a bit of official business."

I knew exactly what they were.

"Change of ownership," he said, smiling gently. "The car's officially yours now, Emerson."

I pictured all the times I rode shotgun while Winnie hummed along to the radio or told me about weird dreams she had. It's cruel, really, how the most ordinary things become the moments you miss the most. You never think a random afternoon drive will be the last one.

"Oh, hold on, one last thing," Anders said, and he placed another bag on the table. He unzipped it and pulled out the contents. It was an urn, with a hummingbird etched into the side. He looked at me. "Never easy," he said, "but these are Ms. Langford's ashes. She has instructed in her will that they were to be given to you, Emerson. She said you would know what to do with them." He promptly handed me the urn, and I just stared blankly at it.

Winnie assumed I would know what to do with them?

"Thanks, Anders," Henry said, as Anders closed his briefcase. "Appreciate you coming so late." We were all quiet as he left.

I was still clutching the urn when Gill piped up. "You know, we should name our group in Winnie's honor," he said. "Something she would have liked."

Everyone thought for a moment.

"Misery Loves Company," I finally said.

Henry snorted, which made Gill and Rita laugh, and Bobby and Julian too. Wren grinned at me, and Olivia nodded an approval.

"Then it's settled," Max said. "A poetry evening with Misery Loves Company."

January

Chapter 21

Olivia

It snowed on and on in the days after Winnie's funeral. Not the heavy kind that traps you indoors, but the soft flakes that float down like they've got nowhere else to be. Wren and I were walking down Main Street, hands tucked into our pockets, when she suddenly stopped, turned to me, and grabbed my arm.

"Dance with me," she said, her voice excited and playful.

"Here?" I looked around. "In the street?"

"Yes," she nodded, already pulling me toward her. "I've never danced in the snow before."

So we did—under the string of holiday lights and decorations that adorned the lampposts and building facades. The sprinkle of snow clung to her hair, melted on my cheeks, and for a few perfect minutes, there was no pain, no past, no heaviness. Just the sound of our boots crunching on the pavement, and Wren's laugh as our cold noses brushed each other's as we swayed beneath the falling sky.

Then came the holidays.

Wren and I had spent Christmas at Aunt Nell's, surrounded by succulents and Riot's enthusiastic response to Wren's knowledge of all things Harley Davidson. The turkey was juicy, the potatoes golden, the gravy to die for, and the sugar cookies warm—we were still in a food coma by the time New Year's rolled around. Henry had insisted on a little celebration at the library. He strung up paper stars and tinsel in the reading corner and put out mulled apple cider and snickerdoodles. The group came—all of us. Even Emmy. No one really said it, but I think we all needed to feel like we had made it to the end of something. That we weren't alone when the clock hit midnight.

And then, somewhere in that gray stretch of January—the kind of unmemorable week that feels just like the last, I got the call. By some miracle, Riley Novak, the EMT who responded to the scene of Wren and Lucy's accident, hadn't forgotten about me. He mentioned he'd be heading to a nearby campground for a winter fly-fishing trip—something about the tailwaters keeping the river from freezing—and agreed to meet me there Wednesday morning. I walked into the café he'd chosen, scanning the room until I spotted him, a burly man with silvering hair and a weathered face, fiddling with a napkin.

"Riley?" I ventured.

He looked up. "Olivia," he echoed, nodding as he stood to shake my hand. "Nice to meet you. I was surprised by your voicemail, though. Didn't think anyone still cared about that case."

"I care," I replied. "Do you mind if I record this?"

"Go ahead," he said, gesturing for me to sit down.

I set my phone on the table between us and hit record. "So, you were working as a paramedic in July 2024?"

"Yep, I've been a New York paramedic for fifteen years now," he said, leaning back in his chair.

"Impressive," I replied.

He chuckled. "Got first responders all through my family—cops, firefighters. Me? I wanted paramedic work because I don't like guns or dalmatians."

The dad joke caught me off guard, and I gave a polite laugh.

"It had been a long day," he began. "My partner, Maria, and I had barely taken a break. We managed to pull into a McDonald's for a quick bite when we got radioed about a minor fender bender on the highway. We sped off with fry grease still on our hands. The patient there just needed a bandage for a sprained wrist."

He paused, shaking his head slightly, as though he was trying to shake off a bad memory. "We were heading back when the accident with Brooklyn and Lucy happened. It was sheer luck we were there at that moment."

I leaned in. "What did you see?"

His expression darkened. "The Jeep was stopped at the intersection. Then another car, speeding, slammed into it. The impact was brutal—sent the Jeep into an electrical pole. The other car didn't stop; it veered onto the sidewalk, mowed down a kid, a young boy. It was bad."

"Okay," I said, inhaling just about all the air around us. "And Maria, she witnessed it too?"

"No," he replied. "She was hunched over, trying to see if they'd added pickles to her burger. She saw the aftermath, not the impact itself."

"What happened next?"

"We jumped into action, of course. Radioed backup. Maria went to assist the boy, and I approached Lucy and Brooklyn's vehicle. It was severely mangled. Lucy was already deceased, and Brooklyn was barely conscious. We had to wait for the fire department to bring the Jaws of Life to remove her from the wreckage."

I felt a wave of nausea and ran my hands through my hair, trying to steady myself.

"Our training kicked in, and you do what you have to do, but oh boy, that accident site still gives me the shivers."

"Do you know who the other driver was?" I asked. "The one who actually caused the accident?"

Riley shook his head. "No. I never got close to him. The other paramedics on scene tended to him."

"Did you give a witness statement?"

"Yeah," he said with a short nod, his expression hardening. "But it never made it into the official reports."

I frowned. "What do you mean?"

He hesitated, lowering his voice. "The report I gave didn't match what the police were saying happened. When I followed up later, it was like my statement had disappeared. They were pushing a completely different version of events."

"Different how?" I pressed.

"They pinned the whole thing on Lucy, said she was drunk and caused the crash. But from what I saw, her car was stopped at the intersection when it was hit. I didn't see any evidence of reckless driving on her part." He folded his arms. "And, to corroborate, I tracked down Mrs. Lewis—the mother of the boy who was injured. Her version of events seemed awfully in line with mine."

"And you didn't push back on that?"

Riley's jaw tightened. "I'm a paramedic," he replied. "I'm not a detective, and I don't have any say in what the police put in their reports. But I knew something was off when they didn't call me back for a follow-up. It felt like they didn't want my version of events on record."

"Do you have proof?"

"You would need the original coroner's report," he said. "Not the sanitized version they gave the families. The truth is in there."

I reached out and turned off my phone's recording.

"Not sure how you'll get your hands on it, though, since they're sealed," he added, giving me a sideways glance. "Unless you know a guy."

I smiled. Oh, I knew a guy, all right.

"I need a favor," I said, sliding into a booth at Sam's three hours later.

"You always need favors," Trevor replied, taking a bite out of the burger in front of him. Ketchup and mustard were dripping onto his plate.

Trevor Mackerel (yes, like the fish): private investigator, three-time hot dog eating competition winner at Sam's Diner, and father of Hayley Mackerel, my high school girlfriend.

"This one's big," I said.

"They're always big with you," he said, tipping what must have been half the sugar pot into his coffee. "What's the job?"

"I need access to an original coroner's report," I said.

Trevor stopped mid-chew, his burger hovering in front of his face. "A coroner's report? For what?"

"A story," I replied, keeping my tone causal.

"You can't get it on public record?"

"No. It was sealed. I need the original report from the NYPD coroner. The one they didn't want anyone to see."

His brows lifted slightly. "And you think you're gonna blow the lid off some kind of cover-up?"

I nodded. "It's big, Trevor. *Really* big. The kind that changes lives. I think the police altered the report to cover up something, or to cover for someone."

Trevor set his burger down, wiping his hands with a napkin as he studied me. "Liv, you're poking the hornet's nest with this one. If there's a cover-up at that level, it means powerful people don't want the truth getting out. You sure you wanna go there?"

"That's exactly why I *need* to go there," I said. "Can you get it or not?"

He leaned back against the booth, his expression unreadable for a moment before a grin spread across his face. "'Course I can. Might take a day or two, though. These things don't exactly come gift-wrapped."

"Take your time," I said, though my chest burned with urgency.

Trevor stirred his overly sweet coffee, a sly smile playing on his lips. "Hey, by the way, you ever thought about getting back together with Hayley?"

I rolled my eyes. "Sorry, Trev. I'm sort of attached these days."

He sighed dramatically. "I don't particularly enjoy her current partner," he muttered.

"You didn't particularly enjoy me either," I said, stealing a fry from his plate.

He grinned again. "Touché." He tipped his coffee mug toward me. "I'll let you know when I've got it."

Three days later, Trevor came through with the report. He handed it to me as I filled up gas at the station. "We're square," he whispered, sliding the envelope under my arm and disappearing as quickly as he'd arrived. I scrambled to force the nozzle back in place, fumbling into my car and ripping open the envelope. Inside was Lucy's original death certificate. I scanned it, plucking the relevant lines from the document and burning them into my memory.

IMMEDIATE CAUSE OF DEATH: (A) Blunt Force Trauma

DUE TO: Vehicle collision

MANNER OF DEATH: Reckless driving

PLACE OF INJURY: Intersection of Broadway and Houston Street, New York

DESCRIBE HOW INJURY OCCURRED: The deceased was injured when another vehicle, traveling at excessive speed, struck their car while it was stopped at an intersection.

The impact forced the deceased's vehicle into an electrical pole, resulting in fatal injuries.

TOXICOLOGY REPORT: Toxicology results were negative for alcohol, drugs or any other intoxicants.

As I read through the coroner's report, the pieces began to fall into place. The police hadn't just twisted the narrative, they'd buried the truth entirely. By sealing the original coroner's findings and witness statements, like the EMT's, from public record, they created a reality they could control. There was no way for the press, or anyone, to independently verify what really happened. It was diabolically simple. With no accessible documents to challenge their version of events, the NYPD could feed the media whatever story they wanted. Lucy wasn't just blamed, she was framed. But why?

My hands trembled as I tucked the papers back into the envelope. My mind raced with a thousand possibilities, but one thing was clear—Lucy was innocent.

When I arrived at the library later that afternoon to drop off paper plates and cups for the poetry evening, Rita caught me off guard. She approached, waving a piece of paper like it was a winning lottery ticket.

"I got it!" she beamed, bouncing on the balls of her feet. "The number you were after."

"You did?" I replied excitedly, reaching for the paper.

"You know, Livvy," she said, holding on to the paper a moment longer, "I knew the name sounded familiar. Billy Andrews! He dated my sister in high school. Of course, I was younger, so they always shooed me away, but I remember him. He proposed to her once, you know, but she turned him down.

Broke his poor heart. I guess he became the big-shot detective he wanted to be."

Or a fraud, I thought to myself.

"Oh, they were high school sweethearts," Rita continued, her voice filled with nostalgia. "I think Billy might have been the one that got away. He wanted to go off to the police academy in New York, and she wanted to stay here in Everston. So she turned him down. But I think they always held a torch for each other. They used to sing that song by The Beach Boys—what was it?" She paused, her eyes lighting up as she recalled. "'God Only Knows'! That's it. Anyway, they would sing it all the time to each other, and she still sings it nearly every day, even with her mind like it is."

"Well, they say it's usually the long-term memory that remains the strongest," I said, trying to absorb the avalanche of information.

Rita nodded, a satisfied smile on her face. "As soon as I placed his name—I mean, he always went by 'Billy,' but I suppose 'Bill' is more professional—I immediately got in touch with Darla, his cousin who still lives in town. I see her every Wednesday at the nail salon."

I managed to nod along.

"So, I spoke to Darla, and—" Rita hesitated for a moment, looking sheepish, "Well, I told her a little white lie and said that Martha had remembered Billy the other day when I was visiting her at the nursing home. Wouldn't it be so lovely if she could speak with him again? And Darla gave me his number! She said he still lives in New York, but retired from the force . . . oh, about a year or so ago now."

I frowned, trying to comprehend the significance of this information.

"Anyway," Rita said, her face flushed, looking thrilled to pieces, "you tell Billy that Rita Carmichael says hello."

I stared at the paper in my hand, unable to shake the feeling that this couldn't just be coincidence. My mother had always insisted there was no such thing as fate. "It's all chaos," she'd say. "People connect dots where there aren't any." But I had argued with her, young and hopeful, believing that the world had an unseen magic, a design we couldn't always understand.

Standing there with Rita rambling on about high school sweethearts and nail salons, I couldn't help but think about the odds of Wren landing in Everston, a town where Billy Andrews, the detective in charge of investigating her accident, had dated the sister of a woman who was part of the very grief group Wren joined to help her heal. It felt like too much to be random. How could I explain this strange convergence of events? Wren, this town, our grief group, we'd all found our way to each other.

Maybe it was for something we didn't yet understand. Either way, I had a direct line to Billy, and it was time to reel him in.

Back in the office, I settled behind my desk, pretending to be engrossed in paperwork to avoid drawing Colin's attention. The number Rita had given me was tucked into my notepad. With a deep breath, I dialed, my heart thudding in anticipation.

"Bill Andrews," came the gruff, slightly hoarse voice on the other end.

"Hi, Detective Andrews. My name is Olivia Piroso. I'm a reporter with High Country Broadcasting in Colorado," I said, trying to keep my tone steady.

"I'm retired," he interrupted sharply.

"I understand," I replied quickly. "However, I'm working on a story about a car accident that occurred in late 2024, at Broadway and Houston Street in New York?"

There was a beat of silence. "I worked a lot of traffic accidents," he said curtly. "Email the department if you want details."

I pushed forward. "This accident was widely covered in the media. It involved author Brooklyn Paisley, a young boy named Alec Lewis, and an unidentified third person—John Doe in the media reports. It says here you worked the case."

"How did you get my number?"

"Rita Carmichael. She's a dear friend," I said.

There was a long pause. "Rita?" he asked, his voice softening slightly. "How is she?"

His question surprised me, throwing me off track momentarily.

"She's fine," I said. "She mentioned you dated her sister Martha in high school."

"Martha," he murmured, and I knew I'd struck a chord.

"She's in a nursing home now, unfortunately," I continued, evenly. "She has dementia, but Rita says she still sings 'God Only Knows' nearly every day."

The line was quiet for a moment before he sighed. "What do you want, Ms. Piroso?"

"The truth," I said plainly. "The media reports say that Lucy Halloran, Brooklyn Paisley's fiancée, was intoxicated and lost control of her vehicle. But the toxicology report says otherwise. Lucy wasn't drunk, and the original coroner's report confirms that."

"How did you get access to that report?" he asked, his tone tightening again. "It was sealed."

"So it was sealed on purpose, then?" I said, ignoring his question. "Why? Why wasn't the real cause of the accident ever made public?"

"The Brooklyn woman was famous. She asked for the reports to be sealed. We couldn't control what the media reported."

I scoffed. "You don't expect me to believe that."

"It was an open-and-shut case," he replied. "John Doe's vehicle hit Ms. Halloran and she crashed into the boy, sad story all around."

"With all due respect, Mr. Andrews, the media reports said Lucy's car hit John Doe's car and then the boy."

"Yes, well, it's been years—"

"It's been less than two years, Mr. Andrews, not long enough for your memory to be that bad." I tried to contain my anger, but it wasn't working. "Can you really live with yourself knowing that the real victims are still suffering, and that a dead woman has been blamed for something she didn't do?"

There was another long pause before he spoke, his voice low. "We knew who the offending driver was. He wasn't a John Doe. His name was Mark Lerwick, an off-duty officer and the son of Deputy Police Commissioner Daniel Lerwick. He was drunk."

I gripped the phone tighter. "So why wasn't that reported?"

"You don't know the kind of pressure we faced in the department," Andrews said. "The commissioner was up for reelection. Mark had a history of reckless behavior, and this would have ended his career, and his father's—"

"So, you let an innocent woman take the fall?" I asked, incredulous.

He let out a heavy sigh. "I was six months from retirement. They threatened my pension, my reputation, everything I'd worked for. It was either go along with it or lose it all."

I pressed a hand to my forehead, trying to process his words. "You do realize the consequences of what you allowed, don't you? Lucy's name was dragged through the mud. Brooklyn has been living with the lie that her fiancée caused the accident and hurt a small child. Alec Lewis is paralyzed, and his family still doesn't know the truth."

"You think I don't know that?" Andrews snapped, his voice cracking slightly. "I've lived with that guilt every day since. And for what? Mark Lerwick ran a stoplight three months ago and hit a cyclist. He's in jail now. The commissioner? He resigned."

I squeezed the bridge of my nose.

"What would you have done in my position?" he continued, his tone bitter. "Imagine dedicating your entire life to something, only to have it taken from you at the very end."

I thought about the anchor job. I didn't have an answer for him.

"You didn't get all this from me," he said abruptly, his voice hollow. The line went dead before I could respond.

I sat back in my chair. My head felt heavy, and my ears were ringing. I stared at the phone, letting the weight of the conversation sink in. I ached for Lucy, for Wren, for Alec Lewis. All innocent people, their lives completely upended, and they didn't even know the full truth.

As I struggled to make sense of it all, Josh appeared at my desk, startling me with a paper bag in hand.

"Panini," he said simply, dropping it front of me.

"Thanks," I muttered, unwrapping it absently. "Did you add olives?"

"You bet," he replied.

I bit into it, the first thing I'd had all day other than some Mentos and a coffee.

"You've been at it for hours on end," he said, leaning against the desk.

I moved my screen slightly from Josh's line of vision, but he only peered around it. I shut my laptop more forcefully than I intended and he scowled at me.

"You've got a story, don't you?" he pressed. "You're going for the anchor job?"

"I don't know," I replied. "Maybe I don't want it. Cassie can have it."

Josh snorted. "You really think Cassie would make a better anchor than you?"

I shrugged. "She seems to think so."

"That's because she's delusional," he replied. "Tell me what the story is!"

I took another bite of the panini and muffled something completely inaudible through a mouthful of bread, meat, and olives.

"Fine," Josh said. "Have it your way, but keep writing it, Liv! This could be your comeback story."

It wasn't a question of whether or not I *could* continue writing the story—I had enough details, reports, and sources to blow it right open. The words would come easily enough, but it wasn't the story that was hard to make sense of. It was what I felt for Wren. For years, I had lived in the clarity of deadlines and headlines, turning chaos into order with a byline. But meeting her had unraveled something in me, something raw and unguarded. She made me feel in a way I hadn't let myself in a long time. I cared for her deeply, maybe even in ways I wasn't ready to admit. I cared for the grief group too; our lives had all been woven together in the fragile hope of something new. This wasn't just about ambition, or about the anchor role and proving I had what it takes. And yet, I couldn't ignore that I was my mother's daughter, shaped by her relentless drive, her belief that success was the only proof of worth. I wrestled with that truth, with the part of me that still longed for her approval, even now that she was gone. But there was another part of me, whispering that sometimes the world needs more than ambition. Sometimes, it needs heart.

That afternoon, I knocked on Wren's front door. When it eased open on its own, I stepped inside, calling out as I did. The house smelled faintly of something warm—cinnamon maybe? I found her in the back bedroom, a mess of paint cans and plastic sheets strewn across the floor. Bob Dylan played softly from her phone, his voice filling the otherwise quiet space. A small bundle of roses sat haphazardly on the windowsill, a card poking out from the leaves.

"Do you need help?" I asked, as I stood in the doorway.

She nearly knocked a paint can over in surprise but brightened when she saw me. "I didn't hear you come in." She smiled. "But yes, I could use the help. I seem to be able to wield a pen, but not a paintbrush."

I laughed and stepped inside to reach for a spare brush, but then paused in front of her instead. "Just one thing first," I said, pulling her toward me. I kissed her soundly, with a need that felt like it had been building for weeks. I felt the breath leave her body.

"What was that for?" she asked, flushing, as we pulled apart.

"I just needed it," I replied, picking up the paintbrush and twirling it around my fingers. "This is the wall you're working on?"

She nodded and handed me a paint tray. She hummed as she went back to painting, and I couldn't help but think how adorable she was. I dipped my brush in the emerald green paint and tried desperately to focus on the task, but I was distracted by everything I had learned. The injustice of it all—the lies, the false reports, the smear campaign against Lucy—was almost too much. Losing Lucy was already an unbearable grief for Wren, but to have her memory tarnished and the truth buried? It was unforgivable. There had to be some sort of justice. For Lucy. For Wren.

"Earth to Liv?" Wren's voice broke through my thoughts. I realized I had stopped painting, the brush hanging limply in my hand. She was standing next to me, her hand resting gently on my waist, her expression concerned.

"Sorry," I said, setting the brush down. "I got lost there for a minute."

"Where did you go?"

I sighed, running a hand through my hair. "I have to tell you something," I said, turning to face her.

Wren looked at me curiously. "You don't like the color I've chosen?"

I glanced at the deep-emerald paint on the wall and gave a small smile. "No, I like it. It's not about that . . . It's about Lucy."

Her smile faded, and she straightened, confused. "Okay . . ."

"I met with the EMT," I said, the words coming out quickly. "One of the first responders at the accident."

Wren's breath hitched. "You did?"

"Yes," I replied. "And he confirmed some things I've been looking into." I took a deep breath. "The accident was not Lucy's fault," I said, firmly. "The third party involved—the John Doe—he was an off-duty police officer, Mark Lerwick, also coincidentally the son of Deputy Police Commissioner Daniel Lerwick. He was drunk driving that night. He hit your car, sent it into the pole, then skidded and hit Alec Lewis on the curb. The police covered it up."

Wren's face froze, as though she couldn't quite process the information.

"And it gets worse," I continued. "Mark Lerwick also had a number of other incidents on his rap sheet—multiple DUI's, repeated racial profiling, accusations of excessive force, and even complaints of harassment. All swept under the rug because of who his father was. They needed to find a scapegoat, and they chose Lucy. They sealed the reports from public record, and they fed the media a false story."

"And you have proof of all this?"

"Yes," I said, "I do. And I'll write the story, Wren. I'll get justice for Lucy, for Alec, and for you. I mean sure, perhaps I'm about to take on the NYPD, but who cares? I mean, this is a full-blown cover-up, Wren. Someone *has* to be held accountable."

"You can't," Wren said suddenly, her voice sharp. "You can't take on the NYPD, Olivia. That's just not going to happen." She stood abruptly, pacing a few steps across the room. Her hands were shaking, her movements tight, almost frantic. "I don't want that," she continued, her words tumbling over each other. "I can't have the press know where I am. I've worked so hard to rebuild my life again."

"Under a different name, though," I replied, exasperated. "You could be you again, you could write again, and you can tell your story! We can get the truth out there."

Wren crossed her arms tightly, her eyes clouded with fear.

"You said you liked the name Wren," she whispered.

My heart felt like it was about to fall out of my chest. "I do," I replied. "Of course I like the name Wren."

"Why didn't you talk to me about this first?" she asked, the words quieter but no less charged. "This isn't just some old story. It's my life."

"I know," I replied gently. "I'm sorry, I just want to do what's best for you."

She moved into my arms, holding me close to her. "This is what's best, Liv," she whispered against my neck. "A new life. Here, in Everston, with you, where nothing can hurt us."

I held her tighter, knowing she needed this moment. Knowing, perhaps, that I needed it too.

February

Chapter 22

Henry

For a long time after my brother's death, I could still see him. Sometimes he was standing in the doorway, other times it was as though he had passed me by in the street, or I'd catch glimpses of him between the aisles of the library. It felt like he was somehow visiting me, like a ghost, if you believe in those sorts of things. I wasn't sure why, but one day I stopped seeing him. It was as though he had died all over again.

Last night I dreamed of Winnie. We were all together. I was standing in her kitchen helping her make her famous chicken pot pie. Emerson sat at the dining table, deep in a board game with Wren and Olivia, their laughter carrying through the room. Gill and Julian were wrapped in conversation with Bobby, their voices blending into the background, while Max and Rita were giggling over something indistinguishable. It was simple—celebrating the new year, wrapped in the kind of comfort that comes from knowing you belong.

But now, there would be no more chicken pot pie, not the way she made it. No more evenings with her, no more of her wry humor, her knowing glances, her way of making everything feel electric and steady at the same time. We would never be together again. And that's what grief is, isn't it? It's missing everything about a person in a way that hurts the most.

"Are you okay?"

I blinked at the screen I had been staring at and looked at Wren.

"Yes," I said, shaking my head slightly. "Sorry, I was just lost for a moment."

"I'm sorry," she replied. "I don't know why I am so excited about brass doorknobs, they're probably the most boring thing on Earth to you."

I patted her shoulder. "I am thrilled you've found the original brass doorknobs for the house. Truly." I grinned, and then it faded. "I was just thinking about Winnie."

Wren's shoulders slumped slightly. "I know," she replied. "I think about her too."

I glanced back at the book file on screen, the final version of *Thinking of You*, ready to be uploaded. We'd managed to collect everyone's poems early, without too many questions. Rita, of course, had peppered me with suspicions about the sudden deadline, and I'd sheepishly told her it was to get everything cleared by the library board.

"I feel guilty you're helping me with this," Wren said. "You're at work, after all."

I scanned the nearly empty library. "Do you see any patrons begging for my expertise right now?"

She looked around, then shook her head. "Well . . . no."

"Then let's just get this book uploaded and ordered," I said. "This is going to be a nice surprise for the group."

"Thank you for looking at this," Wren said. "I honestly feel a little guilty for not helping more with all the admin."

I raised an eyebrow. "Wren, I'm a librarian. Admin is literally my job. Besides, you were putting together a *whole book*. Perhaps a new career path for you?"

A nervous smile tugged at her mouth, but as we finalized the upload, something shifted in her expression. She had done everything herself—it was formatted, structured, polished. All I'd done was offer a few thoughts and figure out how to print the thing. And honestly? She'd barely needed my help.

"Seriously, Wren, you're good at this," I said, watching the progress bar load. "I'm impressed you knew how to do it all, and I'm even more impressed with your writing."

She hesitated, fiddling with the sleeve of her sweater. "Maybe it's what I did . . . in another life."

Something about her tone made me pause. Wren was sharp and quick, but the moment anything related to publishing or writing came up, she went quiet. Distant. I didn't know why, but I knew better than to press. If you pressed Wren, she may very well disappear. I turned back to the screen to look at the cover art. I'd contacted Merrill, a local artist, to create an illustration for the book cover, a raven and a bluebird together, as envisioned by Wren.

"I love this drawing," Wren said softly.

"Me too," I replied. "I've liked helping with this project, you know, even if only a little."

"You're a natural. Maybe you should work in book publishing?"

I smiled. "Jacob always thought that I'd make a good editor," I admitted, leaning back slightly. "I always wanted to be a librarian, but editing would've been a great job too."

"Why can't you be both?"

I waved my hand. "I can't say I know too many authors, much less any who would need my editing services," I replied.

That was the moment she pulled away again. It was like she was physically still in the room, but her mind was elsewhere, somewhere she didn't want to go.

"Done," I said. "Now we wait."

She let out a slow breath, as if letting go of something heavier than just the book.

"Now we wait," she echoed.

A moment of silence settled between us before Wren finally

spoke again. "I'm doing the right thing, aren't I? This book, it was meant as a gift, but I'm not sure how it will be received."

"I think it's special," I replied. "And more than that, Wren, I know it meant something to you to write it. That matters, too, doesn't it?"

She studied me for a moment, like there was something she wanted to say but couldn't seem to find the words to say it.

"You know, Max used to say to me, 'Other people's grief doesn't belong to me,'" I said.

"Max is very wise." Wren grinned.

"He is," I replied. "But I think it can be both. Other people's grief doesn't belong to us, but maybe it helps us to find belonging in each other."

Suddenly, the library door opened and my wiry sculptor friend strolled in. I sunk so low in my chair, I nearly slid right off. Next to me, Wren immediately ducked down with a look of pure confusion.

"What is it?" she whispered, her voice a flurry of urgency.

"The sculptor," I hissed, nodding toward the growing collection of his "art" cluttering the front desk.

Wren peeked over the desk, eyes scanning the ever-growing lineup—FrankenFrog, of course, plus an owl wearing a tiny wizard hat, and a cat with an impressively coifed mustache.

"Oh dear," she murmured, her shoulders shaking with suppressed laughter.

"Shhh!" I shot her a desperate look. But it was too late.

"Ah, Henry!" The sculptor—whose name I'd only recently learned was Otis—strode toward the counter with his latest masterpiece: a lumpy teapot with feet.

"Thought I'd bring you something special. What do you say, waive a few more of those late fees?"

Wren and I exchanged a long, pointed look—her eyes sparkling with amusement, mine filled with suffering.

"You know," Wren said, smiling. "This might be the best one yet."

Otis puffed out his chest, beaming.

And for a moment, everything felt a little lighter.

I was elbow-deep in coffee machine parts, battling a clogged filter and wondering why caffeine held such power over humanity (especially where there was literally a café across the road), when I heard my name.

"Henry!"

I turned to see Olivia standing in the doorway, breathless, her cheeks flushed from what I guessed was a brisk walk, or a maybe a quick sprint.

"I found you," she said, as if she'd been searching the entire town.

"Well, where else would I be?" I replied, straightening up and wiping my hands on a towel. "What's wrong?"

"Nothing," she said quickly, then added, "Well, not *nothing*. But not urgent either. I need your advice."

She was worked up more than usual, and her tone carried a kind of nervous energy.

"I need help to make a choice," she continued, stepping into the room. "And considering it's your fault I even joined this grief group in the first place, I'm making you the one to do it."

I stared at her, baffled. "Olivia, what in all of the San Juan Mountains are you talking about?"

I'd never said that phrase in my life. It wasn't even a real phrase. Clearly, I was spending too much time around emotionally charged middle schoolers and broken appliances.

"My redemption arc," she said with an exaggerated sigh, and then—ignoring all protocol—she plopped herself down on one of the staff room chairs. I glanced nervously at the door. If Lana or Dev walked in and saw Olivia commandeering our little break room, I'd never hear the end of it. She slapped two hefty binders on the table in front of her, their spines labeled in bold black marker.

"What are these?" I asked, wiping coffee bean residue off my hands. I really hated the stuff.

"Two stories," she replied, her voice quieter now. "One is a story that could get me the anchor job at the station. The other . . . well, the other is a puff piece. But it's mine. I love it."

I sat down across from her, reaching for the first binder. She swatted my hand away with a glare.

"I have to choose," she said firmly.

"Well, that's easy. Choose the one that gets you the job," I said, as if the answer were obvious.

Her face fell, as though she was devastated at my suggestion.

"Why wouldn't you?" I asked, genuinely confused. "Are you okay?"

She sighed, leaning back in the chair, her hands falling to her lap. "No," she said softly, almost like she didn't mean for me to hear. "I think I'm falling in love."

I blinked, utterly lost. "I see . . ."

"The first story," she continued, her voice gaining strength, "could hurt someone I've come to care deeply about. The second story . . . it's about the grief group. It's about how it has changed my life."

I stared at her and, for a moment, the noise of the coffee machine and the chaos of the library faded into the background. Here was Olivia, this ambitious reporter—steadfast and strong—but she hadn't started out that way, not here. When she first came to the grief group, she showed up sporadically, always late, lingering near the edges like she wasn't sure she wanted to stay. She rarely spoke, and when she did, her words were guarded, unsure if she was ready to share. It had taken her a long time to open up, to let us in. But now . . . now she was someone who leaned in to the vulnerability, who showed up every week, on time, ready to listen and be heard. She loved everyone in the group in the way only someone who'd lived through pain could. And Olivia had known pain. I'd heard enough of her stories about her mother to know that life hadn't always been kind to her. But here she was, flourishing. Stronger. Braver. And she was saying, out loud, that the group had been a part of that. I felt something swell in my chest—pride, warmth, maybe even gratitude for her honesty.

"Well," I said carefully, "sometimes people get hurt in life."

"Oh, not like this," she murmured.

"You've worked so hard for your career, Olivia," I continued. "You've wanted to be the anchor at HCB for so long. I know how much it means to you."

She sighed, her eyes clouding with uncertainty. "It does mean a lot," she admitted. "All I ever wanted was to be out of my mother's shadow. But the group means a lot too."

I hesitated, my voice softening. "Which one are you going to choose?"

She reached across the table and placed her hand over mine. Her touch was steady, her gaze earnest.

"You really are remarkable, Henry," she said, her lips curving into a soft smile. "I hope the world knows that someday."

"I'm just trying to help," I replied, though the words felt inadequate.

"And you do," she said. "More than you know."

For a moment, it looked like she might say more, but instead she pulled her hand back, stood up, and gathered the binders into her arms.

"Sometimes," she said, pausing in the doorway, "it's not about choosing the right story. It's about figuring out who you are in the middle of it."

I opened my mouth to reply, but she didn't wait for an answer. And with that, she was gone, leaving me sitting there, unsure which story she meant or what decision she'd made.

March

Chapter 23

Wren

Everston had eased into the quiet rhythms of early spring—morning runs through trails edged with snow, sleepy weekends tangled in blankets with Olivia, biweekly Tuesdays with the grief group, Henry insisting peppermint hot chocolate be added to the usual tea and snacks, and countless pancakes shared at Sam's Diner. In seven months, I had torn down walls in the old house, just like I had dismantled parts of myself. I had replanted the garden, and in doing so rediscovered myself. I had repainted rooms, and in the same way I had become someone new. In those seven months, I had gone from being hell-bent on running from my pain to slowly letting it in, because it was the only way I was ever going to begin to understand it. Grief, as it happened, was not a linear thing; it didn't follow a clear line from start to finish, rather it pivoted and curved like a winding road through the mountains. Sometimes it was a calm journey, other times not, but I found my way through it.

That particular afternoon, I opened my front door to find Henry standing on the porch. Just behind him, the rest of the group had gathered—Emerson holding a bouquet of dahlias (my favorite); Rita balancing a basket of still-warm cinnamon rolls; Gill, Julian, and Max each carrying colorful gift bags in varying states of crumple; and Bobby holding a very large *Happy Birthday* balloon that wobbled in the breeze.

"Happy birthday!" they called out, more or less in unison.

Emerson sighed audibly. "We practiced that," she muttered. "Evidently not enough."

I laughed as she breezed past me, heading straight for the kitchen where Olivia was overseeing the lemon and herb roasted chicken we'd been preparing together. I'd made my homemade pesto to drizzle over the warm potato and green bean salad, much to Olivia's delight. I stepped aside to let the others in. The entryway had become one of my favorite spaces in the house—a tall ceiling crowned with pressed tin, now freshly painted in soft cream. The old hardwood floors gleamed, and I'd lined the hallway with vintage frames I'd found in the antique shop up near Norvale. Where once there had been peeling wallpaper and water stains, now there was warmth.

Henry hugged me tightly. "Happy birthday, Wren," he said. "We love an Aries."

"One with excellent taste," Bobby added, glancing around approvingly. "This front entrance? Immac."

I greeted each of them with a hug, and the house filled with chatter and laughter as they filed inside.

Gill hovered behind, marveling at the changes. "I barely recognize the place!" he said. "I didn't know if you had it in you, but boy I have never been so happy to be wrong."

"I have something for you," I said, and Gill's eyes brightened. "It's not chocolate, I'm afraid," I added, but he chuckled.

"I think Henry has you covered in that department; the boy always brings me chocolate."

"That he does," I agreed. "What I have for you is in the library."

I led Gill through the front hall, and into the parlor I had converted into a library. I'd spent six weeks constructing the shelving and then filled it with the books Gill had stacked from floor to ceiling in the basement. Henry had also contributed nearly an entire row of books himself. I moved to the window, gently drawing back the curtains. Behind them, I'd had a custom stained-glass window put in, with the colorful outline of two opossums embracing each other.

Gills eyes went misty. "Oh, Wren," he whispered. "This is just . . . Edith would love this."

"I thought she might," I said softly. We stood there for a quiet moment, Gill staring up at the window, a small smile of wonder on his face.

"Thank you for letting me stay, Gill. I was so lost when I arrived here—broken, really. But I found Sam's Diner, and I found you. And this house gave me the space to begin again. You welcomed me when I didn't feel welcome anywhere. And you led me to Henry's grief group, too, which has helped me more than I could ever explain."

Gill's eyes softened. "You brought life back into this house, Wren. Into all of us, I think."

He cleared his throat, blinking back emotion. "Now, come on," he said. "I can smell whatever delicious thing you and Olivia have been roasting."

We walked back through the hall toward the kitchen, the smell of rosemary and lemon wafting through the house. The kitchen opened up just past the archway, with tall windows that overlooked the garden and let in the last of the fading afternoon light. I'd kept all the original floorboards, the wide molding, and the antique ceiling rose, but I'd updated the broken kitchen cabinets with pale sage cupboards, those brass handles I'd found, and open shelves lined with dishes and jars of dried herbs. Everyone had gathered around the reclaimed farmhouse table, set with mismatched plates, linen napkins, and jam jars holding handpicked wildflowers. Olivia was bent over the oven, carefully lifting the roasted chicken from its tray, the golden skin crackling as it hit the cutting board. A flush had crept into her cheeks from the heat, a wisp of hair falling loose at her temple. I'd grown to love the way she moved so easily through my kitchen now; after countless nights cooking together, after learning my pesto sauce, after rolling pasta dough across the counter while we laughed and danced to music. I stepped beside her, unable to help myself.

"You okay?" I asked, brushing her hair behind her ear.

"I'm perfect," she replied, smiling without looking up. "I happen to have graduated from my Easy-Bake Oven days." I leaned in, pressed my lips to the corner of her mouth, and listened to her sigh in response. "Go and sit," she murmured, her eyes filled with affection. "Emerson and I will start serving."

As I sat down at the table, I thought of Lucy. She would've approved of this birthday party. And the thought of her didn't make me sad. It made me happy. I felt like I'd finally arrived at the next chapter, the one where the heaviness had begun to lift. The house was no longer just a project or a distraction, it was a home. The garden was beginning to bloom again, and so was I. Some of my favorite people were here, the kitchen smelled of rosemary and cinnamon, and there was a birthday cake cooling on the counter. The poetry evening was just a couple of weeks away, and we were all looking forward to it. When I was finalizing the book, I had decided that the final poem in *Thinking of You* should be Winnie's poem. She had taught us that a heart could be both broken and full at once, and that was the most human lesson of them all. That night, I had decided to gift everyone their copy. There was a time I thought I might never write again—that poetry had left me along with everything else—but, it turns out, the things we love the most have a way of coming back to us.

"There you are," I said, stepping onto the porch. Olivia sat on the swing, legs tucked beneath her, a glass of red wine in one hand and a half-eaten slice of birthday cake balanced on a napkin in the other. She wore a soft cotton dress that slipped slightly off one shoulder, and from where I stood, I could see the edge of her lavender tattoo peeking out, inked just below her collarbone. A delicate trail of purple buds, the stems curling like they were still growing. I thought of how many times I had traced it with my fingers, learning its shape, understanding what it meant to feel steady with someone again.

I sat beside her, draping a blanket across our legs, letting the swing rock gently beneath us.

"Did you see Emerson's face when I gave her a copy of the book?" I smiled.

Olivia grinned and took a sip of wine. "Honestly, I never thought I'd see the day Emerson Coleman was rendered speechless."

"I hope she likes it," I said. "I hope they all do."

"They will," Olivia said, with the kind of quiet certainty I hadn't heard in a long time, the kind I used to hear when I read my poems aloud to Lucy. The kind that made me believe I could do and write anything. "You are the most thoughtful person I know."

I leaned toward her, and she pressed a kiss to my lips. "Happy birthday," she whispered, and it was soft, happiness pouring from one soul to the next.

"Thank you," I murmured. "For everything."

She tilted her head, looking at me curiously.

"When Lucy died, it left a gaping hole inside me," I began. "I felt as if all the light had been snuffed out, and I was left stumbling around in the dark, trying to find it again."

Olivia reached for my hand. "I know what you mean," she said softly. "Loss does that. I've been in the darkness for a long time myself."

"Being with you, it feels like the world isn't so dark anymore. I feel sparks of joy, moments when I can actually smile and mean it. You've given me hope that it's possible to move forward."

A small smile played at the corners of her mouth and she reached out, tracing her thumb along my lips. "You give me that too," she whispered. "We're finding our way out of the darkness together."

"Maybe you're my second chance," I replied.

She leaned in and kissed me again, slower this time. "Only if you're mine."

As we sat, swaying slightly, the stars seemed softer, like spring was slowly starting to stretch open, reminding us that, despite our past, we had found something beautiful in each other.

I had learned many things from Everston, but the most important of them all was that, rather than running from grief, I was supposed to feel all of it—the pain, the suffering, the unending waves of heartache. There was no time limit on when the anguish would end and the healing would begin, because they were intertwined. One day I woke up in the morning and could see how far I'd moved along the road. That's what living with grief was: you just had to keep moving.

Chapter 24

Emerson

When I was eleven years old, my brother, Sebastian, and I convinced ourselves that we could build a time machine. We spent three weeks raiding the old Miller junkyard for materials: scraps of tin and metal, cardboard, wood, old milk bottles, tangled wires, anything we thought might work. We were so sure we'd figure it out, excited by the possibility of going back in time. Sebastian wanted to stop Dad from leaving. I wanted to convince Mom to keep our dog. We both wanted to secure tickets to a Fall Out Boy concert we'd missed (never mind the fact we couldn't have afforded them, anyway). We'd begun our project together, spending nearly every waking hour on it, until, halfway through, Sebastian developed a crush on some girl in his class. Her name was Blair Calihan, and our grand plans shriveled up like skin after a long bath. It was never really about the time machine. It was about fixing things that felt broken, things we couldn't fix in real life. There were so many times I'd wished for that time machine. The day Dad walked out; the day my goldfish died and I cried for, like, seven hours; the time I fractured my ankle and missed six weeks of gymnastics, including a competition. The accident. Winnie's illness. So many things. More than anything, I just wished I could go back in time because maybe the answers were there. Maybe *I* was there.

Winnie used to tell me that fate was like a whisper. It nudged you toward where you were supposed to be. I'd scoffed at the idea, telling her that fate was just coincidence dressed up to feel important. But now? Now I wished I could go back and ask Winnie if she thought it was fate that life had turned out this way, that I had decided to let the gymnastics scholarship go. It was the hardest decision I'd ever made. I could see the disappointment in Coach Tillman's eyes, even though she said she understood. For so long, gymnastics had been my safety net. Without it, I felt like I was free-falling with no idea where I would land. Maybe I wouldn't feel so lost if Winnie were still here. Life was so much harder without her. I missed her all the time—more than I'd missed anyone in my entire life. And I wished I could ask her what I should do with my life. But if I'm honest, I already know what she would say—go, try, see what's out there. Which is why I'm in Denver. I spent the morning on a campus tour at the University of Denver, seeing if I could picture myself here. Now I'm back at the hotel, curled up on the lumpy couch by the little bar fridge. Rain tapping against the window, steady and soft. The perfect reading weather. I mean, let's be real, any weather is reading weather, but there's something about rain and a good book.

On the list? The. Book. Wren. Wrote!!! Like, Wren actually wrote me a book. Well, truthfully, she wrote it for all of us in the group, but she dedicated it to me. Seriously, there was a page at the beginning that said, *For Emmy, one day at a time.* I still couldn't believe it. I didn't even know Wren could write poetry. I mean, I knew we were all working on our poems for the poetry evening, but she wrote a whole *book*—Rita would be super surprised by this—and had it published. Henry helped her. There was a raven on the cover, all dark and mysterious, plus a bluebird—grief and joy. I cried when she gave it to me.

I settled into the couch cushions and flipped open the book. It was called *Thinking of You*. The poems hit hard. Like, rip-your-heart-out-then-give-you-a-hug hard. I could almost hear Winnie reading them out loud, pausing every two seconds to debate what they *really* meant. But then something weird started happening. The words felt . . . familiar. Too familiar. The rhythm, the tone, the whole vibe. It was giving B.W. Paisley. Which was insane. Wren was not Brooklyn-freaking-Paisley. Right? Except the more I read, the more my stomach did this weird floppy thing. Because it wasn't just similar. It *was* the same.

The language was so distinctly *her* that it couldn't belong to anyone else. Maybe Wren had contacted Brooklyn for advice, how cool would that have been?! No. Impossible. Brooklyn Paisley must be far too busy and important. What if Wren had just copied them? No. Wren wasn't like that. And more to the point, I'd already read everything Brooklyn had published! I stilled for a moment as a small thought crossed into my mind. I put the book down, scoffing, and pushed off the couch.

There's no way, I thought.

I paced toward the little bar fridge, yanked it open, stared at the nearly empty take-out containers of last night's dinner, as though they might hold answers, then slammed it shut again. My eyes darted to the bed, messy with blankets and in-room dining plates shoved to one side. I hunted for my phone in the chaos, fingers fumbling until I found it. I swiped for Instagram. I hadn't used the app in forever; I'd avoided social media as much as possible. The thought of posting myself, of my scars being frozen in a photo grid, sitting there for people to comment on, whisper about, it had made me want to crawl out of my skin. But this was different. I typed "B.W. Paisley author" into search and found her profile. Verified. Eleven million followers. There've been maybe three moments in my life when my jaw has practically hit the floor: the time my mom accidentally bleached my prom dress, the time Brady tried to convince me he was as good as Patrick Mahomes, and the time my jaw nearly detached as my car hurtled across the road (sorry, super dark, I know).

But believe me when I say my jaw was *on the ground* when the search results came back . . . in fact, it was probably fifty feet *below* the ground. Because those photos *were* Wren. Okay, not *exactly* Wren. B.W. Paisley had long, dark hair, and glasses, her whole vibe screaming "put together" in that effortlessly cool New York way. Wren had chopped hair, highlights, and was always in baggy overalls and oversized T-shirts, the whole "please don't notice me" thing. But it was her. The more I stared, the more I knew.

I sucked in all the air around me. "Oh my god," I whispered to no one, pressing my hand against the scars on my neck like that would steady me.

Of course, Wren had always seemed familiar. I must have seen her in those tiny thumbnails that pop up when you google authors' books. But I'd never really looked closely at them, had I?

I started pacing again, my thoughts spiraling, thinking about everything this meant. Wren was B.W. Paisley. Wren, who I'd poured my heart out to in the grief group. Wren, who had written a book just for us. Wren, who'd sat quietly in meetings, listening like she really cared, like every word you said mattered to her. I thought about all those times we'd stayed after the group had wrapped up, lingering in the library, trawling through books, me rambling about how hard it was to move forward with these scars that refused to fade. I stopped pacing for a moment, staring at the angry marks down my neck and arms in my reflection in the glass of the window—an untamed road map. I thought back to one night after a doctor's appointment, when he'd told me it was unlikely I'd ever be able to do gymnastics again. I'd gone home and locked myself in my room, curled up in the corner like I could just disappear into it. I felt so ugly, so broken. I didn't want anyone to look at me ever again.

And then I'd reached for one of B.W. Paisley's old poetry books. I don't even know why. It wasn't like I thought it would fix anything, but I'd picked it up anyway, holding it like a lifeline.

I remember flipping to a poem about finding beauty in imperfection, and I'd started crying so hard I could barely read the words. It wasn't some magic cure-all, but it felt like a person had reached through the pages and told me I wasn't alone. Her books had felt like a friend when I had none. And all this time, that same person was *right here*. She had listened to me, even when I hadn't known how to say what I was feeling. She'd laughed with me, she'd offered to help me get back behind the wheel, she'd given me advice. And she'd never once told me who she really was. Why didn't she tell me? Was it because she didn't trust me? I felt a twinge of hurt. Hadn't we bonded? But then I thought about the way she carried herself, her hesitation, the way she flinched whenever someone brought up the past. She had always avoided talking about herself too much. I remembered the day she gave me the book, how she looked at me like it wasn't a big deal, but her hands had been shaking.

Maybe I should've felt hurt. But mostly? I felt like I was buzzing out of my skin. This was huge. B.W. Paisley was *here*. She was part of our grief group. She'd written this beautiful book. Winnie would've loved this. Rita would lose her mind. And Henry? I mean, he was probably going to faint. So what now? Do I just casually start following Wren? Send her a DM? Hey, guess I found the real you. Yeah, that wouldn't be weird at all. This was so stressful. What do you even do when you realize your friend is secretly a famous person? My thumb hovered, brain short-circuiting, and in the end I bailed and exited the profile. And then suddenly there it was. The very first post in my feed. Brady. Smiling like an idiot, his arm slung around some girl, her hand shoved in front of the camera to show off a diamond ring.

We're engaged.

Engaged? The F?! Since when? My vision blurred as I stared, until a laugh barked out of me, morphing into a snort. Of course. Of course the forever he promised me would end up belonging

The Last Poem

to someone else. Heat rose in my chest—anger, jealousy, and the sheer audacity of it tangled together. Petty? Absolutely. But did I care? Not even a little. If Brady could parade around like his life was perfect, then so could I. Before I knew it, I had Wren's book in my lap again. I snapped a photo of the last poem in the book—my favorite, "Winnie's Lesson"—then scrolled through my camera roll until I found a selfie I'd taken with Wren outside the library. *Perfect*. I mashed the upload button and typed out a caption:

> B.W. Paisley wrote me a book, because not only is she the best person ever, but also the greatest thing to happen to Everston, Colorado.

I mean, fate had brought her here, right? Surely, it had to mean something. And anyway who was even going to see this? My five hundred followers? But Brady would.

Posted.

PART III

Chapter 25

Wren

They ruined the crocuses—the first signs of spring—their delicate purple blooms crushed as paparazzi and internet sleuths stood in the garden beds, trying to get a better view through the windows. From the street it sounded like wild bison charging down the mountain. The air buzzed with urgency as voices clamored, shouting my name, their intensity shattering the stillness of the morning. Flashes erupted from all directions—cameras, iPhones, anything that could capture an image—illuminating the kitchen where I had stood, mindlessly washing last night's dishes. I froze, soap dripping from my fingers, and stared in horror as the official news crews clustered at the curb, tripods bristling—while a paparazzo's SUV barreled up the driveway. It plowed through the potted geraniums and sent garden statues toppling like dominoes. My sanctuary, my hidden refuge, had been discovered, and now it lay in ruins.

They had found me.

Even in my shock I managed to close the curtains, but the shouting didn't stop. Questions banged against the windows. An accusatory voice cut through the noise, riding above the rest: "How does it feel to be hiding in the mountains while the boy your fiancée ran over is still paralyzed?"

My legs buckled. I grabbed the edge of the kitchen counter for support, my breath shallow and ragged. My phone on the counter buzzed with a missed call, and then another one, and another one. On and on messages pinged. A relentless stream of calls from people I had left behind. My agent. My publicist. Even my parents. They had respected the distance I had asked for after Lucy's death. But now, their messages were urgent. The internet was alive with speculation. *Where has B.W. Paisley been? Why is she hiding? What is she hiding?*

I didn't wait to hear more. My hands shook as I fumbled with my keys. I bolted out the back door, ducking past the chaos in the front yard. I slammed the car door and narrowly missed people and cameras as I sped away. The house, the one I had spent seven months restoring, disappeared in my rearview mirror as dust kicked up behind my spinning wheels. My sanctuary—the garden, the porch, the life I had built here—felt trampled, as broken as the crocuses they'd crushed beneath their feet.

I didn't know where else to go. There was only one place in this town where I believed I might be safe—the library. When I burst through the entrance, my legs felt like lead, as though they wanted to root themselves to the carpet beneath me. I staggered toward the front desk where Henry sat, calm as ever, speaking into the phone.

"Henry," I gasped, breathless. "I need to tell you something."

He ended the phone call, his eyes lifting to meet mine.

Henry's gaze was different, distant and almost unrecognizable. It was as though I had suddenly become a stranger to him: not the person he had spent hours planning the poetry evening with; not the friend who had shared wine and late-night conversations about loss and grief; not the one who always had paint in her hair and asked him for advice about what color would match the drapes Gill insisted on keeping; not the person who had shared all the fears in the very depths of their heart. Without a word, I knew he had found out.

"I need a moment," he said quietly, his voice calm but laced with something unreadable.

I nodded, though my heart was breaking.

He adjusted his glasses, locked his computer screen, and fiddled with the collar of his shirt, like it suddenly felt too tight.

"I'm sorry," I whispered, my voice trembling. "I'm sorry I didn't tell you who I really was. But the press, they've found me. They somehow found Gill's address and are all over the front yard. I couldn't stay there."

Before he could respond, the screech of tires outside made us both turn. A news van came to a halt in front of the library, its doors flying open as a camera operator leaped onto the pavement, adjusting their lens for a shot.

Henry's expression didn't change, though his eyes never left the scene outside. "It would seem they're everywhere," he said flatly.

"Please, Henry," my voice cracked. Flashbacks of the relentless press after the accident, the constant hounding and invasive questions, the torture on social media, rained down on me like shards of glass. I was dizzy, breathless, and spiraling. "Please, help me."

Henry's jaw tightened and, without a word, he pressed the intercom button on the front desk. His voice, steady and authoritative, filled the library. "Patrons of Everston Library, please note we are urgently closing due to a family emergency. Please exit in an orderly fashion through the front doors."

There weren't many patrons, and those who were there shuffled out with confused glances. Henry marched to the front doors and locked them just as the press surged forward, cameras and microphones thrust toward the glass. Their muffled shouts were barely audible through the heavy doors. I retreated to the staff room, my steps unsteady, the world spinning around me. The walls seemed to cave in as I leaned against the cabinets, trying to catch my breath. My pulse pounded in my ears, my chest rising and falling in frantic rhythm. *Please slow down*, I begged my heart silently.

Henry appeared in the doorway, his face clouded with something unreadable. Was it shock? Hurt? Anger? I couldn't tell.

"That was Rita on the phone just before," he said, his voice carefully controlled. "She said someone from *Us Weekly* cornered her at Sam's early this morning. They were asking about Brooklyn Paisley. She told them she had no idea who that was. But then—" He stopped, leaning on the doorframe; I could clearly see the hurt across his face. "They showed her a photo on their phone, and she said, 'Oh no, that's Wren. She's probably at Gill's.'"

My breath caught, and I felt the room still. "She gave them my location?" I whispered.

"Well, not on purpose. She didn't know what it meant. She thought they were here for the poetry evening. Not for . . ." He stopped again, his eyes searching mine. "Brooklyn Paisley."

The name sounded so foreign, distant, like someone I used to know but didn't anymore.

"Henry, I didn't want this. I didn't mean—"

"Well, what *did* you mean?" he replied, his tone harsher now. "Because from where I'm standing, the woman we thought we knew—Wren—the one who was a friend, who we shared our deepest grief with, isn't who she said she was."

"It *is* me. Wren is my middle name," I said softly. "You have to believe—"

"What the hell happened in New York to make you come here?" he interrupted. "What are you hiding from? And why here? You could have gone anywhere, why Everston? Why did you infiltrate our town?"

Infiltrate. I felt a lump rise in my throat as tears stung my eyes. "It wasn't like that," I said. "I wasn't trying to infiltrate anything. I just . . . I just wanted to disappear. To start over."

Henry's face slightly softened, but the confusion and hurt remained. "Disappear from what?"

"It was the accident," I said again, forcing myself to meet his gaze. "The one that killed Lucy. The police said she was drunk, that she crashed into another vehicle, injuring the man inside, and then mounted the curb, hitting a young boy. But I struggled to remember it that way. Lucy wasn't drunk. She wasn't reckless. But the press didn't care about the truth. They wanted a story, a scapegoat. And Lucy, even though she paid with her life, wasn't enough. They wanted to bury me too. They weren't going to stop until I was ruined. I just ran."

Henry stood silently, absorbing what I was saying.

"It wasn't until a few weeks ago that I learned the man in the other car wasn't just some random person. He was an off-duty cop, and the son of the police commissioner. He was drunk that night. He crashed into us, sent our car spinning into a pole, and then *he* was the one that mounted the curb and hit the boy. But the police covered it up to protect him. They sealed the reports. Hid it from the public and fed the media whatever they wanted."

Recognition suddenly dawned in his eyes. "*You* were Olivia's story!" he exclaimed.

"What?" I asked, my stomach knotting.

"Olivia came to me," he said. "She told me she had two stories she was working on. One about the grief group—which I really thought she would do as a favor, but the other was massive. Big enough to get her the job as anchor. That was you, wasn't it? Your story. She knew."

The world tilted. A ringing filled my ears, drowning out everything but the sound of my heart shattering. The weight of it all exploded. The woman I loved, the one I thought had given me a second chance, had just stolen it all away.

Chapter 26

Olivia

One moment, I was standing in the wine aisle at the grocery store, staring at a bottle of pinot noir, debating whether it would pair nicely with the casserole I planned to make for Wren that night. The next, my phone was ringing, and Colin's voice was exploding down the line.

"You better get your ass back to the station, Piroso!" he roared. "How the hell is the *Daily Mail* running articles about B.W. Paisley hiding out in Everston, and we didn't know? Worse, you've been fucking *dating* her for the last three months, and you didn't think to tell me about it!?"

I dropped the wine bottle. It smashed all over the crisp white floors. Red wine spread quickly, creeping toward my sneakers. A store employee poked his head out of the break room, his eyes narrowing at the mess. He grabbed a mop, muttering something under his breath. The TV in the break room was showing the news. Through the gap in the door I saw "B.W. Paisley" splashed across the screen and I launched myself forward, through the opening.

"Where's the remote!?" I said frantically. "Turn the volume up!"

The young man recoiled slightly, looking at me as though I was unhinged. I didn't blame him.

"The remote!" I repeated.

"Who are you?" he spluttered.

I saw the remote on one of the tables and lunged for it, turning the volume on full blast. The headlines screamed at me.

"Where is B.W. Paisley? Mystery Solved as Author Emerges in Colorado After Months of Silence"

"From Bestseller to Recluse: B.W. Paisley Found Living in Seclusion After Fatal Crash Sparks Scandal"

"B.W. Paisley Retreats to Colorado Mountains Following Public Scrutiny Over Fatal Accident"

They rolled over the top of each other, one by one, a hideous pastiche of the media frenzy that had erupted. The screen showed images of Wren, the car accident, of Everston . . .

"Ma'am, you can't be in here," a voice appeared beside me. "This is for staff only."

I turned to find the manager standing beside me, hands on her hips, looking at me as though she wasn't sure whether I was having a nervous breakdown. There was a strong possibility I was. My phone buzzed incessantly in my pocket, messages from Colin, Josh, even *Cassie*. I stumbled out of the store, my vision swimming. In the car, I turned the radio on, blasting the sound to drown out the ringing in my ears. My hands trembled as I started the engine and roared out of the parking lot, way too fast. But I had to get back to Everston. I had to get to Wren.

The last time a big story like this broke in Everston, I was nineteen. My mother spearheaded coverage of the entire thing, which involved a tourist who had gone missing while hiking in the nearby mountains. It was the kind of drama that gripped the town for months. The young woman had come to Everston the way most do, for a quiet retreat, but her sudden disappearance turned everything upside down. My mother took charge of the investigation; our sheriff didn't stand a chance. She spent countless hours interviewing the missing woman's friends and family, anyone who had seen her in the days before she vanished. She pored over maps of the hiking trails, consulted with search and rescue teams, and even hiked some of the trails herself, trying to piece together what might have happened. The breakthrough came when a witness mentioned seeing the woman arguing with a man in the diner the day before she disappeared. My mother's reporting led to a composite sketch of the man, which circulated widely. The media pressure and her relentless pursuit of the truth forced the man to turn himself in. He confessed—said it was an accident, that the woman had fallen during a heated argument. My mother was suddenly a legend. The woman who had singlehandedly solved the mystery. What no one knew was that I had sat with her late into the evenings, poring over maps. That it was me who hiked with her along the trails, searching for clues. And it was me, not her, who had first connected the witness to the story.

When I reached the house, Gill's front lawn was covered in paparazzi. Some were even from our own station. They'd ruined the flower beds that Wren had spent months putting back together, carefully watching over every plant as it regrew. They'd kicked over paint cans, spilling emerald green pigment across the driveway. I hadn't been able to reach Wren on her phone, and my anxiety grew with every missed call. Emerson was in Denver for a college tour, and even Henry hadn't picked up when I tried him. My heart pounded as I fought my way through the throng of reporters, screaming at them to move, until I managed to squeeze through the back door. Inside, the house was eerily quiet despite the commotion outside. The sink was filled with cold dishwater, suds clinging to the edges. Our wineglasses were still on the table from last night, when everything had felt so simple, so perfect. Just as I reached the foot of the stairs, my phone buzzed with a text from Henry.

> She's here with me,
> at the library

I'd never driven so fast down Main Street in my entire life. My tires squealed as I pulled into the alley behind the library. I slammed the car door shut, ignoring the shouts of reporters crowding the building. Elbowing through the back entrance, I found Henry standing by the door. His usually neat hair was a mess, his face pale with tension.

"Break room," was all he said, his voice clipped and distant.

"Wren," I breathed, as I charged through the break room door, moving to wrap her in my arms. Instead, I found her standing rigid, trembling with barely contained fury. Her eyes, usually so soft and expressive, now blazed with a fire that could burn down the entire library.

"You revealed me," she hissed, her words full of venom. "How could you do this to me?"

The accusation slammed into me like a high-speed train. "I would never," I said, my voice sharp with disbelief. "I didn't tell a soul, Wren."

"Brooklyn, actually," Henry interjected from the corner, his tone colder than I'd ever heard it. "But I suppose you already knew that."

My stomach twisted as Wren's eyes filled with tears. "I didn't mean to hurt you," she said, her voice breaking as she pleaded with Henry. "I wanted to tell you."

"But you didn't," he said, his gaze hardening. "You didn't trust me. All this time I believed you were someone else."

Wren turned back to me, her fury rekindled. "You're right. I decided to trust the wrong person."

I reeled backward.

"You don't mean that," I replied.

"You just wanted that job," Wren said. "That big promotion to anchor. You must have been over the moon when you found out who I really was. I knew you were too good to be true. You were just using me."

Her words shattered something inside me. "You're scared and angry," I said, forcing myself to stay steady. "I know you don't believe I would do this. You know me better than that."

"Do I?" she yelled, her voice vibrating off the walls. "You pushed and pushed for me to share the story. Over and over again!"

"To help you!" I cried, desperation creeping into my voice. "To clear Lucy's name. She was innocent!"

"Don't talk about Lucy," Wren snapped, and it felt like she had slapped me. "You didn't want to help me. You just wanted to further your career. I can't believe I ever trusted you."

My heart splintered into a thousand jagged pieces. "Wren, listen to me," I pleaded, stepping closer. "I love you. I didn't break that story. I didn't tell anyone who you really were."

"I don't believe you," she said, tears streaming down her face. Her voice was raw, broken. "You've ruined everything. I have nowhere to hide."

"Maybe you shouldn't be hiding anymore!" I replied. "You don't have to hide. *We* don't have to hide."

Her eyes burned into mine, filled with grief. "That wasn't for you to decide!"

"Wren, I—"

"Like mother, like daughter," she said coldly. "I'm sure she would be proud."

She turned on her heel and stormed out of the room, her words hanging in the air like thorns, cutting deeper and deeper.

I stood there, stunned, barely able to breathe. "Henry," I said, but he turned away as well.

"The library is closed."

Chapter 27

Henry

In our first group meeting, Winnie had posed a rather unusual question to Max: "What is the saddest story you have ever heard?" At first, I found this question quite peculiar, almost intrusive. But the longer I thought about it, the more I realized Winnie wasn't asking out of morbid curiosity; she was searching for some answer to her own pain. Perhaps if she heard about someone else's grief, she might better understand her own. Max, ever patient, had recounted a story about a mother traveling with her family during the holidays. An oncoming four-wheel drive collided with their car, killing her three children in the back seat and leaving her gravely injured. For years afterward, Max explained, the woman told anyone who asked that her children were alive. She had built a world in her mind where they grew up, went to college, got married, moved overseas. She had created an entire alternate reality—an escape from a truth too unbearable to live with. Max explained that grief can be so overwhelming, so all-consuming, that we sometimes construct parallel spaces to exist in, where the grief cannot follow.

I had never forgotten that story.

It was all I could think about as I tried to unravel what I had learned about Wren. Had she done the same thing? Had she rebuilt herself piece by piece, brick by brick, not as Brooklyn Paisley, literary sensation, but as Wren—the friend who brought croissants to me on Friday afternoons after a long week of work; the woman who stayed late after grief group to rearrange chairs and wash empty mugs; the person who always smiled at the dog-eared copy of *Jane Eyre* I kept on my desk, teasing me that I'd read it more times than anyone could count? She had slipped into this version of herself so seamlessly, so convincingly, that none of us had questioned it. I felt a pang of heartache that settled in my chest, heavy and unwieldy. How could she have hidden this from me? From all of us? How had I not seen it? And yet, as I sat with the thought longer, Max's story echoed in my mind.

When people choose to believe something, others often go along with it, unquestioning. Wren presented herself as someone ordinary. A woman trying to heal in a small town. And we all believed her, because we wanted to.

After I lost Jacob, if I'd had the opportunity to run, to recreate my life, to become someone else, who would have I become? Perhaps Henry the baker, waking up at dawn to knead dough and hand out pastries. Or Henry the editor, sipping espresso in a sleek office as I nurtured stories into the world. Or maybe Henry the carpenter, building something tangible, something solid, something that wouldn't collapse under the weight of loss.

I lay awake, staring at my ceiling as the darkness dragged on through the night. I thought I knew Wren. Hell, I thought I knew Olivia. How could she have done this to Wren? Olivia was vivacious, strong, and opinionated—but cruel? I'd never known her to be cruel. But then again, I was starting to question how well I knew anyone. Eventually my anxiety about the poetry evening began to creep in too. What if the press turned it into a spectacle? What if it overshadowed everything we'd worked for? Max's words floated back to me: *Grief changes people. Sometimes we create spaces where the pain can't follow. Grief reveals the truths we would rather not face, but it also reveals the ways we both run from and return to ourselves.* As the clock ticked past midnight, I felt more uncertain than ever.

The Last Poem

*

I arrived at the library earlier than usual, just as the first light of dawn began to break over the mountain. The sight never failed to strike me—the way the sky unfurled into a palette of pinks and purples, clashing beautifully with the motley painted buildings along Main Street. I loved this town; I loved the way it felt tucked into its own little corner of the world, cradled by the mountains' shadow. The smell of coffee already wafted down the street from the café, mingling with the smell of fresh rain from the night before. But today, something felt off, like the town itself noticed an absence. As I approached the library return box, the morning air was cool against my skin. I opened the metal lid with a slight creak, half expecting some sort of firecracker to go off, but all I found was a note. The paper was neatly folded. I recognized Wren's handwriting immediately. I inhaled deeply as I opened the note.

> I'm sorry for everything, Henry. But I am not sorry to have met you, to have been part of this group that you created. You are and will always be the glue of it. Everston saved my life, and I will never forget you. I have returned to New York, so I will not bother you again.
> Be well, Henry.

Hours later, I was still staring at Wren's handwriting, too distracted to even reprimand the teenagers scribbling in library books—an offense that usually earned my swift and stern intervention. Suddenly, Emerson burst into the reading corner, narrowly avoiding one of the new lamps I'd placed on the table just the other day. Her thick, wavy black hair was escaping from her ponytail, and her cheeks were flushed, as if she'd run the whole way here.

"Nobody tells me anything!" she exclaimed, breathless. "No calls, no texts, nothing. I'm gone for, like, three days, and all hell breaks loose. And nobody bothers to call me?"

She bent forward, hands on her knees as she tried to catch her breath. "Well, nobody except Gill, who is a mess, by the way. And Rita, she thinks it's all her fault for telling that reporter about Gill's place. Bobby and her had this huge fight about it, because Bobby said she shouldn't have said anything. Now Rita is with my mom, crying her eyes out, because her and Bobby were supposed to perform their poem together. And Julian is dealing with some family emergency—which could mean literally anything. Olivia's phone is off. And here you are, staring at the floor like the pipes have burst again."

"We didn't want to worry you," I said. "There was nothing you could've done anyway, Em, you were in Denver. Why worry you when you were hours away?"

"Because I would have come home sooner. I would have started punching those reporters!" she retorted, straightening up. "I would've come in swinging."

"I'm sure assault charges would look fantastic on your college applications."

She huffed and crossed her arms. "But it's one of us, Henry. One of *us*!"

"Well, how much of an '*us*' could she be, when we didn't even know who she really was?" I said. "Besides, they weren't here very long anyway. As soon as they realized no one was going to give any interviews, they left."

"This is unbelievable," Emerson muttered, flopping into the armchair beside me. "Where is she?"

"She's gone," I said, the words unexpectedly catching in my throat. "Wren. Or Brooklyn. Or—I don't even know who she is."

"She just *left*?" Emerson asked, her voice low, as if saying it too loudly might make it more real.

I nodded. "Back to New York, if that's even where she lives."

Emerson sighed heavily. "She *does* live in New York," she said. "The accident was bad, Henry. Like, really bad." She paused, her fingers absentmindedly brushing the deep scar that ran along her neck. "But the press that followed? That was way worse."

"How do you know this?"

"Because obviously I have now googled the crap out of her," she replied, as if it were a no-brainer. She pulled out her phone, her thumb swiping purposefully across the screen, before leaning closer and holding it out to me. "Look," she said softly. A video started playing, shaky and chaotic, like it had been recorded by someone shoving their way through a crowd. There was Wren, emerging from a building. Her movements were slow, labored, her body hunched as if every step took monumental effort. A large gash ran across her forehead, dark-purple bruises pooling beneath both eyes. Bandages were wrapped around her wrists, and gauze peeked out from beneath the collar of her shirt, covering her neck and arms. She looked utterly destroyed, both physically and emotionally.

"That's a rehabilitation facility," Emerson interjected. "She was trying to get well, and faced this every day."

Paparazzi swarmed around her like vultures, their flashes blinding and relentless. The shouting was deafening, overlapping questions and accusations hurled at her without mercy.

"Brooklyn, how does it feel to know that boy will never walk again? Do you think your fame is protecting you from justice? Are you hiding behind your dead fiancée's memory?"

Amid the chaos, other voices rose, angrier, crueler.

"Why aren't you paying for the boy's care!?" someone shouted. "Celebrities think they're above the law!"

"You should be in jail, bitch," another jeered.

"I'm glad your stupid fiancée died." Wren visibly flinched at those words, her face crumpling. She clutched her arms, as though trying to shield herself from the barrage.

"God," I whispered.

The video continued, showing her being ushered toward a waiting car. A security guard tried to hold back the crowd, but the shouts followed her, pounding against the windows as she was driven away.

Emerson scrolled through the comments, and they were just as bad.

"They're ruthless," she murmured. "It's like they found joy in her grief. Imagine people glad that Jacob had died because it meant they could see you fall. It's gross. It's the worst parts of humanity."

I rubbed my hands down my face. "So are friends who turn their back on you," I said bitterly.

She looked at me. "Huh?"

"I was hurt that Wren didn't tell me who she was. I thought she didn't trust me. Selfishly I made it all about myself. But . . . of course, she would be hesitant to tell anyone," I said, gesturing toward the video on Emerson's phone. "She would have been terrified of reliving all that."

I stood up, beginning to pace across the rug. "I just don't understand how the press found her. She changed her appearance, she's thousands of miles away, and she's been living quietly for almost a year, in a town no one would think to look. How does someone like that get discovered in Everston, of all places?"

Emerson suddenly made a sound, halfway between a gasp and a groan. She was staring wide-eyed at her phone. "This is my fault," she cried. "It was me."

I froze mid-step and turned toward her. "What are you talking about?"

Tears sprung to her eyes. "Oh god. I posted a picture," she explained. "When she gave me the book—the one you helped her with, *Thinking of You*. I recognized her writing. It felt so much like . . . her."

"You recognized her as B.W. Paisley?"

Emerson nodded. "At first I looked her up on Instagram, which you know, I've avoided for so long, and I see this photo of Brady and he's engaged!"

"I—what?" I stammered.

"I know!" she continued, "I was so annoyed. He's so annoying. And I wanted to show I was okay. That my life was just as good too. So I posted photos. I shared a poem from the book, and then a photo of Wren and me outside the library."

She looked at me, breathless. "And I hashtagged Everston, Colorado."

My chest felt heavy. "I see," I replied.

"I'm obsessed with her books, Henry," Emerson continued, her words tumbling out. "I could hardly believe Wren was . . . her. I just didn't think! I mean, I only have, like, five hundred followers. I haven't posted in forever. I didn't think anyone would even care. Okay, side note, I did kinda want Brady to see it."

She glanced down at her phone again, the screen's glow lighting her face, flustered and bewildered.

I leaned closer, catching the sharp rise of her breath as her thumb scrolled. There were more than a million likes on the post. *You've got to be kidding me.*

She paled slightly.

"What is it?" I asked, dread flooding my veins.

"She wanted me to drive her car!" Emerson gasped. "Can you imagine if I had crashed it? I could have wrecked B.W. Paisley's car!"

"Let's focus," I said, holding up my hands, trying to regain control of the conversation as we both spiraled into wild theories about what we did or did not say in front of *Brooklyn Paisley*. My stomach churned as I tried not to think about the hour-long conversation I had with Wren about how good at editing I thought I would be. *As if she hadn't worked with the best editors in the industry*—god, what else had I said? Did I try to explain rhyming couplets to her once? Oh, I definitely did. I could feel my face heating at the thought.

Emerson was ranting about Rita not being able to dare question the success of contemporary poets when she had been living and breathing beside B.W. Paisley when I pulled us back into line.

"We need a plan," I said firmly.

"Well, isn't it obvious?" she replied. "We need to get Wren back." She stood so quickly she nearly knocked the table lamp off again. "If Olivia isn't answering her phone, then I'll go to her apartment."

"That won't work," I said, sighing.

Emerson appeared incredulous. "How much do I not know?"

"Wren thinks it was Olivia who told the press," I explained. "Olivia was working on a story about Wren's accident. As it happens, the driver truly responsible for it was an off-duty cop, it was covered up, but Wren begged her not to run it."

Emerson looked like the roof had just caved in. "A police cover-up?" she stammered, "What kind of—"

"That's a whole other story," I interrupted, rubbing the back of my neck. "The point is, Wren thinks Olivia betrayed her."

She shook her head. "But Olivia loves her. Like seriously, she looks at Wren like she's *made* of poetry. How could she think Olivia would sell her out for a headline?"

I laughed bitterly. "Pain doesn't care about logic. It feeds on doubt. When you've suffered enough, you'll believe the worst, even from the people who love you the most." Guilt twisted in my chest. I had doubted Olivia, too, even when I should have known better. Clearly, I wasn't winning any awards for friend of the year.

Emerson let out a slow, shaky breath, processing everything. "So, now Wren's gone, Olivia's vanished, and we're left with . . . this."

"It would seem so," I responded. "And," I added, my stomach in knots, "our poetry evening is in just a week. Two of our most important people are gone, and Olivia's promise of reporters? Out the window most likely. Mayor Ashcroft is expecting a big event and I'm not sure how we're going to pull it off."

"I'll fix it, Henry," Emerson said. "You just focus on the poetry evening. Make sure everyone else is ready."

"Where are you going?" I called after her as she tore through the library, knocking over a stack of books in the process.

"I've got this, Henry!" was all I heard, as Emerson disappeared in a flurry out the front doors and onto Main Street.

April

Chapter 28

Wren

When I had first discovered Everston, it wasn't really on purpose. I'd been searching for hours, my GPS stubbornly out of range. The map on my phone was little more than a pixelated guess, the roads seemed endless and tangled, leading me to dead ends both literal and metaphorical. Each turn that didn't lead me to Everston only amplified the gnawing doubt: why was I even trying to find this place? On all the other stops on my journey, each marked by Lucy's coasters, I had found no trace of her. Did I really think Everston would be any different? I was chasing a ghost. Just as I was ready to turn back, something caught my eye—a bird perched on a weathered sign by the side of the road. At first, I thought it was a wren. Lucy, of course, loved wrens, and in excitement to feel closer to her, I'd pulled over. But as I stepped closer, I realized it wasn't a wren at all. It was a bluebird, its plump body fluffed against the breeze, perched delicately on a sign that pointed toward Everston. I stood there, staring at it, as if the bird were daring me to follow. So, I did. I veered off the highway, down that long, winding road that hugged the mountain, not knowing that this place, this tiny dot on a map, would change my life forever.

Now I was back in New York, and everything felt different. I'd left Everston the same way I'd left New York—in a hurry, without a plan, and in a desperate attempt to just *escape*. Half my things were still at Gill's, and I'd abandoned my car in the long-term parking lot at the Denver airport. When I landed and took in the city, it hit me like an old, familiar song. The jagged high-rises pierced the skyline, their windows glittering, a stark contrast to the sloping mountains I had grown used to in Everston. The air carried its own signature—warm pretzels and roasted chestnuts from the corner carts mixed with the faint metallic tang of subway tracks, the faintest trace of hot asphalt lingering. The streets buzzed with energy, a constant hum of people moving, heels clicking against pavement, snippets of conversations overlapping in countless languages, taxis honking in frustration, and the deep rumble of delivery trucks moving through it all. This was the New York I knew. The pulse of a city I once called home. But how could I still call it home when I had undoubtedly left my heart somewhere else? It felt like nothing fit anymore. New York demanded something from you. It always had—a certain grit, the courage to carve out your own space in the middle of chaos. I needed something, anything, that could make me feel as though I belonged, so I jumped in a cab, and before I knew it I found myself standing outside my parents' house. There was something in the peeling paint on the doorframe, and the sound of the neighborhood kids playing kickball in the street, that wrapped around me like an old, frayed sweater. When my mother opened the door, her face froze for a moment, as if her mind couldn't quite process what her eyes were seeing. Then her expression softened, her surprise melting into a flood of overwhelming relief. She didn't say a word, just pulled me into her arms. It was the kind of hug that undid me completely. I let myself crumble in her embrace, collapsing into her. A moment later, my father appeared in the hallway, his footsteps slowing as he registered the sight of me. His brow furrowed in disbelief before his lips parted in an almost inaudible exhale. Without hesitation, he joined us, wrapping his arms around both of us. I felt myself expel the weight of everything that had happened these last few months as I buried my face against them, and sobbed into their arms.

*

When I opened my eyes, soft morning light seeped through the linen curtains of my parents' guest room. Dust motes floated lazily in a haze, suspending the stillness. My phone sat untouched on the nightstand, still powered off—a small barrier I had chosen for my own self-preservation. I rose slowly, dressing and making my way downstairs. Mom was nestled in her favorite armchair. A steaming cup of tea rested on the side table, its gentle curls of vapor drifting upward. Her face was hidden behind the pages of a well-worn book, her brow lightly furrowed in focus. She glanced up at the sound of my footsteps entering the living room, her eyes narrowing slightly as she took me in.

"Are those paint marks on your overalls?" she asked, a faint smile tugging at the corners of her mouth.

I looked down, noting the splashes and flecks of color decorating the fabric from my thighs to the chest pocket. "Yes," I said simply.

Moving to the couch opposite her, I sank into the cushions and dragged one of the crocheted pillows onto my lap, hugging it tightly.

"So," she said, "were you a painter these past months?"

I smiled, thinking of Gill and all those hours spent sanding furniture, finding new railings, gardening, and repairing the gutters. "Not quite," I replied. "I was helping a friend renovate their house."

"Oh," she replied, arching an eyebrow. "Finished?"

I scrunched my nose, thinking of those opossums. "Not quite," I admitted.

"I suppose you might want to get back to it then," she said, delicately.

I sighed, leaning back into the couch. "I can't go back, Mom," I said.

"I see," she said softly. "What about your place?"

I shook my head. "I don't want to go there either."

She paused for a moment, before setting down her book

and moving to sit beside me on the couch, wrapping her arms around me. "We loved Lucy," she whispered. "We loved you and Lucy. And Lucy loved you. Nothing—not even death—will ever change that. But, sweetheart, it's because of how much Lucy loved you that I know she wouldn't want you to keep running."

The truth of those words settled deep in my chest, and I felt the sadness rising, spreading like wildfire through my veins and engulfing my body.

Lucy wouldn't want me to keep running.

The street was alive with the quiet hum of a New York morning. A cyclist zipped past, nearly clipping my shoulder as I stepped off the curb. On the corner, the bodega was already bustling. Its faded awning casting a shadow over buckets of fresh flowers spilling onto the sidewalk. The scent of coffee and toasted bagels drifted from the door. A group of teenagers sat on a stoop across the street, talking and laughing with each other. My parents had taken care of my brownstone while I had disappeared into Everston. Despite my months and months of mostly silence, they hadn't abandoned it like I had. Standing on the sidewalk, I noticed small touches that weren't mine: a neatly arranged planter overflowing with ivy by the front steps, and a little owl statue perched by the door—no doubt my father's attempt at keeping rats away. The sight reminded me of the garden statues I had peppered Gill's front garden with, and the quirky clay creatures that sat atop the front desk at the library. I pushed the thought away as I fumbled for my keys. Inside, the air smelled faintly of lemon. It was like stepping into a time capsule. The world had continued moving, but inside these walls, time had stood still. Dust clung to the sleek lines of midcentury furniture, and the high ceilings echoed my hesitant footsteps.

I moved from room to room, drinking it in. I had taken down almost every photograph, the memories too painful, but there were still touches of a life once shared: our collection of mismatched mugs, a book left open on the coffee table, and some of Lucy's favorite artworks still hung on the walls. In the bedroom, a pale light filtered through the curtains, casting long shadows on the hardwood floor. The space felt colder than I remembered, the emptiness magnified. Shivering, I crossed to the wardrobe to fetch a sweater. As I pulled open the drawer, my fingers brushed against something soft. I lifted it: a red scarf, slipping through my fingers. It had been Lucy's. I brought it to my face, inhaling deeply. The faint scent of her perfume still lingered, and it filled my senses. Grief has a way of condensing time, collapsing the years into a single breath.

"What do I do, Lucy?" I whispered to the empty room.

Her presence was sudden and quiet, like a whisper of wind through an open window. She was there, sitting on the edge of the bed, as clear as ever.

"You're here," I said, drawing a breath.

"I am." She smiled.

I lowered myself onto the bed beside her, the ache in my heart easing, if only slightly. "I think I have ruined everything," I murmured. "Everston, Olivia, my new friends . . ."

Lucy tilted her head, her eyes kind. "Things that are meant to be have a habit of working out."

"How so?"

"You were always supposed to find Everston," she replied, "but not to find me. To find Olivia."

"A second chance?"

"Yes."

I looked down at my hands, brushing over where my engagement ring once lived on my finger. The indentation had long since gone. "It still feels strange sometimes," I said. "To let myself feel happy without you."

"Wren," Lucy's voice broke through my thoughts, softer than

The Last Poem

before. "Grief and happiness can live together. You've learned that. Moving forward doesn't mean leaving me behind. I'll always be with you."

I studied her closely; the edges of her figure seemed to blur into the background, like an old photograph fading in the sun.

"You're going," I said quietly, but there was no panic. Only understanding.

"It's okay," Lucy assured me. "I'll always be part of your story. It's not goodbye; it's just making space for what's ahead."

I swallowed the lump in my throat.

"What if I can't do it?"

"You can," she said, her smile warm and certain. Her gaze flicked to the pocket of my overalls. "The answer is already with you."

Confused, I reached into the pocket and pulled out the coaster. The one of Everston. Its circular shape framed an illustration of the colorful buildings on Main Street, a pickup truck filled with flowers parked in the foreground, while mountains rose in the background against the clear blue sky.

The memory came rushing back. Lucy coming home from a work trip, her cheeks flushed with excitement as she handed me the coaster.

"You wouldn't believe this adorable little town," she said. "It's the kind of town that steals your heart, Bee. The kind of place you go when everything feels like it's falling apart."

"Oh," I replied, smiling at her enthusiasm. "What's there?"

"The best cinnamon rolls you'll ever taste," she grinned, her eyes sparkling. "And mountains, and bluebirds, and a sky that stretches forever. The Main Street has every building in a different vibrant color, and there's only one traffic light in the whole place. There's quaint little stores and a beautiful old library. It's magic."

I laughed, as I continued folding our laundry. "Maybe I'll have to go sometime."

"You must," she replied. "If ever you can't find me, I'll be there."

I blinked back tears as I clutched the coaster tightly in my hand. I closed my eyes, and exhaled. When I opened them again, Lucy was gone.

The doorbell rang, pulling me from the haze of my thoughts. I moved through the house, back to the front door, and opened it to find Peter, my literary agent, standing on the stoop. His expression was a mix of exasperation and determination. He stepped inside and charged into the living room without waiting for an invitation, holding a stack of papers and his ever-present phone.

"Brooklyn," he began, already pacing. "When you said you needed time—to get the writing juices flowing—I thought, great, she's finally coming out of her self-imposed retirement phase. But nearly a year!? My god, do you know how much damage control I had to do?"

I folded my arms. *Self-imposed retirement phase?* I was still *grieving*. "Nice to see you, too, Peter."

He ignored my sarcasm, continuing to pace the room, gesturing animatedly with his phone and papers as he spoke. "The press is having a field day. They've been speculating about your disappearance for months. One outlet had the nerve to infer that you'd been abducted by aliens."

I scoffed. "That would have been interesting I suppose."

He glared at me. "This isn't a joke, Brooklyn. Your editor is still ready and willing to publish the poetry book, despite your disappearance, and your complete disregard for media appearances, interviews, festival panels, charity events, everything you had committed to. We need to address this head-on."

I sank heavily into the couch, running a hand through my hair. "I can't do this right now, Peter."

"Yes, you can," he said. "I've spoken with Dana"—my heart rate doubled thinking about her; she was my friend and I'd ghosted her—"we've organized a press conference. Just one. With your name, it's not hard to make it happen quickly. Thank god. You answer some questions, clear the air, read some of that poetry you sent me all those months ago, and we can move on."

"I'm not ready," I whispered, my voice barely audible.

"You don't have to be ready," he replied. "Besides, this press conference could generate great publicity. It's a win-win. You'll have a chance to tell your story on your terms, and we'll reignite interest in the book."

Of course, this was about the book. The same one that sat unfinished since the night Lucy died. Until I'd landed in Everston. That partial manuscript had transformed into the book I wrote for Misery Loves Company. Peter had no idea that I'd managed to finish it. I wondered what my editor would say if she knew I'd published *Thinking of You* myself and printed copies for a grief group in Colorado.

I sighed, too tired to fight him. "Okay," I said. "Do whatever you need to."

Peter nodded, already typing something on his phone. "I'll handle everything. You just need to show up."

In all that time, not once had he asked how I was. And it struck me—people who truly know grief don't shy away from it. They see it, hold it, and honor it, because they understand its weight. But people like Peter? They don't ask, don't care, and don't linger. To them, loss isn't something worth acknowledging, it's just an inconvenience, a silence they're too afraid to fill. And that silence? It said everything. You know who wouldn't have done that? A certain group of people in Everston, Colorado.

Chapter 29

Emerson

Let me tell you about the first time I drove after my accident. It was in the afternoon. The sun was shining, not a cloud in the sky. I climbed into Winnie's old car, buckled her urn into the passenger seat (yes, I used the actual seat belt), turned on the ignition, and let Nirvana carry me out into the street.

And then I drove to New York City.

Okay, obviously I didn't just drive to New York City. First, I drove to St. Louis. I drove for sixteen straight hours with only two stops for gas—and an almost-meltdown because it was dark, I was alone, and I was sort of regretting my decision to drive 2,113 miles with my dead friend's ashes buckled into the passenger seat. Somewhere in the middle, I ate a protein bar, talked myself into calming down, and kept driving until I collapsed at a Holiday Inn. I even grabbed the complimentary slippers, something to soften the blow when my mom inevitably yelled at me for what I had done.

When I finally got to New York, I definitely regretted driving through the city. The GPS routed me seven times, I had to shut off the radio to concentrate, a cabbie flipped me off for merging (with plenty of room, thank you), and I almost ran over a cyclist (his flipping off, totally justified). My heart rate was through the roof, I thought I might have an actual heart attack. But I didn't. I got through it. Just like Winnie always said: *You'll get through it, Emmy. No matter how big the storm, you'll find a way through.* I'm almost mad at her for being so right.

The reason for this impromptu, wildly irresponsible road trip? Wren—or should I say, B.W. Paisley—was doing a book signing and media conference at the Strand Bookstore. The minute I rushed from the library, I went home and decided I would stalk her Instagram for any sign of life. Brooklyn may have had a ton of questions to answer, but so did Wren. And my plan was to go get her, beg for forgiveness, and bring her back to Everston. She needed to be there for the poetry evening, to stop everyone from freaking out. Plus, Olivia was, like, heartbroken. She sent me one text—a heartbreak emoji—before all my messages went undelivered and calls silenced. I felt so bad, because it wasn't her fault, and she was too stubborn to let me explain. This was *my* fault. So, I was going to tell Wren this. I was fully aware that she was a super-famous author who just bounced out on a bunch of commitments, fans, and a whole team of people, but Wren was also my friend and I just wanted to make sure she was okay. Because that was what we did in Misery Loves Company, we looked out for each other.

The last time I was in New York was for a gymnastics competition at Willow High School, about an hour outside the city. The only "sightseeing" we did was Times Square. Overrated to be honest, although the singing cowboy was funny. But you don't forget the smell of New York City, or its pizza slices. I furiously inhaled a margherita slice as I power walked toward the Strand on Broadway and 12th. The event started in half an hour, and I had no idea what to expect. Would there be a line around the block? Did I need to pay? Was security going to stop me? I'd never been to a book signing before. As it turned out, the event was free, and the line wasn't outside because everyone was already packed in on the second floor. The room was filled with at least a hundred people, squished in like sardines. I squeezed through to the back wall and found a spot with a decent view. There was a small stage at the front with a table and two chairs. A moderator—Charlie, according to his name tag—thanked everyone for coming on short notice. If this was the scale of a last-minute event, I couldn't imagine the chaos of something planned in advance. Charlie announced Brooklyn, and the crowd erupted into applause. Some people hooted and hollered, one girl in front of me looked like she might pass out. Brooklyn stepped onto the stage, and everything went quiet. She looked . . . polished. Like, super polished. The kind of polished you only see in magazine spreads or on movie stars. She had on a tailored Chanel blazer with a blouse tucked neatly underneath, and sleek black pants that fit her perfectly. Her shiny, pointed heels clicked softly against the stage floor as she walked.

"She cut her hair," someone murmured next to me.

"Yeah, it's so much lighter now," another added.

"Where are her glasses?" the first person asked, more of an accusation than a question.

I bit the inside of my cheek; for a moment, it felt surreal. I mean sure, she looked different, more like the author who belonged up there under the lights. Like she was the person the world expected her to be. But they didn't know her. They didn't know the Wren who had worn baggy overalls nearly every day and spent weeks sanding furniture in Gill's front yard, or the Wren who had offered me driving lessons in her super-expensive car. They didn't know the Wren who baked a lemon meringue pie for our first meeting after Winnie was gone, or the Wren who leaned in close as I ugly cried over a slice and whispered that Winnie would always be with us. They didn't know the Wren who went bird-watching with me or spent hours helping Bobby sew rhinestones onto his denim jacket. They didn't know the Wren who had all the time in the world for people like me—people who were lost and sad and just trying to find their way back. It was weird seeing her like this.

At this point, I didn't have a plan. My original plan—the one I ran over and over again in my head on the longest, most exhausting drive of my life—was just to get to New York. To find Wren. Also, not to crash. But that was it. Turns out, twenty-seven hours on the road, give or take, isn't nearly enough time to figure out what to say to someone whose hiding spot you just accidentally exposed to the entire world. Watching her onstage, with the entire room staring up at her and hanging off her every word, I felt completely out of my depth. Like, standing-on-the-edge-of-a-diving-board-with-no-clue-how-to-swim levels of out of my depth. But I had to do something. I just had no idea what.

The event started with Wren pulling *Thinking of You* from her tote bag. I recognized the cover, the same one I had posted all over my social media. She explained that the book was special, something she had started a long time ago but hadn't been able to finish until just recently. There was a man off to the side filming everything, whispering with someone in an expensive-looking suit. He had a weasellike air about him; he was squinting at the book as though perplexed by it. I immediately did not like him.

Wren opened the book and began to read.

"You remind me what it feels like to live again, to breathe and believe. You make me want to stay when all I've ever known is how to leave." Her voice faltered, just briefly, before she cleared her throat and carried on.

After Wren finished reading—to rapturous applause—Charlie told the crowd that she would be taking questions, and I saw her take a long, deep breath. The first two were softballs about her inspiration and writing process, but it didn't take long for the mood to shift.

"Why were you in Colorado?" someone asked, his tone sharper than it needed to be.

Wren hesitated for a moment. "I was taking a break," she said, her voice steady but guarded. "But I am healed and ready to get back to writing and talking about the next book."

Healed and ready? I snorted so loudly that five people in the row in front turned to glare at me.

Wren didn't seem to notice the disruption.

"Are you worried about what the media is saying?" another person asked. "About the accident?"

Wren shifted in her seat. "There are certain tabloids that will write whatever stories help sell their publication. I cannot stop this from happening, but I can tell you that what was reported wasn't the truth."

There was a slight murmur throughout the crowd.

Another hand shot up, and Charlie pointed to them.

"What were you doing in Colorado all that time?"

She hesitated again. "I . . . I was actually helping to plan a special event," she said. "But they don't need me anymore, so I returned to New York, where I belong."

"That's not true!" I blurted, before I could stop myself, tears springing to my eyes. "Winnie would've wanted us to see it through, together. We were counting on you."

The room went dead silent. Wren's head snapped up, her eyes scanning the crowd.

"Emerson?" she said, her voice mixed with urgency and disbelief.

"You need to wait your turn," Weasel Guy snapped.

"No, she doesn't," Wren shot back. She left the stage, weaved her way through the crowd, past all the curious onlookers, until she found me. And then, contrary to all the ways I thought she would react to me being there, she pulled me into her arms.

"Oh, Emmy," she whispered, exhaling a long, relieved breath. "I'm so glad to see you."

I didn't even care that everyone was staring, that I was a sweaty, tear-streaked mess, or that my hair probably looked like I'd been through a tornado from power walking to the event. Wren was happy to see me, and that made every mile of the drive worth it.

Chapter 30

Wren

The clinking of cutlery and the soft murmur of conversation filled the air at Momo & More. The place still had its hole-in-the-wall charm, with warm amber lighting that cast a cozy glow across the dark wooden booths, and delicate lanterns that hung from the low ceiling, their intricate designs casting soft, dancing shadows across the walls. The air was rich with the aroma of steaming dumplings, fresh ginger, and a hint of chili oil that lingered like an open invitation.

Emerson was hunched over the menu, her brow furrowed in deep concentration as though choosing between each dumpling variety was a life-or-death decision. I sat across from her, absently stirring the ice in my glass of water, my gaze drifting toward a booth near the back corner. It was where Lucy and I always sat. Every birthday, a random Friday night, or when we just had a craving for dumplings. We'd order the same thing every time—classic pork and chive for her, chicken and ginger for me—and laugh about how predictable we'd become. The seat was empty now, a quiet reminder of what I used to have. Strangely, though, I did not want to be sitting there. I looked at Emerson, who had crossed eight states to get to me. She hadn't just *driven*; she'd faced her biggest fear, crossed highways, mountain passes, and miles of uncertainty—all for me.

"How did I get this so wrong?" I asked quietly.

I had assumed the worst of Olivia, the person I was falling in love with, and it was enough to expel the breath from my lungs.

Emerson set her menu down, her fingers fiddling with the little soy sauce pots on the table. "Well, it wasn't your fault," she said. "It was mine."

"Emmy, we've been over this. I'm not angry at you."

"I know," she replied, "but it *is* my fault for posting the picture. The press found you because of me, not Olivia."

I sighed, leaning back against the booth. "Yes, but I jumped to conclusions because I was scared. That's on me."

Emerson grinned lightly. "Max would be so proud of us."

I picked up my phone and tried calling Olivia again. Straight to voicemail. My heart sank a little further, and I stared at the empty screen, wishing it could give me some kind of answer. I'd texted her, left her messages, begged her to call me back. But there was nothing. I couldn't blame her, because I'd done the same thing. I'd ignored everything and everyone. Grief, as it happens, is so powerful it can make a person disappear into a void, even in a world that is always connected.

"She's just not answering," I said dismally. "No matter how many times I call, nothing."

"Well, we can't change that tonight," Emerson said, her attention already back on the menu.

"But what about the poetry evening?" I said, the words coming out as more of a plea than I intended. "Do you think she'll come?"
It may be my only chance to see her.

"Yeah, I do," she said simply.

I frowned. "How can you be so sure?"

"Because she's hurt," she shrugged. "And that's how we all ended up together in the first place."

The waiter arrived and placed two bowls of steaming miso soup in front of us. He jotted down our dumpling order, plus a green tea for me, and disappeared back to the kitchen. Emerson slurped down her soup, wincing slightly at the temperature.

"Oh," she said suddenly. "I almost forgot—I loved the book. *Thinking of You*. It's my favorite book of yours to date. Everyone in the group has already read it too. Julian asked if we could just read those poems out during the poetry evening."

I softened. "Really?"

"Absolutely. For someone who hasn't written poetry in ten years, I think you've still got it." She cleared her throat, and ventured, "I know Winnie would have liked it, especially the last poem."

She returned to her soup, blowing gently to cool each spoonful.

"You should let me post on social media for you," she said suddenly, her tone casual but her eyes excited. "I mean, I know the whole 'posting the poem you wrote for Winnie' thing kind of ruined your life briefly, but it *did* go viral, so . . ."

I set my soup spoon down, looking at her in interest. Surprising us both, I slid my phone toward her. "Do your best," I said.

Emerson's face lit up as she grabbed my device.

"You know," I said, watching her face, dimly lit by the screen, "I used to feel tied to this place, like it was some tether to Lucy. But now . . ." I trailed off, glancing around the restaurant.

"Now what?" Emerson asked, slightly distracted by whatever she was currently typing into my phone.

"Now I feel like my life isn't here anymore," I admitted. And it wasn't. It was back in Everston, with a group of people who had somehow, without my realizing, saved my life.

Emerson looked up and leaned forward, her eyes soft. "So, let's go home."

I smiled, nodding. "Let's go home."

*

By the time we arrived back in Colorado, the sun was just beginning to rise, casting pinks and oranges over the mountains. The air filled my lungs; I felt fresh and alive. Emerson and I had left Winnie's car outside my apartment and had taken the first available red-eye flight out of New York, and I spent the better part of the night quietly watching the clouds out the window. At Denver International, we found my car right where I'd left it in the long-term parking lot.

As I went to open the driver door, Emerson stopped me, a smile on her face. She wiggled her fingers and asked for the keys. I handed them over wordlessly and we got into the car. She adjusted the seat, turned up the radio to a decibel level that was far too loud, and pulled out of the lot as though it were *her* car. As we drove, the monotony of the highway lulled me into a restless haze of worry, but looking at Emerson, calm and collected, I also felt proud in a way I didn't know how to explain.

It was late morning by the time we reached Everston. As we pulled up to Emerson's house, she turned to me. "I need to go deal with my mom," she said, her voice steady but tired. "Will you be okay?"

I nodded, trying to muster a smile. "I'll be fine. I think I'll head to Gill's for now."

"Call me if you need anything, okay?" she said. "But I'll see you tonight."

The poetry evening. "Yes," I replied, firmly, and she squeezed my shoulder. "Tonight."

As Emerson hurried away, I reached for my phone, ignoring the barrage of missed calls and unread messages that cluttered my screen. Instead, I opened Olivia's contact. My texts to her still sat undelivered. The silence was stretching further between us. I tried calling her again, holding my breath as the phone rang. And rang. And rang. Straight to voicemail.

"Olivia, it's me. Please call me back when you can. I was

wrong. I was so wrong and I'm sorry. I need to see you." My voice cracked at the end, and I quickly hung up. I sat in the car, staring out at the mountains, their peaks soft and powdery. Aiden Callaway came on the radio, one of the songs that Olivia and I loved and listened to as we made dinner. I saw her so clearly in my mind: barefoot, messy hair, wearing one of my oversized T-shirts and handing me chopped garlic with a smile that could undo me.

I turned off the radio, and the silence felt deafening. The thought of sitting in Gill's house, alone with my guilt, was unbearable. I had to do something. I shifted into gear, and before I realized it I had pulled up outside of Olivia's apartment building. I climbed the stairs, my heart pounding with every step, and knocked on her door. Nothing. I knocked again, louder this time, and called out, "Olivia?"

Still nothing.

The hallway echoed with more of my knocking, before I heard a door creak open. I turned to see a woman, older, her hair pulled into a neat bun, peeking out from the apartment next door.

"She's not in," the neighbor said. "She left town, oh . . . early this morning? Seemed like she was in a hurry."

I murmured a thank you, and turned back toward the stairs.

I drove into town, parked outside the diner, and wandered along Main Street, my thoughts circling. I was considering taking one of the trails up the side of the mountain and screaming into the forest, until I spotted a small shop I'd somehow never noticed before. Its colorful door and window frames glistened in the sunlight. The hand-painted sign above the door read: *Merrill's Art and Gift Shop*. Could it be the artist from the book cover? I immediately pushed open the door. The shop's interior was a riot of color, too, and complete chaos. Bright yellow and lavender walls framed shelves crammed with the strangest assortment of items. Whimsical T-shirts and socks hung next to pottery and hand-carved figurines. Traffic signs leaned against antique clocks, and a bin of stuffed toys sat beside vintage radios. The creaky wooden floors groaned with every step as I drifted toward a wall of paintings, my eyes drawn to their intricate details. Each piece depicted Everston in some way, and they were all painted on an assortment of different objects, from guitars to mugs to vases.

"They're beautiful, aren't they?" a voice behind me said, startling me.

I turned to see a middle-aged woman with silver-streaked hair standing behind the counter. She smiled warmly.

"Incredible," I said, my gaze lingering on one particular painting of a bird perched on a delicate branch.

"Oh, those are by Merrill herself," the woman said. "She's ninety-two, and still paints every day."

"Ninety-two?" I echoed, impressed.

The woman nodded. "She's upstairs if you'd like to meet her?"

I hesitated for a moment. "Sure," I replied.

She led me to narrow staircase, and I climbed up to a small studio above the shop. The space was cluttered in the best way: canvases leaned against walls, jars of brushes and paint tubes scattered across tables, and a faint smell of turpentine in the air.

Merrill was perched on a stool, a walking stick nearby, painting an old acoustic guitar with steady hands that defied her age. Her brush moved with precision, creating intricate designs that wound their way across the wood. She was painting the mountain.

"Merrill?" the shopkeeper called softly. "You have a visitor."

The old woman turned, her face lighting up with a warm smile. "Oh, hello there! Come in, don't be shy."

I stepped into the room, taking in the details around me. "Hi," I said, feeling a little awkward but charmed by her talent. "I was just admiring your paintings downstairs and the lady thought I might like to meet you."

She waved a hand. "My daughter." She laughed heartily. "She's always sending poor folks upstairs, thinks I don't get out much and need the social interaction." She tapped her head. "Keeps the mind working, apparently."

I smiled. "Well, your work is incredible. It feels . . . alive."

"Thank you," she said, gesturing for me to take a seat on a worn-out armchair near her. "I try to capture the things most people miss. The quiet moments. The little details. Life moves so fast, don't you think?"

"Too fast," I admitted, glancing at the half-painted guitar she was working on. "That's beautiful. Is it for a special project?"

She looked at the guitar, her hands resting gently on her lap. "It's for me. Something I've been tinkering with for a while. Music and painting, they're both ways to tell a story."

"That's quite true," I said.

Merrill observed me for a moment, studying me with curious eyes. "You have the look of someone carrying a story of their own. Are you a painter too?"

"Not a painter," I replied. "I . . . I write."

"Writing is just painting with words, dear. Do you find it helps? With whatever's weighing you down?"

Before I could respond, I saw it—a small, worn business card sitting on the edge of a cluttered table. My breath caught in my throat. I'd recognize that card anywhere. It was Lucy's business card.

I stood, and picked it up with trembling hands. "How did you get this?" I asked, my voice barely above a whisper.

Merrill looked at me with her brow furrowed, but then softened when she noticed the business card in my hands. "Oh, a lovely young woman from New York gave that to me a couple of years ago. She came in after reading about my work in a news article. What was her name . . . Lucy, I believe?"

My heart dropped. "Lucy, you said?"

Merrill nodded. "Oh yes. She was so enthusiastic about my art. She said she had read an article by a local reporter, now what was *her* name . . ." She paused, squinting as though thinking. "Olivia Piroso," she finally continued, "and so she just needed to come see it for herself. Said she'd email me about buying a piece. But I never heard from her. Such a shame."

The air felt heavy around me as I tried to force my words out. "What was the piece?"

She gestured to a painting propped against the wall. It was of a wren, its feathers rendered with such detail it popped from the canvas. The background was a soft, muted blend of blues and greens, the forest below the mountain.

"Is it still for sale?" I asked, my voice trembling.

Merrill smiled. "Oh yes, dear," she said. "It's been waiting for the right home."

I bought the painting on the spot, cradling it in my arms as I made my way back downstairs. There was one person I knew who would marvel at this seeming work of fate, and that was Henry. I hurried down the street toward the library, not knowing exactly what I was going to say to him, or how he would react to seeing me after I'd disappeared with only a note. But I knew I had to show him the painting. Weeks ago, when the snow had finally melted, Henry and I had planted pansies in window boxes, the flowers' petals soft against the lingering chill of early spring. As I approached the library, I saw them blooming—bursts of purple, yellow, and white reaching eagerly for the light. A pang of warmth and guilt hit simultaneously. Oh, I loved this library.

I spotted Henry outside. He was at the book return box, hanging up a sign that read: *Poetry Evening Tonight*. There were no odd items shoved into the return slot this time, no fireworks, no giant sticks, no birthday cakes, no items of clothing—just Henry, focused on his task. His expression shifted from concentration to surprise as he noticed me approaching.

"You're here," he said. "Emerson . . . she . . . she said, well . . ." he trailed off, shuffling his feet awkwardly.

"I'm so sorry I ever left," I blurted. "And I'm so sorry I didn't tell you who I was."

Henry sighed gently, his usual warmth returning to his face. "I took it personally, you know. That you couldn't tell me your secret. I thought perhaps it was because you didn't trust me. It was silly, really."

"Henry, that isn't why I didn't tell you . . ." I began.

"I know," he replied, smoothing the tape over the edges of the sign so it laid flat. There was a beat of silence before he spoke again. "A few days after Winnie's funeral, I wasn't having the best day. So, I just walked out of the library. Imagine that, Everston Library with no librarian! I was gone the whole day. I went up to the Overlook and just sat there, staring at the mountains, trying to make sense of everything. Lana kept calling, even Emerson texted me, *Where the hell are you?* But I didn't answer. I couldn't."

I watch him thoughtfully, listening.

"I was just so lost," he admitted. "And I have a secret of my own, Wren. I've sold you all some fabricated story that the state was paying for free grief sessions. But the truth?" He smiled sadly, shaking his head. "It's been me. I've been footing the bill, and I can't keep up with it."

I stared at him, a mixture of admiration and disbelief flooding my chest. "Henry, why didn't you say anything? Why go through all that alone?"

He sighed, glancing at the sign he'd just hung as it fluttered in the slight breeze.

"Because I wanted to help. I thought maybe if I just kept going, I'd figure it out. I had tried to get funding—reached out to a few local organizations, talked to a few people in town, emailed some places—but it didn't pan out. It turns out grief isn't exactly a line item most budgets want to cover."

"Is that the real reason for the poetry evening?" I said. "To raise funds? To impress the mayor so much that you can finally secure proper support?"

He nodded, his gaze distant for a moment. "Yes, originally. But it's turned into more than that. It's about showing people what we've built here, what it means to the community. If they can see that, maybe they'll understand why it's worth saving."

"I've worked with all kinds of people, Henry. Business types, artists, donors . . ." I let out a small breath. "I've been to those funding galas, the kind where you raise more in one night than some people see in years. And even then, it's never easy."

"What do you mean?" he asked, tilting his head.

"It's a whole song and dance. You make your case, hope they care. Sometimes they do. Sometimes they don't. But you just keep going. Because if it matters to you, then it's worth it."

Henry paused, gathering his thoughts. "Yes, well, as I sat up there at the Overlook that day, quite literally having absolutely no idea what my next steps should be, mourning Winnie, still thinking about Jacob, wondering if I should just disappear into the mountains and become a caveman—you texted me."

He smiled at the memory.

"First, you sent me a meme—something about renovations—and then you sent me a poem you were working on for the book."

I blinked, trying to recall. I truly had hundreds of renovation memes at that point.

"If I remember it right, it went something like," he went on, *"In the murmur of the leaves, in the quiet of the sky, in the clouds that form and the rain that falls, hope is born again each day. In the laughter of a friend, in the warmth of a smile, in the love that never ends, we will always find our way."*

His words hung in the air, in the way poems do, especially when they catch you off guard. "You wrote about finding hope in delicate things, Wren. In little, everyday moments. Even in all the crappiness that life can offer sometimes, there's always a reason to come back. There are always people worth coming back for."

He stepped forward, and hugged me, squeezing lightly. "You just need to find people worth coming back for," he said softly. "And Wren, just so you know, you're worth coming back for."

I tried not to let the hot sting of tears well in my eyes as I hugged him back, clutching the painting between us. "You really are the glue of our group, Henry," I murmured.

He pulled away, his eyes suddenly lighting up with barely contained excitement. "You know," he said, practically bouncing on his heels. "It's April."

I tilted my head, watching him with amusement. "Yes," I said slowly, waiting for the punch line.

"It's poetry month!" he exclaimed.

I let out a soft laugh. "Of course it is."

Henry clapped his hands together. "Do you know what this means?"

"That you're about to suggest something dramatic?"

He gasped, feigning offense. "This is the perfect excuse for more poetry readings, themed library displays. We could even get one of those cardboard pop-ups of you, and brace yourself, you could host a town-wide haiku contest!"

I laughed. "Let's just start with a poetry evening by Misery Loves Company?"

He nodded, still in thought. "How do you feel about an impromptu sonnet battle?"

Before I could answer, there was a commotion on the opposite side of the street, and suddenly Julian appeared, a small child in tow, and half the members of Misery Loves Company trailing behind him. Their faces lit up when they saw me.

"Wren!" they called in unison.

"Hi, everyone," I replied, and I felt as nervous as I did that very first time I sat in the corner, listening to them all.

Bobby was carrying an enormous water dispenser, balancing it on his hip like it weighed nothing. He grinned. Julian stopped in front of me and placed a hand gently on my shoulder.

"I guess I should've asked you for advice, shouldn't I? When I was writing my poem," he said, with a wry smile.

"Well, you know," I replied lightly, "poetry is subjective."

Julian chuckled, the sound warm and familiar. "That's exactly what Emerson said. Let's hope the audience is just as kind."

Before I could respond, Bobby shifted the water dispenser to one arm and wrapped the other around me in a hug. "Do you like being called Wren?" he asked, his voice low and sincere.

I nodded, the tears returning to my eyes. "Very much," I whispered.

He nodded. "Then that's all that matters."

Gill stepped forward, rummaging through his oversized coat pockets like he was searching for treasure. Finally, he pulled out a small bottle of maple syrup and held it out to me triumphantly.

"I couldn't shove any pancakes in my pocket," he said, with a small wink, pressing the bottle into my hand. "Nothin' no one can say, Wren. Don't matter about your past. You'll always be my favorite person to eat pancakes with."

The knot in my chest loosened a fraction, and I clutched the bottle like a lifeline.

Rita popped out from behind Gill. She was dressed to the nines, her sequined black dress catching every bit of light, shimmering like the surface of a lake. Thick gold bracelets jangled on her wrists, and an oversized necklace that looked like it belonged to a queen from some ancient dynasty rested on her chest. Her heels clacked on the pavement as she approached.

"Well, don't just stand there gawking," she said, smoothing down her dress with a flourish. "I know I look stunning, but we've got bigger fish to fry."

She narrowed her eyes playfully at me. "Wren, do you have

any idea what *Us Weekly* would pay for an exclusive interview with you?"

I blinked, unsure how to respond. "I . . . what?"

She grinned, leaning in conspiratorially. "I'm joking," she said. "No tabloid in the world could ever truly know you, but we do." Her voice softened as she placed a hand on my arm, her bracelets clinking. "And we support you."

A loud bang interrupted the moment, as a car bumped against the curb with a slight skid. The door swung open with a creak, and Emerson emerged, adjusting her sunglasses and inspecting the front of the car. She was wearing an outfit that screamed *Winnie*—a slightly oversized blazer, a colorful scarf, and boots with just a hint of scuff. Her thick, wavy black hair bounced as she shook her head.

"Man, my brother would kill me if I damaged his car," she muttered, sighing dramatically.

Henry's mouth was wide open. "You're driving," he said, blinking at her in disbelief.

"Duh," she replied, rolling her eyes playfully. "How else do you think I got Wren back?"

She sauntered over, wrapping me in a tight hug. "Sorry I couldn't hang this morning," she said, pulling back slightly. "My mom wanted to have this *long* talk about New York and leaving Winnie's car there. I mean, technically she gave it to me but—do you think I'll get a parking ticket outside your brownstone, or—?"

Henry's expression shifted from gobsmacked to something verging on apocalyptic. "You drove!" he shouted. "To *New York*? In Winnie's rusty old Bug? I thought you flew there and back. Are you kidding me?"

Emerson shrugged nonchalantly, hooking her thumbs into the pockets of her blazer. "Relax, Henry. I'm here, Wren's here, and the car is, like, mostly fine."

He was still spluttering indignantly and peppering her with

questions as she led the way toward the library doors. "Are you kidding?" I heard him exclaim as they disappeared inside. "Driving all that way—you could've—you what—you took her ashes—did you bring them *back*?"

I pushed the doors open and followed them inside. The familiar warmth of the library enveloped me like an old sweater, soft and comforting. The faint scent of books and polished wood lingered in the air, and the marigolds caught the afternoon light, glowing like tiny flames. It felt unchanged, constant, despite everything that had happened. There was still so much to do before people started arriving for the poetry evening. But, as I looked around at the people bustling about, the ones who stood by me, I felt a flicker of something I hadn't felt in a long time—hope. Perhaps Henry was right. Perhaps I was worth coming back for. Perhaps Olivia would eventually think so too.

I was in the middle of helping Lillian from Sweet Moments unload her pastries onto the serving table when I heard someone call my name.

"Brooklyn?"

I turned, and there, standing with his usual air of quiet confidence, was Archie Beecher from *The New York Times*. He'd written several profiles on my books and career over the years and was a friend in the professional sense. Unlike so many others, Archie had never written about Lucy's death. For that alone, I was grateful.

"Archie," I said, surprised to see him here, of all places. He stepped forward and hugged me warmly.

"I'm so glad to see you," he said. "I was at your press conference in New York, hidden in the back, of course. I wanted to try and catch you afterward, but I couldn't manage it. Did you get any of my emails?"

I paled. "To be honest, it's been a difficult time. I haven't been great at keeping up with correspondence. But I am working on opening that back up again."

He flashed a smile. "I presume that young woman in the crowd at your press conference has something to do with that?"

I laughed. "Yes, you would presume correctly."

His expression hardened, a flicker of understanding in his eyes. "I lost my father a year ago. Ended up spending three months in the Himalayas at a retreat, just trying to find my footing again. You do what you have to."

"What brings you here?" I asked.

His face brightened. "Well, when I heard about this exclusive poetry evening—something you've been involved in, no less—I had to see it for myself. The intersection of grief and creativity, particularly in a small-town setting, is a fascinating concept. What this town is doing here is remarkable, truly. Poetry as a means of healing . . . it's inspiring. I wouldn't miss it."

Before I could respond, he squeezed my shoulders affectionally. "I'll go find a seat," he said. "But I'd love to catch up afterward. It's good to see you back."

With that, he slipped into the growing crowd, leaving me standing by the table, a tray of pastries in my hands, wondering how far this tiny event had reached, and how much further it might go.

The library was aglow, soft, twinkling fairy lights casting a golden tinge over the walls from where they were draped over the bookshelves. Chairs were arranged in neat rows facing a small makeshift stage, complete with a microphone. Henry had even draped curtains from the ceiling to create a side stage for us all to huddle behind. Guests had been filtering in steadily, and I could hardly believe so many people could fit inside the space. At seven p.m. sharp, Henry walked onto the stage and addressed the crowd in the way only Henry could—with enthusiastic clapping.

"Welcome, everyone!" Henry began. "I'm so thrilled to see you all here tonight. As many of you know, this is our first unofficial poetry evening, and I do hope we can host many more in the future, here at the library."

The audience clapped, the sound mingling with the soft chatter and laughter that had filled the room moments before.

"Everston Library has always been a place for stories, community, and knowledge," he continued. "But tonight it transforms into a house of poetry. I wanted to thank our wonderful Mayor Ashcroft for joining us this evening." He gestured toward the mayor, who gave a polite nod.

Henry's face softened as he took a small breath. "Many of you know about our grief group that meets here regularly. Perhaps what you don't know is that we have been using poetry to express and process our emotions, to find a way through our grief together. We wanted to share a bit of that with you this evening, in the hope that we can continue this work here at the library for others."

As Henry spoke, the room seemed to breathe with him, the atmosphere thick with understanding. Somehow, it felt like people just got it; that pain, while deeply personal, was also a source of togetherness we so often left unspoken.

Henry concluded with a beaming smile. "So, sit back and enjoy some delicious snacks and refreshments from the lovely Lillian of Sweet Moments, and let's celebrate the power of poetry."

As he began adjusting the microphone, I slipped away behind the shelves to find Emerson huddled in the reading corner with the rest of the group, but still no Olivia.

"Wren," Gill said, reaching out a hand. "Emerson is helping us warm up our voices."

"You're a vocal coach now, are you?" I asked, and she smirked.

"Haven't you heard? I wear many hats—vocal coach, poet, social media assistant . . ." she replied.

"Just how many reporters did you contact?"

She shrugged. "I don't know, like ten?" She coughed. "Or maybe it was more like fifty."

"Emmy!" I hissed. "We agreed on three!"

"What?" she replied. "You said we had to get the word out, to help Henry. Get as much attention on this night as possible. I mean, I only DM'd the ones you were following. I figured if you were following them, you liked them. You know, like, over half of them replied right away. You got clout, girl."

I couldn't even respond.

"Also," Emerson added, "I know you have, like, millions of followers, but seriously, Wren, it's not cool to use so many emojis these days. Just leave your socials to me, hmm?"

I groaned as the others burst into laughter.

As Rita and Bobby walked out onto our little makeshift stage to give the first performance, I spotted Max in the corner. I made my way to him, weaving through the crowd.

He looked at me pointedly. "Does it make sense now?" he asked.

"Does what make sense?" I responded, puzzled.

"Your loss?"

I thought for a moment, feeling the weight of the question. "No," I replied truthfully. "But I don't think it's supposed to."

Max nodded, knowingly. "I knew you'd get there."

"What were you writing in your notebook?" I asked him. "All those meetings, you were always writing in a notebook."

Max peered at me through his glasses, a light smile tugging the corners of his mouth. "Would you like to see?"

"Notes on me?" I asked, curiosity piqued.

He smiled, handing me the notebook he'd had with him during all the meetings at the library. I opened it carefully, wondering if he was breaking a zillion patient confidentiality laws. But there were no notes on anyone in our grief group. There weren't even any notes about me. There were just poems. Dozens of them. They were *my* poems, from various works I had written over the years.

I stared back at him, astonished.

Max shrugged. "I knew who you were," he replied. "I've been a fan of your writing for a very long time. I recognized you immediately. Your poetry helped me grieve my relationship with my daughter—she died, but she was a fan of your work, too, and reading it always made me feel like we were still somehow connected."

"You never said anything," I murmured.

"Of course not," he replied. "You were reinventing yourself, why would I get in the way of that?"

I nodded, wondering what the me from a year ago would think of all of this. She'd been lost, fighting her way out of a dark hole; if I'd told her then that she would somehow find the light, I wondered if she would have believed me. But perhaps that's the point. You have to sit in the darkness—learn it, understand it—so that when you finally see the light, you'll recognize it.

As though he could read my mind—a superpower I have often wondered if therapists have—Max said, "Brooklyn would be proud of you, Wren."

As the night unfolded, Rita and Bobby read their joint poem, a tender reflection on learning to accept heartache, to let it shape them instead of break them, and how it had unexpectedly guided them toward healing. Julian followed, his voice trembling as he did what Emerson had told him to do; he'd written a letter to his family. His wife, sitting in the front row with his daughter, cried. Gill lightened the mood with a poem about opossums, and

Mayor Ashcroft gave a heartfelt speech about the importance of the arts in fostering community as a gateway to mental health initiatives. Then Henry—steady, kind Henry—read a poem for Jacob, and for the library. Finally, Emerson closed the round with a bittersweet piece about Winnie, weaving in the lessons she'd learned about how love can outlast loss. Her mom was beaming. Emerson, being Emerson, took her time onstage not only to share her poem but also to deliver an impassioned commentary to the media present on the resurgence of contemporary poetry and its profound role in fostering personal healing and emotional growth. I could see Archie Beecher scribbling away on a notepad and made a mental note to introduce them. As applause filled the room, I knew it was almost my turn. I leaned against the edge of a bookshelf.

And then I saw Olivia.

She rushed through the library doors, hair curled slightly at the ends, dampened by the light drizzle that had begun to fall outside. Her face was flushed and breathless as she scanned the room. When her eyes found mine, she weaved her way through the crowd, never breaking our gaze until she was standing right in front of me.

"Wren," she said, her voice soft but full of emotion. "You're here."

I swallowed hard; my chest felt fluttery. "I shouldn't have left," I whispered. "I tried to reach you, I'm so—"

"Sorry," she said. "I turned my phone off. I was . . . hurt," she admitted. "It's something I used to do with my mom when I was younger . . ." She paused. "Actually, it carried right through until she died, if I'm honest. When she'd hurt me, I'd just go radio silent. Sometimes for days, sometimes for weeks."

I nodded. "I shouldn't have said those things," I said, my voice breaking. "They were awful. I didn't mean them, Liv. I was just scared, and hurt, and confused. You are nothing like your mom."

She reached out, her fingertips brushing mine, warm and soft, sending a quiet ache straight to my chest. "I know," she said gently. "I know you were. I wasn't thinking clearly. I drove to Denver," she admitted, her cheeks flushing. "I was trying to get a flight to New York. Silly, right?"

"Liv . . ." I started, but she squeezed my hand.

"I didn't really have a plan. I just needed to find you. Then I turned my phone back on, got your messages, and—well, of course my phone died. And then I remembered the poetry evening tonight." She laughed lightly. "And I'm late, as per usual."

I exhaled, the tension around us falling away. "I shouldn't have doubted you. I was wrong for jumping to conclusions."

"It's okay," she replied. "You know, if I've learned anything, it's that when you hurt for so long, it's all you really know, so you just assume it's going to happen again."

I stepped toward her, our faces inches apart. "Can we start again?" I asked, my voice barely above a whisper.

She smiled, her eyes soft and full of light. "Of course," she said, lifting my hand to her lips and kissing my knuckles.

I pulled her into me, burying my face into the curve of her neck. Her arms wrapped around my shoulders, anchoring me in a way only Olivia seemed to be able to do. The library faded away, and, for a moment, it was just the two of us.

Henry's voice crackled over the microphone, drawing us back to the present. "There are still plenty of cinnamon rolls, folks," he said, his tone cheerful, "but not if you keep eating four each. Yes, I'm looking at you, Gill."

Olivia grinned, pulling back just enough to meet my gaze. "What is the name of your poem?" she asked, her voice a whisper meant just for me.

I looked into her light-filled eyes and laced my fingers between hers. "*Second Chance.*"

June

Chapter 31

Olivia

My mother's gravestone sat beneath an oak tree, its branches swaying gently in the breeze, casting dappled shadows across the polished granite. The sunlight softened the edges of everything, even the truths I'd spent years trying to hold in my hands. Maybe, in the end, death softens us too. I placed a bouquet of daffodils, her favorite flowers, beside the stone. A honeybee hovered, drawn to their bright-yellow petals—a tiny reminder of life continuing, even here, where time felt suspended. It was hard to believe so much time had passed. I had my mother's inscription updated. At the time of her funeral, I'd only inscribed her name:

Bonnie Anne Piroso
1964–2024

But now it read:

Bonnie Anne Piroso
1964–2024
In our hearts.
Your memory lingers, fond and true.
There is not a day that we do not think of you, Mom.

What I'd learned in those months was that grief wasn't just about what you lose, it was also about what you find. You can still have a relationship with someone even after they're gone. I talked to my mom more than I ever did when she was alive. I told her stories, asked for her advice; even if I didn't hear an answer, I liked to think she was listening. Some days, I told her about Wren. About the way Wren's courage made me braver too. Other days, I talked about our little grief group—about how they'd helped me learn to let go of the anger, and, somehow, hold on to the love.

I had a dream last night. In it, I was seven years old, scared and desperate for my mom. Then I was sixteen, so angry I wanted to scream, wanting justice for every day she hadn't chosen me. And then I was me, as I am now, standing quietly beside her. I didn't know if it was healing or just the passage of time, but I finally found a way to listen to each part of myself—the young girl who needed a mom who was never there, the teenager who rebelled out of anger and hurt, and the adult who understood that sometimes people can't give you what you need, even if they love you. I finally let go.

There was a burial happening on the far side of the cemetery, framed by a small group of people dressed in black, their voices blending softly with the wind. A caretaker nearby tended to the weeds around a gravestone. When he saw me, he straightened up, brushed dirt from his hands, and smiled in recognition.

"Always loved watching her on the TV," he said, nodding toward my mother's name. "Brilliant journalist, she was."

I looked down at the gravestone, tracing the words with my gaze. "Yes," I responded, "she was."

Weeks earlier, Wren and I had sat in her Cabriolet, waiting for Emerson to return with coffee. The drizzle outside blurred the world through the windows. Some faint pop song hummed through the radio. Wren had been unusually quiet, her fingers tapping absentmindedly against the steering wheel.

"Are you worried about Emerson driving?" I asked.

Wren turned, startled out of her thoughts. "Huh?"

I smiled, brushing my fingers through her hair. "You seem far away." I shrugged. "I just wondered if you were worried about an overcaffeinated Emerson driving your precious baby?"

Wren snorted with laughter. "I trust her," she replied. "I've just been thinking—"

"Oh," I replied. "About what?"

"About you," she sighed. "And the story."

I glanced at her, confused. "What story?"

"*The* story," she replied, firmly. "About Lucy's innocence. About the cover-up. The boy and his family deserve justice."

I stared at her. "But we don't know how far this could go. What if it brings everything back? The press, the scrutiny . . . all of it?"

Her hand found mine, a quiet reassurance. "Then we will face it together. You're the only one who can tell it."

As Wren's words often did, they stayed with me for the entire car ride back, even as Emerson rattled off bird facts at lightning speed in the hope we'd spot a black rosy-finch—a bird so elusive it may as well be Bigfoot's pet. Those same words—*You're the only one who can tell it*—swirled in my mind for days afterward, a heaviness I couldn't shake.

Cassie didn't get the job as anchor. She was informed just before going live on air, and, whether it was the years of scheming catching up to her, the misplaced assumption that I might get the position, or simply the pressure of it all, she snapped. Her meltdown unfolded spectacularly during her segment. The silver lining? I was officially off the hook for the station's most embarrassing on-air moment. In the aftermath, Colin called me into his office. Bracing for some sort of vitriol, I was caught off guard when he offered something entirely unexpected: an apology, something I don't think anyone has ever gotten from Colin. He leaned back in his chair, running a hand through his beard, his expression unusually reflective.

"Olivia," he began, "I owe you an apology."

I'd blinked. "You do?"

He sighed, shuffling things around on his desk. "I've lied to you," he said flatly. "I actually didn't like your mother. Bonnie was . . . a powerhouse, sure, but she was ruthless. And there were many occasions she had professionally screwed me over. But the powers that be loved her, and so I had no choice. Every time I saw you, I saw her. And it just . . ." He took in a deep breath. "To be frank, you just pissed me off."

"I—"

He held up his hand. "It was wrong. It was unfair. It was unprofessional. I was too hard on you. You're nothing like her."

I didn't know how to respond.

"You chose integrity," he continued. "Your mother would have absolutely thrown B.W. Paisley under the bus. Hell, she would have thrown *you* under the bus for a career-making story. But you didn't. I admire that about you, Liv. Which is why I'm offering you the promotion to anchor."

What I said next blew my own mind.

"I don't want it," I replied. Colin stiffened, just as surprised.

"What I want," I said, "is to be head of investigative journalism. That's what I care about, uncovering truths."

Because I knew the story I was going to pursue. And I was going to blow the lid off it.

After a long while, Colin grinned at me. "All right, Piroso. It's yours."

I couldn't predict the future any more than I could have predicted the winding path that brought me here. I didn't know what would happen when the story was aired—whether it would be met with truth and justice, or whether it would dredge up all sorts of darkness. But that uncertainty is part of living. There would always be things I couldn't control, things I couldn't know. But here's what I did know: I was never late for our grief group meetings anymore. Rita still happily took my *Us Weekly* magazine offerings. I found a strange kind of freedom in sharing my grief, letting it breathe in a room filled with people who truly understood. Wren bought Gill's property, and I leased my condo to officially move in with her. On Wednesday mornings, we always had breakfast at Sam's—three pancakes, stacked high, with butter and syrup smeared in the middle. I knew that was still the best way to have them, and I knew Gill would always remind us if we forgot. Sometimes Emerson joined us when she was home from college, and, when she did, we took long drives through the mountains. We talked about Winnie, about Lucy, and about my mother. Because that's all we could do for the people we had lost.

We couldn't bring them back. We couldn't rewrite who they were. But we could remember them. We could keep talking about them. I knew that the sun would still rise and set over Everston, painting the sky with colors that could take your breath away. I knew that the old steam train would still operate to and from Norvale in the summertime. I knew that the grief we carried would soften over time, but never disappear.

And I knew that I loved Wren.

The afternoon sunlight followed me home as I drove down Ducks Crossing Road. The wildflowers had begun to dot the side of the road once more, the butterflies returning. Wren was sitting on the porch swing as I pulled into the driveway, her hair catching the golden light of the setting sun. She held a mug in her hands, the steam curling softly in the air. The sight of her always made my heart skip, the kind of skip that felt like falling, but in the best way. She glanced up at me, her smile gentle, as though she had been waiting for me all along. The tray of fresh succulents

I'd picked up on my way home wobbled precariously on the passenger seat, and I loaded everything into my arms before walking toward her, careful not to spill the soil.

"Have you noticed this?" she asked, gesturing to the swing.

"Noticed what?" I replied, as I set the tray down near the steps and moved closer to her. I kissed her cheek, soaking in its warmth.

She ran her fingers along the edge of the swing, her touch reverent. "There's an inscription," she replied. "It says, '*Gill, I am not here, but I am still here. I love you always, Edith.*'"

I leaned in, following Wren's fingers across the delicate carving. "How have we not noticed this before?" I wondered. So many nights we had sat out on this swing, watching the fireflies pepper the garden edge and the evenings roll in.

Wren nodded, her expression wistful.

"Everything okay?" I asked, noticing the faraway look in her eyes.

"I was just thinking about bluebirds, actually," she admitted.

"Oh?" I tilted my head, leaning against the swing's armrest.

"Did you know they sing to each other during nesting season? Kind of like they're serenading their partner."

I laughed. "Is that so?"

"Marvelous, aren't they?" She grinned, and ran her thumb across my lip, humming a tune, before leaning in and kissing me softly.

"Are you ready to tackle our wall project?" she asked.

"I guess I have to be," I responded. "It's not going to renovate itself."

The wall in question was in the upstairs hallway. The old plaster was cracked and peeling, and we'd decided to open it up to expose the original woodwork underneath—a plan that might have been overly ambitious but felt worth the effort. Gill had been quite right about one thing, there was always something that needed fixing. Upstairs, Wren ran her fingers over the uneven surface of the wall. She grinned mischievously. "Imagine if we find treasure behind here?"

I shuddered. "I'd take diamonds over anything sinister."

Wren laughed. "You've been reading too much true crime."

We started peeling away the plaster, dust filling the air as chunks of the wall came loose. Wren and I worked side by side, the rhythm of our movements in sync. She talked animatedly about all sorts of ways we could decorate the room, but our banter was cut short when a section of the wall suddenly gave way with a loud crack. A screeching sound erupted from the hole, and we both froze. Staring back at us, wide-eyed and utterly unimpressed, were the very opossums that had made themselves persistent guests in this home.

Wren and I squealed in response and stumbled backward. We tripped over each other, the tarp we had laid out, and the various tools around us, and landed on the floor in a heap of tangled limbs. For a moment there was only silence, save for the rustling of the opossums retreating farther into the wall.

We looked at each other in disbelief.

"Oh my god, they got us," Wren exclaimed.

We burst into laughter. The kind of laughter that doubles you over and makes your stomach ache. We couldn't stop, our giggles filling the room, and spilling into the house like sunlight through windows.

Life has a way of handing us these small, unexpected, messy, perfectly imperfect moments. They are easy to overlook in the chaos of our daily lives, but they are also the ones that matter. And maybe that's all life is—a collection of memories, of love, laughter, resilience, and connection, stitched together to make us whole. Grief may silence us at first, but it also reminds us of why we go on living.

And, as long as we're here, we can still choose to tell the story.

August

Chapter 32

Emerson

Some days, I felt like Winnie had come back to visit me. It was usually in those in-between moments—like when the light first broke over the mountains and chased away the shadows, or when the wind rustled the leaves just right, almost like they were carrying her voice. It was in the quiet pauses between heartbeats, the stillness that accompanied a deep breath, or when the sunlight hit the rearview mirror as I was driving her old car. Those were the moments I knew Winnie was with me.

It was the small stuff I missed the most. Bird-watching, reading poetry, cooking in her kitchen. I could handle the big things, like when Wren and I spread her ashes out the window as I drove along the Million Dollar Highway (which, by the way, was terrifying). Or when I got accepted into the University of Denver, and we threw a party—Gill even shared his chocolate with me. Or even when my doctor told me I didn't need any more surgeries, and my mom and brother surprised me and took me out for dinner. I knew what to expect in those moments. Winnie couldn't be a part of them anymore, and yeah, it sucked, but grief would always suck.

What got me was the little things. Like hearing a hummingbird call and being reminded of her, or catching a whiff of freshly made lemon meringue pie, or seeing brightly colored beads in the window of a store. That's when I felt the empty space she'd left behind the most. Henry said that when people die, we tend to say we *loved* them, like it was a thing of the past. But the love doesn't stop. You don't have to leave it behind; you can carry it with you. We would all still love Winnie, and that *love* was alive in us.

It was the end of summer here in Everston. The days were still hot—like, why-did-I-wear-jeans kind of hot—but the nights were starting to cool just enough that you could pretend fall was on the way. In a couple of weeks, the town would be packed with tourists for our harvest festival. The birds were starting their migrations south, which was basically the Super Bowl of bird-watching. Species that spent summers in the mountains—like warblers, flycatchers, and tanagers—were passing through, along with shorebirds stopping over on their way to the coast. You never knew what you might see. Olivia promised she'd come bird-watching with Wren and me, as long as I only shared one bird fact an hour instead of fifteen. I said I'd try. No guarantees, though.

These days, my plate was pretty full. School would start in September and UCLA was no longer on the table; I guess I just didn't want that dream anymore. The University of Denver felt right—still in Colorado, *and* they had a great creative writing program. It wasn't what I had planned, but maybe that's the point. I also ran Wren's social media accounts now. Turns out, I was actually really good at it—who knew? I even did a little PA work for her, which meant bossing people around on her behalf. Mostly Dana, her publicist, but that was fine because she loved me. It's funny, I used to think my life was over when gymnastics didn't work out. I thought I'd lost my one shot at a future. But it turns out life doesn't end when one dream does. Winnie was right. Dreams can change, and they can be just as amazing, sometimes even better.

I went back to New York. First, to get Winnie's car—it couldn't just stay parked outside Wren's brownstone forever, and second, because Wren wanted to lease out her place and bring her things back to Everston. Yep, she officially moved here. She even went by Wren now—not like, in print, because even Henry said that would be very confusing for readers—but to her people, she was Wren. That's right, I was one of her people. The trip was so great. Henry came with us, and so did Olivia. Wren showed us some of her favorite food spots in New York, and then we jumped in Winnie's car and drove back to Everston. We stopped at a bunch of places from Lucy's coasters along the way. And guess what? I drove part of the way. I was a pro now (well, sort of). It really did get easier.

Oh, and I met someone too. He hated football, made homemade ice cream, and made me laugh the way Winnie used to. He accepted every part of me, scars and all. I know she would've liked him. She was right about my scars—they were never going away, but that wasn't the point. I was so busy trying to get back to my old life and the old me that I didn't realize those versions of me were gone. But that was okay. A new me showed up. And I liked her. Maybe there'll be more versions along the way, but the point is, I was still here. I got to choose who I wanted to be and where I wanted to go.

Oh, and ravens were still my favorite bird—but honestly, bluebirds were pretty cool too.

October

Chapter 33

Henry

Everston Library was bustling with activity. To be fair, it had always been busy for our little town, but lately it was alive in a way I'd never seen before. The tables were filled with laughter and conversations; the shelves practically hummed with movement. Just a few weeks earlier, a couple from Switzerland came through after reading about us online. It was wild to think about. The poetry evening had sparked something I don't think any of us could have anticipated. The evening garnered lots of attention from the press. Mayor Ashcroft was so impressed, she allocated a portion of the town's budget to mental health initiatives. That funding made it possible for Max to come out of retirement and help me establish Everston Library's first-ever officially run grief counseling group.

Misery Loves Company had grown. Tenfold! We ran sessions four nights a week! Of course, our name had to be changed to something a little more professional, so we decided on The Winnie Group. A fitting name if there ever was one. But Tuesday nights, twice a month, remained sacred. No official timetables. No new faces. Just the ones who had been there since the very beginning. It was still Gill, whose eyes lit up every time I handed him a chocolate bar; Rita, who was slowly amassing an impressive collection of *Us Weekly* magazines thanks to a certain head investigative reporter; Julian, who couldn't stop beaming about the arrival of his new baby with his wife; Bobby, who now knew that the hardest acceptance is sometimes of yourself; Emerson, who carried her scars like badges of wisdom, not shame, and who also drove a certain Volkswagen through town with the music blaring; Olivia, who learned that leaning on others didn't make her weak; and Wren, who finally stopped running and chose to stay.

And then there was me. I would always miss Jacob. I would always grieve the years I didn't get to spend with him. But somewhere along the way, I learned that I could still live for him too. And, of course, perhaps most importantly, we still read poetry.

The library was particularly busy, filled with chatter and footsteps that blended into the comforting rustle of turning pages. Kids sprawled on beanbag chairs in the children's section, their noses buried in brightly colored books, while a group of teenagers chattered animatedly in the designated "talk zone" (much more preferable than scribbling in books). Over by the computers, a woman was typing furiously, her headphones firmly in place, while someone else was playing solitaire (excellent choice).

I had fully embraced fall: paper leaves draped over bookshelves, a *Cozy Mysteries & Pumpkin Spice Reads* display near the entrance, and a banner over the front desk that read *Fall into a Good Book* (that was Wren's suggestion, admittedly). The scent of cinnamon and chai tea lingered, thanks to the complimentary brew we'd offered patrons all week. Near the front desk, Lana was delicately explaining late fees for the hundredth time to our resident sculptor, who, as usual, had brought another creation to add to an array of whimsically crafted clay creatures in lieu of actually paying the fine. The collection had become its own exhibit featuring FrankenFrog, now sporting a tiny beret, a giraffe holding a bouquet, a house with no windows, the owl with the wizard hat, the mustached cat, and—perhaps my favorite—the lumpy teapot with feet. Across the room, sunlight streamed through the large windows, catching the dust motes in a golden glow. I breathed it all in as I made my way to the back of the library, where a certain group of people had gathered upon my request.

The new dedicated space for The Winnie Group was finally coming together. The room, tucked in the back of the library, had been cleared out entirely for this purpose. Now, it was a blank canvas—a literal one—with paint rollers, brushes, and trays scattered across the floor.

Gill stood a few steps up on a ladder, his paint roller tapping the ceiling with a suspicious glare. "You sure the pipes are sturdy above here, Henry?" he asked. "Hate to have them bursting after all this work."

Rita chimed in from across the room, where she was busily arranging new notebooks in a cabinet. "Yes, I wondered about that, too, Gill," she said. "Henry, perhaps you should climb up there and hang off them, see how sturdy they are?"

"The pipes are fine," I insisted. "No one is doing acrobatics on them. It's a counseling group, not a circus."

"Could've fooled me," Emerson quipped, crouched in the corner by a bookshelf. She was arranging poetry volumes with the same precision you'd expect from a jeweler setting diamonds. As per a group vote, the whole bookcase was being meticulously curated by our resident poetry major from the University of Denver.

"Are you adding any traditional poetry to those shelves?"

She scoffed. "Why would I—"

I raised my eyebrows at her, and she groaned.

"Yes, I will add some," she replied. "But only the good ones."

Across the room, Bobby and Julian were hauling armchairs through the doorway. The chairs were mismatched—one a rich burgundy, another a soft beige, and another a deep emerald green—like the group itself, each of us different in our own way, but tied together through our shared struggles. Julian grunted as they finally set the chairs down. "These are heavier than they look," he commented.

"Are we getting hazard pay for this?" Bobby asked, grinning.

"I don't mind volunteering," Gill said brightly, "so long as Henry doesn't volunteer his life savings again." He gave me a pointed look.

"Yes, yes. Point taken," I replied, sheepishly. I was probably never going to live that down. "We've come a long way since then."

I glanced over at Wren and Olivia. They were painting the far wall, their laughter bubbling like music over the hum of conversation. Olivia swiped her roller lightly across Wren's overalls, leaving a streak of pale blue paint. Wren retaliated with a playful flick of her brush, sending specks of paint onto Olivia's cheek. They were so entirely wrapped up in their own world, it was almost like the rest of us didn't exist. I suppose our lives were much like this room we were creating: sometimes we start with a blank slate, sometimes we're rebuilding over what came before, but either way, it's the people we fill it with who make it meaningful.

"Are we really going to add polka dots to that feature wall?" I called, and Wren looked over at me.

"Of course," she replied. "It's what Winnie would have wanted."

As Wren and Olivia leaned closer, whispering something I couldn't hear, I thought perhaps Jacob had been right about something. Life doesn't promise certainty; it offers possibilities. Grief and love, endings and beginnings—they all coexist. And no matter how mismatched or messy the pieces, there is always room to start again.

"You know, Henry, I wouldn't mind some tea," Rita said, her voice cutting through my thoughts. She had moved from the cabinet and was now steadying the ladder, looking up at Gill.

I clapped my hands together. "I think I can manage that," I replied, before mouthing *Get him down from there* in her direction.

"Coffee for me, please, Henry," Julian rumbled, adjusting an armchair into the corner.

"Tea, coffee, cookies—coming right up," I called as I headed for the staff room. The sound of their chatter and banter continued behind me as I slipped away. The warmth of their voices echoed in my chest, and I smiled to myself.

The coffee machine made some sort of angry gurgling sound, followed by the dreaded slosh of black sludge. I grimaced.

"Not again," I muttered.

Wren poked her head into the staff room as she tied her hair back with paint-speckled fingers. "How's the tea and coffee coming along?"

"The tea is fine!" I remarked. "It's always the damn coffee."

She gave me a quizzical smile, before I handed her a tray of cookies. "Here," I said. "Will you man the tea and cookies while I pop across the road for coffee?"

"Can you add some cinnamon rolls to that order?" she called after me.

I grinned. "Naturally."

As I stepped into the sun-drenched afternoon, I thought of Winnie. She really would have loved all this.

The coffee shop was filled to the brim with people. Outside, an entire fleet of bicycles was perched, their owners inside, chatting and enjoying their drinks of choice, alongside an array of cakes and sandwiches. The barista gave me a strained look as I walked in, silently warning me that there may be a bit of a wait. As I scanned the crowded room, I spotted Lillian from Sweet Moments standing third in line. I hadn't seen her since she catered the poetry evening, and to my surprise, I found myself smiling.

She noticed me too. "Henry," she said brightly, as I approached her.

"How are you?" I asked.

"I'm great," she responded. "Just picking up some supplies. How's the library?"

"It's been bustling lately," I replied. "Ever since the poetry night."

"Oh, it was fantastic, Henry," she said. "I tell so many people about it. Such a wonderful thing you did for this community. And B.W. Paisley!" She gushed, "I cannot believe she was there! Even I know who she is." She giggled at herself.

"She lives in Everston now," I said. "I know her quite well."

I could almost hear both Emerson and Olivia snickering over the fact that I just name dropped our famous friend into conversation, and I felt almost guilty. Almost, because Emerson was constantly sliding into conversations that she drove B.W. Paisley's Cabriolet on the weekends.

I watched as Lillian placed her order: a large oat milk latte, with a single shot of espresso and three pumps of caramel syrup.

"My brother used to drink his coffee like that," I remarked.

"Really?" Lillian responded, smiling thoughtfully. "I had a friend who drank his coffee this way too. We met in the oncology ward. He always insisted it was best with three pumps of caramel."

I felt a tingle in my chest.

"What was your friend's name?" I asked.

"Jacob," she replied.

Of course it was.

"Do you drink coffee?" she asked. "My treat."

"Yes, actually," I said, after a moment. "I'll have what you're having."

Everston Library Presents

A Poetry Evening

with

Misery ♡ Loves Company

$15 per ticket   Refreshments & snacks provided

All proceeds support mental health initiatives in Everston

A Silver Lining

Rita Carmichael and Bobby Prescott

Rita

For many days, I stood alone,
my sister's mind adrift, her memories flown.
Once we shared secrets, laughter and tears.
Now, I hold her hand, through foggy years.

It took me so long, for missing lasts forever,
but acceptance blooms like a late summer flower.
In the garden of our lives, hour by hour
I cherish the moments, though they will fade away
For even in our silence now, love still lives.

Bobby

Finally, despite it all, I found my truth,
A heart that beats differently, unmasked youth.
From the despair of judgment, I stepped into light.
With friends who embraced me, I finally took flight.

Acceptance whispered like a gentle breeze.
In the embrace of love, I found my ease.
Leaving behind the echoes of disdain,
in my chosen family I broke free from pain.

Together

From grief something new can be born,
A silver lining amid the ache and mourn.
From the shattered pieces of broken dreams,
joy takes root, at first timid, unlikely it seems,
until blooming freely, unafraid to flow,
love finds its place and begins to grow.

For in every ending, there's a new start;
in the rhythm of change, we find our heart.
Older and younger, different paths we tread,
together, we walk to a future ahead.

Yours

Julian Foster

My love, how to put into words, a grief like this, when the pain takes up so much space. A letter to you, from a broken heart, a grieving soul, but a hand that reaches for yours. The heartbeat we lost, so faint, so new—a whisper, a promise of life within, now silenced. I think about the dreams we wove together, how they shaped themselves into tiny clothes, names we murmured soft in the dark, futures built with promise and hope. I remember your hands, cradling your growing belly. How anticipation bloomed with every kick, every flutter, our secret language that only we could understand. Then, a quiet moment, a shadow passed, and the world tilted, leaving an emptiness behind. Grief settled in the hollow spaces, a presence of absence, words unsaid, songs unsung, a love that had no time to grow. In the stillness, I watch your tears fall, and though mine are quieter, they fall too—silent prayers to the stars, for the one we never met, but will forever hold. Time moves forward, relentless and indifferent. Yet, in the quiet of the night, I feel you close, heartache for what might have been, but a reminder of the strength we carry together. The grief may always stay, taking up less space over time, and in this space between sorrow and love, we will endure—for always your heart is my heart and my heart is yours.

An Opossum Love Poem

Gill Huxley

In the quiet of nightfall, when the world slows,
Two opossums wander, where the wild grass grows.
With fur a wee bit grizzled, and eyes that still gleam,
They shuffle through memories, as if in a dream.

Side by side they scavenge, for morsels and more,
In the garden of life, where love's treasures are stored.
They've weathered the seasons, from spring's tender green,
To the chill of late autumn, when frost's touch is seen.

He recalls their first meeting, under moon's gentle light,
Her eyes bright as stars, that first summer night.
Together they've journeyed, through joys and through strife,
In the dance of the dusk, as husband and wife.

With each gentle nuzzle, and soft, caring glance,
They share the quiet comfort of love's tender trance.
No need for grand gestures, or words deeply spun,
Their bond is the night, the stars, and the sun.

Through years that have passed, their steps may be slow,
But their hearts beat as one, with a warmth that still glows.
In the twilight they linger, with love softly hummed,
Oh, two opossums in life, forever as one.

Grief Is the Lesson

Henry Briggs

It's been so long since I lost you, and yet it feels like yesterday. All this time, navigating a world that suddenly felt tilted, like a picture frame hung just slightly askew. We were two sides of the same coin, and when you left, it felt like half of me vanished. The grief was an anchor, pulling me into depths I never knew existed, and for the longest time, I didn't know if I wanted to resurface. Grief has a way of making time elastic, stretching moments of despair into a forever, while compressing all the joy into fleeting snapshots. I avoided our favorite places and memories, hoping to dull the pain, yet this only drained the color from my life. But over time, I felt a shift, a sense of understanding. I knew that grief was teaching me a lesson. It was as though you were right there beside me. I knew then that I would always carry you with me—in the stories I told, the smile I had, the way I lived. The grief didn't have to be an anchor. It could be a bridge instead, to you, all that you were and all that I could be. Life moves forward and so do I. Your laughter echoes in my mind, your strength gives me courage, your love reminds me I am never truly alone.

Halves

Emerson Coleman

On a tree branch, outside my window,
a raven perched, eyes glinting
like the shadows in the night.
It reminded me of all the days
I thought would never end—
grief is a heavy weight.
A suffocating quiet.

I would watch the raven, wings like a cloak.
It echoed emptiness, a reminder of loss,
A picture of endings.

And then one day, a bluebird came—
tentative and bright.
A song of something new to come.
A hint of sun after years of rain,
a promise to start again.

It took all that I was becoming to break free
from the dark, and the lingering shadows.
The raven had such a grip.
But I learned to listen to the bluebird's song,
to allow it into my heart.

Now, I see them both, the raven, and the bluebird.
Two sides entwined together—death and life.
For neither exists without the other;
and in their contrast, I find my strength.
The raven still comes, its presence part of me,
But the bluebird's song is louder now—
I live with both.

Rhyming Is Hard, Loving You Isn't

Olivia Piroso

There once was a heart filled with dread,
Haunted by ghosts in her head.
Then she found golden light,
honey eyes, burning bright—
Now hope lives where fear used to tread.

Second Chance

Wren Paisley

Life as I had known it ended one day—abruptly. It all came crashing down in a single instant. I had closed my eyes, and as I dreamed, my soul was still my soul, but then I awoke, and I had been irreversibly changed. With this new becoming, a grief arrived that I had never expected, a hollow nothingness that shattered all that I had been to pieces. My heart was filled with an ache that seemed to last an eternity. As it happened, a new road appeared before me. It spoke to me in soft sunlight and warm skies. It whispered of a new way to be. I was fearful: Who would I be along this new path? Where would I go? What would I do? And that was the point. I was lost, but change would find me again. My heart unfurled in the moment I met you, and I understood second chances.

Winnie's Lesson

Winnie Langford

This is what I always want you to know—

Grief, I have learned, is a relentless tide. It comes and goes with the moon. And yet, I have found strength is much the same. How wonderful that even in sorrow, there is space for joy.

You must embrace your quirks, your whoopsie doos, your over-the-top, out-there everything-ness. For in our quirks lie our sparks for life. Cherish the unexpected paths—they lead to the most wondrous adventures.

Loss is not an end, but something new. Even if it fills you with despair, dread, and heartache, you must unearth these things, understand there is transformation in between.

Love deeply, without reservation. Love the people you care about, fall in love, forgive when forgiveness is needed. Forgive yourself often, even if it is difficult.

Dance—in the rain, in the living room, in the middle of the kitchen. Dance with your friends, throw your hands up and shake all the worry from your body. These are small moments that will never be returned to you. Hold them, so that the memory lives on forever.

Poetry is a lighthouse. When the nights feel too long, read until you find your way again.

Be kind, especially to yourself, for self-compassion is the root of all healing. When you are kind to yourself, you are kind to others.

Hope is stubborn—keep it that way. Even on the days when it feels foolish to believe, believe anyway.

Live, even when it's messy. *Especially* when it's messy.

That's where you'll find yourself.

Acknowledgments

When I first started this journey of wanting to become an author, I had every intention of publishing novels. And I did, I published two, even if I had no idea where that would lead. What I wasn't anticipating was that for nearly ten years I would be sidetracked with poetry. A journey I have loved, but all the while I held onto the dream of returning to stories like this. Stories that, hopefully, make you feel something. After all, storytelling is how we connect, how we relate, and how we find hope.

Now that I am here, I am reminded that to write a book is one thing; to finish one, polish it, agonize over it, and put it into the world is another thing entirely. I would never have reached this point without the love, guidance, and generosity of so many people.

Firstly, to Anthea and Kirsty, thank you for believing in me and in this book, thank you for your vision, your advice, and for always reminding me why this story mattered. Our collaborations over the years have led me here, and I am endlessly grateful.

To the teams at Atria/Simon & Schuster and Andrews McMeel, from sales and marketing to design, production, and every hand that shaped this project in ways readers will never see, thank you for championing this story and making it real. Andrews McMeel has been my publishing home for poetry for so many years, and it feels fitting that we've taken this next step together. And to the incredible team at Atria/Simon & Schuster, thank you for welcoming me into this new chapter of my career.

To my dream-team editors, Katherine, Jarred, Danys, Dayten, and Liz, books don't exist without editors, and this one certainly wouldn't without you. Thank you for your patience, your brilliance, your sharp eyes, and your steady faith in this story. You caught what I couldn't, turned what was rough into something better, and reminded me to trust myself when I second-guessed myself. Every page is stronger because of you.

To James, this was a long time coming. From where we started to where we are now, I'll always believe we make the best team. You, too, should be proud of what we've accomplished.

To Justin, my illustrator, and my friend. We've worked together for many years, and when I first began talking about this novel, I thought: no one gets me without Justin, we're a package deal. Thank you for a yet another wonderful cover; it was everything I could have hoped for!

To my early beta readers and friends who let me test scenes, reminded me of looming deadlines, and encouraged me every step of the way, your time, feedback, and effort were invaluable. Thank you.

To my partner Claire, thank you for loving me through all the late nights, the doubts, the suggestions, and the edits. For your little smiles over Wren and Olivia, and for being a wonderful writer and editor yourself. Living life with you is one of my greatest loves, and I will always be grateful that my forever is a book girly. Mum and Dad, Nick, Brie, my nieces Evelyn and Charlotte, and all my family, thank you for always supporting me and never stopping cheering me on, even when it means listening to me talk endlessly about fictional people as if they were real. To Kate, my mother-in-law, thank you for going line by line with a pencil and circling every typo. Some people might call that generous, but I know it's just who you are. Love you to bits.

And finally, to you, the reader. Thank you for picking up this book and giving each of these characters a place in your hands and heart. Stories come alive when they're shared, and I am so grateful you chose to share in this one.

Love always,

Courtney

Book Club Questions

1. In *The Last Poem*, the characters use poetry to express grief and connection, and poems are woven throughout the story. Has poetry played a role in your own life, or, if not, do you feel inspired to read more poetry after this book?

2. Imagine you could step into Everston, Colorado, for one day. What would you want to experience or discover there?

3. *"It's like grief is this . . . weird, unofficial, shitty club"* (page 154). This book suggests that grief can be both deeply personal and shared. How do you think community plays a role in helping us carry loss?

4. Which character from Misery Loves Company would you want to grab a coffee, tea or wine with, and why?

5. How did *The Last Poem*'s exploration of grief reflect or differ from your own understanding of loss?

6. Is there a particular line or metaphor that stayed with you after reading? If so, why do you think it had such an impact?

7. All the characters from the grief support group are mourning a loved one, or are dealing with a traumatic experience. Yet they also find joy in what they have, or what second chances come their way. What does this suggest about the ways love and memory live on?

8. At Misery Loves Company's first meeting, Max uses the extended simile of the stained jacket (page 186) to illustrate that grief changes over time. Could you see that happening with any of the characters in this story?

9. According to Wren and Emerson, ravens symbolize death, change and rebirth, whereas bluebirds symbolize joy and hope. Can these two ideas coexist? *The Last Poem* explores both grief and joy—did parts of this book make you laugh, or cry, or both?

10. If *The Last Poem* was a mood, what would it be: a rainy day with tea; a sunset hike through the mountains; a cozy late night by the fire; or something else?

11. If this book had a soundtrack, what song would you add to it?

12. If you could place *The Last Poem* in the hands of someone in your life, who would it be, and what do you hope they would take from it?

13. What's one word you'd use to capture how you felt when you finished the book?

Wished you could read Wren's poetry book, *Thinking of You*?
Luckily for you, it's soon to be a reality.

Coming soon.

About the Author

Courtney Peppernell is an internationally bestselling author, known for her moving poetry and storytelling. Her beloved Pillow Thoughts series, along with *Watering the Soul*, *I Hope You Stay*, *Time Will Tell*, and more, have resonated with readers around the world and have been translated into many languages. Blending themes of love, healing, and self-discovery, Courtney's work spans both poetry and fiction, leaving a lasting impact in contemporary literature. She lives on the south coast of New South Wales, Australia, with her partner and spends her days writing, always accompanied by her beloved dogs and chickens. For more, follow Courtney on Instagram and TikTok at @courtneypeppernell.

I'd love to hear from you. Write to me:
courtney@pepperbooks.org
www.peppernell.com